SEDUCE ME IN SHADOW

TEMPT ME WITH DARKNESS

"Excellent story . . . wonderful characters . . . You won't want to put it down."

—*Romantic Times*

"This orgasmic paranormal . . . will have Black's fans panting for the next installment."

—*Publishers Weekly*

"Fast-paced, emotional, and thoroughly addicting."

—Romance Junkies

"A hot, exciting romance filled with intriguing characters and a great storyline. I can't wait for more in this imaginative series!"

—Lara Adrian, *New York Times* bestselling author

"Shayla Black's writing is pure magic. Gripping, sensual, absolutely delicious."

—Cheyenne McCray, *New York Times* bestselling author

"Compelling, unique, a paranormal romance with 'epic' written all over it!"

—Jaci Burton, national bestselling author

These titles are also available as eBooks

Other Doomsday Brethren Novels
from Shayla Black

Tempt Me with Darkness

Seduce Me in Shadow

Possess Me at Midnight

Anthologies

Haunted by Your Touch
(with Jeaniene Frost and Sharie Kohler)

ENTICE ME
AT
Twilight

SHAYLA BLACK

POCKET BOOKS
New York   London   Toronto   Sydney

Pocket Books
A Division of Simon & Schuster, Inc.
1230 Avenue of the Americas
New York, NY 10020

This book is a work of fiction. Names, characters, places, and incidents either are products of the author's imagination or are used fictitiously. Any resemblance to actual events or locales or persons, living or dead, is entirely coincidental.

First Pocket Books paperback edition November 2010

POCKET and colophon are registered trademarks of Simon & Schuster, Inc.

For information about special discounts for bulk purchases, please contact Simon & Schuster Special Sales at 1-866-506-1949 or business@simonandschuster.com

The Simon & Schuster Speakers Bureau can bring authors to your live event. For more information or to book an event contact the Simon & Schuster Speakers Bureau at 1-866-248-3049 or visit our website at www.simonspeakers.com.

Cover illustration by Juliana Kolesova

Manufactured in the United States of America

10   9   8   7   6   5   4   3   2   1

ISBN 978-1-5011-0259-2
ISBN 978-1-4391-6680-2 (ebook)

For Bonnie Hoffmaster

Thanks for being such an unwavering fan of this series and my writing, for all your encouragement, gentle prodding, and overall sunny sweetness.
You're simply wonderful.

ACKNOWLEDGMENTS

I must thank some of my usual cast of characters: Natalie, Laurie, Denise, and Annee. You guys keep me sane and motivated. I'd be lost without you. A special shoutout to Heather L. for last-minute beta reading, good insight, and overall cheerleading. I would be remiss if I didn't thank Jane Burns for responding to all my wacky (and no doubt annoying) queries about things particular to the UK. You're always thorough, helpful, and timely. Big thanks! As always, to the wonderful Kris Cook, the other half of my brain. Where would I be without you? You always have the right answer, even if it's to say nothing and listen to me ramble until I find the solution on my own. Thanks very much to my agent, Kim Whalen, for believing in this book and supporting me one hundred percent. And to my family, for more than I can enumerate here, but most especially all the love.

CHAPTER 1

PRESENT DAY—ENGLAND

"YOUR TIMING BLOODY SUCKS," Simon Northam, Duke of Hurstgrove, said as his boots crunched on the snowy field. Charred ruins rose like specters in the foggy distance. Fat gray clouds and evening mist promised more bad weather.

"Tell that to Mathias." Bram Rion brushed back his tawny wind-blown hair.

"True," Duke, as Simon preferred to be called, conceded.

There was no convenient time for Mathias d'Arc to attack Bram's home. But weeks ago, he and his Anarki army had descended on Bram's residence in the hopes of eradicating the Doomsday Brethren, a group of wizards devoted to ridding magickind of the evil sorcerer and his minions. Mathias preached equality to the Deprived class of magickind, but it was a ruse. He dealt in torture, plunder, and murder—all for ill-gotten power. The attack had nearly taken Bram, the Doomsday Brethren's leader, and the rest of the warriors by surprise. They'd barely escaped, and had been forced to abandon the house—their headquarters—to stay alive.

Now, Bram had gathered Duke and two other warriors together at the estate's remains. Duke dreaded sifting through the piles of blackened stone, plaster, and brick scattered among so many discarded personal effects. It looked like the aftermath of a natural disaster. But there'd been nothing natural about this.

"You're missing my point." Duke raised a brow at Bram. "Today is damn inconvenient for you to drag me here. Yesterday? Tomorrow? Either would have been splendid."

"So sorry I didn't consult your social calendar." Bram's tone dripped sarcasm.

"If I'm late to Mason's wedding, my family will kill me. He's my brother."

"Half-brother," Bram pointed out none too gently. "This won't take long, your highness. You'll be at Lowechester Hall long before the big event."

Duke smiled. "I'll string you up by the balls if I'm not."

"You've got time. The ceremony isn't until midnight, yes? Odd time."

"It's New Year's Eve. New beginnings, and that sort of rubbish." Duke shrugged. "What I'm wondering is why you demanded we come here *tonight.*"

"I only discovered hours ago that I can no longer teleport inside my own home. Or enter in any other way. There are several possible reasons." He sighed. "None of them good."

"Such as?"

"Think you, the great Bram Rion, will explain himself?" Marrok leaned across the line of warriors, his blue-gray eyes full of mirth. The gargantuan Arthurian warrior loved teasing Bram.

"Without his usual dodgy charm?" Ice Rykard, Bram's brother-by-mating, raised a dark brow that nearly disappeared beneath his black skullcap. "Why would he start now?"

"The lot of you can piss off." Bram pressed ahead to the blackened, leaning house in the distance. "Other than the recent attack on the Lowery family, Mathias has been like a church mouse since he failed to defeat Ice for a Council seat. We know he won't abandon his quest to overtake magickind. So his nearly three weeks of silence makes me itch."

Agreed. The Doomsday Brethren was the biggest stumbling block between Mathias and ultimate power. None of them liked it when they couldn't guess the vile wizard's next move.

With a ripe curse, Bram ranted on. "The Council gave us—and us alone—the mandate to kill Mathias . . . but to do that, we must find him."

"We will." Duke hunkered into his brown Italian wool overcoat, then drawled, "I hope he doesn't feel compelled to ring in the New Year with a bang. Tomorrow is much more convenient for me to fight mayhem."

As was often the case, humor was lost on Ice. The warrior's mood was as black as his turtleneck sweater. "Fucking bastard needs to be put down. But how do we kill a man who was already once dead?"

"We will—somehow. But first we must gain entrance to my house. There's too much information inside that could help him."

Ice shot Bram a stunned glare. "Not your grandfather's writings?"

Bram didn't say a word.

"You left Merlin's work *here*?" Duke nearly choked.

"I was unconscious when Mathias attacked, if you'll recall," Bram said defensively.

A sick feeling settled into Duke's stomach. Merlin had been the greatest wizard ever, dating back to the time of King Arthur. "If those writings fell into the wrong hands, magickind would be totally buggered."

"Completely," Bram admitted.

"Fuck," Ice muttered. "Any chance Mathias doesn't know you have Merlin's texts?"

Bram shrugged. "At the very least, I'm sure he hopes I do. And of course, I have no idea what Shock might have told him."

Their supposed double-agent Shock Denzell . . . whose loyalties no one could quite seem to pin down. Dodgy bastard.

Duke sighed. "Fine, then. We'll try to enter the house and look for Merlin's books. I can stay an hour now and return tomorrow, if necessary. Mason extended an olive branch by asking me to be his best man. We haven't been on speaking terms for roughly a decade, so I really can't be late."

Not that Duke particularly wanted to attend the festivities. Felicia Safford would be a stunning bride. White would only heighten her air of innocence. Her blue eyes would dance with life and fire that she'd do her damnedest to repress.

The thought of Felicia made his blood stir, his breathing ragged. *Bloody hell*.

At their first official meeting last night, when Felicia had slid the soft skin of her palm against his, he'd felt a jolt. Duke suspected then that she didn't belong with his brother. But she'd chosen Mason for reasons he couldn't fathom, so Duke would grit his teeth through tonight's ceremony, hope he could keep his stare off the bride, and tamp down his guilty urge to strip her bare and take her to bed.

"Best man." Ice scoffed. "All the pomp and ceremony of a human wedding sounds absurd. Why don't humans simply speak words, like the Call, and be done?"

Duke hid a smile. "They speak vows, but the pomp, I suspect, is for the mothers. Mine is in her element, planning Mason and Felicia into oblivion."

"If you and Mason don't get on well, why did he choose you as his best man?" Bram's tawny brow wrinkled in confusion.

"I'm certain our mother had a hand in it." Plus, as Duke knew, his presence—given that he'd been labeled one of

England's most eligible bachelors by the human tabloids—would mean lots of press. Damn, where was a noose when he needed one?

"Are you feeling well enough for the festivities?" Bram frowned, staring at the space just around Duke. "I noticed earlier that your magical signature seems a bit faded, like you're unwell. But shiny 'round the edges. Never seen that."

His signature was off kilter? The magical aura around every witch or wizard told all others about the person's state of being. If someone magical was mated, their colors blended with their love's and visually proclaimed them bonded. If they were magically very weak or strong, a wizard's or witch's signature would reflect that with the choice and intensity of colors. Likewise, if one of magickind ailed, their signature would appear faded. But shiny edges?

Sometimes, growing up human only to discover at age thirty that he was actually a wizard was a detriment. He often didn't understand magic's subtleties and intricacies any better than magickind understood those of humans.

Duke frowned. "I feel fine."

"Something is definitely off."

Something other than the fact he'd awakened in a cold sweat last night, thinking about Felicia being his brother's wife, thinking of her smiling up at Mason as he sank deep into her body? Imagining her with him made Duke want to demolish buildings with his bare hands.

"You low on energy?" Ice asked, crossing thick arms over his massive chest.

Duke winced. Among magickind, energy was best derived during sex. Frequent, raw exchanges of pleasure powered their magic. Last night, he'd bedded a witch he'd met at a pub. Pleasant enough. He'd already forgotten her name, but remembered her dark blond hair with honey streaks and her shining blue eyes. She'd made it easy to close his eyes and pretend.

"I said I'm fine," he bit out. "Let's focus on why Bram is unable to enter his house."

"Once we reach what's left of the walls, we'll find out," Bram vowed as they strode through the night.

Suddenly, they hit an invisible barrier inches from the crumbling ruins. Marrok stopped short, shoving at the unseen obstruction with a massive shoulder. Ice pushed with brawny hands. Bram poked and punched it, cursing and kicking when he couldn't break through. Duke probed it mentally. The barrier didn't budge.

"The bastard put up his own barrier to prevent me from getting inside," Bram cursed. "I think he lives to torment me."

"Who?" Marrok asked.

"Shock." Bram skimmed his fingers across the wall, then nodded. "His magic is all over this place. He wants me to know that—"

"My magic surrounds your house," said the wizard in question, now standing directly behind them. "You're not getting in until I say so."

They whirled to find Shock Denzell dressed in black from head to toe, ever-present sunglasses shielding his eyes, a leather duster falling to his calves, vicious combat boots covering enormous feet.

Behind him stood a half-dozen undead corpses—a small fraction of Mathias's Anarki army. Their evil glares made them look exactly like what they were: human zombies whose souls had been sucked out and replaced with Mathias's twisted thoughts.

Shock's younger brother, Zain, stood in front of the undead creatures, a superior smirk lifting his scruffy goatee. A

T-shirt that read *Do I look like a fucking people person?* sagged across his chest.

Bram seethed, staring daggers at Shock, who strode past, stepping closer to the walls. He towered above all the Doomsday Brethren except Marrok.

Personally, Duke didn't believe Shock was secretly fighting for good while pretending to serve evil. Shock merely placated both sides, knowing the winning side would put him in a cushy position eventually. The fact that Zain was one of Mathias's most fervent supporters didn't lend Shock any credibility cither.

"Protecting my house for me or keeping it safe for someone else?" Bram raised a sharp golden brow in challenge, his tan cashmere coat flapping in the wind.

Shock sent him a mocking grin. "You have some interesting stuff in here."

It didn't escape Duke's notice that Shock had failed to answer the question.

Ice snarled. "What have you taken, you fucking bastard?"

"Fucking bastard?" Shock's dark brows raised. "Here I thought we were friends."

"Always knew you were a delusional wanker," Ice snarled.

"Your choice of friends leaves something to be desired." Bram's gaze ran over the Anarki in their robes. Their rotting faces sat deep in their hoods. But there was no missing the chill they radiated or the eyes that glowed with bloodlust.

Shock crossed thick arms over his chest. "Given your friendship with Lucan MacTavish, I could say the same."

"He's my best friend, and you stole his mate."

"Former mate," Shock corrected, holding up a meaty finger. "And I didn't steal Anka. Mathias did. After she escaped, she chose *me*, not Lucan, to protect her."

"Protecting isn't the only thing you're doing to her." Ice's piercing green eyes said he was ready to rip Shock's head off. Which might improve both their moods.

Sighing, Duke ran a hand over his jaw, grimacing at the two days' worth of growth beneath his fingertips. He needed to leave, shave, and get ready for this blasted wedding. God knew, this conversation was getting them nowhere. He'd almost rather perform his familial duty—calm his mother, greet guests, and dodge the paparazzi—than listen to this blah, blah, blah.

Or was it that he'd simply rather be near Felicia?

"Lift your magical protections around Bram's house and let us in," Duke demanded.

Shock raised a scathing glare to him. The expression slid off, morphing to something like astonishment, as the wizard stared at him. No, at his signature.

Had the witch last night failed to charge his power? He felt well enough, but . . .

"You." He pointed to Duke, the surprise on his face replaced by a glower. "Come here and make me."

Duke hesitated. Not that Shock scared him. Yes, the wizard did his best to intimidate, but what disturbed Duke was that Shock had singled him out. Usually, the leather-clad goon antagonized Bram, Ice, or Lucan. So why did Shock want to fight *him* now?

Exchanging a glance with Bram, who shrugged, Duke stepped forward. "You're an annoying bastard."

Shock sent him a dismissive glare. "You're barely better than a human."

"You rattle off your mouth unwisely," Marrok, himself human, bit out as he tossed back his dark hair and readied for a fight.

With a dismissive wave, Shock addressed the warrior. "You've redeemed yourself by mating a very worthy witch and living among magickind. Mr. High-and-Mighty over there,"—Shock nodded rudely in Duke's direction—"he's got one foot in both camps. He's a bloody duke. Who among magickind has use for such worthless human titles? He even smells human."

"Better than smelling like a backstabbing arsehole," Duke quipped.

Thunder crossed Shock's face, and he raced forward and struck Duke, an open palm cracking against his cheek. Duke recoiled. Shock had slapped him, not punched him like a warrior. He felt the insult all the way to his bones.

With a lazy gait, Shock backed up a few paces and sent Duke a challenging glare. "I'd hit you with a spell . . . but your human blood would probably curdle."

Gritting his teeth, Duke told himself to stay calm. Shock was baiting him. The question was, why?

Clenching his fists to keep a handle on his temper, Duke squared off with Shock. "As fascinating as your juvenile behavior isn't, we're simply here to take stock of the contents of Bram's house. Kindly remove your . . . protections and let us in."

"Fuck off."

Clenching his fists, Duke repressed the urge to attack. Shock wanted something—not from Bram or Ice or Marrok. But from *him*. When Shock had made more of a pretense of fighting on their side and actually attended the Doomsday Brethren's meetings, he'd barely spoken to him. To be singled out this way was confusing.

But Denzell wanted a fight. Fine. Duke would play along until he figured out this rubbish.

He drew his wand from his overcoat and whipped it in Shock's direction.

Before he could conjure a spell, Shock shook his head.

"I won't fight you like a wizard; you barely are one." He sneered and crooked his finger. "Come here and fight like the dirty humans you were raised with. Show me what you know."

With a glare, Duke sheathed his wand again and approached Shock. He struck the other wizard with a lightning quick open-palmed slap, tit for tat. Shock's head snapped to the side. The big wizard laughed.

The elder Denzell brother had long been regarded as crafty and violent. Today, he seemed flat insane.

"Is that the best you've got?"

Duke shook his head. If Shock was itching for a fight so badly . . .

Without another thought, Duke fired a right cross at the leather-clad wizard, who blocked the punch and shoved one of his own at Duke's gut. As he leapt out of the way to avoid having his guts knocked into his spine, pandemonium erupted around him. Bram attacked another Anarki, tearing his robe away to reveal a greenish-black creature with a sunken face, rotting flesh, and the body temperature of an ice cube.

"Ugh!" Ice groused as he reached for the knife in his boot. "Dead fish floating in the Thames smell better."

The wizard didn't exaggerate. Anarki were nasty all the way around.

Marrok engaged two zombies, who circled him, hoping to take him down. Duke flashed a fist out and clipped Shock on the chin. As the other wizard grunted and stumbled, Marrok yanked his ever-constant sword from his scabbard and skewered one of his opponents. Bram kicked the knees out from under his. As the zombie crashed to the ground, his entire body disintegrated, the silky robe fluttering to the ground in his wake.

Shock's younger brother emerged from the pack of Anarki with a snarl.

"Zain," Bram called out. "It's been far too long since you came for a . . . visit."

At Bram's sly reference to Zain's prior captivity, the younger Denzell bristled. "You no longer have a filthy, cold dungeon in which to keep me chained." Zain cast a dismissive glance at the ruins of Bram's house. "Pity."

Bram snarled a curse. He'd been short-tempered since Mathias had attacked him with some mysterious spell a few weeks back that had since faded but not broken. That Emma, his mysterious new mate, had abandoned him, only made matters worse. This could get ugly.

Zain whipped out his wand. Bram followed suit. Ice tackled an Anarki between them, a dagger in his meaty fist. Flying punches and kicks brought everyone nearby tumbling to the ground.

As the melee ensued, Shock pounced on Duke, grabbed him by the throat, and dragged him inside the circle of protection, against the crumbling walls of the house.

"Listen to me." Shock squeezed Duke's throat.

"Piss. Off," he croaked.

"Take a swipe at me." Denzell relaxed his hold.

Shock was inviting him to hit him in the face? With a mental shrug, Duke pounded a fist into the other man's left cheekbone.

"Bugger!" Shock thundered. "Don't knock my face off, you stupid fuck. I'm trying to help you. Mathias has a new plan."

Was this a ruse . . . or the reason Shock had singled him out? "Go on."

"At least pretend to struggle while you listen," Shock muttered.

That wasn't too hard, since he wasn't fond of Shock's palm pressing on his windpipe. He managed to shove a fist into Shock's stomach.

"Barmy fuck!" he growled, then lowered his voice. "Mathias seeks to resurrect Morganna le Fay."

The air and the fight left Duke. Resurrect one of the most evil witches in history? If this story was real . . . "Is he out of his bloody mind?"

"If Mathias succeeds, he believes he can control her power, perhaps even absorb it."

Which would make him virtually unstoppable. "Bloody hell . . ."

"Exactly. Hit me again."

Making full use of his free pass, Duke unleashed his frustration with another fist to Shock's gut. The other wizard paid him back with a mean jab to the eye that sent him reeling.

Duke shook off the pain. "To resurrect Morganna, Mathias would have to get into her tomb. It's supposedly guarded by impenetrable magic. No one would make it alive."

"Except an Untouchable." Shock took another jab at Duke's jaw, connecting with a harsh blow.

An Untouchable, a human completely immune to magic? Were they mere folklore or actually real? Duke wiggled his jaw, grimacing. This was when growing up human hindered him.

He plowed a fist to Shock's gut again. "Why tell me?"

The other wizard grunted. "Your signature indicates you've come into contact with one in the past day or two."

Then Bram's words tripped Duke's memory. *My signature is faded and shiny.*

"Bingo."

Hell. Duke had forgotten that Shock could read minds.

And how did Shock know of this signature anomaly when Bram didn't? Because Bram didn't use dark magic? And more important, who was the Untouchable?

Around them, the others fought. Zain and Bram rumbled close. Duke joined in with a square thrust right at the tall wizard's nose.

Shock tackled him into the wall and hissed, "If Mathias manages to resurrect Morganna, life as we know it will be over. Zain has *seen* you. He won't keep the fact you've had contact with the Untouchable to himself. You've got a few hours at most to figure out who it is before Mathias pounds on your door."

Every human Duke's mother had recently introduced him to had some association with Mason and Felicia's wedding. Zain kept up with a bit of human news; he'd know about the event. That knowledge could threaten hundreds of family, friends, and the press—all of whom would be under his roof for the ceremony. *Shit.*

Shock got in his face, teeth clenched. "Find the Untouchable before Mathias does."

How?

"And get him or her deep into hiding." The older Denzell brother delivered another blow to his cheek.

Damn it, that throbbed like a thorn in a lion's paw and made him roar as loudly. He stumbled, his ears ringing.

"The Anarki are dead, and your chums are chasing Zain," Shock said. "Last chance. Hit me hard."

"Gladly." With a grimace, Duke reared back to deliver a punishing left hook.

At the second of impact, both Denzell brothers disappeared, teleporting out.

Damn it! That punch would have made him feel loads better.

Shoving his frustration aside, Duke realized Shock had left him *inside* the protections around Bram's house. On purpose? Perhaps . . . one never knew with the elder Denzell. But now Duke could let the others past those protections so they could search for Merlin's tomes.

As he mentally opened the barriers, Ice ran to Duke's side. "Devious Denzell bastards."

Bram nodded, fists clenched. "Shock won that round, I fear. Your face looks terrible. You all right?"

No. Duke was terrified for the Untouchable. Whoever the unlucky human was would be at his house tonight for the wedding, and Mathias would soon know that.

"According to Shock, Mathias has plans to resurrect Morganna."

"He *told* you that?" Ice's jaw dropped. "Is he barking mad?"

Duke frowned. "Shock or Mathias?"

"Mathias . . . but I suppose the question could apply to both," Bram said.

"Think you there is any answer except aye?" Marrok stomped toward them, sweat dripping as he sheathed his sword.

Bram shook his head. "Impossible. He'd have to open her tomb. No one but my grandfather knew for certain how to do that, or whether the old tale about her essence remaining there had a shred of truth. He was responsible for Morganna's demise, after all."

"'Tis likely he would have written such down," Marrok pointed out.

Cold dread slid through Duke. "And you kept Merlin's writings here."

A heartbeat later, Bram cursed. "That's why Shock has been poking around here. He was looking for Merlin's books."

Duke nodded. "And for a way to help Mathias bring her back to this plane."

"Horn-swined lout," Marrok groused.

Bram shook his head. "Still, Mathias would need an Untouchable to open Morganna's tomb. They only come once every thousand years. Mathias is looking for a proverbial needle in a haystack."

Duke grimaced. "Apparently, without trying, I found that needle."

Bram's gaze zipped over to him. "That's what's wrong with your signature."

"How does Shock know about the Untouchable's effect on someone magical?" Duke asked, hoping the double agent was merely unhinged or yanking his chain.

"His great uncle. Utterly mental and violent. Rumor is, he killed the last Untouchable, then talked incessantly about the change in his signature after touching her."

"Why would Shock admit any of this to me, unless . . ."

"He's on our side?" Bram shook his head. "Wishful thinking, I fear. I'm sure being 'forthright' serves some purpose of his we'll never know. Rather than puzzling him out now, we must focus on finding the Untouchable before Mathias does."

"This must be someone involved with the wedding. I've met any number of people recently." *The photographer, the caterer, the florist . . .* "Does this person have any characteristics?"

With Duke's help, Bram tore into the house, picking through the ruins until he came to what remained of his office. They held their collective breath, hoping Merlin's writings hadn't been ransacked.

Bram quickly unsealed the protective spell he had previously placed. The ground opened up and a box emerged. The blond wizard tore open the lid and reached inside, grabbing a stack of ancient, yellowed tomes. They all heaved a sigh of relief.

Bram clutched them tight. "I'll skim these, see if there's any information."

"No time," Duke insisted. "We have to find the Untouchable now. Looks like you're all invited to my brother's wedding."

Bram gestured to their ripped, mud-streaked attire. "Won't we fit in."

"Who bloody cares? If we don't act now, there may be a slaughter."

CHAPTER 2

FELICIA SAFFORD LOOKED UP to see her fiancé, Mason Daniels, stride into her changing room as she adjusted her veil. "Why are you here? Impatient as usual?"

A sly smile drew up the corner of his full mouth, reaching all the way to his dark eyes. "You know me . . ."

That she did. For six years now. Mason had never looked more dashing. His inky hair gleamed in the golden lamplight. They were roughly the same height when she wore heels, but Mason's devotion to a workout regimen showed in the way he did a tuxedo proud. That little scar on his jaw gave him a rakish air. He turned heads wherever he went, but Felicia felt blessed to be one of the few who truly knew him from the inside out.

Over the years, they'd become best friends. His proposal a few months back had surprised her. They'd never so much as dated, but his persuasive arguments about a solid rapport being the foundation for a wonderful family someday made perfect sense and tapped into her longing for that kind of loving safety. They got on famously, respected each other, shared many values, even liked the same music. On top of that, he was a talented barrister.

So she'd said yes.

Felicia didn't seek the roller-coaster ride of all-consuming romantic love, and Mason was well aware of that. They would remain friends, but become partners in life. They'd both agreed it was the perfect arrangement.

Mason gave her a long, low whistle. "You look beautiful. Lace suits you."

It was probably the best she'd ever looked in her life, and given her adoptive mother's penchant for dressing her like a doll, that said something. But Felicia knew Mason liked her not only for her exterior, but for *her*.

Everything was perfect, except her niggling anxiety. What if marriage changed everything between them?

"Uh oh. You've gone quiet on me. Thinking of Deirdre, darling? Wishing she could be here?"

That, too. Felicia clutched the locket she wore about her neck. For nearly an hour this morning, she'd stared at her sister's picture tucked inside, barely able to hold hot tears at bay. She'd half-heartedly chosen an old school chum as her maid of honor, but Deirdre's absence created a gaping hole in Felicia's chest. She missed her sister every day, but today. . . Felicia felt as if she bled grief. If she admitted that, however, Mason would only worry.

"I'm fine. See?" She flashed her dimples at him, doing her best to shove her abyss of sadness aside.

He frowned. "That's not genuine."

Felicia sighed. Mason knew her too well. "I'm trying. It's just that . . . not having her here makes everything feel incomplete."

"It's natural to miss her."

"Yes. But I'm angry. Her absence is a black spot. Deirdre should be here, and she chose not to be."

"You feel abandoned. I know. You have good cause." Cupping her cheek, he murmured, "Focus on us, on our future. We're going to be happy."

"Yessir." She sent him a mock salute, trying to lighten the mood. "If I didn't say so, you look stunning."

He chuckled. "Thank you. I should go. If Mum knew I'd

seen you before the wedding, she would prattle on about bad luck and all that."

"Our friendship is much too thick for us to worry about such things."

He'd supported her through uni after Deirdre's shocking death. With her sister gone, Felicia had faltered, drowning in grief, and she'd lost her scholarship. Mason had arrived, a knight in a white sedan, brought Chinese takeout, and helped her pick up the pieces of her life. After that, they'd gone from close to inseparable.

Now all that stood between them and a comfortable tomorrow was a short jaunt up the aisle in the windowed chapel overlooking the Duke of Hurstgrove's extensive garden, and an exchange of vows as the New Year rang in. In theory, a piece of cake.

But what if things weren't that simple?

"We are very close." Mason squeezed her hand, his gaze direct—disconcertingly so. "Full house, by the way."

Felicia groaned, withdrawing her hand and pressing it to her stomach. "I'm so nervous."

He tensed. "About marrying me?"

She shouldn't be. Good looking, good family, good salary. Her parents, had they lived, would have approved of everything about tonight, even down to the Alita Graham gown. Its modest elegance and the satin ribbon about her waist hinted of a bygone era that fit the wedding's historic location. The three-quarter sleeves suited the late December date. But she couldn't stop wondering if committing herself, even to her best friend, was really a good idea. After what Deirdre had endured, what if she was making a mistake?

No. It was just nerves and sorrow. She had to put them behind her.

"About tripping!" She forced a grin. "This train will likely be the death of me. Why didn't we elope?"

Mason relaxed and grinned. "Because Simon shows no signs of marrying soon, and my mother wanted at least one wedding to organize. Don't worry. You'll be brilliant."

As he gave her one of those lazy smiles she knew had helped him shag his way through uni, she thanked God it didn't impact her. Then she realized that he wasn't heading toward the door. Instead, he sauntered closer to her, and something in his eyes warmed, darkening in a way she'd never seen.

"Stop frowning, darling. You'll be fine. *We'll* be fine." The suddenly deep tone of his whisper shivered down her spine.

That I've-had-a-night-of-rough-sex voice was Mason's?

Her eyes widened. Dread flared as he raised a brow and leaned closer, wearing a determined expression. Frozen, she watched as he raised his palm to her jaw, cradling it. She tried to inch back, but Mason's fingers curled around her nape, staying her. His mouth hovered above hers, his eyes growing sharp with desire.

Oh God! This wasn't what they'd agreed to. This was exactly what she'd feared about marrying him—changing everything. Ruining their friendship.

"Mason, stop. What are you—"

"Shh." He leaned even closer, so close the scent of his aftershave bombarded her. His smooth-shaven cheek caressed her own. Then he pressed his lips to her jaw.

Mason had kissed her many times. Hello. Good-bye. Always a friendly peck. Never had his lips lingered, seduced. As if he *wanted* her.

Felicia sucked in a breath, her heart pumping wildly in panic.

He desired her, after all these years? Yes, logically she'd

known they would share a bed eventually once married. They both wanted children, after all. But she'd imagined even sex would be friendly, fun, never seductive or hungry, like Mason's expression suggested now.

Firm lips feathered their way across her cheek. His breathing turned uneven. Felicia tensed. Anxiety and confusion raced through her blood, chilling her. He urged her closer . . . to his mouth.

Felicia started to protest when he silenced her with a firm press of his lips. Everything inside her froze. For the sake of their marriage, she tried to relax.

With a groan, Mason urged her lips apart. Slowly, he dipped inside, cajoling her with a sweep of lips, a slide of tongue. An embrace of passion. The kiss of a lover.

Never in a million years had she thought Mason felt any true desire for her. The sense of security she'd always felt with him suddenly disappeared, yanked out from under her minutes before their wedding. Relaxing into his kiss was impossible.

She wrenched away and gaped at him, so many thoughts and conflicting feelings bombarding her that she hardly knew where to start.

Mason's breath was choppy. His hands shook. Desire flushed his cheeks as he pressed his forehead against hers. "I've wanted to do that for a very long time."

Seriously?

Yes.

All her life, she'd had the uncanny ability to sense lies. For her, they had an acrid smell that made her slightly queasy. No terrible scent lingered to indicate that Mason had been anything but bluntly honest.

Felicia recoiled.

"This isn't what we discussed. We're . . . friends, Mason,"

she cried as she tried to pull away, form a coherent reply. "We've always been friends. I . . . I—"

"We will always be friends. But we're about to be more. I'm sorry if that was too much, too suddenly. We have our whole lives to be together. I won't push you, darling. I know how you feel about love after what happened to Deirdre. But you're no more like her than I am like that bastard she fell for. Let yourself fall in love with me, Felicia." He cupped her shoulders in his hands and stared right into her eyes. "It won't hurt, I promise."

Anger, as fast and hot as lightning, thawed her chill. The last thing she wanted to do today was talk about Alexei, the scum who had destroyed her sister. The fact Mason had even mentioned falling in love ten minutes before she pledged her life to him, when Deirdre weighed so heavily on her heart, ratcheted up her fury—and her fear.

"No. We are *friends*," she insisted.

"We still are. But Felicia, we're about to become spouses, as well." He caressed her cheek. "I should be able to tell you that I love you."

Felicia's heart stopped. He *love-loved* her? She sniffed, praying to scent his lie. Nothing but the slight burn of gas from the furnace. Even without her unusual gift, one look in his melting chocolate eyes told her the answer.

Mason was in love with her.

Bloody hell! How had she missed it?

The air was suddenly gone from her lungs, and she tried to gasp for a breath. "H-how long have you felt this way?"

He hesitated, heaved a reluctant sigh. "Almost from the beginning. I-I wanted to give you plenty of time and space to truly know me, be certain I would never hurt you, before—"

"You think learning that you kept your feelings from me

for years doesn't hurt?" Betrayal and panic overwhelmed her. Her one safe haven had become the very thing she feared most.

What the devil was she supposed to do, now as a houseful of wedding guests awaited them?

He inched forward, cupped her cheeks. Shoving against his chest, Felicia backed away. "Don't. Just . . . don't."

"You're panicking, and there's no need. This is *me*! You know everything about me, from my favorite songs to the sorts of socks I prefer."

Yes, she had known everything about Mason . . . except what was in his heart. The fact that he'd spring this on her now made her wonder how much he really understood her or respected the agreement they'd made.

Most women would be thrilled with his sudden revelation, but it terrified Felicia. She didn't need a psychologist to understand why an orphan would crave a family of her own. She'd wanted one, provided she didn't have to risk her heart. Now? She clenched her fists, dread coiling in her heart.

As she tried to grapple with a world gone topsy-turvy, Mason grabbed her and pressed a quick kiss to her lips, startling her all over again.

She pulled away. "Don't do this."

"I thought I could keep my feelings to myself, but . . ." With a solemn stare, he shook his head. "I want all of you, not just the parts you're willing to share. I'm sorry I'm changing everything we agreed to, but with time, I know you'll love me back."

"Mason, I don't think I'm capable of reciprocating and I don't want to hurt you."

"You *are* capable. In time, you'll see I'm right." His expression softened, imploring her—something his adversaries in court never saw. "The ceremony starts in a few minutes.

Please be there with a smile. Everything will work out, I promise. At the stroke of midnight, we'll start a new year and our new lives together."

He pressed a soft kiss to her cheek and left the room. Felicia watched him, anger and fear tangling inside her. For weeks now a voice had been niggling in the back of her head, asking her if marrying Mason was a mistake, and she'd been denying it. He was a wonderful man, would make the most attentive of fathers. They wanted the same things. How could they lose, right? They'd agreed that love wouldn't enter into the equation. But now . . .

What if she ended up hurting her best friend?

Felicia swallowed. That was the last thing she wanted to happen. What the devil should she do to prevent it? Backing out now would pain him. But if she married him to spare him, would he wake up one day, after they'd had a child or two, and realize his love would always be unrequited? How much more would that hurt?

Her first instinct was to break the engagement, but Mason was the first person with whom she shared any accomplishment or problem. The one who told her—before anyone else—of his triumphs and disappointments. Mason's voice was the one she most looked forward to hearing each morning, and the one she needed to hear when nightmares of Deirdre plagued her. If she broke the engagement, and broke his heart, would he ever speak to her again? What would they do without each other?

Her stomach seemed to drop to her toes. She either had to accept his feelings or call off the wedding—and she must decide quickly.

Before she could puzzle it out, Mason spoke in the hallway outside her bedroom. "Hello, Mother."

"Mason!" the Dowager Duchess of Hurstgrove and Felicia's future mother-in-law exclaimed, shocked. "Were you—" she sputtered. "Did you see Felicia before the ceremony?"

"I did, and she looks lovely. Did you need something?"

His voice made a hundred emotions collide inside Felicia. Resisting the urge to cry, she crossed her arms tightly over her chest. She'd sought marriage to a friend who would care about her, work with her to build a solid future. A good husband, a nice job until the children came, a house in a quiet suburb, weekends in the park, holidays at the shore.

With a few words, Mason had changed everything. That fact was like a hot knife to the chest. Her future had become a frightening chasm.

"Have you seen your brother?" the dowager asked.

"*Half* brother," Mason muttered. "The freak."

This wasn't the first time she'd heard Mason's opinion of His Grace. She'd met the man once, just yesterday, so Felicia couldn't comment except to say he deserved his status as England's most eligible bachelor. He was titled, rich, and dangerously good looking. Many women fancied themselves in love with him. For a chance to win His Grace's heart, these stupid cows gave away their bodies and opened up their hearts. Felicia shuddered to think how many of them he'd crushed under his very expensive boots.

"Mason," his mother chastised. "He *is* your brother."

Except for their similar coloring and eyes, Felicia would have never guessed it. The brothers' personalities were night and day.

Mason sighed. "No, I haven't seen him. I told you he wasn't reliable."

Thoughts racing, Felicia bit her lip. If His Grace failed to appear for the ceremony, perhaps they'd have to postpone it. That would buy her time to think about her dilemma with Mason.

"Hello, dear." The Dowager Duchess peeked her head inside the room. "You look lovely, but terrified. Smile."

Felicia glided toward her on numb legs and did her best to comply, though it felt wooden. When Mason edged closer, he saw through her façade. His stare asked what she was going to do. She didn't have a clue.

The dowager turned and wagged a bejeweled finger in Mason's face. "Simon will come, and when he does, you boys will get along. No fighting. Do I make myself clear?"

Mason slanted his mother a long-suffering smile. "Indeed. What shall I tell him?"

"I need him in the sanctuary right away."

"Of course," Mason put a hand to the small of his mother's back and escorted her to the stairs. "I'll send him straight on."

The dowager looked at her younger son over the shoulder of her beaded, pale blue dress. "Come. You're not supposed to see the bride before the ceremony. It really *is* bad luck."

"Give me one moment," he pressed, his understanding smile disappearing the moment she fell from view. Then he faced Felicia. "Why did I let her talk me into this silly notion that we'd achieve instant family harmony if I asked Simon to be my best man?"

Because Mason tried to please his mother, and no one could fault him for it. Down to his core, he was good and decent. Over the years, he'd comforted her during some of her lowest moments. Felicia could almost believe they could salvage their future together. Almost. Why couldn't he be content to remain her friend?

Mason cursed. "Simon must stop shagging his tarts long enough to get presentable and greet our guests."

Felicia had read the tabloid accounts of His Grace's *very* active dating life, the lewd suggestions. No proof, but there were always pictures of him with beauties at this function or that. Of course he had no trouble finding women willing to have sex with him. His Grace had even made her belly flip when she'd first met him. Their handshake had given her a jolt—literally. One touch, and her skin had heated, her heart stuttered.

Sophisticated, gorgeous, insanely masculine—everything about the man sent up her danger signals.

"Tarts, plural?"

"Indeed. He once shagged four women to exhaustion in less than thirty-six hours."

The tabloids had never mentioned *that*.

"His thirtieth birthday present to himself," Mason sneered. "In the middle of the party, he sneaked upstairs with his girlfriend. As the party went on, they were rutting away. My poor mother tried to make excuses. He never did blow out his candles. And a few hours later, he—"

"Hours?"

"Indeed. His supermodel of the moment, Cara, actually passed out, and Simon lurched down the back stairs into the kitchen, half-mad. He grabbed another woman—my French tutor, of all people! They disappeared for more than a few ticks of the clock. At the end of the party, a few women still loitered, I think hoping to be nearby when the very eligible Simon Northam appeared again. And they were. And still he kept rutting, even through an odd sort of earthquake that brought the upstairs roof down. He barely even noticed!"

Since there was no stench or nausea, Felicia knew what Mason said was true. Many women were bubble-headed enough to care only about His Grace's pretty title, face, and bank balance. On one level, she understood. Something about him was . . . compelling. But Simon Northam clearly took advantage of his appeal. What sort of man treated women so disrespectfully? A selfish wanker who led a life of privilege and assumed no one was as important as he. A practiced seducer accustomed to having his every whim fulfilled, with little care whose heart he broke. The type of cad who had been Deirdre's death knell.

By contrast, Mason was a good man. He'd never use and discard women like toothpicks. Even so . . . could she marry him, knowing he had vastly different expectations for their union? She *did* care for him. Was it fair to walk way without trying to love him? If she married him, he would do his utmost to treat her well. If she left now, eventually she would have to date. The singles scene would be filled with sharks like Hurstgrove. What the devil was she going to do?

"Felicia, darling." He grabbed her hands. "Stop worrying. I know your concerns. I've no doubt your mind and heart are racing madly—"

The door behind her fiancé opened, and Mason whirled around at the intrusion. The Duke of Hurstgrove lurched into the hall, looking utterly disheveled.

Felicia gasped. Her heart jumped in her chest.

Dark hair fell into his unshaven face, which looked as if it had been used as a punching bag. One eye was blackening. A cut rent his lip. His bow tie sat askew, and his shirt gaped open, exposing flashes of a bronzed chest. He swayed on his feet, gripping the door frame for support, his knuckles bleeding. Every muscle in his torso rippled. Distress and heat washed over Felicia.

He and Mason had the same glossy brown hair, chocolate eyes, and strong jaw. Despite the dozen years between them, they looked the same age. But the resemblance ended there. Rather than Mason's boxer's nose, a strong, aristocratic one bisected Hurstgrove's face. A cleft dimpled the duke's square chin. High cheekbones slashed each side of his face. When he wasn't arguing a case, Mason exuded an affable charm. His Grace put off something darkly riveting, an air of mystery. And charisma. The man oozed sex. Just looking at him caused electricity to sizzle across Felicia's skin.

Damn it, she refused to be attracted to him, even in passing. He was the sort of man she detested—lascivious, selfish, completely unaware of the pain he left in his wake. Her odd, visceral reaction to him made little sense.

"You're late," Mason spat to his brother. "You've been . . . fighting? Bloody hell! Shave and get dressed so we can carry on."

Hurstgrove grabbed Mason by the lapels and shoved him against the wall. "I need a list of every guest attending and every person working this wedding."

Mason pushed him away. "What you need is to piss off and get dressed. You can't go anywhere like this. You look like a ruffian."

His Grace's fists tightened in Mason's lapels. "I need that list. *Now!*"

Felicia frowned. What the devil was wrong with the man?

"I'm getting married and spending the rest of my life being happy," Mason growled back. "You might try doing the same before you disgrace all of us."

"I'm not letting go until you get me the damn list!"

"I have it," Felicia hissed at Hurstgrove. "I'll give it to you, if you'll take your hands off him."

In an instant, he released Mason and turned all his formidable attention on her, his gaze heavy, hot, burning. Fury and impatience and something she couldn't identify hit her. She swallowed and stiffened her spine, resisting the urge to step back.

"Get it," he snapped. Then, to her surprise, he added more gently, "Please."

Felicia cast a glance at Mason, who nodded. Rattled by fury and a dark thrill she couldn't explain, she stepped past the men and entered the bedroom she'd used to dress. Inside her tote she found her master lists. Why would His Grace want them? To make certain she hadn't invited the paparazzi? Lord knew they hounded the man. Whatever the reason, if surrendering the list kept him from strangling Mason, she'd do it. Then she'd give him a piece of her mind.

As soon as she figured out whether she should continue with the wedding.

When she returned to the hall, another man had crowded into the little landing area, this one tall and blond, wearing muddy jeans and boots. His authoritative air and razor-sharp gaze gave her pause.

"The bride, Miss Safford," Hurstgrove said to the new-comer.

She waited, but His Grace didn't bother to introduce his friend to her. Not that it mattered. But did the man think her beneath him and his chum? Felicia gritted her teeth, shoving the thought away. Reconsidering her pending marriage to Mason was far more important.

"She has the list," he told the blond man as he grabbed it from her and began to scan.

"Stop." Mason's demand was low, cold. "It's one thing for you to be rude to me. We're hardly best mates anymore. But you will not behave so badly to my wife."

"My deepest apologies, Miss Safford." He looked directly at her with those dark eyes that made her shiver. Then he turned to Mason. "She's your *fiancée*."

"A quarter-hour will change that." Mason's eyes narrowed. "Don't you *dare* think differently. I know you too well."

Hurstgrove raised a haughty brow.

"Leave Felicia alone, or I swear I will never speak to you again, Mother be damned," Mason threatened.

Was Mason implying that his half brother wanted her? Hurstgrove met her stare, his expression carefully blank. That's exactly what Mason meant. Felicia's stomach flipped again.

Foolish. Why should she care if she was one of many who inspired his erection?

"Don't you have guests to greet?" Hurstgrove suggested, his tone silky, lethal.

"Indeed. Clean up and get to the sanctuary. We'll discuss your abominable behavior later," Mason vowed, then offered her his arm.

Felicia took it, dragging her gaze away from His Grace and chastising herself. She had more than enough problems without her thoughts lingering on the unsettling duke.

Gaze firmly forward, she walked down the stairs with Mason. True, they shouldn't be seen together before the wedding, but finding someplace quiet to discuss their future was more imperative than convention, especially with so little time left to decide what to do.

As they reached the corridor at the bottom of the stairs, a half-dozen women, all dressed to kill, screeched at the sight of *the* Simon Northam. They sprinted up the stairs, tearing past her and Mason, their short skirts and long curls swishing.

As she rounded the corner, Felicia glanced over her shoulder. Lace, giggles, and feminine fawning surrounded His Grace. And he didn't look as if he was trying terribly hard to escape. In fact, he wrapped an arm around the nearest girl, put his lips against her ear, and spoke.

Would he have sex with one—or all of them—tonight? At the thought, something ugly and painful jabbed her. Did the man simply roll about the sheets with anyone possessing estrogen?

That answer wasn't much of a mystery, unlike his demand for the guest list. Regardless of why he wanted it, Felicia knew that having Hurstgrove here would be trouble.

After Bram arranged a distraction, enabling Duke to lose the gaggle of ever-present "ladies" looking for a trophy husband, the Doomsday Brethren leader yanked him back into his bedroom and slammed the door. Beside him stood Marrok and Ice, whose expressions ranged from disinterest to mild puzzlement. Finally, Ice shrugged and turned his attention to magically repairing their clothes—or trying to.

"Bugger!" Ice cursed as the tear in his shirt widened to reveal one enormous shoulder. "Where is my mate when I need her?"

"Aye," Marrok concurred with a laugh. "Sabelle can mend my trousers. You, I trust not."

"Sod it." Ice shrugged. "I'm not here to impress the humans."

"You'll scare them, more like," Bram drawled, then turned to Duke. "We need to work around Mason's enmity for you and deal with the crisis at hand."

"Indeed." Duke paced his large room, moonlight glowing through the balcony's French doors. He tamped down the urge to chase after the bride and press his lips to hers. "I have Felicia's lists. Let's hope they're complete."

Duke strode across the hardwood floors and their thick decorative rugs. When he reached his massive desk, he yanked open a heavy drawer and rummaged around for a pen. Hearing the tick-tock of time slipping away and knowing that Mathias was likely hot on their heels, he stared hard at the guest list, checking off the names of all new human acquaintances over the past week.

He thrust it at Bram. "We'll split into pairs. One will

shake hands while the other observes. In theory, the moment we come into contact with the Untouchable, our signatures should reflect that, yes? And Marrok's mating to Olivia should give him enough of a signature to be impacted, despite the fact he's human."

"Absolutely. You take Ice, and I'll go with Marrok. You obviously know your way around the house better, so you and Ice head to the kitchens and anywhere else the wedding staff might be. Marrok and I can follow the path of guests to the wedding and shake hands with those attending, including the bride—"

"Don't touch her." Duke tried to swallow down a seething rage at the thought of any male experimenting on Felicia. Based on the other wizards' surprise, he failed miserably.

Bram swore, then exchanged a glance with Ice. "You're possessive of your brother's fiancée."

God, he hated being so transparent. "Protective. I won't touch her, either."

"Someone must, in order to rule her out." Bram pointed out. "Mating ensures that Marrok has no designs on any woman other than Olivia. Besides, she would string him up by the balls if he did. Same with Ice, only in this case, I'd help Sabelle since she's my sister."

"Never happen," Ice assured Bram. "Sabelle is my world."

Ice could be a right scary bastard, but no one could deny how much he loved his mate.

"Though I've no idea where Emma is, I am still mated."

And like every other mated wizard, Bram had no desire nor the ability to bed another female. Duke often felt sorry for the poor sod. His woman had answered his Call in order to steal the Doomsday Diary, the most powerful book in their realm. Then she'd abandoned him after a single night, sneaking away with the book while he slept. In the nearly two months since, they'd recovered the book but found not one clue to her whereabouts.

Bram smiled grimly. "So you see, Felicia is safe from any lascivious intent on our part. I'm not certain that's the case with you. Besides, she's already touched you. Your signature is already altered. What if another touch doesn't show?"

In his head, Duke knew that. It didn't make looking at another man being close to or touching Felicia any easier. Even watching her walk away on Mason's arm had been torture. "Let me be the one. Let me try. Please."

"He's got it bad," Ice muttered.

Duke swallowed—and didn't say a word. Why refute the truth?

"All right, then," Bram relented, clearly against his better judgment. "Marrok and I will find the people on the guest list you've marked. Thankfully, that's a mere handful. You deal with the workers and Felicia. Meet us in the chapel in ten minutes."

Though he disliked it, Duke didn't have any more appealing options. He must find the Untouchable and whisk him or her away before Mathias and the Anarki descended.

"I should call off the wedding entirely, for safety's sake." Duke liked that idea—a great deal.

"Can't," Bram argued. "If you do, people will leave, and you'll never find the Untouchable. As soon as we discern their identity, *then* we'll halt the wedding and send everyone home."

"Indeed." Then reality hit him. How could he do that without disappointing his mother? Mason would hate him even more. And the stunning Felicia? He grimaced.

Did he have a choice?

Bram clapped him on the back. "I know this is difficult, but it's for the best."

Right. Then why did he have this knotted feeling in his gut that his life was about to change forever?

Knowing the die had been cast, Duke turned and left his bedroom. At the bottom of the stairs, Ice fell in step at his shoulder, wearing an expression that said *poor bastard*. Duke did his best to ignore it.

Quickly, he hunted up the florist, the cake decorator, and the wedding planner, all of whom his mother had insisted he meet in the past few days, hinting that she hoped he might require their services soon. One by one, he quickly reacquainted himself with them, ostensibly to ensure everything went smoothly. After he touched each individual, Ice simply shook his head. Within minutes, they'd run through most of their list and come up empty-handed.

"It must be one of the guests," Ice declared as they left the kitchen.

"Or the minister." *Or worse, the bride.*

The thought of Felicia in the middle of this war made Duke sick as hell. *Please God*, anyone *else . . .*

Exiting the kitchen, they headed for the chapel, his guts in knots. Duke had walked perhaps twenty meters down the corridor when the flock of young beauties darted for him again. He groaned. *Not now . . .*

Through the window behind him, a flashbulb went off. Paparazzi, damn them. Duke had little doubt these images would appear on some tabloid or another come morning.

At his side, Ice chuckled. "Right hell to be so popular. Are these the same girls who surrounded you earlier?"

"I think so." He hadn't looked that closely.

Searching for a gentle but insistent way to throw them off, Duke said, "Ladies, there will be plenty of time after the—"

One pressed her lips to his, cutting him off in mid-sentence. Another stepped behind him and wrapped her arms around his middle, then whispered exactly what she'd like to do to him if only they had a bit of privacy. She wasn't shy. The rest swarmed around, not allowing him an inch of air.

Bloody hell! Not that he hadn't experienced such unladylike behavior before, but at his brother's wedding, steps outside the chapel?

As he tried to jerk free, someone shoved the women aside with a feminine growl, then grabbed him by the arm and whirled him around. Felicia, in white lace, surrounded by a halo of golden curls. And she looked furious.

"Are you mad or simply unable to control your libido for a few minutes? I'm attempting to have an important conversation, and your behavior is disruptive. I don't know how your mother or brother abide this. Mason says you're forty-three; you act sixteen."

She sent a severe scowl to the women still hovering about, trying to gain his attention. "You all have seats somewhere. Find them!"

The women backed away—though not happily. At the moment, Duke could have kissed her for freeing him. Hell, he wanted to kiss her anyway. Deeply. Lips, tongues, clothes dropping to the floor as he lowered her to the bed . . .

No, I must not think that about Mason's bride.

"You will *not* embarrass Mason or your mother this way," Felicia vowed in a low-voiced breath. "This stops now, or I'll throw you out myself."

Too bad Duke was too distracted by the fact that, this close, he could see the glistening of Felicia's pouty red lips under their gloss . . . and right down the front of her gown to the sweet swells of her breasts. Heat ripped through his blood. Need compelled him. *Grab her. Take her. Possess her.* The words were a chant in his brain, loud and getting louder until he could scarcely remember why he was resisting.

Honor. Family harmony.

Damn it. He sighed.

Felicia gripped his elbow tighter and pursed her plump lips in displeasure. Bloody hell, she smelled like gardenia and woman. Duke only got harder. Blast it, he hoped his dinner jacket covered that. Somehow, he had to keep his hands to himself because her light floral-musky scent was driving him mad.

"Are you listening?" she demanded.

At his side, Ice cleared his throat and cast a sidelong glance at Felicia, then a meaningful glance at Duke's magical signature. "We have a winner."

CHAPTER 3

FELICIA GLARED AT HURSTGROVE, trying to rein in her temper. A sharp rebuke sat on the tip of her tongue. She pursed her lips together to hold it in, refusing to create an even bigger scene.

God, but the man got under her skin. Moments ago, she and Mason had been in a quiet corner, and she'd been desperately trying to decide her future. Marry Mason . . . or not? She'd been interrupted by Hurstgrove's antics. Even the friends he'd brought along caused gasps and raised brows. His blond chum had been intimidating enough, but she certainly would never have pictured His Grace running about with a tattooed, stubble-headed giant who looked more at home in back alleys. What the devil was going on?

Hurstgrove stared back. Blood flooded her cheeks, and her chest rose harshly with each agitated breath. Unfortunately, her reaction wasn't entirely fueled by anger. Though she released his arm, she still couldn't manage to cool her sizzling blood.

"You're certain?" His Grace demanded of the other man, his mouth tight.

The scary one crossed enormous arms over his chest, making one shoulder bulge through his filthy, torn sweater. "Yes. Sorry."

Hurstgrove clenched his fists and swore. Something grim and furious crossed his angular face.

Felicia blinked, stared. Were they both touched in the head?

"I've no notion what you're on about with this 'winner' comment, but could you give us some privacy, please?" She glared at the black-clad ruffian.

The burly man shot Hurstgrove a look she couldn't decipher. "Duke?"

Felicia frowned. Cheeky form of address.

"It's what my friends call me. A joke," Hurstgrove explained, shoving his hands in his pockets. He tapped his toe in agitation. "Give us a minute, Ice."

"You have less than that. The clock is ticking," he said, backing away.

Felicia was inclined to like Ice a bit more when he shooed the hovering flock of women toward the chapel, leaving her and Hurstgrove alone.

Grabbing hold of both her temper and her wayward response to him, she paced into the shadows of the corridor, out of sight of any passing wedding guest. He followed. As soon as he hovered above her, all wide shoulders and dark stare, she drew in a shaky breath. Why had she imagined shuttling into a dark corner with Hurstgrove was wise?

She fought against the edgy awareness that cramped her belly. "Cease this appalling behavior. As if arriving late after a brawl wasn't rude enough, your friends are wreaking havoc. I was attempting to sort through my future and—"

"With the ceremony due to start any moment?" Hurstgrove looked at his watch.

She bristled. Her indecision about marrying Mason was none of his affair. "Your mother and Mason are now attempting to deal with *your* friends, one of whom is a veritable giant wearing a sword. At a wedding! He's forcing people to shake his hand."

His Grace grimaced. "Felicia—"

"And you allowed those women to . . . molest you a few

dozen meters from the altar." The sight had burned itself into her brain, hurting when she knew it shouldn't. And that only made her more angry. "It's unforgivable."

He frowned. "I have never touched any of those women in my life."

She detected no acrid scent, and felt no unsettled stomach. So, he told the truth—this once. Small comfort. "Hardly noteworthy, given your generally deplorable behavior."

"I apologize, but I must talk to you about—"

"When I'm finished." She poked a finger in his chest. "The paparazzi are peeking through the windows and having a grand time photographing the shocked expressions of your mother's friends. She's quite beside herself. I know everyone bows and scrapes to you, and women throw themselves at your feet. Don't expect either from me."

Her face turned even more grim. "It's not my aim to upset you. This is . . . necessary."

A fresh wave of anger crashed through Felicia, and she welcomed it, hoping it would hold her awareness of him at bay. "Are you so arrogant that you must have attention? Do you need the cameras, the women, and the notoriety to feel fulfilled, Your Grace?"

"What?" He recoiled, looking perplexed, then furious. "*No.* I'm trying to tell you something but . . . bloody hell. I've gone about this the wrong way. Sorry."

"Indeed."

He shrugged. "I'm only human."

Felicia opened her mouth to argue with him. Then a familiar, biting scent burned her nostrils. An instant later, her stomach turned, and she put a hand over her queasy belly to steady herself.

Hurstgrove lied—and the stench hadn't presented itself until his last three words.

Not human? Impossible. Felicia's mind raced. He looked like any other attractive man, though younger than his forty-three years suggested. Perhaps the whole evening—having Mason reveal his true feelings and His Grace making a scene—had thrown her senses off?

"What did you say?" she demanded.

"I'm only human. I make mistakes."

Immediately, Felicia's nostrils burned wildly again. Her stomach pitched as if she were in a rowboat in the midst of a hurricane. Gasping, she stared at him, wide eyed.

The Duke of Hurstgrove was *not* human. What, then, was he?

The horror on her face must have shown, because he grabbed her shoulders, his touch feverishly warm. A flurry of tingles barraged her. "What's the matter? Are you nervous? Faint?" Understanding dawned, and he backed away. "No, you're frightened."

Of you.

If she admitted that, how would he react? What was such an intimidating non-human capable of? If he knew that she'd figured out his secret, what would he do to her?

Heart pounding so hard she couldn't hear her own voice, Felicia muttered, "I-I must . . . repair my lipstick."

Before he could respond, she tore from his grasp and ran.

As she disappeared up the stairs, Ice, who had been loitering outside the chapel, sauntered across the marble tiles toward Duke. "Apologizing, are you? Not a particularly effective tactic to tell the woman she's in danger."

Duke snorted. "You would have grabbed her and run without any thought of alienating your family, causing a scandal, or scaring the hell out of her."

The other wizard shrugged. "I don't have any family to

alienate, I don't give a damn if I cause a scandal, and I'd rather have my woman frightened than dead."

"She's not mine."

A sly smile crept across his face. "Is that what you're telling yourself?"

"Piss off. I can't do what you would have done. My situation is more complicated."

Ice didn't say a word, just took a long look around him at the marble tile, perfectly plastered walls, and muraled ceilings. The original estate had been built by one of Duke's ancestors in the mid-sixteenth century. Over the years, the house had been expanded, altered, sections demolished and rebuilt. The chapel was part of that original structure, now overlooking the lush gardens his mother took great pains to oversee. The rest of the house maintained that stiff, museum-quality look. Duke had considered turning the estate over to the National Trust, but his mother loved living here.

Now seeing the estate through Ice's eyes, a wizard who had grown up in a series of caves . . . Duke winced. Ice couldn't possibly understand his responsibilities.

"I always thought Bram had ostentatiousness down to a fine art, but you make him look like an amateur."

"I didn't decorate—" Frustration crashed in, and Duke raked a hand through his hair. "Never mind. Focus on Felicia. I don't want her out of our sight. The Anarki may appear at any moment. We'll try this your way, but I must persuade Mason to call off this wedding so we can get everyone else out of here."

Ice raised a dark, bushy brow. "How?"

"No idea." Regardless of what anyone said, Mason would likely refuse.

Damn it, Duke wished he could simply confess that he was a wizard. But Mason would only think him a nutter.

Even if he could convince his brother, Mason wouldn't even abide having a Liberal Democrat in the house, so Duke couldn't imagine what he'd think about someone magical.

With a slap on the back, Ice shot him a pitying look. "Good luck. Would you like me to fetch Felicia?"

Duke's first instinct was to refuse. *He* wanted to be the one to watch over her, keep her safe from danger. But that wouldn't stop Mathias from crashing this wedding and potentially hurting his family or guests in his quest to find the Untouchable. He had to empty Lowechester Hall. While he wouldn't be skimping on the drama, he had to hope the plan saved lives. And that he could avoid the tempting Felicia as much as possible.

"Yes. I'll have a word with Mason."

"Make it thirty seconds or less." Ice bounded down the hall and up the stairs toward the family's rooms.

Head swimming, Duke darted toward the chapel.

Mason stormed toward him, greeting him at the door. "Where the hell have you been? We were set to start ten minutes ago. You should have been lined up in the anteroom long before. Your friends are disturbing the guests. Mum can't find Felicia, and somehow I know you're to blame."

Entirely. "I'll address my friends. Felicia is fixing her lipstick." *And avoiding me.* "But I must talk to—"

"Did you have anything to do with her lipstick being mussed?" Mason's dark eyes narrowed.

No, but God, he'd love that. The thought of kissing her made him hard all over. Again. Duke tugged at the bottom of his dinner jacket. "No. She seemed flustered when I ran into her in the hall. But that's not important. Listen to me, Mason. Felicia is in danger."

* * *

In her hiding place behind an armoire door, Felicia listened as Hurstgrove's words penetrated her brain. She clapped a hand over her mouth to hold in a gasp. Truth bathed His Grace's expression. The absence of a stench or a burning belly told her senses that he believed every word he said.

Danger?

Was he delusional? Mistaken?

Or, God forbid, right?

After slipping past the scary, stubble-headed man, Felicia had sneaked back here. Thankfully, no one had noticed her lurking in the shadowed corner of the corridor. And here she would stay until she was certain Hurstgrove wouldn't guess that she knew his secret.

Biting her lip, Felicia held her questions. Mason, a barrister well trained in cross-examination, would ask what was necessary. She'd listen and smell and decipher truths from lies. Besides, Mason wouldn't be rattled by Hurstgrove's compelling demeanor or the fact that he wasn't human. Felicia would bet a year's salary Mason had no clue his brother was anything but a normal man.

"*What?*" her fiancé exploded. "Danger? Of what sort?"

"Felicia is the target of a madman. He will take her from you and by the time he's done, she'll beg for death. Any moment, he and his . . . terrorists will descend."

Felicia prayed to smell the awful stench that turned her stomach. Only the roses and jasmine of her wedding flowers wafted to her nose. Still, Hurstgrove's perception didn't make it reality. She prayed he was wrong.

"Madman? Terrorists?" Mason scowled. "How would *you* know this? Do you have any proof?"

Hurstgrove paused. "I met with one of his underlings, who told me—"

"You, meeting a terrorist's underling?" Mason shot him a skeptical glare.

Felicia thought it unlikely as well. Except her ability told her his words were fact.

Hurstgrove hesitated. "I know him through my friends. Listen to—"

"Do you?" Mason cocked his head. "The skull-capped thug or the big bloke with the sword?"

"Neither. Did you hear me? This madman *will* torture and kill her."

Again, Hurstgrove told the truth as he knew it. *Dear God . . .* Why her? Felicia tried to grapple for any reason why she would have come to a madman's attention. Retribution for some criminal Mason had helped put behind bars?

"So this person offered you information? And you believed him? Without proof?" Mason scoffed.

"Damn it! He has no reason to lie."

"Just as you have no reason to ruin my wedding with this ridiculous assertion?" Mason's voice rang thick with sarcasm. "How could this criminal possibly know Felicia?"

"I . . . don't know."

The scent of Hurstgrove's lie smacked Felicia in the face. He knew exactly how this villain had come to be aware of her. So why was he keeping the answer to himself?

"She is a bloody nursery school teacher. I've known you to go to ridiculous lengths in the past to bed a woman who made your cock twitch, but this is low, even for you," Mason growled, then shook his head. "A terrorist looking for Felicia. Don't take me for stupid."

Hurstgrove hesitated, looking agitated and bleak. "I'm not making this up!"

"Rubbish! You cooked up this fucking charade to ruin our wedding."

"I'm trying to protect her," His Grace insisted. "Damn it, we don't have time to—"

"If she's in danger, why didn't you come forward before now?" Mason raised a dark brow, back in barrister mode.

"I just learned of it an hour ago. Mason—"

"Why did you want the guest list if you knew she was in danger?"

Hurstgrove paced the elegant floor, moonlight bathing his strong profile. Felicia's heart stuttered at the sight. The most insane urge to get close to him, curl up against him, press her mouth to his, overcame her. She shoved the schoolgirlish reaction aside. He wasn't human. Her life could be in peril. What the hell was she doing lusting after the man?

"It's complicated," the duke finally answered.

Mason raised a dark brow. "I'll manage."

Hurstgrove raked a hand through his mussed hair. "We've no time for this now unless you want her to die."

"She'll be in a whole other sort of danger with you. I'm not budging until you give me proof."

His Grace clenched his jaw, telling her he fought long and hard for patience. "I knew what they sought, not who. I'd hoped it wasn't Felicia . . ."

But it was, as least in Hurstgrove's mind. Fresh panic set in. Who was this madman? What could he possibly want with her?

Mason scoffed. "How thick do you think I am? What does she have that a terrorist could possibly want?"

Hurstgrove hesitated. "I'll explain when she's out of danger. Now, I must take her into hiding—"

"*You* won't take her anywhere."

"Felicia will *die* if she doesn't leave with me now!"

She watched their rapid exchange, her heart pounding. Everything Hurstgrove said was true, so she *should* leave. Felicia stepped forward to say as much, but Mason cut in first.

"By all means, you and your shady friends go. If Felicia needs protecting, that is my job and my right. After the wedding—"

"She may be dead before you finish the ceremony! These aren't your average thugs. You can't protect her."

Felicia hung back as a new possibility washed over her. Were these terrorists non-human like Hurstgrove? That possibility showered her in a horrific wave. Dear God, if so, who else but Hurstgrove could keep her safe?

"You have the audacity to suggest we postpone the wedding?" Mason thundered.

"I'm not suggesting; I'm insisting."

If she was truly in danger, Hurstgrove's plan sounded not only logical, but imperative. Yet . . . if she didn't marry Mason tonight, would she ever? Or would that door close? Without a husband, how would she achieve her dreams of her own home and family? Then again, none of that would matter if she was dead.

"You bastard." Mason hurled. "You've inherited a title, an estate, a vast fortune, and have the world at your feet. You shag a different woman every night. I want *one* for the rest of my life, to protect and cherish. You merely seek to add another notch to your bedpost."

"That's not true."

Murder crossed Mason's face. "So, you don't want Felicia?"

Hurstgrove frowned, hesitated. "No."

A moment later, an overwhelming stench hit her, so debilitating, she clutched her stomach. Her eyes watered. Hurstgrove *did* want her—very badly. Felicia swallowed. His response was like a flash fire, blistering her veins. She tried to push her reaction aside. Foolish. Inappropriate. Destructive.

How much more complicated could her life become? Loved by one brother, desired by the other, who wasn't even human . . .

Suddenly, Hurstgrove's friends crowded into the corridor like a walking wall of testosterone. Individually, they each spelled trouble. Together, they looked downright menacing.

The trio sauntered toward Mason.

"Where is she?" His Grace demanded of Ice.

He smiled tightly. "Here in the room, eavesdropping on you."

Felicia gnawed her lip. She'd done nothing to give herself away, but he might not be human either. Did Ice know where she'd hidden? Fear detonated in her belly.

Then the blond one spoke. "Time is up. Duke, now."

"Then go," Mason spat and turned back to Hurstgrove. "I will not postpone my wedding based on hearsay. I'm marrying the woman I love tonight. And you won't stop me."

"I regret that saving Felicia will further deteriorate our relationship, but not enough to risk her. You shouldn't either, if you truly love her."

"How *dare* you suggest . . ." Fury etched his face, then his voice turned deadly calm. "Leave. You're no longer invited."

"Throwing me out of my own house will not keep her safe. This . . . criminal is more depraved than you can possibly imagine."

Another truth.

Felicia had more than enough information to be certain of her next move. Time to speak up—and make her choice.

"Why me?" she asked, stepping out of the armoire, into the light.

Hurstgrove whirled toward her, visibly relieved to see her in one piece. "I'll explain later." Then he reached for her. "If you want to live, take my hand and come with me now."

His gaze was electric. Everything jumbled inside her. The security Mason gave her clashed with the foreign excitement his half brother wrought. She didn't like the way Hurstgrove made her feel, vulnerable and so aware of her femininity, fragile and desirable at once. She'd elected to marry Mason in part because he never engendered such feelings in her. He would make a stable partner, a wonderful father. Hurstgrove was rich, titled, good-looking, and notoriously good in bed—built for a night, not forever.

"Felicia," Mason said sharply. "You don't believe this rubbish, do you?"

She'd never told him about her bullshit barometer. In fact, she'd never told anyone but Deirdre. Most people would never believe such a thing, and Mason, who made a good living by dealing in evidence and facts, was less likely than most.

"I have a . . . sense that he's being honest."

"Are you mad? He constantly seduces women, no doubt with lies. This is absurd!"

At her side, Hurstgrove tensed, then glanced at Bram, who nodded. What sort of signal was that?

In the next moment, His Grace surged forward and hooked an arm around her waist, lifting her, wedding dress and all, into his arms and against his chest. Lest she fall, Felicia instinctively locked her arms around the strong column of his neck. Her bridal bouquet slipped from her fingers and fell to the floor.

He strode toward the exit at the rear of the house without a backward glance.

"What the hell are you doing?" she asked.

No answer. He simply marched away from his friends, her fiancé, their wedding.

She wriggled in his grasp. "Put me down! I said I was inclined to believe you. I never agreed that I would come along."

His arms tightened around her. "Sorry. I won't risk you."

Hurstgrove was abducting her? Her breath stuttered, and her belly turned over again. In that moment, it wasn't only her safety she feared for.

Felicia opened her mouth to protest, but the sincerity of his dark eyes silenced her.

If not for the danger, she would have fought him, punching, biting, scratching . . . anything to avoid putting herself in his path and potentially under his spell. But His Grace risked family censure and scandal to protect her from a deadly threat. And he wanted her.

Which motivated him most?

"Put her down now!" Mason demanded.

Hurstgrove didn't slow his pace a bit. "Sorry. Trying to pop out the back before the paparazzi catch on. I assume you prefer not to have pictures of this splashed across the rags?"

Felicia glanced over his shoulder to see his friends restraining Mason. They were "other" too, she suspected. None of them looked mad or otherwise deranged, but rather almost too powerful to be human.

"You fucking bastard! Bring my bride back!" Mason bellowed.

His mother appeared at the bottom of the stairs, mouth agape. "Simon!"

"I'll ring you later, Mum," His Grace threw over his shoulder, trying to shield Felicia as paparazzi flashbulbs began to stream through the windows and lit up the corridors. Most likely, these images would be front page news. Horror gripped her as she buried her face in Hurstgrove's shoulder—and inhaled a complex scent of sandalwood, citrus, and man that went straight to her head.

At the clatter of shoes against the marble tiles, Felicia

raised her head, fastening her gaze on the chapel doors in the distance. Most of her guests stared now, faces slack with a shock she discerned even at a distance. Some snapped pictures with their mobiles. Her friends and coworkers all stared, mouths agape. Hurstgrove cursed.

"Stop!" she ordered. "If danger is coming, Mason—"

"Can't help or protect you. *You* are the target. Mason can only be a liability. If you want him safe, leave him here."

It sounded like a convenient excuse, and she would have thought so if not for the absence of any cloying, burning scent.

"This is mad!"

"And the tabloids will eat the scandal up, which I fear may expose you to . . ." Hurstgrove paused, sighed regretfully. "Too late now. I know what this monster is capable of and I promise, I won't let him touch you."

She absorbed his protective vow. Why would the self-absorbed playboy care?

"W-when can I return home? To Mason."

He grimaced as he pushed his way into a small parlor, crossed the room in a handful of steps, then muscled his way through French doors and outside.

Freezing air pelted her, slipping under her dress insidiously. Fresh snow dusted the ground. Wind whipped through her curls, tearing at her upswept do, penetrating her lace sleeves with chill. Hurstgrove wrapped his arms more tightly around her. The warmth of his skin seeped in. His male scent pummeled her senses again. She heard his beating heart, his even breaths. He felt so human.

"Perhaps a few days." He shook his head. "I don't know."

An ugly truth. The idea of being so close to Mason's compelling half brother for even that long petrified her.

"Over there!" she heard through the wind's howl, then

looked up to see a swarm of paparazzi sprinting behind the estate, across the snowy lawn and toward them, flashbulbs popping with each step.

Hurstgrove picked up the pace, darting for the outbuilding that held his autos. He showed no signs of tiring. Under his tuxedo, he was solid muscle.

"I can walk," she protested.

"The snow will ruin your dress and shoes."

Likely, but a slight stench told her that wasn't the only reason he carried her. "Be reasonable. I'm not exactly a feather. If we're rushing to safety, and you're going to fatigue—"

"Not for some time."

Under her hands, his shoulders and arms were spine-tinglingly hard. Felicia shoved the thought away. "Clearly, you exercise, but—"

"Marrok is like the most demanding personal trainer. On fast forward. In an endless loop. Trust me; he's ensured this is little effort."

"I understand that I'm in danger. I won't run from you."

He shot her a regretful glance. "Sorry. I'm not convinced."

Before she could argue, Hurstgrove shouldered his way inside the building, then kicked the door closed behind, stooping to lock it. As he turned, she saw Bram. How had he beaten them here?

He sat behind the wheel of a very expensive black Italian sports car. Convertible. Who owned such an impractical vehicle in a climate that got nearly as much rain as sun?

A duke.

Bram revved the engine, then ducked out of the driver's seat to stand beside it. "Get her in. You'd best leave quickly. I have a bad feeling."

His Grace strode to the passenger door, slid her into the seat, buckled her in, and shut her inside. Black leather. Flawless. Powerful. Imposing.

She grabbed at the door handle, scrambling to find a way out, but Hurstgrove blocked her path on one side, Bram on the other. "Agreed. I'd rather use my . . . usual method of transportation."

"Try it?" Bram asked.

"Useless, which I expected. Try it yourself."

What the devil were they talking about?

Felicia leaned across the seat and watched as the blond man stood very still and closed his eyes, straining slightly.

Bram expected *that* to take him someplace? Like "Beam me up, Scotty"? What were Hurstgrove and his friends? Aliens?

The other man opened his eyes. "Totally nonfunctional. Damn. You'd best go. Your signature has damn near become a beacon. Meet us at Ice's?"

"Hopefully by tomorrow afternoon." Hurstgrove slid into the driver's seat, buckled up, and rolled down the window. "I'll ring you along the way."

Bram pressed a button and raised the garage door. "I should come with you. Safety in numbers."

Hurstgrove looked in the rearview mirror, then swore. "Too late. Get the guests out of the chapel, to safety. You'll have to stay and fight."

Felicia whipped her head around to look out the driver's window and saw a mass of black-robed men marching toward the house.

CHAPTER 4

FELICIA GASPED. "WHO IS *that?*"

Duke ignored the question and sent Bram a grim glance.

This rescue was going to hell fast. He had a reluctant hostage, an infuriated groom, and paparazzi following him round the back of his supposedly private estate. Trespassing bastards. He could only hope that Zain skipped a day or two of reading the tabloids. If not, Mathias would know quickly that Duke had spirited Felicia away and guess why.

"Go. Now," the other wizard ordered. "Whatever it takes to keep her safe . . ."

Absolutely. Duke would do it, no questions asked.

Rolling up the tinted windows, he backed out of the garage slowly, lights killed. He couldn't attract attention.

"Duck," he demanded of Felicia.

She didn't. Wide-eyed, she stared out the back window at the hooded figures amassing in the gardens. "There are so many of them! Who—"

"Duck!" He grabbed her neck and pulled her head down.

Her cheek hit his thigh, and he felt Felicia panting through his trousers. He got hard. Again. *Damn it.*

"What the devil are you doing?" She struggled against his hold.

"Hiding you from a madman. Stay the bloody hell down!"

A moment later, Mathias emerged from the middle of the Anarki pack. Duke's fingers tightened in Felicia's hair. Horror gripped him as the wind whipped the evil wizard's long hair away from his deceptively youthful face, revealing a smile of evil glee. It took everything inside Duke not to turn back to protect his family and their guests when Mathias raised his hands to the wall, as if readying to demolish it with a spell.

To Duke's surprise, no bricks tumbled to the ground.

Holy hell! He glanced down at Felicia, her shoulders hunched beside the gearshift. He'd known magic would be impossible when she was near; that was the nature of an Untouchable. But Mathias was at least two hundred meters away.

Her suppression of magic was that strong? That made her a force to be reckoned with. And a huge target for Mathias.

Even before tonight, Felicia had been someone Duke was willing to protect with his life . . . and he didn't want to think too hard about why. Now that he knew she was the Untouchable, he'd move heaven and earth to keep her safe.

He eased down the drive to the dark road. Once he hit the little lane, Duke jammed down on the clutch, threw the gearshift into first, then stomped on the accelerator. Rapidly, he shifted up to second, third, fourth . . . still feeling Felicia's breath on his thigh. Checking the rearview mirror, he was relieved to see that no one appeared to notice his departure in the mayhem. He floored it, putting distance between them and Mathias, every muscle in his body tense, his heart thumping in his chest.

As he rounded the first corner, one of the walls of the six-teenth-century chapel crashed down under Mathias's spell. Duke closed his eyes and held in a curse. Dear God, please let everyone be unharmed, especially once Mathias realized the Doomsday Brethren had spirited the Untouchable away.

As the house slipped from sight, Duke flipped on the headlights and released Felicia, fighting the urge to run his hand through her soft honey hair to ensure she was unharmed. "Sorry if I hurt you. Are you all right?"

"Who were those people in the robes? Were they the villains trying to—"

"Yes." He didn't want to elaborate now. And he didn't want to talk about Felicia being hurt or killed. The other female corpses he'd seen after Mathias's torture were too horrific to contemplate.

Panic raced across her face. "What about the wedding party and the house?"

"Bram, Marrok, and Ice will protect everyone."

"Three people aren't enough to fight that army. We must call the authorities. Go back! Mason and your mother and—"

"The police can't help them." Duke pressed his lips together regretfully, shifting again as the car jetted through the inky night. "We can't go back."

"They need our help!"

"I'll make certain they get it, but you must be safe at all costs."

"I won't leave Mason there to die!"

"He'll be fine." Duke gritted his teeth at the sound of his brother's name on her lips, spoken with such devotion. "It's not him they want. It's you."

Privately, he worried about his family and guests, but he saw no need to admit that to Felicia and worry her more.

Grabbing the phone from his pocket, he thumbed through the menus, then found the number he sought.

Tynan answered on the first ring, "You all right, Duke?"

"Close call, but I'm fine."

"Did you find—"

"Indeed. My brother's bride is with me."

"Shit! She came with you voluntarily on her wedding day?"

"Not . . . exactly. Listen, Tynan. Mathias and the Anarki have descended on my house. Bram, Ice, and Marrok need backup."

"Got it. Ronan is handy. Caden, can you go with us? Right, then. He's in as well."

"Lucan?"

"He's . . . not having a good night."

Duke winced. "Angry, despondent, or insane?"

"Depends on which moment you ask."

Damn it! "So, not battle ready?"

"Not even close," Tynan said.

"Keep him there. I don't need him regressing instead of saving the wedding guests. You and the others get to my house posthaste."

"Will do."

"Please, find my mother and my brother. Make certain . . ."

God, if something happened to them because he hadn't revealed the fact he was a wizard and hadn't properly protected the place, the guilt would crush him. He'd always been afraid that putting magical protections around his house would announce the fact that a wizard lived there and be an engraved invitation to Mathias. Now, Duke regretted the decision more than anything.

"We'll keep them safe."

"One more thing," Duke interjected. "Is Sabelle available?"

"Somewhere around. I'll put her on."

A moment later, Duke heard a sunny, feminine voice. "Hello. All well?"

"That remains to be seen. Anytime Mathias crashes a party, it's not good."

"Can I help?" Concern laced her voice.

Duke downshifted for the next turn in the winding road, cursing the long, deserted lane they must travel before reaching the motorway. "I'd like you to research a bloodline for me. Her name is Felicia Safford."

"What?" his passenger screeched. "You have no right—"

He held up a palm, cutting her off. "Who are her ancestors?"

"In other words, make certain she is *the* Untouchable? Got it," Sabelle said in his other ear. "I'll need details. Birth date, birthplace, parents' names . . ."

Moving his mobile from his mouth, Duke said to Felicia, "I'll explain everything shortly. But—"

She wrinkled her nose, then narrowed her eyes at him. "Rubbish! You aren't planning to explain anything."

How had she known that? Explaining the situation would only drag her deeper into danger, and Duke wasn't in favor of that. "We've no time to argue now, damn it! What's your birth date?"

"My—" She huffed in frustration. "Mason and your mother may be dying, and you're driving in the opposite direction, asking inane questions?"

"Your. Birth. Date. Now."

She shook her head, her expression mulish. "You *will* explain or I won't say a word."

Duke hesitated. No one magical made a habit of revealing themselves to a human. But how did he explain that the more he dragged her into this war, the more difficult it would be for her to resume her life? For a woman Mason had described as sweet and caring, Felicia had a surprising stubborn streak.

"I'm asking for a very good cause that could save more lives, I swear. I can't spare the time to explain now." Even if he could, the truth was too dangerous.

Felicia sat back in her seat, stared suspiciously, then, of all things, she sniffed. "June twenty-eight, nineteen eighty-five."

"Where were you born?"

"Newham General Hospital, London."

"Parents' names?"

She bit her lip. "I'm adopted. My birth parents' names are sealed."

He froze. "Your adoptive parents are listed on the birth certificate?"

"Yes. Margaret and Rowland Safford."

Nodding, Duke put the phone back to his ear. "Did you hear that?"

"I'm on it now," Sabelle promised.

"Thank you. Have Bram call me when the fight is over."

After Sabelle agreed and they rang off, Duke pocketed his phone, very aware of Felicia beside him, clenching her fists. Her jaw tightened, and he could almost see her thoughts turning in her head.

"Why does this madman want *me*? I heard what you told Mason, but I know there's more."

Duke hesitated. How could he say more without exposing magickind and endangering her further? "You're . . . special."

"Oh, please." She rolled her eyes.

"Different," he clarified. "Hopefully, Sabelle's research will uncover the answers we need."

Her brow wrinkled. She had intelligence, this one. She'd figured out quickly that she was genuinely in danger. She had a knack for knowing when he was less than honest. Duke feared what she'd figure out next.

"You think my birth parents were important in some way?"

Not in the manner she meant, but . . . "Until we have the facts, I can't say. But my mission was—is—to keep you safe, no matter what. I know leaving Mason behind to face danger was difficult. But it was necessary. Until we can find some way to throw Mathias off—"

"That's his name, the leader of all those hooded creatures? And his group is the anarchy people."

Duke winced. She'd been listening to his call. He hadn't meant to let any of that slip. But it was late, his nerves were unwinding. Felicia distracted him until he could scarcely think. He *must* be more careful in the future.

"It's not important."

She wrinkled her nose at him. "That's a lie! Because of this man, my life is in shambles—"

"I'm doing everything I can to stop him. Until then, you must stay close to me. Bram and the others will help."

"So we won't be . . . alone?"

Duke whipped his gaze to Felicia. Anxiety filled her expression.

So, she didn't want to be alone with him. Duke knew why. He'd become very adept at reading the subtlest signs of a woman's interest, and Felicia blared them against her will. He'd bet his last penny she was aware of him as a man.

Duke's gut tightened. Being with Felicia was like getting closer to a shimmering ocean, beautiful, inviting, almost irresistible. But getting entangled with her would be like falling into a drowning pool. As much as his magical senses may decree otherwise, she belonged to Mason, loved him. Felicia would be a part of this war only briefly, and in a limited fashion. If he didn't want to lose his family or keep her in danger, he had to shove his instincts aside.

"Once we reach safety, we won't be alone," he assured.

"Good." She sighed. "Th-that's good."

He gripped the wheel tightly and stared at the shadowed road. "Felicia, I know you're Mason's. I respect that."

Or he was trying to.

"Thank you," she said stiffly. "Who will be with us? The friends you brought to the wedding? This Tynan and Lucan, who's evidently not quite sane?"

Damn she had been listening intently. "Likely."

"Who is Sabelle?"

Did he detect a note of jealousy? The possibility jolted him with an unexpected thrill. He should strive to alienate Felicia romantically. But he couldn't bring himself to do it.

"Ice's . . . wife." And he'd already said far too much. The less she knew the safer she'd be. "Get some sleep. We have a long journey."

An hour later, Duke's phone rang. Bram. He answered almost instantly, hoping not to wake Felicia.

"Talk to me."

"I'm glad that fucking nightmare is over. Your mother and Mason are safe. Ronan and Marrok escorted the guests into your library, away from windows overlooking the gardens or chapel so the humans wouldn't see all the magical activity and lose their minds. It was a good plan."

Despite the positive news, Bram's tone told Duke everything had gone to hell. "But?"

"The Anarki halfheartedly fought us. Very odd. We cut through them in minutes. I think Mathias brought them merely to distract us. As soon as he could perform magic, he realized the Untouchable had gone. I chased him through the house as he teleported from room to room until he found the guests."

Duke's heart beat in his chest. Mathias with a roomful of humans. He wouldn't bother to show them his magic, just kill them. The possibility sickened him. "And?"

"The good news is, Mathias didn't show his parlor tricks

to the humans or use them for target practice. The bad news? Mathias realized quickly that the bride was gone, and guests gave him her name. He knows Felicia is most likely the Untouchable."

The words were like an earthquake in his chest. Everything inside Duke shifted. Any hope that she could easily return to her life imploded, turning to rubble. He'd known that letting go of his potential mate would be hell, but he'd been prepared to do it for Mason's sake . . . and Felicia's. But now that Mathias knew her identity, the game had changed irrevocably.

"Damn it," he cursed in a low voice. "What now? We cannot just wait a few days, then return her to her world with a simple guard. She'd be in constant danger, along with every child she watches at her nursery school and—"

"I know." Bram sighed heavily. "Take her to Ice's. We'll discuss the future there."

"What's there to discuss?" Duke's mind raced. "She can't simply be a human again until we find some way to neutralize the threat to her safety."

Bram paused. "Does that really break your heart, the thought of her in our world, so near you?"

Even now, Duke was doing his best to tamp down his inappropriate thrill at that realization. "She doesn't belong with us. With me. She's not *safe.*"

"She's no longer safe anywhere."

Duke smashed his palm on the steering wheel, then winced as Felicia stirred. "I don't want her in danger."

"You may not have realized this, given your life of privilege, but you don't always get what you want."

"Fuck you," he growled.

"That make you feel better?" Bram challenged.

Dragging in a breath, Duke tried to rein in his temper.

Bram was merely the messenger in this situation, and as much as he wanted to tell the wizard off again, it would do little good. Felicia had been inexorably dragged into their world, and he had no idea what to do next.

"I want to talk to that prick who ran off with my bride," Mason shouted in the background. "Right now! He will return Felicia to me or so help me God . . . Give me that!"

After a loud fumbling, Mason hissed into the phone, "Simon?"

"Or you'll what?" Duke returned. "Beat me for keeping Felicia out of danger?"

"She's *my* bride. *I* should be the one to keep her safe, you horse's ass! But you snatched her from me. Now the tabloids are atwitter about the fact you abducted Felicia from our wedding. She's the subject of the worst innuendos. They captured some very clear pictures of the two of you. I saw how you were looking at her."

Mason paused, clearly hoping Duke would bow, scrape, or otherwise apologize. He didn't say a word.

"Bring Felicia back," Mason demanded. "I'll protect her. I don't trust you. You've already banged every attractive woman from London to Edinburgh. You even seduced my French tutor, despite my crush on her. Nothing I feel matters one whit to you, and I know you'd think nothing of using this danger to lure Felicia to your bed."

The French tutor? Yes, his thirtieth birthday. His transition from man to wizard. Duke barely recalled touching the woman. But that weekend, he could have shagged an entire sorority and been unaware of it.

"I'm sorry."

"Too little, too late. You shagged Nicolette and the others for hours and returned them exhausted and dehydrated. I won't let you do the same to Felicia. Or worse."

Duke grimaced. He'd never meant to hurt Mason, but after that fateful weekend, their once close relationship had given way to animosity. Until now, he'd never known why.

Mason went on, "Given the way these people demolished the chapel, I can't deny there's danger. If it's directed at Felicia, I know very important people in the government who can keep her safe. You're not trained—"

"The man who attacked you earlier is looking for her now. Your government friends can't help Felicia at all. I can. I won't release her until she'll be safe."

"That's absurd. I have connections to highly trained individuals at MI6 and—"

"Even MI6 can't fight this. The danger can only be fought by people I know," Duke countered. "They understand this madman. I promise, she will be safe with me."

"How? If MI6 can't protect her, how can an aimless playboy like you? You'll do anything to get into a woman's knickers, and this just proves it."

"I have no iniquitous purpose," Duke insisted. "I've duly noted that she is yours and have no plans to seduce her. That is the last you will hear from me on this subject."

No way could he promise he'd never touch Felicia. Of course, he'd try like hell to keep his hands off, but Duke knew he wasn't strong enough to promise it. Half of his thoughts revolved around keeping her safe. The other half fixated on stripping her down to her skin and loving every inch of her.

"You fucking—"

"Would you like to speak to her?" Duke cut through Mason's outburst. Responding to it would only prolong the argument.

His brother cursed. "You know I would."

Duke hit a button to mute the phone, then turned to the lovely Felicia at his side, sleeping restlessly in her seat. Her honey hair was loosening from its French twist, wisps of golden strands curling at her neck and temples. She looked so soft, so female. And so exhausted. His heart jolted, and he jerked his eyes back to the road, swallowing hard.

"Felicia?"

She didn't stir at all. Nor did she when he called her name again, this time louder.

Bloody hell. He was going to have to touch her.

Duke didn't like the way his hand shook as he reached out and cupped her shoulder. The contact was like a lightning bolt through him. He tugged his hand away, but when she didn't stir, he drew in a shuddering breath, then wrapped his hand around her shoulder again.

Steeling himself against a hot flood of desire, he jostled her. "Felicia?"

She moaned and turned her face his way, lashes fluttering slowly over her blue eyes, now sultry with sleep. As if he needed another slam of arousal coursing through him.

"What?" Her sleepy voice sounded husky and rough, and Duke couldn't help but wonder if that's how she'd sound after a night in his bed.

He cleared his throat. "Mason is on the phone. Would you like to speak to him?"

That news brought Felicia's eyes open wide. She sat up straight, looking startled. "I fell asleep? Blast it!"

"Mason?" He held out the phone.

"Yes. Please."

Duke held in a curse as he unmuted the phone and handed it to her.

Felicia grabbed it tightly. "Are you all right?"

"Darling, are *you*?"

In that moment, Duke regretted that he had very good hearing.

"Fine. A bit rattled. Worried about you. I saw the robed men. What did they do?"

"I don't know precisely," he said bitterly. "Simon's odd friends dispensed with them. After the attackers demolished the chapel with their bloody bare hands—which I still can't comprehend—I had my hands full keeping the guests calm and reviving Mother after she fainted."

Felicia gasped. "But she's all right? You and everyone else are well?"

"Quite. It's you I'm worried for. We should be together tonight, husband and wife, making love."

"Mason . . ." Felicia flushed and shot a furtive look across the car before her glance skittered away.

No doubt Mason had experienced all the joys of her body, but the notion of his brother in Felicia's bed made Duke homicidal. He gripped the steering wheel to keep himself from ripping the phone out of her hand and kissing her senseless.

"Be careful with Simon, darling. He's *very* much like Alexei."

Her gaze strayed his way, measuring, before jerking her stare back to the dark road. "Thank you for caring."

"I do. I have for six years, since I saw that bus douse you in the rain."

"And turn me into a drowned rat." She smiled wistfully. "Still, you came to my rescue, as you have so many times."

"I always will. Please, return to me safe and ready to be my wife."

She pressed her lips together, her expression turning pensive. "We'll talk soon."

"If you want, we'll elope next time," Mason rushed to

say. "Someplace warm and tropical. I know how you love the heat."

A vision of Felicia in white on a sandy beach with swaying palm trees and love in her eyes gripped Duke by the throat. The vision shattered when she extended her hand to Mason, not him.

Fury boiled. Mason with Felicia, it was wrong. Duke suspected—*knew*—that if he kissed her, if he tasted her at all, his instinct would identify her as his mate and he'd be bloody tempted to speak the Call.

But she'd belonged to Mason first. If Felicia had agreed to marry his brother, she must love him. For family harmony and her happiness, he would somehow find the strength to return her to his brother untouched.

Desolation seethed inside him. How many decades—hell, centuries—would he spend alone if he allowed his one true mate to slip through his fingers? Yet how could he live with himself if he stole his brother's fiancée?

Squaring his shoulders and focusing on the winding road, Duke shoved the thought away.

Mason murmured, "We'll get married somewhere tropical, darling. Just come back to me."

Felicia teared up, bit her lip. Those tears, along with the idea that he'd stolen something from her that she very much wanted, were a stake through Duke's heart.

"I will," she choked out.

Mason sighed. "I'll call you tomorrow. Let me speak with Simon again."

"All right. Good-bye, Mason."

"I love you," he murmured.

Before Felicia could say anything, Duke ripped the phone from her hand and jerked it to his ear. "What do you want?"

"Two days, you bastard. You have two days to bring her

back so I can get her adequate protection or I'll report you to the authorities and charge you with kidnapping. Plenty of witnesses. And that will be nothing compared to what I'll do to you personally."

Duke knew he could avoid all that by faking his own death and disappearing into the magical world. He'd have to someday, before people started questioning why he, like most wizards, looked perpetually thirty. In fact, he'd already begun making arrangements.

Enacting his plan now was tempting. After tonight, there would be scandal, which would be ten times worse if the authorities sought him. Another challenge the Doomsday Brethren didn't need. And what would all this strife do to his poor mother? Failing to return Felicia in two days could forever mar his already shaky relationship with Mason. And Duke felt certain that his brother's fiancée would never be interested in him now that he'd abducted her against her will. Mason had warned her off, compared him to some wanker named Alexei. An ex-boyfriend?

But he couldn't abandon his family to Mathias's whims before ensuring everyone's safety. He couldn't cause his mother grief by "dying." He couldn't bring himself to sever all ties with Felicia.

Fucking hopeless.

"I'll do my best."

But deep down, Duke knew it would take far longer than a couple of days to make Felicia safe now that Mathias knew she was the Untouchable. She'd be with him day and night. How could he possibly resist her?

CHAPTER 5

AS THE CALL ENDED, Felicia risked a glance at Hurstgrove's profile, illuminated by the dashboard's lights. She didn't know what Mason had said, but she didn't imagine it was friendly, given the way her captor clenched his jaw and gripped the wheel. Restraining the urge to ask—she knew Mason and could fill in the blanks—Felicia winced and looked at the clock. Two-fourteen a.m.

A new day, a new problem. She'd been abducted from her wedding. By someone not quite human.

Happy New Year . . .

She rubbed her eyes, trying not to smear the professionally applied makeup she'd paid for hours earlier, then plucked at her veil until it came free. Draping it across the dashboard, Felicia sighed. She could feel every seam in the heavy, form-fitting wedding gown. Her hopes of a happy family and future lay in shambles. And damn it, she had to use the loo.

Exhaustion beat at her. Nerves had kept her awake most of last night, and she felt every minute of that sleeplessness in the warm car that jetted through the dark night to "safety." Wherever that was.

"Felicia?"

Shocking how gentle Hurstgrove's tone could be. How warm. But then, she supposed it came in handy, seducing as many women as he did.

Across the small sports car's leather interior, his dark

stare scorched her. He touched her shoulder. Desire darkened his eyes, tightened his face.

Against her will and better judgment, Felicia's heart stuttered. Her body heated. She edged away. He dropped his hand with a sigh.

Aside from their one meeting prior to the wedding, Hurstgrove was a complete stranger. Still, he hadn't lied about her safety. Though he had abducted her, she knew he would never harm her.

Seduce her? That, she suspected, he would try. But would he really abduct her merely to do so, as Mason had accused?

Felicia frowned. That didn't add up. Hurstgrove couldn't want her *that* badly. He didn't know her. At most, he saw a pretty shell, but he bedded actresses and models, women clearly far more beautiful than she was. Though her adoptive parents had praised her looks too often for Felicia to think ill of herself, and male students at uni had frequently asked her out, she didn't believe she was pretty enough to motivate a duke to risk scandal and alienate his family. And was he so lacking in bed partners that he'd have to stoop to this length to get one? No.

Nor did she think he'd done it merely to annoy Mason. Their rivalry was obvious, but her built-in lie detector told her that Hurstgrove had not gambled his familial connections for a fleeting affair.

It would be so easy to be angry, to wonder why Hurstgrove had done this *to* her. But he'd abducted her from her wedding *for* her, and at great expense to himself.

Why?

He might not be the most honorable man ever. He objectified women and didn't seem to care much about resolving Mason's animosity. But he had risked much to help her, attempted diplomacy, then took quick action when talking no longer worked. He wasn't afraid to do what needed to be done. In a weird way, Felicia admired him for it. Beyond the fact he wasn't human—what sort of "other" he was, she had no idea—there was more to Hurstgrove than she'd previously imagined.

What would he be like in bed?

The question came from nowhere, unbidden, unwanted. A thousand sensual images pelted her at once: his hand fisting in her hair, the other gripping her hip; his lips on hers; hard muscles sliding over her skin, covering every inch of her body; his shoulders bunching under her nails as he slid deep inside her . . . and she lifted her hips in welcome, arching her back and hissing with pleasure.

Felicia lifted shaking hands to her hot cheeks. *Oh goodness.* She was breathing too fast. How could that one little fantasy—the one that would never actually become reality—affect her so quickly?

He was her fiancé's half brother, her abductor. He wasn't even human, yet . . . she couldn't *not* be aware of him. Every time he drew near, her body lit up like a Christmas tree. Of course she was grateful that he'd saved her from Mathias tonight. But it wasn't gratitude making her breasts ache or her knickers turn moist. Why? She should hate everything about his rich, womanizing ways. But she couldn't hate him.

Did that non-human part of him draw her in? Did aliens possess such powers? Or maybe he was something else from myth or lore? Did such beings truly exist? It seemed fantastical...but she knew, in this case, real life was stranger than fiction.

She took a deep breath and turned to him. "What are you?"

He stilled. "*What* am I?"

"Yes. I know you're not human. Your conversation with

Bram in the garage . . . It's clear your normal mode of transportation isn't an auto. He tried to simply concentrate, as if that would transport him to another location. That's not normal. Not . . . human."

Duke gripped the wheel tighter. "I don't know what you're talking about."

Another lie, but accusing him would get her nowhere. "I'm not stupid. You claimed I'm in grave danger from a madman I've never heard of and that only you and your friends can protect me. Then a lot of robed villains arrived unexpectedly and in minutes demolished a building that had stood for hundreds of years. What am I to make of that?"

Hurstgrove winced. "The evening has been harrowing. I'm sorry."

"You're missing the point. There are holes in your story, and I want the truth."

He sighed. "Felicia . . ."

"You're too high-profile to be a government agent. You don't need money, so you'd be barmy to deal in drugs or arms. Nor does—"

"I would never do either!" He cast her an outraged glance. "I obey the laws."

"Except those pertaining to kidnapping," she pointed out, brow raised. "Besides, even if you regularly broke laws, I've never seen drug dealers or third-world generals crash a wedding with an army in black robes. Not a very inconspicuous way to do business. But all that is very human, which you're not."

"This is ridiculous, Felicia."

"Is it? Why else would you imagine that you could close your eyes and beam yourself to . . . Tahiti? So I ask myself, who—or what—would imagine they could? Are you an alien? Do you have eight arms or tentacles or—"

"*What?*" A frown of incredulity cut deep into his brow. "Of course not. Don't be mad."

So he wasn't an alien. "A ghost?"

"Do I look dead?"

No, very much alive. Healthy, gorgeous, so masculine her pulse wouldn't slow— Bad train of thought. "Answer the question."

"This is absurd. Stop—"

"When I get the truth, I will. Should I protect my jugular around you? Invest in a garlic necklace?"

Hurstgrove downshifted, took a curve a bit too fast, and swore. "Vampires are nasty creatures, a small step up from cannibals. I'd destroy myself first."

Right, *then*. "Do you turn furry during certain phases of the moon?"

"Oh dear God." He rolled his eyes. "This is preposterous. Lupines don't eat meals with utensils. Do you think I could be a member of the peerage and photographed as often as I am if I couldn't manage a fork?"

Did that mean he knew one? Or did he answer questions with questions simply to throw her off? "So, not a lupine?"

"Definitely *not*. I like to shower more than once a decade. I'm plain human."

She wrinkled her nose at the stench. "You're not. Zombie? Demon?"

"Christ! I haven't risen from the grave or come from hell." He glared at her, his patience clearly running thin. "Though I feel as if I'm there now."

She harrumphed. "Elf? Fairy? Some other magical creature?"

He let out a long-suffering sigh. "Stop. In three minutes, I've gone from a street thug wielding dime bags to a pale midget with pointed ears. I'm exhausted."

Felicia sent him a mulish glare. True, Hurstgrove looked tired, but it was mostly an excuse not to answer her questions. And still, her nose told her that she hadn't hit on the truth . . . yet.

Felicia tapped her chin in thought. Duke couldn't help but stare. She looked adorable when she was tenacious.

She cocked her head and speared him with another probing stare, one that made him hot. "Your Grace—"

"Simon," he corrected. He hated being called "Your Grace," as if he was a damn ballet dancer. But even more, he wanted the intimacy of hearing his given name on Felicia's lips. "No more questions."

What was the point in confessing that he was a wizard? Around her, he couldn't prove it. Since she was likely the Untouchable, any sort of *abracadabra* was impossible. So if he divulged his abilities, Felicia would think him a nutter. More than she already did. Besides, magickind only revealed their existence to humans in extreme circumstances. Though this was perilously close to qualifying, the less she knew about magickind, the safer for her.

Felicia frowned. "But—"

"No."

She glared at him. "You can't shut me up indefinitely."

He sent her a tight smile. "I can try."

Crossing her arms tightly across the lush swell of her breasts, she looked out the passenger window. Duke breathed a sigh of relief. She'd given up—at least for now. He wasn't fool enough to believe he'd heard the last of her questions.

"Where are you taking me exactly?" she asked into their thick silence. "In all the commotion, I never asked."

Duke hesitated. Felicia had been through so much today. He'd whisked her away from the man she loved. He'd withheld the truth about his magic. But she'd already figured out that he wasn't human, damn it. That likely terrified her. The least he could do was comfort her with one truth.

"We're going to Ice's caves. They're in Wales."

She cast him a furtive glance under the thick fringe of her lashes. In those blue eyes was pique. And something curious, breathless, that aroused him far more than he cared to admit.

Had she imagined them together in bed?

Felicia shifted in her seat, turning away slightly. Her pose spoke volumes.

Of course she hasn't thought of you sexually, you fool. She's marrying your brother. Stupid, wishful thinking. She wasn't his to take.

One night. He had to get through one night alone with her, then never allow himself this temptation again. He and Mason might not be best chums anymore, but Duke didn't poach, especially where he wasn't wanted. And he refused to hurt his brother and disappoint their mother . . . at least any more than he already had.

"Why there?" She frowned.

It was the temporary headquarters of the Doomsday Brethren. But he couldn't say that. "The location is isolated and secure. Don't expect many creature comforts. We've had a few mattresses brought in, but it's nothing posh, I assure you."

Felicia frowned, clearly puzzled.

He dated dozens of women—sometimes all at once. But this one fascinated him like no other. She didn't behave in whatever way she thought he'd like. Felicia was purely herself.

"Tell me what you're thinking."

She raised a pale brow. "Does that usually work for you?"

"What?"

"*Demanding*, rather than asking."

He couldn't stop a half smile from lifting his lips. Sometimes his aristocratic upbringing made him a bit bossy.

Duke rubbed at the stubble shadowing his jaw and cheeks. "Deepest apologies. Will you please share what you're thinking, Felicia?"

"You have money and you're used to far better accommodations than a cave, so why stay there with Ice and the others?"

Damn it, more questions. He should have known. "Why not?"

"Because according to Mason, besides Lowechester Hall, you have a flat in London, a home somewhere along the shore, and a hunting lodge in Scotland," she went on. "Given that, why stay in rustic Welsh caves?"

Had Mason neglected to mention the Manhattan apartment? Duke shook his head.

She'd already asked *what* he was, not lingering on the who and why of tonight's events. Those were mere scenery. Felicia had focused on the big picture, as if she'd known that his being a wizard was key to comprehending the catastrophic evening. Now she sought more answers. Did she always ask such clever questions? He usually dated the most vapid human women he could find because they were incapable of guessing what he was and never attracted him for long.

Beautiful, saucy—and too damn smart, Felicia was exactly the sort of woman he avoided.

"Just staying with friends for a bit," he lied.

She grimaced and clutched her stomach.

"Something wrong?" Concern raced through him.

"When you're ready to be honest, let me know. Is there a loo anywhere near?"

Glancing at the clock, Hurstgrove wondered how she

could see right through him. "Sorry. It's been a couple of hours. We've another few at least before we reach Ice's place. We should stop for the night."

But where? Duke winced. Wasn't much alongside this stretch of the M4.

The next few minutes passed in tense silence until, finally, he pulled off the motorway at the only bit of civilization visible. A few scattered cottages, looking as old as the tiny village itself, squatted on a dark, narrow road. At the end, nestled in trees, a plain mid-century house appeared, only visible because his headlights reflected off the front windows.

As Duke steered the convertible closer, he noted a faint air of lonesomeness. He pulled up in the drive and turned to Felicia. "Wait here."

He hopped out of the car and sprinted to the little cottage door. A few envelopes bulged out of the mail slot. A peek through the window revealed newspapers littering the floor. No one had been home for days.

Praying the inhabitants were away for the holiday, Duke returned to the car, then followed the drive around the back of the house. He cut the lights and the engine.

"Who lives here?" she asked, frowning.

No idea. "A friend. Let's go."

Felicia grabbed his arm as he began to climb out of the car. "You're lying."

How could she know that? "We'll only be here a few hours. Come on."

"We can't just barge into someone's home!"

"This is life or death. We haven't time to be polite."

She dug in her heels. "We're staying in separate rooms, yes?"

It would be wiser for his self-control, but . . . Duke shook his head. "I'll do my utmost to respect your privacy. But I can't let this . . . man get his hands on you, Felicia. I won't risk you. 'Depraved' is too kind a word to describe him."

She hesitated, then sighed. "All right."

Her acceptance of the situation relieved him and made him a bit proud. She was smart and practical . . . and driving him mad with lust.

As he walked around to help her out of the car, he murmured, "Stay close to me."

Felicia exited, shivering as she scanned their surroundings. He slung an arm around her and drew her against his side.

Bristling, she backed away. "Unless you're concerned about a stampeding sheep or cow, I'm perfectly fine. There's no one about."

"You'd be surprised by the things that go bump in the night." He smiled grimly at her. "Besides, you're freezing. Let's go."

The moment they stepped away from the car, the January wind whipped through them anew. She shivered in the delicate lace of her dress and crossed her arms, huddling into herself to keep warm.

Stubborn woman. Duke shrugged out of his coat.

"Oh, no. You don't—"

Felicia didn't even finish her protest before he settled his dinner jacket over her shoulders. Almost instantly, she sank deep into the warmth of the coat.

"Warmer?"

Felicia buried her hands in the lapels and inhaled deeply. Duke was already hard, but his erection turned painful.

Cheeks red, she lifted her face from the garment and nodded. "Th-thank you."

At the door, Duke hesitated. If Felicia weren't with him, he'd simply wave a hand and let his magic open the door.

He couldn't send her two hundred meters away now. Too dangerous. So in addition to kidnapping, less than four hours later he'd be adding breaking and entering to his criminal repertoire. *Won't Mum be proud?*

He reared back to elbow out a little pane of glass above the handle when Felicia tapped his shoulder. She held the key in her hand.

"Where did you find that?"

She gestured to her feet. "Flower pot. I keep my spare there as well."

Very smart. Duke grabbed the key and stepped forward to open the door for Felicia. They crowded together on the tiny stoop. Her wide blue eyes lifted to his face, searching, aware. The pulse at her neck beat rapidly. Her face was so close, he felt her warm breath against his mouth.

Duke's stomach clenched, and he resisted an insane urge to crush her between the door and his body, to cover her lips with his, press deep inside, and roll her sweetness on his tongue. He didn't dare.

Slowly, he stepped back.

Tearing her gaze from his, Felicia squeezed between him and the door, then stepped into the cozy little house with its neutral colors and masculine touches. Duke closed the door behind her and locked it. Just in case, he tried to magically secure the door . . . but nothing. Damn. He'd have to keep her close and take other precautions.

Silently, he followed Felicia into the slightly cluttered space. Discarded newspapers and sports magazines were everywhere. Rows and rows of books lined the dark wood shelves around the perimeter of the room. He continued trailing her down a narrow hallway that smelled faintly of cedar and mold, through an arch in the stone wall, and up a steep flight of stairs. Her slim hips swayed. His desire flared to heated life again, gnawing at him. He hung his head, pressed his shoulders down, trying to relieve some of the tension. Problem was, it wasn't in his neck.

At the top of the landing, Duke wrapped his fingers around her delicate wrist, staying her. "Let me go into the rooms first, just in case."

Felicia thrust her hands on her slender hips. "We're safe. There's no one here, Your Grace."

"Simon," he corrected again. "And simply because it appears we're alone doesn't make it so."

"The door was locked."

That meant nothing to magickind. Even with Felicia here, Mathias could break in the human way just as effectively.

Duke shot her a warning glance. She sighed, muttering about high-handed men, and flattened herself against the railing.

He passed her on the narrow stairwell, his body brushing hers at the chest and thighs. He steadied her with his hands on her shoulders. All right, it was an excuse to touch her. The yearning to press her bare flesh against him and unleash his need for her pounded him again, growing dangerously with every moment they were together. Only thoughts of Mason and Mathias enabled him to release her and trek down the narrow hall.

He stopped at the first door on the left. A quick glance inside revealed a small music room with electronic equipment, a keyboard, drums, and a trumpet all scattered about.

Duke turned to the door across the hall. A slightly musty scent drifted out, as if no one had slept here in a few days or weeks. He flipped on the nearby lamp. The room was stark, masculine, minimal, and very small. The owner had squeezed an armoire, a wooden bench, and one narrow tester bed into the room.

It was going to be a long night.

Biting back a curse, Duke ushered Felicia into the bedroom. He took another glance at the little bed. His gut tightened. "Would you like the shower first?"

Awareness shadowed her glance. "If you don't mind . . ."

Duke gestured to the adjacent room, and she edged past him, flipped on the light to reveal glossy black tiles lining a stark white shower, then turned. His gaze locked with hers, squeezing the air from his lungs, until she closed the door between them.

Letting out a breath, Duke tore off his shoes, coat, tie, and shirt. He'd rather strip down and ease this aching erection, but Felicia was forbidden, and wanking off to thoughts of her would not be helpful, he knew from experience. Besides, he must stay focused on her safety.

Lifting the dark wooden blinds, he looked outside at the night around him, alert for any signs of menace. He couldn't see a damn thing beyond the trees, but Mathias was out there searching, waiting for him to fuck up and expose Felicia to danger. Cursing, Duke pulled out his mobile and hit the button to dial Bram.

"What?" he panted into the phone after the first ring. In the background, Duke heard feminine moans. Bram was with a woman?

"You found Emma?"

"No," he snarled.

"How is sex with someone else possible when you have a mate?" he blurted.

"I'm not shagging her, you dolt."

Of course not. As a mated wizard, Bram couldn't. He must be siphoning off the woman's sexual energy—a necessity after facing Mathias and the Anarki earlier. A wizard had to keep his magic powered somehow. So how did Bram soak in her pleasure if he wasn't touching her? Duke decided he didn't really want to know.

"It's nearly three in the morning. What the hell do you want?"

Duke cleared his throat. "Felicia and I are stopping for the night somewhere west of Magor."

"Where is that?"

"Exactly."

Bram cursed. "Hold on."

A fumbling sound, another feminine groan, a beep, then silence. Duke winced.

Moments later, another beep signaled Bram's return. He was breathing even harder. "You and Felicia alone. Is that wise?"

Of course not. "She's exhausted. I won't take advantage of a sleeping woman."

Bram scoffed. "I don't care what you do with the girl; that's between you, her, and Mason. But you're with an Untouchable and have no protection."

"We won't stay more than a few hours. I don't think Mathias followed us."

"But you don't know that for a fact. I'll send reinforcements, just in case."

"Thank you."

"Have you told Felicia what you are?"

"No." Duke plowed a hand through his hair. "I'd rather not. The less she knows about us, the better for her safety. But she is full of questions."

Bram grumbled. "I don't think you can avoid the truth for long, but we'll deal with it later. Focus on keeping her safe now. I don't need to tell you how valuable she is."

Not at all. "See you tomorrow."

Duke rang off as Felicia opened the bathroom door and

peeked out, her face hesitant. "Can you help me? I hate to ask . . ."

"Anything," he vowed, crossing the room to her.

She bit her lip. "My dress . . ."

Then turned her back to him. A row of small satin buttons secured the lace gown from her neck to her waist—twenty of them, at least. And she wanted *him* to unfasten them? Unwrap her like a package?

A fresh wave of desire swamped him, nearly overwhelming. Dear God, how could he touch those buttons—her skin—and not take more?

Felicia cast a nervous glance over her shoulder again, moving the thick tumble of golden curls that had fallen from her twist out of his way.

Duke did his best to school his face and soothe her as he closed the distance between them. His heart revved, his palms turned damp. He wanted her so badly, he could hardly walk right.

She's not yours.

With shaking hands, he reached for the first button at the creamy flesh of her neck, just below the wispy curls rioting near her hairline. Another button, then a second, a third . . . revealing the line of her spine and the softest skin. With each button, Duke exposed more and more of her, and his greedy gaze ate up every inch. The dress fell away, baring the delicate slopes of her shoulders, her upper back, the hint of her small waist.

His breathing turned ragged. As close as he was, Felicia couldn't possibly fail to notice.

Two buttons left. He reached for the first, and couldn't resist caressing one fingertip down her spine. She shuddered and looked back, wide-eyed, pupils dilated. Red colored her cheeks. She bit her plump bottom lip between her teeth.

Her breathing also sounded harsh in the silence between them.

Dear God, she was aroused.

Grabbing the last button, he twisted it, sliding it free of its mooring. He had to get away from her before he did something they'd both regret.

The dress sagged forward, and she caught it—but not until it fell from her bare shoulders and slid toward her hips, revealing a bit of the white lacy knickers he yearned to rip from her body.

"Thank you," she breathed.

"You're welcome." His voice sounded rusty, as if he hadn't used it in years.

Walk away!

But he stood, rooted. Staring.

Felicia retreated—until her back hit the portal. With one hand, she grabbed the edge of the door. To steady herself? To shut it? With the other, she clutched her dress to her breasts. Duke still saw the shadow between them, pale, plump, tempting . . .

His gaze jerked up to her face. She stared back.

The lust thickening his blood nearly knocked him over, and Duke gripped the door jamb above her head for support. In forty-three years, he'd never felt anything like this. Not during his privileged adolescence, where the right glance and a bit of title-dropping got him any girl he wished. Not during his tumultuous transition from man to wizard. Certainly not recently, when sex had become mechanical, nothing more than a way to power up for the next battle against Mathias.

This was totally unfamiliar and beyond his control.

Duke shuffled closer. Her body heat grabbed him across the mere ribbon of space between them. He leaned in, tilted his head, his gaze zeroed in on her lips, thoughts of tasting her storming through his head.

He was about to make the biggest mistake of his life.

"Stop me," he murmured.

Felicia stared, breathless, silent.

Heart revving, Duke inched closer, enough to see the little line bisecting that lush lower lip and smell the peppermint of the holiday candy he'd given her in the car. "Felicia, stop me."

But she swayed closer, her eyes fluttering shut. Her hand left the door and latched on to his bare shoulder. Her touch jolted his system, a lightning rod charging through him. Thought stopped, desire flared.

Yes, he was going to hell, but he'd go with her sweet taste on his tongue.

He fused their lips together, covering her mouth with his own. So soft. Her gasp hit him in the chest as her fingers tightened on his shoulder, nails biting. Duke pressed his body against hers and urged her mouth open, instinct roaring at him to taste her. Felicia hesitated, then slowly, her lips began to part.

He willed patience, his fingers clutching the wood above her head until splinters dug under his skin. He wanted to touch her so damn badly, stroke his hand down her delicate flesh, and caress her. But with need roaring through him, Duke was incapable of being gentle just now.

Using his free hand, he yanked her dress off her hips, unable to hear whether he'd torn it over the drumming of his heart. It pooled at her feet.

Then, finally, her lips parted completely, all the sweet treasures inside his to taste. He skimmed her lace-clad hip, her naked waist, until he settled the bare curve of her breast in his palm, her nipple burning his flesh.

Desire burst like fireworks inside him, loud, bright, impossible to ignore.

Duke crushed her mouth under his and delved deep, not wasting the time to sample. He inhaled, her sweet gardenia scent filling his senses like a drug. Her tongue brushed his shyly. She shuddered, her hand searing its way up his shoulder to clutch the back of his neck, her fist grasping at the short strands of his hair. The pull on his scalp told him that he affected her, and that revved him up.

Then instinct flattened him. Like all wizards, Duke sensed his mate by taste. After a single kiss, he knew for certain that Felicia was meant to be *his*.

He didn't waste another instant before he pressed his entire body against hers, their bare chests hot against each other, intimate. He devoured her as if she was the most sumptuous flavor he'd ever rolled across his tongue. As if he'd starve without her. Both were true.

Words stormed through his head, familiar despite the fact he'd never spoken them. Significant words. Life altering. He couldn't wait to say them. To speak the Call and make her his.

Then as Felicia moaned and pushed at his shoulder, he remembered that she loved his brother.

Fuck! The scandal. His mother. Mason, who would never forgive him . . .

Duke tore his mouth away, panting. Still, the words were a chant in his brain. *Become a part of me, as I become a part of you. And ever after, I promise myself to thee . . .*

Not going to happen.

Felicia snatched her hand from his neck as if his skin burned and dived down for her dress, clutching it to her chest. "W-we . . . can't do this."

Duke couldn't argue with that.

Already, he was biting the words back, the effort painful. If he spoke the Call, he would belong to her irrevocably and forever. Her heart would always belong to another.

Backing away, he watched as she clutched her dress to her chest, which rose and fell with each hitched breath. Her eyes, so blue, looked somewhere between stunned and accusatory.

He had no one else to blame. Everything was his fault.

"I'm sorry." Duke forced himself to step away, putting more space between them.

She wrinkled her nose and stared for a long, stilted moment. What the hell was she thinking?

"No, you're not."

Her harsh breaths rent the air, one after the other. In the air, he smelled the faint hint of arousal. Duke couldn't stop himself. He stepped forward again, his palm skimming up her so-soft arm, around her shoulder, sweeping across her bare back.

"Felicia . . ."

She gasped, jerked away, and slammed the door between them. Then locked it.

As the shower started, he cursed bitterly and paced toward the window across the room—as far away from Felicia as he dared go.

Outside, he spied Tynan O'Shea huddled in a long trench coat, lounging against a tree. Marrok paced the yard near the road, his sword flapping with each booted step. Ronan—he could only tell which Wolvesey twin from the dark hair—walked a circle about the house, passing just under Duke's window. He'd have to apologize later for their misery, but at least he knew Felicia was safe tonight.

From everyone but himself.

More than once, he'd heard friends say that love was a bitch. He'd never understood until now. Granted, he shouldn't know Felicia well enough to love her. But in her kiss, he'd sensed even more about her. Soft. Sweet. He'd bet she adored children and baking…but she had a hint of tartness. From that, Duke suspected that she possessed more than a hint of vixen that she only showed those she trusted most. Already, he'd seen glimpses of the quick temper she tried to hide beneath her polite British façade. She was clever, very genuine, and, her delicate face told him, confused about that kiss.

Knowing that she was meant for him but that her heart belonged to Mason was the most shattering pain he'd ever endured. If felt like losing the sun forever, sending him into deep freeze. Duke frowned, that truth hacking at his heart.

Even if he managed to hold back the Call, he'd never be the same again.

CHAPTER 6

THE SHOWER PELTED FELICIA, steaming up the small, black-tiled bathroom. Though she wasn't cold, nearly five minutes after Hurstgrove's kiss, she couldn't stop shaking. That hadn't been a simple meeting of the lips.

What have I done?

Felicia could scarcely process the fact that she'd been in the arms of two brothers in one night, and had reacted very differently to each one.

Mason's kiss had surprised her. Though he'd tried desperately to both seduce and reassure her, she'd been unable to hide her shock and distress. Since then, she'd been awash in guilt. The man had held her hand through her adoptive parents' funeral, then Deirdre's two years later, forever lending his support and smiles . . . and she'd been unable to respond to him on their wedding day? If he was going to father her children, shouldn't she be able to enjoy his touch? When Mason had kissed her, Felicia suspected that her fears had locked down any passionate response and the suddenness of his romantic feelings had overwhelmed her too quickly for her to adapt.

His brother blew that myth to hell.

She was barely acquainted with Hurstgrove and knew of him only through Mason's accounts and what she'd read in the tabloids, all of which told her that His Grace was the last man she should ever want. Yet when he'd ravished her mouth, had she been stunned, repulsed, or afraid? No. The first touch of his lips had been blistering hot. Then she'd melted into him, her head spinning, her heart pounding. Instantly, she'd been desperate for more.

Then he'd deepened the kiss, turning it into something that felt like a vow, blindsiding her with a sense of connection even deeper than the tug she'd felt at their first meeting. It made no sense. Hurstgrove was the master of temporary flings and tawdry affairs. How could she possibly desire him? Felicia couldn't explain it, but denying her response to him was pointless. Just thinking about his kiss made her belly tighten. Even lower, an ache settled in and throbbed, precisely where she didn't want it.

Pressing her thighs together, she let the hot water slide over her. Hurstgrove's seduction had been slow, controlled—but she'd felt his hunger seething under thin restraint. Holding back had cost him greatly and done nothing to disguise the fact that he'd been ready to shove her against the wall and have his way with her. With him, she'd become a trembling mess in seconds, a stranger to her own body, aching for more of his forbidden touch. She'd nearly allowed him anything—and everything—he wanted.

Why Hurstgrove? Why didn't she respond with such ardor to familiar, reliable Mason? Whatever the reason, she must get the man, or whatever he was, out of her head and focus on staying alive.

Felicia scrubbed her skin until it felt raw, but she couldn't erase the feel of Hurstgrove against her, his palm swallowing her breast. Regardless of the stunning pleasure, he could not touch her again. Though her relationship with Mason was up in the air, she owed him everything. He'd been willing to give her his name, his life, his support, his patience, and the family she craved. After mere hours apart, she'd repaid him by nearly succumbing to his playboy sibling. That fact flayed her with shame.

There had been only two people in Felicia's life with whom she could discuss a dilemma of this magnitude. Deirdre was cold in the ground, and the last thing Mason wanted to hear was that his half brother's kiss sent her up in flames.

Felicia swallowed back her tears. Wallowing never accomplished anything, and she couldn't hide in the shower forever. She must face Hurstgrove.

With a palmful of shampoo, Felicia scrubbed away the hairspray, tearing out the remaining pins in her hair. She took a deep breath, willing herself to calm. When she finished, she would cover herself as best she could, then sit the man down and explain the boundaries of their rapport in no uncertain terms.

Feeling clean, if not better, Felicia emerged from the steamy shower. She donned her bra and panties—she'd insist on clean replacements tomorrow—then noticed a white men's T-shirt folded on the faux marble counter. She froze. Hurstgrove had been in here while she'd been naked and thinking of him?

A wave of heat and fury jolting her, Felicia yanked the shirt over her head. Then stopped. Oh God, it smelled exactly like him. Sandalwood, slightly citrusy, something sinful. It *was* his.

Hating the way she trembled for him, she found a new comb inside a drawer and yanked it through her hair, then emerged to set the ground rules.

As Felicia stepped out of the bathroom, surprise rippled through her. He lay, not on the very cozy bed that a man his size would practically eclipse, but curled awkwardly and half-bare on the wooden bench at its foot. Her anger drained, and she frowned. Wouldn't a selfish bastard simply take the bed? Wouldn't a Casanova insist they share it?

Instead, her gaze staked over his bare bronzed shoulders

bulked with muscle, even at rest. Bulging, corded arms that had carried her effortlessly, shouted the fact he was all male. His calves and large feet hung over the edge.

Again, she couldn't help but wonder *what* he was. Given how much he affected her, Felicia's theory that he was somehow magical made sense.

Lying on his side on the short bench with his legs tucked close to his body, Hurstgrove looked bloody uncomfortable. Inviting him to the bed would be both detrimental to her sanity and her future. To make matters worse, the old house was drafty, and winter's chill had definitely invaded. No doubt, he was in for a long, miserable night. Guilt tugged at her.

"Y-you should stoke the fireplace."

"Go to sleep, Felicia," Hurstgrove murmured. His voice was low, scratchy, intimate. Shiver-inducing.

"It's freezing in here." She crossed her arms over her chest.

"Get under the blankets. They'll warm you."

"I'm concerned for *you*. If you start a fire—"

"Neighbors may see smoke from the chimney and get suspicious. Same with Mathias if he followed us. Go to sleep."

So he would forego warmth to keep her safe? And give her the very shirt off his back to keep her covered? Neither had he taken any of the pillows or blankets from the bed for himself.

It made no sense. Hurstgrove was a duke. A wealthy, entitled man. Mason had described him as both womanizing and selfish. Yet His Grace had stolen just one kiss, which he'd begged her to stop. He'd given her the shower, left her the comfort of the bed.

Who was he, really?

Biting her lip, she wrestled with herself. But she couldn't leave him to shiver for the rest of the night.

Felicia grabbed a soft down pillow in one hand and the quilt off the bed with the other, and approached Hurstgrove, draping the thick blanket over his hard, elegant frame.

He lifted sooty lashes to look at her. "What—"

"I don't want you to catch your death." She cradled his head and slid the pillow beneath. The intimacy of the act—his soft hair sliding across her palm, the stubble of his cheek tickling her fingertips—washed over her. Butterflies fluttered in her stomach. She sucked in a stunned breath as desire surged anew. What was it about this man?

He grabbed her wrist, his fingers a hot vise. "Don't."

His harsh whisper made her insides knot, her most secret flesh ache. "It's cold. Let me at least provide a bit of warmth since you left me the bed."

Hurstgrove cursed, then stared at her, dark eyes burning with lust.

She gasped. He wanted her. Badly. Relentlessly. And he either couldn't or didn't bother to hide it.

Felicia backed away, her heart racing, nipples beading with forbidden need. "Your Grace—"

"Damn it, it's Simon. Go to sleep."

"Not yet. What happened earlier can't happen again."

"Agreed." No arguments, no hesitation.

Good, she thought. Then she frowned, suddenly distraught at the thought of never kissing Hurstgrove again.

She shook her head. It wasn't like her to be contradictory. Perhaps she was simply tired or having difficulty adjusting to the recent, dramatic events.

All that was true, but deep inside, she knew she reacted solely to the man.

Hurstgrove gathered the edge of the blanket around his chest, his gaze unwavering. "We'll leave shortly after dawn. Sleep now. Tomorrow will be a long day. I'm trying like hell to resist you, so don't look at me that way. And don't come near me again."

Sunrise came a sleepless three hours later. Felicia eased the skirt of her voluminous dress into the small black convertible as she settled in the seat beside Hurstgrove. He gripped the wheel and stared grimly at the tree-lined road shrouded in fog, studying every inch of his surroundings, as if expecting a ghost—or Mathias—to jump out at any moment. He'd already rebuffed her attempts at conversation twice. The uncomfortable silence between them settled like a lead weight in her stomach.

Surprisingly, the black eye, lacerations, and bruises he'd sported last night were completely gone. Normal people didn't heal in a day. What the devil was he?

Hurstgrove revved away from the house, and she stared at the passing scenery, trying to ignore the tension between them. She turned on the radio, pretending interest in the latest pop songs. Though she trained her eyes away from him, she felt Hurstgrove beside her, intense, larger than life. He put off heat, as if he had a raging fever. Being this near him made her skin flush, her lips tingle. The ache between her legs returned with a vengeance.

After an hour, he still hadn't spoken a word. And it wore on her nerves. What had she done last night that was so deplorable, give him a pillow? Or return his kiss?

"You can't punish me for last night," she blurted into the silence.

He zipped a sharp stare at her. "I'm perfectly aware that I'm to blame. You asked me for a favor. I took advantage of your proximity, then put you in the uncomfortable position of refusing me. I'm sorry."

Of all the things Hurstgrove could have said, this she

hadn't expected. Just as he had with her abduction and his yielding of the bed, he surprised her. No selfish lothario would bother feeling remorse, much less shoulder the blame.

"You're not entirely at fault. I-I should have said no or pushed you away sooner."

"If you had, restraining myself would have been easier." A grim smile twisted his full mouth. "But without my overtures, you could have showered and slept without all that self-castigation."

Felicia turned a stunned gaze to him. "How . . ."

". . . did I know?" He rolled his eyes. "It was nothing I wasn't feeling. Besides, guilt was all over your face."

Felicia looked out the window, away from Hurstgrove. Still, his tangy midnight scent filled the little car. It was too cold to roll down the windows. And they were so close, nearly elbow to elbow. How long before he saw her lingering desire and curiosity, the pull toward him she couldn't explain? What would happen then?

"Would some breakfast and a trip to the loo be possible?"

"You needn't try so hard to avoid me that you refuse to look at me," he demanded.

Reluctantly, she did her best to school her features and turned. But his scorching gaze dipped to her elaborate lace wedding dress he'd helped her don, then caressed her face and the wild fall of her curls. Felicia feared he could see right through her to the desire she suppressed.

His jaw tightened. "Sorry. Let's get you fed."

He pulled off the motorway at the next village, just east of the Welsh border, and stopped in front of a bakery lining a narrow street. The Tudor-style storefront, complete with climbing ivy and a thatched roof, stood sandwiched between an aged brick building and a nondescript tailor's shop whose whitewash had faded yellow. BAKERS AND CONFECTIONERS read the awning over the door. At this hour, the sleepy town's streets were empty.

Anxious for a few minutes away from Hurstgrove's overwhelming presence, she reached for the door handle.

"Stop," Hurstgrove snapped. "Wait here."

He gave off a forbidding vibe. She bit her tongue and sank back in her seat.

As he stepped from the vehicle and pulled his mobile from his pocket, freezing air took his place. His blindingly white shirt and black pants were rumpled, and dark stubble shadowed his lean cheeks. Something bleak tightened his body as he leaned against the car, speaking into his phone in low tones. She rolled down her window just slightly, hoping to overhear. No such luck. But even without words, she felt his watchful concern bleed into the air as he hovered over the car.

He couldn't be this protective with every woman. Was he simply reacting to the danger? Or something more?

A few moments later, he pocketed the phone and opened the door. "A moment more."

Suddenly, two figures emerged through the thick fog, their ground-eating strides reaching Hurstgrove quickly. Where the devil had they come from? Did they live here? Were Ice's caves near?

The first man she recognized from her disaster of a wedding—blond, commanding, and determined to get his way. Bram. Today he'd dressed in well-worn denim and a midnight blue sweater. A brown coat hugged his shoulders, falling to mid-thigh. He carried a large paper sack by its handles.

The other man Felicia had never seen. Dark hair gleamed to his shoulders. A gray henley stretched across his powerful torso. His black coat, black trousers, and black expression all matched. But his blue eyes, dissecting her with one unnerving glance, gave Felicia pause. He was dangerous, had nothing to lose. And wasn't human. Shivering, she looked away.

Bram opened the handles of his sack. Hurstgrove peered inside, nodded, then shot a rancorous stare at the stranger. "I asked you to bring Felicia a change of clothes because she's too conspicuous to use a public loo in a wedding dress. Why bring Lucan?"

The unstable one? Felicia met then man's blue eyes again and had no trouble believing that.

"Extra protection in case you were followed."

"Protection?" Hurstgrove growled. "He all but molested Sabelle a few weeks ago!"

Lucan grabbed Hurstgrove's shirt. "I have control of myself now."

"Do you?" Duke stared pointedly at Lucan's fists in his clothing. "Last week, I heard another female in your cave screaming."

Wild blue eyes narrowed as he released Hurstgrove. "Before or after the two in yours?"

Two? She flinched. That wasn't a lie. Felicia tried to shrug. It hardly mattered who Hurstgrove shared his sheets with.

And *that* was a big, fat lie. Jealousy gashed through her chest as if someone had shoved a blade deep and ripped her open. She struggled to breathe.

Ridiculous! She barely knew the man.

But rationalizing didn't make the pang go away.

"When did you develop a problem with Lucan?" Bram challenged.

"His problem isn't with me." Lucan smirked at Hurstgrove. "Is it? Your problem is female."

"Leave Felicia out of this," Hurstgrove snarled.

Lucan was talking about *her*? Felicia listened more carefully. Perhaps the men might divulge something important, such as when she could return to her life and escape the mysterious pull Hurstgrove had over her.

Bram stepped between the other two. "Enough. Lucan, get everyone something to eat at the bakery."

Shooting a homicidal glare at Hurstgrove, Lucan whirled away.

As soon as he was out of earshot, Bram *tsked* and shook his head. "And I thought Ice was overprotective."

Hurstgrove rolled his lean shoulders and sighed. "I know. Sorry."

"I expect you'll deal with this interesting complication."

"I will. I need to . . . think."

"While you do, you have no argument with Lucan."

"He shouldn't be here." He tensed, clenched his fists. "Near Felicia."

Was Lucan really a threat to her? Bram didn't behave as if he was. But why else would Hurstgrove be *over*protective? Did she matter to him because Mason cared for her? Or because she mattered to Hurstgrove in some way? That possibility shouldn't excite her. He was everything she shouldn't want. But as much as she tried to push the feeling away, it settled deep in her chest.

Down that path lay dangerous heartbreak. She refused to suffer Deirdre's torment.

"Lucan is not yet stable enough for battle, and I must involve him or he truly will go mad. You know what losing Anka has done to him. Perhaps now you have a new appreciation for what he's endured."

Suddenly, the blond man turned her way. When Felicia saw his pointed stare through the driver's window, she whipped her gaze back to the deserted lane.

Settling a hand on Hurstgrove's shoulder, Bram murmured, "Here comes Lucan. Talk to him. You know what Marrok says about effectively fighting Mathias if we're too busy fighting amongst ourselves."

Hurstgrove turned his dark eyes to her. His frustration and heat blasted her all the way to her toes.

"I won't leave her unprotected," he insisted, arms over his chest.

"I'm right here. We will draw more attention if you and Lucan brawl in the middle of the lane. Go bury the hatchet."

Hurstgrove growled something, then walked away.

Felicia shoved the car door open and climbed out. Bram darted around the auto and blocked her.

Planting a palm on his hard abdomen, she pushed him aside. "What the devil is going on?"

"Good morning to you, too." Bram smiled tightly. "Thank you ever so much for eavesdropping. I see your mood isn't any better than his."

Felicia glared in return. "Nor is it likely to improve until I get some answers. I want to know what's going on and when I can go home."

He stilled. "Duke hasn't told you?"

"Not a bloody thing."

"Damn it." Bram stood tall in the foggy mist, looking tense, his gaze darting suspiciously all around. "Not here. Not now. Do you want clean clothes?" He held up the bag.

Felicia snatched it from him. Black trousers, a warm sweater, trainers. Even a new pair of knickers.

"Yes. Thank you."

"Thank my sister. Sabelle is pure genius when clothing is involved. Want to change now?"

Absolutely. Though the dress was heavy, its lace did nothing to block the biting wind. And since they'd stopped, black clouds had rolled in. Drizzle now fell, along with the temperatures. "Where?"

"Backseat. I'll turn away. Lucan and Duke are too far to see you. The windows are tinted. There's no one else in sight."

Clean clothes sounded too good to resist. "All right. I . . . I'll need help with my buttons."

At Bram's nod, she turned. He sighed at the little row of satin buttons and set impersonal hands to them, never touching her skin. When he was halfway through, a scowling Hurstgrove approached at a furious gait, planting himself between her and Bram.

"Problem?" Amusement laced Bram's voice.

"Get your bloody hands off her."

"How did you expect her to change into these clothes without help? I'm guessing, since some of these buttons are hanging by a thread, that you unbuttoned them last night?"

Felicia's face heated as she remembered what happened next.

"Don't touch her," Hurstgrove thundered beside her.

"I asked Bram to help," she offered.

Bram gave off a superior smirk. "Do you want him to finish or shall I?"

She glanced between the two men. No contest. "You, please."

With a curse, His Grace retreated one very small step. His gaze burned her back as Bram bared it and she climbed into the car.

Keeping her back to them, she changed in the cramped space, feeling instantly better equipped to handle whatever happened next. She folded her wedding dress into the bag and stepped out.

"Are either of you going to tell me what's going on now?

Who exactly is this Mathias and why does he want me?" Felicia supplied.

"It doesn't matter. Let me handle this for you," Hurstgrove insisted.

Slamming his fist into the car, Bram cursed. "Are you mad? She needs to know."

His Grace looked as if he restrained a violent urge. "The more she knows the more dangerous it is."

"I can't fight what I don't understand!" she objected. "This is my life and—"

"You're not a warrior. I am." He grabbed her arms tightly. "It's *my* mission to protect you."

Felicia frowned. So he'd said. But why did he care?

"You risk her more by keeping her in the dark," Bram said solemnly. "She stands a better chance of survival if she understands who's after her and why. She may not be able to fight, but fast thinking may mean the difference between life and death."

Hurstgrove sent Bram a snarling glare. He muttered a four-letter word that made her wince. "This isn't your decision."

"When Mathias comes knocking again, it will be too late. Think about that."

Moments later, Lucan sidled up to them. He approached Felicia only long enough to hand her a fruit-filled pastry and coffee in a paper cup. And stare at her with a haunted blue gaze.

"We're done here," Bram said. "Get to Ice's caves quickly. Lucan will ride with you."

"Absolutely not," Hurstgrove objected.

"Your exalted title leads you to believe you get to make the orders. You knew who was in charge when you joined us."

His Grace looked ready to tear someone's head off. "This isn't wise."

"She needs all the protection possible. I had a dream last night of Felicia. With Mathias. Very unpleasant."

Bram told the truth, and Felicia shivered. He'd dreamt something frightening about her and the man who wanted to kill her? If Mathias had destroyed a five-hundred-year-old chapel in a matter of moments, he'd have no trouble destroying her.

Hurstgrove blanched as if he'd seen a ghost. If he'd been concerned before, now he was downright paranoid, his gaze dissecting every part of their surroundings, looking for hidden shadows.

"Do your dreams ever come true?" she asked Bram.

Bram met her stare directly. "Always."

Another unpleasant truth. *Damn.*

"Then you have my cooperation." Fear clutching her insides, Felicia grabbed Hurstgrove's arm in one hand and Lucan's in the other. "Let's go."

By midday, Hurstgrove parked the car near the side of a hill. Just over the rise, the sounds of the crashing ocean carried on the wind. The brisk scent of salt and the winter chill stung Felicia's nose.

As she reached for the door handle, her stomach jumped. Maybe it was the exhaustion, the remote location, or Hurstgrove's taciturn mood, but foreboding washed over Felicia. She suspected her life was about to change forever.

Hurstgrove yanked the keys from the ignition but didn't open the door. Instead, he clenched his jaw and jabbed her with a furious stare. "I don't want this for you."

"Mathias isn't going to rest until he's found me, yes?"

"He's relentless."

"The sooner we deal with this, the sooner I'll have my life back."

Hurstgrove shook his head. "What we're about to tell you will shock you, and I wish I could spare you—"

"But you can't." She resisted the urge to curl her fingers around his hard shoulders and absolve him of guilt. "I can handle it."

"You're strong," Lucan said from the cramped backseat. "Excellent. You'll need it."

Together, they left the car, Hurstgrove standing close, his gaze raking the landscape around them with a watchfulness that made her tense. Lucan crowded her other side, doing the same.

Moments later, a group oozing testosterone emerged to the blustery day from the mouth of the cave, Bram at the front. How had he beaten them here? That mental transportation he'd alluded to at her wedding? Why hadn't they used it with her?

She also recognized Ice from her wedding, along with sword-wielding Marrok. With them were three other men she'd never seen: one with Lucan's blue eyes but an easier mien; a big, dark-haired bloke with gray eyes like a storm cloud; and a smiling fellow with striking green eyes.

"Who are they?" she whispered.

"Let's get inside where it's safer, and I'll explain." Hurstgrove didn't sound happy.

Felicia approached the small crowd, and Ice led the group into the caves. Hurstgrove followed closely behind, ruffling her hair with his hot breath.

The door shut behind them, and warmth enclosed her. The caves, while sparse, were surprisingly homey.

"Some of us, you know. The others . . ." Bram pointed to the blue-eyed man beside him. "This is Caden MacTavish,

Lucan's younger brother. Tynan O'Shea." He gestured to the stormy one, who stared stoically. "And half of the trouble twins, Ronan Wolvesey." Mr. Green Eyes nodded. "Raiden, the other half, is out taking care of an urgent matter."

"Hello," Felicia said to the small cluster of men, then turned to Bram. "Now, tell me everything I need to know."

Before he could say a word, four women filed in. A classically beautiful brunette with stunning indigo eyes introduced herself as Olivia. Next, Felicia met Sydney, a plucky redhead who exuded intelligence. Then Kari, who swung long, pale curls over her shoulder as the diamond in her navel twinkled in the lamplight. Finally, Ice approached another blonde, this one so dazzlingly gorgeous, Felicia's jaw dropped.

The woman threw herself into Ice's arms, and he enclosed her in an embrace. His kiss was so gentle, Felicia could hardly believe it had come from such a fierce male.

When he lifted his head, Ice smiled. "My princess."

This must be Sabelle. Feeling as if she'd just witnessed something intimate, Felicia looked away.

Until Sabelle approached Duke and hugged him. "Thank goodness you're safe."

Hurstgrove kissed her on the forehead, his touch brotherly. "Thank you for your concern."

He wasn't moved by the woman's beauty at all? Felicia frowned. Of the two of them, Sabelle was by far the more stunning. Hurstgrove didn't seem to notice.

Sydney crossed the room and gave him a mock sigh. "Still can't get rid of you, I see."

Hurstgrove smiled wryly. "You're stuck with me."

"A pest to the end. Why am I not surprised?"

Their camaraderie shafted Felicia with a bolt of envy. Hurstgrove liked these women, respected them. The fact she'd never once exchanged an easy word with him chafed her. He wanted her but didn't like her? Or only wanted her because Mason did?

She shoved the ugly thought aside.

A moment later, Caden approached the sassy redhead and tilted her face to his for a lingering kiss.

"You're a flirt," he accused softly, brushing a kiss over her lips.

"Mmm. If flirting gets me treatment like this, I'll do it more often."

"Perhaps I need to take you over my knee, firecracker," he whispered.

Felicia doubted anyone else in the room could hear them. But standing right beside them, she couldn't miss their by-play.

The brunette made her way over to Marrok and looked at him as if he was her moon, sun, and stars all in one. He returned the silent sentiment—along with a good dose of heat. They whispered to each other. Felicia couldn't hear, but their devotion was obvious. In fact, it was all around her. She'd never spent time with couples actually in love. Alexei hadn't loved Deirdre. Her adoptive parents hadn't been in love, either.

Part of Felicia envied their closeness, which made no sense. She didn't want love, didn't want to lose herself as her sister had . . . and yet, there was something so compelling about the obvious commitment these couples shared.

Hurstgrove settled his hand on her waist, above her hip. She jumped at his touch, and swung her gaze over her shoulder. Desire glowed in his eyes.

Sabelle approached her cautiously, then shot a stunned glance to Hurstgrove. "Wow. I can't believe you actually found—"

Hurstgrove shook his head and sent the woman a warning glare.

Felicia wanted to scream. "What are you hiding from me? What is going on?"

"This one speaks her mind," Kari drawled. "A woman I can relate to."

The other women snickered.

"You guys better start talking," Olivia said with a smug smile.

"Quickly." Felicia tried to keep the impatience from her voice. "I've already discerned that you're not human."

Smiles all around the room fell instantly. The air seemed to stop.

"How long have you known?" Bram demanded, jaw nearly scraping his toes.

She bit her lip. "Since he abducted me."

"Hence the twenty questions in the car last night." Hurstgrove winced.

"How did you guess?" Bram snapped.

"Little clues," she said noncommittally.

Felicia had long regarded her built-in lie detector as one of her defenses. The only person she'd ever confessed its existence to was dead. She wasn't giving up the truth to a roomful of people she hardly knew.

"So *what* are you?" she demanded.

"I'm human," Sydney offered softly. "So is Kari."

"As am I," said Marrok.

Felicia's gaze raked over the others. They were the only humans here? Must be; no one else said a word. She let out a deep breath.

"After my quaint game of dodge-the-question with Hurstgrove, I know that you're not vampires, lupines, demons, zombies, or elves."

"Simon," he growled. Again.

"Correct," Bram said cautiously.

Now they were getting somewhere. "In fact, I'm fairly certain that you're magical."

"Smart girl," Ice groused.

"Smarter than I realized." Hurstgrove sent her a long, measuring glance.

She pressed on. "I assume Mathias is magical? And why have I never seen any of you perform magic?"

Bram and Hurstgrove exchanged another glance. The blond man backed farther into the cavernous room and sat on the aged greenish couch. The others followed suit, each choosing a place to sit in the craggy stone room filled with hodge-podge furniture. His Grace rubbed his palms on his trousers and approached her. He took her hand in his.

A thousand volts of pure sexual energy shot up her arm. She jerked away.

Everyone watched.

"You needn't break it to me gently as if someone has died. Just tell me."

He nodded, his dark hair falling across his dark eyes. "Sydney, Kari, and Marrok aside, we're witches and wizards. The wizards comprise the Doomsday Brethren, who fight Mathias and his Anarki army. He hides behind a cloak of helping magickind's lower class, the Deprived. But it's crap. He steals souls to build his army and kills innocents for their life force, all to overtake magickind. God help us—human and magical alike—if that happens."

Felicia took in Hurstgrove's words, heart racing. Every word he'd said was pure truth.

She wasn't sure she wanted the answer to the obvious question, but couldn't afford to bury her head in the sand. "Why does he want me?"

Hurstgrove hesitated, then looked to Sabelle. "What did you find?"

"I'm still checking a few things . . . but Raiden recently uncovered a family tree that gives me every reason to believe your deduction is accurate." The beautiful witch looked at him with apology.

"Thank you, Sabelle. Keep digging and let me know—"

"What deduction?" Felicia demanded. "Don't talk around me like I'm a child. This is *my life*."

He cursed under his breath. "As far as we can tell, you're an Untouchable. Someone who completely dampens all magic near them."

Again, the truth. And this explained why he'd never performed magic around her. "You tried to . . ."

"Use magic?" he prompted. "Yes, I did. Bram did, as well."

"And I," Lucan admitted.

"Last night, while we guarded the house you slept in, I tried a few spells," Ronan admitted. "She's completely effective for a bit more than two hundred meters. Impressive."

Ice whistled, clearly astonished.

Hurstgrove glared at Ice, then approached her in the silence. "Untouchables are born only every thousand years to a very specific bloodline, and since you're adopted . . ."

"The timing is right," Sabelle supplied, rising from Ice's lap. "As is the location. Her effect on your signature and the description of her ability is spot on. I'm trying to determine her birth parents now."

Felicia froze at those words. "They didn't want me; I don't want them."

Sabelle held up her hands, placating. "I understand. We just want to be certain you're actually *the* Untouchable, and not merely a human with a few unusual abilities. Though as long as Mathias believes you are, the facts may be irrelevant."

It was all honest truth, even if lies would have been more believable. The whole thing should have been impossible. Everything felt surreal, like a misadventure happening to someone else. Felicia couldn't wrap her head around it. Panic began to creep in.

"Why would Mathias want someone like me to suppress his magic? Does he view me as a . . . weapon? Does he seek to use me against all of you?"

Hurstgrove paused. "Ever heard of Morganna le Fay?"

She nodded. "King Arthur's half sister, according to lore. A witch, yes?"

"Aye," Marrok piped in. "A more evil bitch has never roamed the earth."

Hurstgrove leaned in. "He became a tad bitter when she cursed him to immortality and took away his ability to . . . well, it's not important. Mathias needs you to enter Morganna's tomb. He seeks to resurrect her and control her power to further his terrible cause."

"Why does he need *me* to bring this dead witch back to life?"

Bram and Hurstgrove shared another glance—and she didn't like their secrecy one bit.

She ground her teeth together. "I won't have you hiding anything from me."

"We don't know for certain," Bram admitted finally. "Lore holds that Morganna's tomb is rigged with all manner of magical traps. Only an Untouchable could bypass those and get inside the tomb."

Oh dear God. This had to be happening to someone else. She'd never walked on the wild side, craved danger—never even had a parking ticket. How could it be that she had powers a magical sociopath wanted?

"Sabelle and I are researching all the surviving information about the tomb," Bram supplied. "As Merlin's surviving grandchildren—"

"*The* Merlin? He was real?"

"Indeed." Bram nodded. "We have his writings. If he noted anything about a way to end Morganna's exile or death, we'll find it."

"Who can tell us something about . . . my kind? Or more about Mathias's plans?"

Hurstgrove and Bram exchanged another heavy glance. His Grace's hand tightened on her hip. "There's one person. But—"

A series of staccato gongs interrupted, sounding somewhat like the start of a nail-biting cinema soundtrack. Though they seemed faint, almost far away.

She looked around for the source of the noise. "What is that?"

Hurstgrove sidled even closer and cursed.

Shaking his head, Bram drawled, "Speak of the devil . . ."

CHAPTER 7

EVERYTHING INSIDE DUKE TENSED at the sound of the magical chime. How the hell was he going to keep Felicia safe now?

"We must hide her," he barked at Bram. Then he turned to Ice. "Where?"

Bram shook his head. "Too late."

"What do you mean?" Felicia tensed.

Duke didn't answer her; he didn't know how to tell her that after he'd tried so hard to protect her, the enemy would soon walk through their front door and see her for himself.

"Let him in, Ice," Bram instructed. "Are your magical boundaries in place?"

"What's happening?" Felicia demanded.

"Only the farthest. Those near the caves . . ." Ice answered as if she hadn't spoken, instead shooting her a pointed stare.

"It's not her fault," Duke defended hotly.

"Understood," Ice agreed. "But how the fuck are we to defend ourselves?"

Felicia winced. "Do I have any means to . . . turn the ability off?"

With a lift of his razor-sharp brow, Ice drawled, "You'll have to tell us. We don't have a damn clue."

"Nor do we have time to find out now. Ice, take Caden and Ronan with you." Bram nodded at the wizards. "Greet Shock cautiously. We don't know for certain why he's come."

Looking at Felicia, Duke knew *exactly* why Shock had come. Fucking bastard.

The three wizards disappeared.

"So not Mathias? And this Shock is a person? Has he come to . . . kill me?"

Scrubbing his face with one hand, Duke wished like hell he could teleport her to Timbuktu—or any safe place. He didn't want to frighten her, but why lie? "Kill you, probably not right away. But don't stand too close. Don't trust him. Don't leave my sight."

"What can one man do against so many?" She scanned the low-ceilinged stone room, bursting with the Doomsday Brethren's collective muscle and brawn.

Duke narrowed his dark eyes. "When Shock is involved, that's always a good question. He'll act like a friend and offer help." Bram crossed his arms over his chest. "Right before he stabs you in the back."

"Fucking mate thief," Lucan growled. He didn't have to say that if he got his hands around Shock's neck, he'd kill the son of a bitch. It was written all over his face.

"He did give you enough information to discern that Felicia is the Untouchable so you could keep her safe," Tynan argued.

"Indeed," Duke snapped. "Likely right before he told Mathias that I'd found her."

Felicia paled. "He knows Mathias?"

"Shock claims to be a double agent," Bram muttered. "Traitor."

"What . . . exactly would Mathias do to me?"

Duke exchanged glances with the others, warning them to shut up. It was one thing to tell her who and what they were. Another entirely to give her the grisly details about Mathias's violence, especially against women.

As usual, Bram did what he wanted. "After he used you to get into Morganna's tomb, he would probably—"

"Shut up!" Duke insisted. "You'll only scare her to death."

Felicia whirled on him. "Stop making decisions for me. I asked because I want the answer, no matter how terrible. You're not my father, husband, brother, or lover."

He knew he should stop himself. Knew it . . . but couldn't. "That last one I can fix. Right now."

She tugged her arm from his grasp, but Duke couldn't miss the reddening of her cheeks or her rapid breaths.

Damn, here they were, deep in the middle of danger, and he could barely think past his need to Call to her and claim her in every way known to man. The need grew every moment he spent near her.

Sighing in frustration, he eased back to put space between them. About two inches of it. More than that he couldn't stand.

"He took my mate from me." Lucan's voice sounded hollow, haunted, just as he was. "He broke our bond, and Anka no longer remembered me. Then he repeatedly raped her and gave her to Shock."

Duke watched the horror wash over Felicia's face and held in a curse. She had good reason to be terrified.

"And Anka was lucky," Tynan intoned, only his eyes giving away the brewing storm inside. "Auropha was to be my mate, but Mathias and the Anarki did much the same to her. And when they'd finished, they dumped her body in front of her parents' house, like trash."

Tynan appeared alive, vital. But inside? If the eyes were the window to the soul, then he was dead. That gray stare looked as if he'd given all to his grief and had nothing left. Felicia's heart went out to him. He'd suffered . . . and still did.

Bram clapped the warrior on the shoulder. "We'll put an end to Mathias."

"It's been weeks since I joined, and nothing has happened," Tynan lashed out. "Even two more minutes is too long to wait to kill that fucker."

To that, no one said a word. There was no arguing with such terrible pain.

Felicia nodded slowly. "If Shock has anything to do with Mathias, I-I'll be careful."

Duke couldn't breathe a sigh of relief. Until Shock was gone, until Mathias was dead, until Felicia was safe, he wondered if he ever would.

A few nail-biting moments later, the trio returned with Shock Denzell in tow. Duke could only imagine what Felicia thought, getting her first look at the wizard decked out in bad attitude and black leather. In a leather duster that stretched tight across monster shoulders and mirrored sunglasses perpetually hiding his eyes, he looked ready to do Mathias's dirty work. The wizard would never pass for nice.

"He says he's alone," Caden offered. "I found no evidence of anyone else nearby."

Little comfort, but Duke nodded.

"I'm Shock." He approached Felicia.

Duke wasn't waiting to find out if the wizard just expected a hearty handshake or wanted to be close enough to grab Felicia. He shoved her behind him. "Get away from her."

Though tangling with Shock was a bit like baiting a rabid bulldog, Duke would have no problem ripping the other wizard's head off if he harmed one hair on her head.

Shock looked Duke up and down, then glanced away with a superior smile. "Honestly, take a breath."

"Piss off! No one invited you here or asked for your commentary."

"I go out of my way to be helpful—"

"For reasons that benefit you far more than us, I'm certain," Duke snarled. "Say what you came to say and get out."

Shock shook his head and looked past Duke. He sent Felicia a long, considering stare. "Amazing."

Her whole body went stiff, and Duke's protective instincts went into hyper drive. He reached behind his back and drew her closer. "Get your filthy gaze off her."

With a snort, Shock said, "She's hard to miss. Her imprint on your signature leaves a trail visible for miles . . . once you know what you're looking for."

Duke's heart seemed to stop. Since Shock knew how that trail looked, if Mathias wasn't yet certain exactly where the Doomsday Brethren had hidden Felicia, he soon would be. And if by some miracle Shock hadn't yet told him, Zain, who had also seen her impact on Duke's signature, would.

Felicia gasped. She was getting a rapid-fire initiation into the ugly underbelly of magickind. Duke wished he could ease her into this—or better yet, leave her out altogether—but Shock's bombshell made it clear that sheltering her from this crap could be fatal indeed.

"I see you're putting it all together." Shock crossed his arms over his chest. "Zain and Mathias are, perhaps, a day behind me—and only because I put a little extra REM in Zain's sleep and assured Mathias I could manage this mission."

This mission. Meaning taking Felicia from them. From him. Instantly, Duke gripped Felicia's hand, glaring at Shock. The rest of the Doomsday Brethren stepped in front of them.

"You won't take her." Duke's heart chugged out of control as fear scratched at his veins.

Shock laughed. "Touching. It would be fun to put that statement to the test, but as it happens, I don't wish to take her."

"Disobeying Mathias's orders, as well as Bram's? Guess you're an equal-opportunity prick," Ice quipped.

"Shut up, Rykard." Shock glowered at Ice, then nodded Duke's way. "I assume the half-human prince told you of Mathias's scheme."

"He's a *duke*," Felicia corrected.

Shock rolled his eyes. "Whatever . . ."

"We know Mathias's plan," Bram assured him. "That doesn't explain why you've followed us, why you've barged in, or why you're supposedly disobeying Mathias's orders."

"Such a stupid wanker." Shock sighed. "Does resurrecting Morganna serve *anyone's* interests?"

"Mathias's," Ice growled.

"I don't think so." Shock frowned. "She wasn't controllable her first time among magickind. No reason to suspect that Mathias will succeed in bringing her to heel when all others, even Merlin, failed. No one needs that bitch back among us, for any reason."

As much as Duke disliked Shock, he couldn't argue with that logic. "You believe Mathias would be in over his head with her?"

"I'm certain of it. He's fantasizing that he'll somehow combine her power with his and use it to control everyone. I think he's delusional."

"Fine. You've warned us that Felicia and I are easy to follow. We'll take precautions. Go."

The big wizard sent him a withering glare. "Such as? What the hell do you know about Untouchables?"

Gritting his teeth, Duke wasn't about to admit the truth Shock had unpleasantly pointed out.

The big wizard shook his head. "I can't stall Zain and Mathias for much longer, so listen closely: My great-uncle killed the last Untouchable, Fayre."

Felicia dug her nails into his shoulder, and Duke felt her recoil. "*Killed* her just for being an Untouchable? And Fayre was my ancestor?"

Shock nodded. "Since the Untouchable gift is passed down through a bloodline, yes. My great-uncle wrote that it took him decades to track Fayre down—once she found a way to disguise her imprint."

Felicia's little gasp shivered down Duke's spine. When she stepped around him, closer to Shock, Duke grabbed her arm and sent her a warning glance. "Remember, he's not to be trusted."

"How did Fayre learn to do that?"

"You're the only one listening, little girl."

She sent the big wizard a hard blue stare, and Duke's appreciation for her courage notched up, even as he wished she'd stay silent.

"Stop patronizing me and give me a bloody answer."

Shock sent him an amused glance. "A little spitfire, isn't she?"

Felicia slipped out of his grip and charged at Shock. Duke lunged for her, but she was too fast.

Instantly, Shock skidded back. "If you want to live, don't touch me."

Duke shoved Felicia out of harm's way, then lunged at Shock. "Don't you *dare* threaten her!"

"I'm not, you barmy fuck! If she touches me, Mathias will know it. Then he will know her imprint for himself. He will have *seen* it. And then no force will be able to keep him from her."

Letting out a pent-up breath, Duke admitted that, as

much as he distrusted Shock, the other wizard was right. Again.

"What are you suggesting?" she demanded. "I don't want to hide. I want my life back."

Shock looked at her with something that almost resembled compassion. "That isn't possible right now. Maybe never."

"Shut up!" Duke growled.

"Is that true?" Felicia demanded of him.

Duke didn't answer. How could he crush her hope? Taking away the life she wanted, putting her in such danger . . . He'd rather shove a knife in his heart.

"Is it?" she demanded.

He cursed under his breath. "Nothing is certain yet."

Felicia flinched, swallowed. Then she lifted her chin with resolution and faced Shock. "How did Fayre hide from your great-uncle?"

"It's not an easy solution. So if you're looking for a quick fix—"

"Tell me," Felicia snarled.

She'd been that ferocious when defending her wedding. Clearly, she wanted her life with Mason back badly. Duke gritted his teeth at the thought.

Amusement flitted across Shock's face. "Fayre mated with a wizard."

Surprise skidded through Duke's veins. "Rubbish!"

God, it had to be a lie, because if it wasn't . . . he couldn't fathom all the complications, except that they would be many and brutal.

A dark brow shot up over the tops of Shock's sunglasses. "Ask her. Am I lying?"

Felicia stilled. "I have no way of knowing."

"Now who's not telling the truth?" His nasty smile held

irony as he looked Duke's way. "This woman engaged to your brother that you're burning to mate? Besides being an Untouchable, she's got another special gift."

Felicia gasped. "I-I don't!"

"Tsk, tsk. Keeping secrets?"

She hesitated, then sent Shock a wary glance. "How would you know?"

"He reads minds," Duke murmured in her ear.

Surprise flitted across her face as she turned to him. "Can you . . . ?"

"No." Duke glared at Shock. "Everyone magical has different abilities. That's not one of mine. Sabelle can. But no one should be able to use that ability around you, including Shock."

The big wizard deflected his implied question with a smug smile. "By the way, Duke, she wants you too, but her desire is all wrapped in guilt and fear. Good luck with that. But don't lie to Felicia. She knows when anyone is being less than honest. Don't you?"

Guilt crept across her face. Duke stared, stunned. He wasn't terribly surprised that she wanted him; he'd tasted desire in her unforgettable kiss. But her ability floored him.

"You know when anyone lies?"

Felicia flushed and looked away.

With a cock of his head and another grin, Shock made it clear he enjoyed imparting this blow. "So when you told her that you were only human? And that you didn't want her? She knew it was crap. Which is why she knows I'm being completely honest when I say that if she wants to disguise herself from Mathias, she must mate with one of you. Today."

Shock's words smacked Duke between the eyes. Felicia knew he had lied. And to keep her safe, now one of the

Doomsday Brethren would have to speak the Call? Quickly, he scanned the room, realizing that in a few short months, most of them had formed mate-bonds. Marrok, Caden, Ice, Bram, Ronan. Now that Raiden had a youngling on the way, Duke suspected he wouldn't be far behind. Who did that leave to do the job, except Lucan, Tynan . . . and himself.

The thought of the broken-hearted madman or the vengeful wizard touching Felicia made him homicidal. No, the thought of *any* man with her sent him into a murderous frenzy. After their kiss last night had roared across his senses, he had no doubt this woman was *his* mate.

Yet how could he steal Mason's fiancée without ending all hope of family harmony?

"Impossible." Duke shook his head. "That can't be."

"If you want Mathias to get his hands on Felicia and use her to bring back the worst witch in magickind's long and sordid history . . . barmy, but your choice. Because you know that once Felicia has served her purpose, Mathias *will* kill her. She's a fantastic liability." Shock shrugged. "My mission here is now accomplished. But alas, I must make my jaunt seem worthwhile to Mathias. I need a volunteer. Who will make the perfect hostage?" Shock's gaze zeroed in on Tynan. "You. Such bloodthirsty thoughts. You want the chance to kill Mathias?"

Tynan's face darkened. "I've wanted nothing more since I saw Auropha's body."

"Who am I to stand in your way?"

Bram, Hurstgrove, and the others had argued vociferously with Tynan, warning him not to leave with Shock. It must be a trap. Felicia couldn't get an exact reading on Shock to know if that was true, which was most odd. He was definitely dodgy. The leather-clad wizard hid layers of secrets behind those sunglasses.

Tynan had barely listened before insisting on going with Shock. Now the two were gone, and Felicia's stomach twisted with today's events.

"Does mating in the magical world mean . . . sex?" She felt her cheeks heat up and did everything possible not to look at Hurstgrove.

"Not precisely," Bram said. "It's . . ."

"Magickind's version of marriage," Hurstgrove supplied.

According to Shock, His Grace was burning to . . . marry her? After a mere day's acquaintance and one kiss? Why?

"Exactly." Bram nodded. "It's a bond. A wizard speaks words to you, the Call. Then a female either Binds to him . . . or Renounces him. But sex plays a role in the bond. Or should."

"If I repel magic, how can a magical ceremony meant to bind me to another take effect?"

"Good question," Bram conceded. "Mating magic is some of the oldest, strongest magic known. Perhaps it supersedes your ability? And perhaps Shock doesn't know what the hell he's talking about and this plan won't work at all. We can't find out unless you Bind to one of the unmated wizards and we see if your imprint on him is altered."

Felicia frowned. "Why would that change my imprint?"

Hurstgrove shrugged. "I didn't grow up with magic and haven't had my abilities as long as the others. The subtleties of magic . . . I don't know."

"I suspect it's because you merge with someone, which, magically speaking, should change your imprint. But I can't say for certain. What we know about Untouchables is very limited," Bram supplied. "Since they're born once every thousand years, that predates everyone here, except Marrok."

Felicia stared at the big warrior. "But you're human. You're a thousand years old?"

He grimaced, and Olivia grinned. "Plus another five hundred. He should be dust by now, but he looks pretty good, huh?"

Amazingly, they were telling the truth. *Wow* . . .

Marrok rolled his eyes, then curled a beefy arm around his wife. "Methinks you should be silenced, wench. Thankfully I can think of many uses for that pretty mouth."

She gave him a huge smile and batted her lashes. "Bring it on."

"Can we focus, please?" Hurstgrove demanded. "Marrok, did you know Fayre? Can you tell me anything about her or her mating?"

Clutching the sword at his side, he looked regretful. "I heard no more than whispers. At the time, I did all things possible to avoid human and magickind alike."

"What about Merlin? Did he write about . . . people like me?" she asked Bram.

"He was brilliant and knew virtually everything about magic. He passed a great deal along to his family, so . . ."

"I'd like to read it before deciding anything."

"Well," Sabelle jumped in, "Merlin pontificated. A lot. He left us volumes upon volumes of his work. Reading them to find that answer won't be an overnight task."

"But they were intact in the ruins of the house?" Hurstgrove demanded.

"Ruins?" Something cold slithered down Felicia's spine.

"Mathias demolished my home a few weeks ago," Bram answered. "Merlin's works were inside, sufficiently hidden, thankfully. I retrieved them recently."

"Let's all start reading," Duke barked. "We must make Felicia safe."

Bram sent him a sharp glance. "Even if we began now, we wouldn't finish every volume for days, perhaps weeks.

Mathias and the Anarki will come knocking long before then. Shock gave you the solution to keeping Felicia safe."

Mate with one of them. Magically marry a wizard. *Oh God*. Felicia swallowed. "I'm already engaged."

"Is your promise to Mason worth your life?" Bram challenged.

No. The word darted through her brain before she could stop it. If she could agree to marry Mason without loving him, perhaps she could mate with one of these wizards and keep her distance. Like a marriage of convenience. Not an awful sacrifice to stay alive. Mason would be hurt, but what were her more appealing options? None.

What if they chose Hurstgrove to be her mate? What of her unruly desire for him? She wasn't certain she could tie herself to her fiancé's brother and not succumb to him. The kiss they'd shared last night haunted her over and over, connecting her to him in a way she didn't understand.

Hurstgrove snapped, "There must be another way. If Mathias was dead, the danger to her would end."

"To all of us. To magickind." Bram tossed his arms wide. "We've been trying to kill him since his return months ago. Olivia nearly succeeded during our first big battle. We invaded his home and cornered him. Ice fought him and was nearly able to deliver the death blow. In every case, he weaseled away. I don't think we can count on killing Mathias before he hunts Felicia down."

Hurstgrove opened his mouth to object, but Ice interrupted, "The planning would take days, at least, and that's if we knew what rat hole he now called home. As Bram said, Shock's given us a simple solution to protect Felicia. We must take it and divert our energy into rescuing Tynan. Stupid, noble git. I know from experience that Mathias's hospitality can be deadly."

Though Tynan hadn't given himself over to Shock for her benefit, his sacrifice might keep Mathias busy until she found safety. Still, she wished he hadn't done it. Though she barely knew the wizard, she ached for him and prayed he hadn't just committed suicide by madman.

"You want Felicia safe, don't you?" Bram raised a cutting golden brow.

Felicia turned to Hurstgrove. Tense, he raked a hand through his hair. His dark eyes latched on to her as he drew deep, agitated breaths. "You know I do."

Though the admission had been reluctantly given, Hurstgrove's words warmed her insides. She mattered to him. Was that why Shock thought he wanted to mate with her?

"I thought so." Bram sounded smug. "Get a taste, did you?"

Hurstgrove charged the other man. "Shut your bloody mouth."

Marrok grabbed His Grace by the shoulders and restrained him. "We cannot effectively fight Mathias if we do naught but fight amongst ourselves."

What was Bram talking about, a taste? And why would it infuriate Hurstgrove so much? They spoke in constant subtext around her, and she was tired of it. "Someone explain what's going on."

No one said a word.

Jerking free, Hurstgrove clenched his fists, but left Bram alone.

"Maybe we're not thinking about this correctly," she said into the silence. "Mathias wants me for one particular purpose, right? To open this tomb and resurrect this witch? Can we not find some way to simply derail him?"

Ice's face lit up. "Open Morganna's tomb on our own and destroy Morganna's essence before Mathias can find you. Brilliant! It might work."

"But warnings about that tomb abound," Sabelle cut in. "Yes, it might work. And it also might kill her."

"What do you mean?" Hurstgrove snapped.

"As lore goes, the tomb was rigged with multiple magical and non-magical traps, designed to eradicate nosy wizards and witches or curious humans. I read something about it once in one of Merlin's tomes." She rubbed her forehead with her palm. "Trying to remember . . . I can only recall something about multiple sections and each being rigged. Each is progressively more dangerous than the last, and designed to kill. Only an Untouchable can bypass that sort of magic. And only someone very bright can pass the human barriers. Even then, nothing is guaranteed."

"Then, no," Hurstgrove returned immediately. "Felicia will *not* step foot near that tomb."

"I am perfectly capable of answering for myself, Your Grace." She anchored her hands on her hips and glared daggers at him.

"For the last bloody time, my name is Simon." Then he shook his head. "You don't understand any of this. Not magickind, not Mathias, and definitely not Morganna. A single wrong move will mean your death, likely a painful one." He shook his head. "I won't put you in a position to die for our cause."

Hurstgrove was angry—on her behalf? He didn't like her pulled into the middle of this and in danger. He wanted her as far from harm's way as possible. Though he'd been bossy and high-handed at times, his protective mien melted a bit of her ire.

"Mathias already did," she countered, placing a gentle hand on his arm.

He tensed beneath her touch, his face a thunderous mix of fury and desire.

"Indeed." Bram paced. "We haven't much time before Mathias comes calling. Entering that tomb should be done cautiously, with a great deal of planning and studying, or we'll be signing more death warrants than yours."

The unvarnished truth—from everyone here. Felicia had wanted this last night when Bram and Hurstgrove and the others had disrupted her wedding and carried her away. But now, she shivered. The truth lurked like a specter, frightening, unavoidable. A very powerful wizard would either use her and murder her, or kill her outright if she refused to cooperate in bringing back a witch who could torment human and magickind alike. Her only possible recourse was a magical "marriage" to a wizard she wanted above all men. Both prospects terrified her.

She knew so little of magickind. Hidden dangers lurked around every corner, it seemed. As surreal as it was, this was her new reality. She must learn all she could, then make quick, sound decisions. Or she would wind up dead and possibly put others in danger.

"Tell me more about this . . . magical marriage," she asked Bram.

He hesitated. "Every unmated wizard, remain here. Felicia must understand who her options are. The rest of you discuss a plan for rescuing Tynan."

Amidst a chorus of affirmative murmurs and back pats, nearly everyone left. Marrok and Olivia, closest to the door, exited first. Ice and Sabelle followed, hands linked. Ronan and Kari whispered furiously, the former tossing a concerned glance back.

"Let me know if you need an ear to bend," Sydney murmured to Felicia before she and Caden left the room.

Suddenly, only Hurstgrove and Lucan remained with her and Bram. The room should have seemed much larger, but His Grace stood too close.

As soon as the door shut, Bram once again began pacing. "Mating is relatively simple. As I said, a wizard speaks the Call. You answer, Bind to him."

Why did she get the feeling he was oversimplifying?

"Hurstgrove and Lucan are the only two unmated wizards?"

"Simon," Duke corrected again.

She ignored him. Though calling the others by name didn't trouble her, it seemed too . . . intimate with him.

"Tynan is also unmated," Bram clarified. "But I don't know if we can recover him in time. Raiden is technically single, but he's currently with Tabitha, the witch who carries his youngling, so . . . no."

"Bram." Lucan's tone held a warning. "My presence here is ludicrous."

"Don't start—"

"Don't *you* start." He shook his head and reached for Bram's throat. "She does not belong with me. Nor I her, and you know that."

Felicia winced at the sight of these two friends fighting because of her. She stepped forward, ready to stop this argument.

Hurstgrove beat her to it, wrapping a harsh hand around Lucan's wrist and squeezing. "Let go. Now."

Lucan cursed, growled, then yanked his hand from Bram's neck. Then he turned electric blue eyes on her. Startling, beautiful, almost glowing, those eyes against his coffee-colored hair and bronzed complexion made Lucan a striking man. Gorgeous. But unstable. His volatility, lurking just under the surface, would explode without warning. It was only a matter of time.

Lucan was in agony without Anka, just as Deirdre had been without Alexei. Having a mate who could never have feelings for Felicia would keep matters simple . . . but she wondered if his sanity could handle bonding with another. Honestly, she didn't think so. She refused to do the one thing guaranteed to push someone broken-hearted over the edge.

"Lucan, it's . . ." She shook her head. "You don't have to say a word to me."

Now, barring a miracle rescue of Tynan, she had only one wizard to choose. The thought made her shivery and hot all over.

"Thank you," he murmured, then sent Hurstgrove a solemn glance. "Duke, I would never subject anyone to the hell Shock has put me through."

Shock. A mate thief, Lucan had said. Was he implying that he wouldn't steal her from Hurstgrove, as if she was already his mate? Shock, and now Lucan, both thought so. *Curious.*

His Grace closed his eyes, his lips flattening into a thin line, but he said nothing to refute Lucan. *Even more curious.*

"We appreciate that, Lucan," Bram began. "But these are desperate times, and—"

"Don't speak to me of sacrifice," Lucan warned. "What have you lost but a pile of stones and a woman you had for one night?"

Bram charged Lucan now, backing him into a wall. "The 'pile of stones' had been in my family for eleven centuries. Though I had Emma for one night, she is still my mate. We didn't have the two hundred years together that you and Anka shared, but we share a bond, just the same."

Felicia sucked in a shocked breath. Lucan and Anka had been mates for two hundred years? "How long do you live?"

"Around a thousand years," Lucan admitted. "I'd spend every one of them with Anka, if I could."

Felicia's jaw dropped. *An entire millennium?*

She turned to Hurstgrove. "How old are you?"

"Forty-three, exactly as Mason said."

"A child by magical standards," Bram quipped. "And before you ask, I'm three hundred ninety-eight. The big four-zero-zero is coming up."

Mind boggling. "If I agree to this magical marriage, how long must the union last? You spoke of Mathias breaking Lucan's bond with Anka, but can the bond be broken voluntarily?"

Bram nodded. "Most mates assume the longer lifespan of the two. So if you mated with Duke, you'd have nine hundred years, give or take, with him. But it's possible to separate once the danger has passed, go back to your mostly normal human existence."

Felicia waited for the acrid burning, but it never came. Perhaps she really *could* return to her normal life.

But the idea of bonding, even temporarily, with Hurstgrove rattled her. His abduction and their heated kiss aside, she'd known him a mere forty-eight hours. And the way he made her feel, he was much too dangerous to her heart.

"Is breaking a bond as simple as entering into one?"

"No. Assuming an Untouchable can truly bond with a wizard, ending the pairing is an uncomfortable process for the female. But once done, you'll recover quickly. And you won't remember your mate at all. You can go on with your life as planned."

"Bram . . ." Hurstgrove snarled at him.

"Not a word. Felicia must know how this impacts *her*."

She studied the Doomsday Brethren's leader. It wasn't what he said that gave her pause; every word rang with truth. "What are you not telling me?"

"Nothing that affects you."

Given the absence of stench, Felicia had to believe him, but the murky way he phrased everything troubled her.

"Say yes," Bram urged. "If you do, you'll have a bond with a wizard who will give his life to keep you safe."

Aware of Hurstgrove's gaze on her, she recoiled. "That kind of sacrifice is something a person only does for a loved one. We won't have that sort of relationship, correct?"

"Saving a mate is a wizard's first instinct, regardless of emotion. Typically, mates develop feelings for each other, but . . . bonds may not be the same for an Untouchable."

Felicia studied Bram with narrowed eyes. "There's no love involved?"

"It's not mandatory or compelled, no."

Another truth. A relief. She'd simply keep her heart—and body—out of the equation. She glanced at Hurstgrove. Well, she'd do her best, anyway. "All right. What do I do?"

"Felicia." Hurstgrove grabbed her shoulders. "Mating is—"

"Good girl," Bram cut in as if Duke hadn't spoken at all. "The Doomsday Brethren have to prepare for Tynan's rescue. It's roughly two hours until nightfall. Rest. I'll return then, so we can proceed."

CHAPTER 8

WITH A COMPASSIONATE SMILE, Sabelle led Felicia through the shadowed cave, holding a candle. "Almost there."

"Thank you."

The witch's smile brightened. "Except for Ice, I'm used to easily reading minds. So odd not to read yours."

A hint that the witch wanted her to open up? Felicia bit her lip. So many thoughts racing through her head. In a few hours, her entire life would change—again. She barely knew Sabelle, or anyone else here. Trust never came easily to Felicia, if at all. Yet they knew about her special gift. They were honest and willing to protect her at the risk of their own lives. She had no one else to talk to, to help her understand what was happening.

Felicia yearned for Mason's soothing voice. Whenever emotions threatened sound logic, he was always there. But she'd bet Mason didn't know what his brother was. Even if he did, how could she ask him for advice before temporarily bonding with Hurstgrove? Mason would never understand.

Finally, Sabelle stopped and opened a door. "Sorry it's so far from the others. Bram hopes that by secluding you deeper underground, you'll be distant enough to allow us to use magic, should it become necessary."

In other words, if Mathias attacked.

Feeling vaguely guilty, despite the fact she couldn't control the power, Felicia nodded and entered the little room nearly consumed by a wide mattress on a simple frame, piled high with quilts. A little water closet with a nearby sink was attached. "Thank you."

"It's not much. We haven't had time to add more than the necessities." The witch shrugged with apology. "Would you like something to eat? Drink?"

She shook her head and kicked off her shoes. "Just some answers, if you please. If you have any information about people like me . . ."

"Like I said, I haven't much. But I'll start looking through my grandfather's writings and bring you whatever I find about Untouchables." Sabelle cocked her head and sent her a considering stare. "I'm surprised you're able to sense lies, since you dampen magic. But there are some races whose traits are genetic, not magical. Vampires, lupines, fae, and I suppose, Untouchables."

"Apparently." Felicia smiled wanly. Silence ensued.

Time to deal with the elephant in the room: mating with Hurst-grove.

How would it affect her relationship with Mason? Was it even fair to contemplate marrying him now that she knew he loved her, when she would never love him the same way in return? Felicia bit her lip. Not likely. But how could she abandon her best friend? Betray him?

In the midst of this upheaval, she couldn't get Hurstgrove out of her head. He'd gone to a lot of trouble to protect her. But he was also the same man who had shagged four women in one night. The same one whose tabloid exploits were legend. If they mated, how long before he snuck away to satisfy his sexual urges with someone else? How much would it hurt?

What a bloody mess.

Concern softened Sabelle's perfect face. "What would you like to know?"

Anything. Everything. Felicia only knew there was much she didn't know—and she had no notion which questions were the right ones to ask. "I . . ."

"I know you didn't ask for my opinion," Sabelle rushed on. "And God knows my brother gave you way too much to think about in a day, but if you're to choose someone to mate with tonight, you should know more about your potential mates."

"Like the fact Lucan is still in love with Anka, and Tynan apparently has a death wish?"

Relief crept across Sabelle's face. "Exactly."

"Not difficult to figure out, really. Lucan seemed unwilling to get involved. And Tynan is irrevocably in love with a memory. And he isn't here, besides. That limits my choices."

Easing the door shut behind her, Sabelle crossed the room. "I think that's best. Romantically speaking, Duke is—"

"Please," Felicia interrupted Sabelle. She didn't need to hear the end of that thought. "I don't want to know about Hurstgrove's love life."

His emotional entanglements should receive the same weight as Lucan's or Tynan's. But she simply couldn't bring herself to hear about Duke being deeply involved with another.

"Duke doesn't have one. A sex life, yes. We all do. In magickind, we must have energy to power our magic or we die. Sex is the most potent, expedient way to get it."

Felicia's eyes popped wide. It sounded so crazy, yet Sabelle told the truth. "Sex is like . . . food?"

"In a manner, yes."

So all of Hurstgrove's sexual exploits of tabloid fame . . . had they merely been the means by which he'd fed his magic? Was sharing sex with someone like sharing a meal to magickind, casual and common? What about their kiss, had that been for energy? Or something more?

"You're still confused." Sabelle looked at her expectantly.

Indeed, Hurstgrove having sex wasn't optional. He must slake his lust—and build his energy—either with her . . . or someone else. She must decide which. Either choice was fraught with its own landmines. "Mulling."

"Duke is an excellent choice of mate for you. He'll care for you well, in every way."

"He's my fiancé's brother."

"I've only known Duke for a few years, but . . ." Sabelle hesitated. "Other than the familial relation, what objection do you have to him as a mate?"

The Duke of Hurstgrove made her want. Feel. Yearn for something beyond the comfort, friendship, and security her head knew made a relationship work. The odd connection to him, her craving for him—that could ultimately destroy her if she let him into her heart. Given that sex was food to him, she'd be crazy to think she'd be the only woman he'd ever eat a meal with again, so to speak. Though he should be nothing to her, Felicia didn't kid herself. His casual snacks would crush her. She'd never had Deirdre's outspoken nature or fiery strength, and look what cheating had driven her strong-willed sister to.

"Hurstgrove and I . . ." Felicia winced. "Not a wise notion." But what other choice could she make?

The witch's blue eyes dissected her. "I don't mean to pry, but . . . did he kiss you?"

Felicia flushed, wondering how Sabelle had guessed. *Kiss* seemed like such an inconsequential word for the scorching, consuming way he'd claimed her mouth and made her ache for what she should never want. Hurstgrove was the sort of man who could easily take a woman's heart with his stunning looks, practiced seduction, and illusion of caring—then rip it to shreds when he moved on.

"It was a mistake," she murmured.

A grin broke out across Sabelle's face. "Not at all. A mating between you two would be brilliant. I've long worried Duke was too disconnected from everyone, everything. He's never shown a preference for one female over another. Until you."

Felicia's heart stopped. Shock and Lucan—and now Sabelle—all seemed to think she belonged with Hurstgrove. Was his urge to protect her rooted in more than merely keeping Mathias from gaining the upper hand against magickind? Had his kiss been more than his playboy tendencies coming out to play or his need for a snack?

"Anything romantic between us is impossible."

"Is it? You need protection. And Duke would give his life for you."

He would; Felicia knew that. Already he'd risked much to keep her alive: his family, a scandal, and now his magical bachelorhood. "That makes no sense. He barely knows me."

Sabelle sent her a long look. "If he kissed you, he knows more than you think."

Duke tried to focus on the conversation around him, but he could only think of Felicia.

In twenty-four hours, she'd been threatened by Mathias, abducted from her wedding, kissed soundly by her fiancé's brother, introduced to magickind, then told to mate with a wizard she barely knew. It was more than anyone should have to deal with so quickly; enough to shake even the hardiest of souls. Yet she'd taken it all in stride, proving again she was a strong, amazing woman.

He wished he could say he'd handled the situation as well. In those same few hours, he'd pried her from the man she loved and kissed her soundly . . . mostly against her will.

Shock's suggestion that she could hide by mating had secretly thrilled him. The need to Call to her coursed through him, crowding out all else. Even now, his hands shook as he suppressed the urge to take Felicia to his bed and make love to her until she admitted that she wanted him even half as much as he craved her.

But that could never happen.

Duke raked a hand through his hair. If he gave in to his urge to claim Felicia, Mason would hate him forever. He recalled sunny days of riding bikes with his brother, the two of them watching cartoons and sharing pranks. The thought of his younger brother hating him for the rest of his days chafed. If he took Felicia as his own, his mother might never speak to him again. He'd loathe his own disloyalty. But his only other choice was to reject the woman intended to be his mate. Which would leave her unprotected. Eventually, she'd marry Mason, and Duke would have nothing left but centuries of loneliness. Fucking no-win situation.

"Are you listening to me?" Bram snapped.

Duke blinked, looked over at the Doomsday Brethren's leader, and grimaced. "Sorry."

"Once Felicia is mated, rescuing Tynan must be our first priority." Bram's booming voice jarred Duke from his thoughts. "Marrok, what strategy did you and the others devise for extracting Tynan from Mathias?"

As Marrok outlined his plan to lure Mathias out of hiding using the Doomsday Diary as bait, Duke's thoughts strayed again to Felicia.

Once they'd spoken their vows, how would he ever keep his hands off her? He'd spent less than two days with her, and already she burned in his blood like a fever.

"Fine," Bram said. "That's the best plan we have for now, though there are a lot of holes."

"Aye," Marrok concurred. "Until we find the lout's location, we must leave more to chance than I like. Methinks we will reconsider much once we know in which hole he hides."

Bram nodded, then sighed. "We need a plan to contain Mathias. Since the Council finally gave us—and no one else—license to kill the bastard, we'd best keep trying."

"It's as if Mathias knows all our plans, even those we don't share with Shock," Ice pointed out. "Because he's the Council elder, that fucker Carlisle Blackbourne insists on hearing the Doomsday Brethren's every move. He's been known to associate with Mathias in the past . . ."

"Indeed," Caden drawled. "I don't believe for a moment that Blackbourne repudiated him. I have no doubt our corrupt Council leader and Mathias are still as thick as thieves."

All this talking did nothing to keep Felicia safe. Duke spit out a nasty curse, and every stare in the room turned to him in surprise.

"Wish to share something now that you're back with us?" Bram glared at him impatiently.

"Blackbourne is a reptile. No one questions that. Why are we discussing it? Let's solidify a plan to kill Mathias. Now. I grow tired of him terrorizing magickind and threatening all we hold dear."

"If you have the solution to our problem, do tell," Bram spat.

Duke didn't give a shit about his mood. "If we're going to lure him out, why not make it to his doom?"

"Perfect. Any ideas on how we can actually kill a wizard who's already risen from the grave? I doubt traditional means will do it."

As much as Duke hated it, Bram made a good point. This conversation wasn't new to the Doomsday Brethren. Truth was, since Mathias had obviously employed some frighteningly dark magic to cheat death, they didn't know exactly how to vanquish him.

That fact had never disturbed Duke half as much as it did right now.

"We haven't yet tried skewering him on a sword covered in Ice's blood." He referenced Ice's fight with Mathias for a Council seat a few weeks prior. "If Ice is incorruptible, then his blood should be poison to Mathias and—"

"And if we can make Mathias stand still whilst we stab him with such a sword, we will. But that isn't really your problem with this discussion. You're worried about Felicia."

Duke raked a hand through his hair. He wasn't behaving like a warrior, and Bram had called him on it. They were supposed to be working toward a common goal, and suddenly, he'd developed his own agenda. "Sorry."

Bram eyed him carefully. "You sense that Felicia is your mate, yes?"

God, why didn't Bram simply ask him to give himself a lobotomy. That would be no harder than admitting he needed his brother's fiancée more than he needed to see his next sunrise. He'd become so bloody transparent.

Feeling the weight of all those gazes, he closed his eyes. "It's irrelevant."

"Clearly not. I understand that being near Felicia and not claiming her, especially when she's in so much danger, is difficult. But your misery will end soon."

No, making Felicia his while knowing that, in her heart, she belonged to Mason, would increase his misery a hundredfold. Somehow, Bram had failed to grasp the situation, or chose not to.

"It will destroy my family."

Bram sent him an apologetic shrug. "Nothing about this war has been easy for any of us."

They'd all made sacrifices. And would continue to.

Lucan sighed. "What time do we leave tonight?"

"Midnight, perhaps. That depends on when our 'information' about the diary's new location reaches Mathias. I've put in a summons for a few wizards who might pass along the word. Should have asked Shock whilst he was here. Now he's not answering."

Naturally. Dodgy bastard.

Then Bram addressed all the men. "I shouldn't have to tell you that rescuing Tynan will be a dangerous mission and may require a great deal of energy and strength. Everyone with a mate, go spend a few hours of quality time with your chosen one."

None of the mated wizards needed to be told twice to find their women. Ice nearly left a trail of fire as he beat feet out of the room. Ronan was hot on his heels, with Caden and Marrok fighting to get out the door next.

Bram sighed at the empty archway moments later. "I've called for a surrogate. Lucan—"

"I'm going out." The wizard's blue eyes looked furious and remote, and Duke wondered if Anka had any idea how badly Lucan pined for her, how much he hated having to touch someone else because she'd chosen Shock as a protector rather than renewing their bond.

Bram nodded. "Be back by ten." Then he turned to Duke with that look of superiority that always annoyed the hell out of him. "Go to Felicia. I don't want to see you again until you're mated, brimming with energy, and have changed her imprint on your signature entirely."

How the bloody hell was he supposed to do that without ruining his life?

"I can't. I'll go with Lucan."

Lifting a golden brow, Bram drawled, "Do I need to ask

some other wizard to mate with Felicia? Blackbourne's son, Sebastian, would enjoy an exotic female to help him build that dynasty he craves. He'd have no qualms about tucking her into his bed from dusk to dawn."

Bram had thrown down the gauntlet, his every word designed to push Duke's buttons and ream his sanity.

If Duke spoke the Call, his urge to make Felicia his in every way would only multiply. The one time he had touched her had nearly decimated his self-control. Far beyond a mere kiss, he didn't even know how to describe the contact. In that moment, he'd been connected to her in every way, felt her goodness, sensed her fear, ached to make her a permanent part of his life.

He'd be damned if Sebastian Blackbourne or any other wizard would touch her.

Clenching his fists, Duke glared at Bram. "Shut. Up. Now."

"Felicia is ours to guard. We can't protect her if you're broadcasting an easy trail to follow. We need you. Man up."

"I don't respond well to coercion or guilt. Piss off."

Duke grabbed Lucan's arm and stalked out of the room, down the hall, and emerged into the blast of the cold night.

With January wind whipping around them, Lucan jerked his arm from Duke's grasp. "What the hell is the matter with you?"

Anger jolted his system, and Duke turned to Lucan, silenced by the other wizard's genuine confusion.

"What would you have me do? She belongs to my brother. I want her, and she knows it. Mason knows it. My family will disown me."

"You know what's at stake." Lucan's blue eyes blazed at him. "I needn't spell it out for you."

Shit. Bram and Lucan were right. Felicia needed a mate.

With a few words, he could protect her, the Doomsday Brethren, and all of magickind. He could speak the Call and solve many problems. Save many lives. Nothing else mattered.

He scrubbed a hand across his face. "I know."

"So what's truly stopping you?"

Duke sighed. "She's meant to be *mine*, but as soon as the danger has passed, she'll break our bond. Because she's female, she'll heal quickly and leave. Return to Mason. You *know* how that feels."

Formerly mated females forgot their previous mates when the bond was severed, so they often sought the protection of another. Anka drifting to Shock was a prime example. Imagining Mason and Felicia together—it twisted deep in Duke's chest until it became a pain he could scarcely endure. The greedy part of him wanted to mate her, then spend every free moment wooing her until she had no will to leave.

"And you fear Felicia will rip your heart out," Lucan finished softly, "leaving you devastated and mad, like me. I wouldn't wish that on any wizard."

Once Felicia left him, Duke knew he would endure an anguish, a possible descent into madness, and a gaping hole in his heart that could take years to heal, if it ever did. Only a few weeks ago, Lucan had been chained to a bed like a madman, thrashing and screaming for his former mate. He'd been so distraught, unable to take energy from the solace of another woman's body, that he'd nearly died. If it hadn't been for Sabelle's tenacity and Anka's healing spell, he might have.

"If I mate Felicia, and she leaves me, I'll have nothing. No family, no mate, no sanity. Nothing but war and vengeance and hate."

"I can't tell you that being torn away from your mate gets easier. But I still wouldn't wish away a second of the time I spent with Anka. Ten minutes with your mate is still better than a lifetime without her. Besides, if you don't mate with Felicia, what will happen to her? Bram dreamed of her in Mathias's clutches."

Duke closed his eyes. Lucan spoke true. He must do whatever necessary to prevent that. Better to lose her to Mason than Mathias.

Even if that meant giving up his family, his sanity. His heart.

"You're right," he told the other wizard. "Go on without me."

Nodding, Lucan shrugged deeper into his coat. Duke darted back toward the cave.

God, this was madness. And in an odd way, he was relieved to have this decision behind him. If all went well, Felicia would be his mate tonight. It was a temporary comfort, and he deceived himself by basking in it. But he had nothing else.

Shouldering his way back inside, he tore from room to room until he found Sabelle. "Where is she?"

Sabelle instantly understood. "Follow me."

Down a series of stairs and narrow hallways they wended until she finally stopped at a closed door. "In here. Reassure Felicia. She's afraid."

"Of being here?"

The beautiful witch shook her head. "Of being with you."

Duke drew in a sharp breath. That fit. Being with her scared the hell out of him. He had no doubt that if he bedded her even once, he'd be addicted. He'd be hers for life. The fact that Shock had read her mind enough to know that Felicia desired him too . . . Duke hardly needed more fuel for his fire.

"I'll do my best."

Sabelle sent him a rueful smile. "I've heard you have very persuasive ways with women. Use them."

Duke swallowed. A vision of his type of persuasion played in his head: Felicia naked on his bed, his fingers clamping her wrists above her head holding her beneath him as he plunged deep, deeper.

No, he couldn't use such methods on Felicia. She might become his mate, but in her heart, she was Mason's. He had to remember that and keep his bloody hands off her. Still, fever burned through him when he thought of her on the other side of the door, alone. Waiting.

Ice hollered for Sabelle. Insistently. A mate's demand. She turned and ran, leaving Duke to face Felicia alone. Fist clenched, he knocked as gently as he could manage.

"Who is it?"

"Simon. May I come in?"

A long pause. Finally, she opened the door a crack. Blue eyes like a Caribbean sea stared back. Pale curls twined around her shoulders and streamed over the sweet mounds of her cotton-covered breasts. He could still taste her sugary flavor on his tongue. And he ached for more. The need heated him from the inside out, and he wondered how he'd ever find the strength to leave her untouched, let her walk away. Somehow, he had to.

Felicia backed away from the door and let him in. The bed looked rumpled and warm. Duke saw the outline of her body on the sheets. And got hard. Damn . . .

"Felicia," he began. "I know this situation isn't optimal, but—"

"You needn't give me your sales pitch. Sabelle already delivered it. You're the most available wizard of the group. But we both know this is a fantastically bad idea."

"Because I want you?"

Felicia blushed, hesitated. "Is that why Shock and Lucan think that you regard me as your mate? Even Sabelle hinted at it."

Duke gritted his teeth. Telling her the truth would do no good, but as Shock had pointed out, he couldn't lie. "That, coupled with my desire to protect you, may have planted the idea in their heads."

"And it had nothing to do with our kiss?"

She was dangerously close to the truth.

He restrained an urge to wince. "I didn't tell them about it. Everyone is on edge . . ."

Technically, not a lie.

Felicia paced. "The problem is, mating with any wizard to protect myself and help magickind betrays Mason, but you . . ."

Would be the worst choice because Mason despised him.

"I won't touch you."

Duke assumed she'd be relieved. Instead, she looked perplexed and a bit agitated.

"How will you get energy? Sabelle explained how you derive it."

Damn it. Sabelle had best not explain more to Felicia, like the fact she was his destined mate and the lengths to which a wizard would go in order to claim his woman. Those facts would only make her more skittish.

"I'll manage."

She froze. "With other women?"

"Does it matter as long as I keep my distance?"

Would she be jealous? Duke held his breath, hoping she'd refute him, hoping she'd offer herself. If it weren't for Mason, he'd be inside her morning, noon, and night. Evening, dawn, twilight—anytime he was awake and she was willing. And that would drag him deeper under her spell and hurt so much more when she left. Mason would hate him even more. Regardless, need pounded inside him, and Duke almost didn't care about Mason or the pain.

Almost.

"Can you? That kiss we shared . . ." She bit her lip, betraying her nerves.

"So help us both. Don't let me . . ." *Touch you, taste you, feel you close around me while you scream in ecstasy.* "I only have so much strength. Stop me next time I tell you to."

Anger tightened Felicia's face. "You overwhelmed me. I had no time to think or breathe or speak."

True. He'd backed her against the door, shoved his body flush against her soft curves, and devoured her tender lips. Her only crime had been responding—a small infraction comparatively. "You're right. Sorry. I'm prepared to Call to you, which I believe is our best course of action, despite the . . . drawbacks."

She looked wary, as if she didn't like the fact he hadn't assured her that he could keep away. *Smart girl.* Duke feared once the words had been spoken and she was his that the fever boiling his blood now would scorch away his restraint. But letting Mathias anywhere near her was far worse.

"We're running out of time," he pointed out.

"Yesterday, I nearly married a man I very much esteem. My best friend. I understand you're suggesting a temporary arrangement, and I'll forget it all eventually. But it's frightening."

"You're not afraid of wizards." If she had been, she'd have run screaming from the lot of them earlier.

"Perhaps foolish on my part, but no."

He stepped closer. God, her scent, wholesome yet so fucking arousing, nearly brought him to his knees. "You know I'm willing to do anything necessary to keep you safe."

Her shaky sigh reached deep inside him. "Yes. And I appreciate it."

Knowing he shouldn't, Duke closed the distance between them a bit more, leaning against the wall, trapping her between him and the mattress. "You're afraid of me. Our kiss."

Felicia tried to hide it, but she was every bit as affected by him as he was by her. That fact sizzled all the way to his core.

She hesitated, stuttered, "It didn't mean anything to you, I know. All your women . . . It was just energy, yes?"

"Magickind doesn't exchange energy through kissing."

"Oh." She swallowed.

Duke frowned. Her reticence went deeper than normal uncertainty in a foreign situation, almost like she feared their attraction, their connection.

A terrible thought jolted him. "Did some man hurt you, Felicia? Break your heart?"

She jerked her startled blue gaze to him. "No. Before Mason, I only dated one other man. Tristan and I parted amicably."

Shoving aside his burning jealousy that his brother and some unknown wanker had touched her, Duke frowned at her words. Though she wasn't a femme fatale by nature, she was gorgeous enough to have men falling at her feet. Since she didn't, there was a reason. Once they'd mated, he'd have time to figure the mystery out.

"Shall I Call to you, then?"

For a long moment, she said nothing, then finally nodded. "How do we . . . proceed?"

No one had prepared her. Damn. "Wait here."

Duke dashed through the hall, looking in several rooms until he found a pen and paper. He jotted down the Binding words, then darted back to Felicia, his heart racing from more than the sprint.

Tonight, she would be his. Perhaps not in every way, but

Duke couldn't deny how wonderful it would feel to call her mate, even if only for a while.

Back at her side, he handed her the scrap of paper, hoping that she didn't see his hands shaking. "Once I speak the Call, you say this in return. Then it's done."

She scanned the words, then glanced up, her blue eyes hesitant. "These sound very . . . permanent."

"In our world, mating is usually sacred. Despite what you may think, mate-breaking is rare. Unions last hundreds of years, and normally we don't undertake a bond for mere protection." He took a risk, grabbed her hand, and squeezed. Damn it, he ached to do much more than comfort her, but he didn't dare scare her away or test his own restraint. "These aren't normal circumstances."

"Of course not. You're willing to help me, and I'm being a ninny. I'm sorry. I—"

"You're fine. Ready?"

She hesitated, then nodded.

Again, knowing he shouldn't, he laced their fingers together. His heart chugged faster as he looked deep into her eyes and swallowed all inflection. If she detected how badly he wanted this, she might run the other way.

"Become a part of me as I become a part of you. And ever after, I promise myself to thee. Each day we share, I shall be honest, good, and true. If this you seek, heed my call. From this moment on, there is no other for me but you."

The rightness of those words slammed over his senses. The fever that had raged inside him since the moment they met skyrocketed. Need scraped across his skin, making him restless. Making him burn. Reminding himself that he couldn't act on it, he clenched his jaw and waited as the silence dragged on.

"Felicia?"

CHAPTER 9

"HELLO." A BEAUTIFUL WITCH with light brown curls and matching eyes entered the sophisticated but unfamiliar bedroom and smiled sweetly as Duke shrugged out of his winter coat. "Clothed or naked?"

He nearly choked. "I beg your pardon?"

She hung his coat over the footboard, then waved her hand in front of her chest. Instantly, the buttons of her blouse came free, exposing plump, white breasts barely concealed by delicate white lace.

A week ago, Duke would have been drawn to this witch. Hell, after that display, he would have gotten her naked and horizontal in thirty seconds. Now, he stared resolutely at her face—and not an inch lower.

"This . . . can be done clothed?"

"Mostly so, yes." Her smile turned from bright to soft. She studied his magical signature with hazel eyes, trying to hide her curiosity. "You've Called to someone?"

It showed. Good. Any alteration on his signature might keep Felicia safe. "Yes."

His thoughts spun back to her little bedroom in the cave, Felicia's hand curled in his, their fingers linked. She'd felt warm, vital, small. And trusting. Granted, her trust in him was limited, yes. But a start.

Into the hushed silence, he'd spoken the Call, forcing himself to deliver the momentous words in calm tones. He'd really wanted to back her onto the mattress, sink deep inside her, then howl out the words as they found pleasure together. Bloody impossible.

"Um . . ." The unfamiliar witch's eyes narrowed in study, her face puzzled. "Are you ill?"

His heart stuttered. Did his signature still appear wonky, shiny? In case she knew anything about Untouchables, he didn't dare ask.

The witch frowned, scanning him. Then she smiled again. "Of course you're not. You look quite healthy. Silly me."

He breathed a sigh of relief at her conclusion. "Just fine."

The witch settled onto the side of the sumptuous bed covered in a sleek black duvet that accented the gray walls. The turquoise of the throw pillows was echoed by modern wall art in the same shade. "The female you Called to spoke the Binding?"

"She did." Right or wrong, every muscle in Duke's body celebrated that fact. Those sweet words falling from Felicia's lips trembled across his memory now, making him ache for her desperately. Obsessively.

He remembered how it had happened with perfect clarity. Felicia had licked her rosy lips nervously, then whispered, "As I become a part of you, you become a part of me. I will be honest, good, and true. I heed your call. 'Tis you I seek . . ."

Then she'd paused again, her fingers tightening on his. She'd glanced at the paper in her hand, at him once more, clearly seeking reassurance.

"You're doing the right thing," he'd whispered, inexorably drawn closer. "One more sentence, and all will be right."

You will be mine.

A ragged exhalation. She pressed her lips together and closed her eyes.

With his free hand, Duke put a finger under Felicia's chin and lifted her face to his. The touch sizzled through his blood. "Look at me, Sunshine. That's good. You're almost there. Say those words to me."

Felicia swallowed. To his surprise, her hand crept up his arm, latching onto his biceps, seeking support. The pulse pounded at her delicate neck. Her gardenia musk wafted between them, nearly driving him mad.

Thick brown lashes fluttered over her vivid blue eyes before her stare snared his with an electric pull. "From this moment on . . ."

His gut clenched when she paused again, her fingers biting into his arm. He leaned closer still, until his mouth hovered inches over hers. Memories of the moments he'd kissed her the night before crashed through his head. Soft, plump lips. Her taste . . . so addicting. Sugary with a hint of sin. Her entire body trembling under his.

Duke moved his finger from her chin, swiping it along her jaw, anchoring his hand at her nape. Pulling her closer. "From this moment on . . ." he prompted.

Her breathing grew more rapid. The tips of her breasts brushed his chest with her next breath. She bit back a gasp and tried to retreat. Scorched all the way to his toes, Duke didn't give her an inch of space.

"From this moment on, there is no other for me but you." She'd looked at him with unguarded blue eyes, spiked with tears. That she'd been moved was a jolt to his chest. She'd *felt* the meaning of the Binding.

Because he meant something to her? Or because she feared she'd betrayed Mason?

Duke gritted his teeth. Whatever. The words were spoken. Victory coursed through him. Every instinct he possessed urged him to use this opportunity to find a way to keep her forever. Cold logic reminded him why he couldn't.

Then Felicia turned her head, pulled away, darting for the other side of the little room.

Duke knew he shouldn't touch her. Knew it, but . . . he still reached out to grab her arm and pull her flush against his body, where she couldn't miss his rough breathing or his aching erection. Her eyes widened. He scented a faint trace of her arousal.

Damn.

It was impossible to resist tasting Felicia again. Everything inside him screamed at him to take in her unique flavor, the one that branded her as his, in any way he could. Reconfirm his intuition, starting with her sweet mouth.

He bent closer to Felicia. Holding his breath, Duke felt the heat of her lips just beneath his. Another fraction and . . .

"Don't," she whispered.

Bugger! All human brides kissed their grooms at the altar. That would be custom in Felicia's mind. The fact she'd refused him even a simple meeting of lips told him that she didn't consider him her husband. Pain sliced through him.

"Am I your first surrogate?" The witch jerked Duke's attention back to the present.

In a manner. He'd had sex with many in the past. Easy, quick, always understanding a wizard's needs and never asking for more than a quick exchange of energy.

This was the first time he'd use one in place of a mate, however. He knew the exchange would be different. Because he was mated, he could no longer have intercourse with another female. But he had no idea what to expect.

"Yes."

That took her aback. "You've been mated how long?"

Duke glanced at his watch, grateful for something new on which to focus besides his torturous memories. "Less than an hour."

"Oh. Right, then." Still, he heard confusion in her voice as she wondered why he was here so soon after making another his for life. "This is unusual. New mates are usually so fixated that—"

"My mate is . . . ill." He grabbed on to the first excuse that jumped in his head.

Instantly, his words erased the question from her hazel eyes and would explain any lingering anomaly in his signature. It also covered his tracks if Mathias ever questioned this witch.

"Oh." Pity tinged her expression. "I'm sorry."

If she only knew how hopeless his situation was. An ill mate might recover. One in love with his brother? He was fucking doomed.

Compassion slid across the witch's lovely oval face. "Then back to my original question, clothed or naked?"

"Clothed, please." *Definitely*.

She shrugged. "We'll try it that way. Doesn't always work . . ."

"Why not?" Did clothing act as a barrier to the exchanged energy?

The surrogate sent him a wry smile. "Wizards are still members of the male species who prefer a lot of visual stimulation."

Remembering that Felicia was his and just how close he'd come to tasting her again . . . "Arousal won't be a problem for me."

"If you change your mind, let me know." She hesitated, then stuck out her hand. "We started somewhat backward. Sorry. I'm—"

"I don't want to know, if you don't mind. Nothing against you."

She dropped her hand with an understanding smile. "Of course."

Duke gritted his teeth. Why the hell had he come here, the magical equivalent of a brothel? Of course, magickind looked upon surrogates more like medical practitioners than prostitutes, which always confused the human side of him. They did provide nourishment and necessary care. He couldn't argue with that. But the delivery of care was completely sexual.

"Now that you're mated, do you know what happens next?"

He must look as lost as he felt, damn it. "Not . . . exactly."

How *did* one siphon sexual energy from a woman he couldn't—and didn't want to—touch?

"Usually, we'll lie on the bed beside each other. In this case, clothed. The idea is to exchange energy, as before, but without bodily contact."

"Yes." *Obviously. But how?*

She must have sensed his confusion. "You pursue your path to gratification while I pursue my own."

His path to . . . "I'm supposed to masturbate?"

A small frown pinched her mouth at his word choice. "Self-pleasure. I do the same. The goal is for us to reach peak in unison."

Lying next to a total stranger when he only wanted Felicia and to feel her sweet body under his, catching her soft moans with his kiss? Maybe arousal would be a problem after all.

Still, he had only two choices: return to Felicia and coax her to his bed or stay here with his nameless surrogate.

Duke had promised not to touch Felicia—then almost immediately broken his promise. If she hadn't put a stop to the kiss, he'd still be at her mouth now, devouring her as he consumed the rest of her body.

No choice. He had to stay here.

Cursing, he walked to the far side of the bed and sat

stiffly. Sighed. He removed his shoes, then forced himself to lie supine, head on the downy pillow.

God, he'd give anything not to be here. Did Bram feel this anger and aversion every time he had to generate energy without his mysterious Emma?

The surrogate sat on the opposite side of the bed and eyed him. "You're welcome to get more comfortable, if you like."

In other words, strip off. "I'm fine."

She shrugged off her blouse and reached for the hooks at the back of her bra.

He looked away. "Is that necessary?"

At his side, she paused. "You don't want to be here; I understand. You may remain clothed, but I must achieve a certain level of comfort to do my job properly. We can turn off the lights, if you wish."

"Please."

With a snap, the interior went dim, and Duke felt the bed dip as she lowered herself beside him, so close he sensed her body heat and smelled the scent of her skin, something like crisp cotton, summertime, and grass. Not unpleasant.

Just not the scent he longed for.

"What's her name?" the surrogate asked softly.

"Felicia." He heard the reverence in his voice and his stomach plummeted to his toes. He was so bloody gone for her.

Rarely had he shared the sheets with the same woman twice. Being a wealthy somebody in the human world and a virtual no one among magickind made for a complicated life. What did he know of commitment or love? But suddenly he felt just that for a woman who had belonged to his brother first. And still did in her heart.

He swallowed. God, he'd known Felicia for two days. He

couldn't *love* her. Admire her, yes. She'd handled the abrupt changes in her life well, all things considered. No hysteria. No screaming or crying. Just acceptance. She'd asked astute questions and assimilated remarkably well. She hadn't judged him for being less than human. She had listened to others' sage advice. And she'd remained amazingly loyal to Mason, even after that kiss Duke had all but forced on her. He didn't like it, but he admired her for it.

"Lovely name," the witch said, then wriggled a bit on the bed.

He risked a quick glance at her. In the shadowed room, he discerned her outline enough to see she'd dropped her little black skirt. She tossed a pair of lacy knickers on the bed between them.

Wincing, Duke scooted farther away, his leg gripping the edge of the bed.

She sighed. "Touch the glass jar on the table beside you. Think of your mate's scent, then light the candle. That's what you'll smell during the process."

Thank God. He eagerly complied.

Within seconds, Felicia's scent filled the air and he inhaled deeply, relaxing for the first time since walking through the door.

Perfect.

Another moment later, the witch at his side whispered, "Um . . . we can't proceed yet. You need to, ah . . . your zip, sir."

Yes, because this terrible train wreck wouldn't be complete until he had to wank himself off beside a stranger.

Biting back a curse, Duke unfastened his trousers, closed his eyes, and reached for his cock. "No offense. Let's get this over with."

"None taken," she murmured as her hands moved over her body in the dark and she moaned.

With the scent of Felicia around him, Duke sank into a vision where she dropped every stitch and welcomed him with open arms, her blue eyes fastened on him as she whispered how much she wanted him and surrendered herself to him utterly.

Getting lost in the fantasy, Duke stroked himself, imagining that he plunged deeply into Felicia's warm wetness and felt her close around him while his spine all but melted with pleasure. His breaths accelerated. The feminine, keening cries around him fed his vision, his fever. His grip tightened, moving faster now, imagining Felicia raising her hips to him in offering, drawing him deeper into her body like she never wanted him to leave.

The fever in him rose. Deep down, he felt Felicia's aching emptiness and confusion. He'd make it better, be a true mate to her in every way, if she'd let him.

Because he loved her.

In his mind, he told her so. Her cries of pleasure nearing peak, she whimpered for him, then whispered that she loved him too.

The ecstasy of those words blew the top of his head off. He shuddered, tensed, screaming through one of the strongest orgasms in memories.

But when his breathing slowed and he opened his eyes, Duke was still in an unfamiliar bedroom beside an unfamiliar witch, his softening cock in his own hand.

The buzz kill was instant. He hadn't quenched his need for Felicia one bit. Instead, he'd only made it stronger.

Cursing, Duke used the appointed towel to clean up. He zipped up his trousers, donned his overcoat, and was out the door before the surrogate could even turn on the lights.

Bram stopped pacing and sat beside Felicia on the serviceable brown couch as he viciously pressed the button to end the call on his mobile. "Duke's still not bloody answering. You mated two hours ago. You're certain both of you spoke all the words?"

Felicia didn't appreciate Bram's badgering. Truthfully, she was still trying to process the enormity of what Hurstgrove had pledged to her: his long life, his fidelity, his devotion. Sacred words, according to him. She hadn't expected that. She'd been required to promise the same in return. Nor had she been unmoved by the vow. As soon as she'd spoken the last of the words, Felicia had yearned to throw her arms around him, kiss him. Merge with him. Cement their bond.

All of that only deepened her desire for him.

Only thoughts of Mason, the wedding they'd nearly shared—and her own fear of a broken heart—had stopped her from acting on it.

Hurstgrove's intensity overwhelmed her. Fighting him felt like trying to stay afloat in a life raft in the midst of a tidal wave. If he ever kissed her again . . . Felicia had no illusions; her will to resist him would crumble.

"He spoke a few sentences, like a vow, then had me say this in return." She uncurled her fist and exposed the ball of paper in her hand.

Bram laid it flat on the dark wooden table in front of them and cursed. "Then that should be everything. I suppose I shouldn't be surprised that you have no magical signature."

After explaining the concept to her quickly, her brow furrowed. "Does that mean the mating didn't take?"

"Normally, that's not a possibility. If the words are spoken, the deed is done, but you . . . are different." He sighed. "Did you feel anything once the Call was issued and the Binding given?"

Other than the insane urge to offer him all that she was, body and heart? Those had been frightening, dizzying moments. He'd been so near, his mouth hovering right over hers, gaze delving deep like he wanted her soul. And she'd wanted to give it—and more—to him. That wasn't magical, she feared, just desire for him asserting itself, as it had since the moment they met.

"I don't think so," she hedged.

"Did he kiss you afterward? Take you to bed?"

Felicia drew back. "I get that you're a right nosy bastard, but that's none of your affair."

He gritted his teeth. "You spoke words, and now he's absent, possibly out in public where others might see his signature. He must look as if he's fully bonded and without any residual trace of your imprint. If the words alone didn't do that, we need to rectify the situation."

How? Did Bram think he could order her to sleep with her fiancé's brother?

An arrow of heat pierced her at the thought of Hurst-grove peeling away her clothing, caressing his way down her skin, claiming her lips with an onslaught of the carnal need she'd seen in his eyes. Of her touching every inch of his hard, male form in return.

Felicia cleared her throat, but it did nothing to dispel the heat swirling in her body.

"Did he even try to seduce you?"

Not for anything would Felicia tell Bram that she had rebuffed Hurstgrove moments after they'd exchanged vows. The last thing she needed from the wizard was a tirade.

"Don't badger her," Olivia chastised as she stepped into the room. "I may not have the magical ability to read minds, at least not yet, but I don't need it to know you're making her uncomfortable. Of course Duke wanted to seduce her. Duh! But you don't know a damn thing about being human. She can't be pledged to one brother, then joined to another without some . . . transition. She needs time." She sighed. "Have you seen Sabelle?"

Felicia blinked, then smothered a smile. Olivia had certainly put Bram in his place. Even he looked surprised.

"Sabelle is likely with Ice." He sent Felicia a pointed stare. "And time is one thing we don't have if we want to keep everyone alive."

"I'm aware of that," Felicia snapped. "I've done everything you've asked."

"Translation: back off," Olivia supplied.

Felicia didn't make new friends easily. Trust was difficult, and she'd always felt different because she cared little for shopping, watching the soaps like *Coronation Street*, or hopping from club to club. She'd always been something of a loner. But Olivia she could like.

Thank you, she mouthed to the other woman.

Olivia winked, then turned back to Bram. "Sabelle isn't with Ice. Most of the warriors have reconvened to run down the details of Tynan's rescue. Any word from Shock? Do you know where to find Mathias or if he's taken the bait?"

"No. If the warriors have reconvened, any chance Duke joined them?"

"Nope, and I don't know where he is." The other woman shrugged. "Not my department. If you all want a hot meal before you go, then I've got to get to the kitchen."

With that, Olivia slid out of the room.

"Cheeky wench," Bram muttered. "If she wasn't destined to be a powerful witch someday, I'd toss her out on her ear."

No, he wouldn't. Felicia heard his fondness for the other woman. The grousing was simply his bad mood talking.

Bram raked his hand through his mussed golden hair. "Where the hell did Duke go?"

So, he was back to that? "I told you, he left without a word shortly after the words were spoken."

Bram turned a prying blue gaze on her. "It doesn't fucking make sense. If he tried to seduce you, what happened?"

Felicia stiffened. "No one said sleeping with him would be required. As Olivia pointed out, I'm still engaged to his brother."

The wizard clutched the arm of the couch, looking as if he'd rather be clutching her neck. "A promise to make a vow to someone isn't more important than the vow you *have* made. You promised from that moment on there was no other for you but Duke."

"Temporarily! It's not as if I've spent my evening having sex with Mason. I haven't broken the vow. But I'll be damned if you're going to force me to disregard the promise I chose to make in favor of the one Fate forced me to."

"Listen up, little girl," Bram growled. "You'd better—"

"Leave her alone."

The deadly command sliced across the room, and Felicia looked up. Hurstgrove.

Her chest tightened at the mere sight of him. Fresh snow dusted the shoulders of his dark coat and hair. He needed a shave, but that somehow added to his appeal. He vibrated with strength and looked beyond brassed off.

Bram stood. His gaze traced Hurstgrove, then he exploded. "Where the fuck have you been?"

Anger on his behalf flooded her. "Don't yell at him!"

"This is at least half your fault for refusing to lie with your mate. Don't butt in unless you're prepared to be helpful."

Deadly calm settled over Hurstgrove's features. "You'll treat her with respect. Or I will take your head off."

"You mated then *left*? You might have asked someone if

speaking the words had changed your signature before you trotted outside where Mathias or any of his goons could see you."

Hurstgrove paused. "Did it?"

"Little has changed."

Gritting his teeth, Hurstgrove cursed. "It must have worked. I *felt* something. There *is* some bond."

"It's barely discernable," Bram grated out. "You should have checked with one of us before leaving."

"After I Called to Felicia and she said the Binding, I searched for you and the others to check my signature. You were closeted with your surrogate. All those with mates were behind locked doors. Lucan had gone." He shrugged off his coat, then shot her a guarded stare. "I thought it best to . . . clear up unfinished business before we go after Tynan."

He wasn't lying, but Felicia frowned at his terminology. What wasn't he saying?

"With your signature skewed, I can't tell your energy level."

Hurstgrove's expression closed up. "I'm fine."

Felicia's breathing skidded to a stop. His energy level . . . attained through sex. Had he acquired it before he'd abducted her or—? She didn't finish her question. But it didn't matter. The notion that he might have touched someone else tonight plunged a knife straight into her heart.

Felicia couldn't conceal her gasp of betrayal. "You've had sex with another woman?"

"No." His clenched fists and a light acrid scent stung around the edges of his words.

He wasn't lying . . . but he wasn't telling the complete truth.

"You went to a surrogate." Bram sounded exasperated. "Bloody hell! We needed to ensure this mating was solid, and instead, you deferred to Felicia's fucking delicate sensibilities and found a substitute for the real thing."

Felicia felt her chest cave in under the pressure of debilitating pain. On the magical equivalent of their wedding night, he'd spent it with another woman? Her ability to breathe ceased for long moments, and she was stunned.

Hurstgrove shouldn't mean a thing to her. But faced with this, she knew better. Why did he affect her so deeply? The man who had sacrificed his standing with his family, tainted his image, given her the magical equivalent of his name, and agreed to fight the most evil of enemies to protect her meant more to her than she'd realized. More than was wise.

"How could you?" The words fell from her lips. A whisper. An accusation.

To reproach him wasn't fair, and she knew it. Yes, they were mated—or mostly so—but he needed energy. She'd refused to provide it, all but made him promise not to touch her. Felicia knew she shouldn't be shocked that he'd turned to another, but the strength of her pain nearly undid her. She wanted him so badly, and could not act on it unless she wanted to betray Mason and risk her heart.

Her feelings weren't logical, she knew. She'd given Hurstgrove few choices. What the hell did she expect?

Hurstgrove glared at Bram. "Are you fucking happy now?"

"Are you?" Bram returned. "Take her. She's yours now. You need to—"

"You don't know a damn thing," Hurstgrove growled. "You trampled all over her feelings with absolutely no thought for how much it could hurt her."

"No," Felicia's voice trembled. "*You* did that when you got naked with another woman."

"Those in a mate bond are unable to have sex with anyone else while mated. I did not have intercourse with her." He crossed the room and took her shoulders in his grip, tightening on her when she tried to pull away. "I would ten times have rather made love to you. If you'd like to now, I'm more than ready."

Felicia paused. The unvarnished truth. Really, what *had* she expected him to do?

Not this, something in her whimpered. She had no right to be upset . . . and yet she couldn't turn off the anger and feeling of betrayal.

"Get the deed done," Bram demanded. "It's the only hope we have of changing her imprint. Both of us together couldn't hurt her as badly as Mathias will if he finds her through you. I realize you don't want to betray your brother. But if you want Felicia alive—"

"Stop playing the same trump card. It's bloody annoying me."

"You tiptoeing around her feelings is doing the same to me."

"Leave us," Felicia demanded. Bram opened his mouth to object, and she plowed ahead. "Stop whatever you're going to say. We know what you want. This is a matter for us to sort out."

Bram glared at her, then scoured Hurstgrove with a scowl. "Fine. The rest of us will see if we can draw Mathias out and save Tynan. Duke, you're staying here. As long as you're carrying her imprint, you can't be seen. We'll be back in a few hours."

With that, Bram slammed out the door. One sort of tension drained away, but Felicia felt another cramp her stomach, this one sexual.

"So the mating didn't work?" She wanted to clarify that point before they said another word.

"Something happened. My signature hasn't altered

enough, but you're certain that Shock didn't lie. Assuming his knowledge is accurate . . ."

"Can we assume that? Do we have any other sources that might corroborate him?"

"Not unless Sabelle finds something in Merlin's books."

"I'll help her look."

"Regardless of what you find, those words we spoke changed me." His fingers tightened on her shoulders, and his dark eyes drilled into her, earnest and demanding at once. "Like all wizards, I have no interest in any female except my mate."

He wasn't lying. He had engaged in some sexual act with the other woman because his kind required energy she had refused to give him. She'd left him no choice, but the fact he'd gone to another without talking to her hurt. An odd mixture of fury, guilt, pain, and desire flooded her chest. Tears stung her eyes like acid. She swallowed them back.

"I've put you in a terrible position." Her voice trembled, and she hated that she couldn't control it. "I'm sorry. I've ruined your life and—"

"Stop." Hurstgrove pulled her closer. "I'm exactly where I want to be. I wouldn't wish away any of this except Mathias painting a target on your back. I know you love Mason . . ."

But she didn't. Felicia bit her lip. Telling Hurstgrove the truth might absolve him of some of the guilt he'd experienced in doing all he had to save her.

"He . . . loves me," she whispered.

Hurstgrove dropped his hand and stepped back. "I know."

She reached up, snagged his sleeve. Even that small touch sent staggering heat blasting through her. Her need for him grew every hour, and Felicia wondered how much longer she could fight it.

"He's my best friend," she whispered.

He stared hard, scanning her face, delving deep into her eyes. "Are you in love with him?"

Hurstgrove moved closer, and she shivered.

Love was too painful when someone left. Deirdre had shown her the despair a broken heart could inflict. She'd been transformed from a vibrant woman to a hollow shell, gouged by need and torment, her confidence shattered, her sanity tested. Her will to live had been ultimately stolen. Felicia didn't want to care about Hurstgrove. But she feared it was too late.

He had sacrificed so much to keep her safe, how could she lie?

"I love him . . . as a friend." She closed her eyes, knowing these words would change everything, but she owed him honesty. "I thought he cared for me in the same way. But moments before you appeared at our wedding, he told me his feelings went deeper."

With a frown, Hurstgrove barged further into her personal space. "Why would you marry a man you aren't in love with? Are you pregnant?"

"No! I want a family someday, but Mason admitting that he loved me was a shock I wasn't prepared for. I-I wasn't even certain if I should go on with the ceremony."

He brushed his fingers across her cheek, and her eyes fluttered open. "Why don't you want him to be in love with you?"

Felicia struggled with the answer. Talking about Deirdre was so . . . painful. Personal. Opening up to Hurstgrove any further would only bring them closer.

"It doesn't matter. Nothing changes Mason's feelings or the fact we've already betrayed him. Anything more we do is merely twisting the knife in his wound."

"You don't think that denying what's between us isn't

hurting me? I think it even hurts you. Is this really how you want it?"

God, no. In that moment, Felicia realized Mason was still her best friend . . . and her best excuse. The real truth was that she was too terrified to gamble her untried heart on Hurstgrove. Yes, he had feelings for her now. But would they last any longer than Alexei's feelings for Deirdre? Hurstgrove would be so easy to fall for—and so hard to get over. Why sign up to get her heart crushed? Just because magic temporarily bound them, didn't ensure that whatever he felt would last once the danger had passed.

"Right now," she murmured, "we have to deal with the situation at hand, not the mess of our feelings. We mated but your magical signature did not change. Bram suggests that consummating our union would, perhaps, do the trick. But Mason has done so much for me over the years and wanted to marry me, despite the fact I don't return his feelings. I can't betray him."

"This isn't about Mason, but *your* fear." He pulled her closer. "And why I scare you."

Felicia's heart pounded. She tore from his grasp and backed toward the door. "Hurstgrove, I—"

"Goddamnit, my name is Simon!" He gripped her tightly, his breaths rough, deep. "I don't know what the hell you're running from, Felicia, but now that I know you don't love Mason, I have no qualms about telling you, *my* mate, that you're more important to me than anything or anyone, even my brother. I won't rest until your heart is *mine*."

CHAPTER 10

She doesn't love Mason.

Those words reverberated in Duke's head as a wide-eyed Felicia backed away from him, terror etched across her delicate face. She shuddered as she retreated another step. "You want my h-heart? No. You need energy, want . . . sex. You—"

He stepped closer, grabbed her shoulders. "Want more from you than sex. *Far* more."

"I-It's the mating. Those words made you feel something that isn't real."

If that's what Felicia thought, he had news for her. "No, I've felt this way since I shook your hand the day we met. It's *you*."

She gaped at him. "And you think you want my . . . love?"

"I won't settle for less."

His words seemed to suck the air from her lungs, and she looked ready to bolt. Duke did the one thing he prayed would remind her how good they could be together: He kissed her.

As his lips covered hers, he urged her to open for him, swallowing her gasp when she did. He gripped her head in his hands, holding her right beneath him as he prowled inside her mouth, tasting her. As he had when he'd kissed her last night, Duke wallowed in her flavor, and its rightness. Sugar, woman, a hint of tartness. *His*—no question about that.

After a moment's hesitation, Felicia threw her arms around him, clutching his shoulders. Pressing closer, she whimpered. It was the sweetest sound he'd ever heard, and as he tilted his head to take the kiss even deeper, his gaze brushed her face. Red lips, half-closed eyes. Desire had wiped the fear from her face, leaving her wanting—panting—just as he craved.

"See," he breathed. "What's between us is good, Felicia. Of course I want your love."

As if he'd dumped a bucket of ice water over her, she blanched and shook her head in denial. She backed out of his arms, toward the door. Her blue eyes teared up, imploring him not to chase her.

"What's the matter? Why does love scare you?"

She didn't say a word, just turned. And ran.

Her rebuff ratcheted up his need to claim her, mark her. His hands trembled, his blood boiled. His cock ached. Duke had never wanted any woman half as much as he wanted Felicia. She was a fever clawing under his skin, driving him mad with desire.

And he knew she wanted him every bit as badly.

Felicia glanced at him over her shoulder. She looked afraid and overwhelmed. He cursed . . . but forced himself to let her go. For now. She needed whatever time he could give her to accept him and their mating, to come to terms with whatever troubled her. Duke would give her what he could, but with danger looming and the fever rising, it couldn't be long.

Since Felicia was impervious to magic, it stood to reason that more than the exchange of a few words might be required to make them a bonded pair, especially on her part. Sex was the next logical possibility.

And he must figure out—quickly—why she feared love.

Leaning against the wall of her bedroom, he closed his

eyes and hissed at the cold stone against his overheated skin. Her addictive flavor lingered on his tongue.

The fact that she didn't love Mason changed everything. Instead of settling for possessing her body to hide her imprint, he had no trouble admitting that he ached all the way to his soul with the need to capture her heart, no matter the cost.

The mobile in his pocket rang. Duke grabbed it and, without thought, teleported out of the cave for better reception. Which told him that Felicia had wandered to some remote corner of the caves, far from him. He tried not to be depressed by that thought.

With the January wind whipping through his hair and clothes, he shivered as he extracted the phone. The name on the caller ID made him swear.

"What do you want, Mason?"

"To speak with my fiancée."

My mate, now and always. "She's . . . sleeping."

Let Mason make of that what he wished. Though he disliked hurting his brother, Duke wasn't above playing dirty to hold on to her.

"Don't antagonize me. Remember, you must have Felicia back to me in a few hours or I will have you arrested for—"

"Kidnapping. I remember. Start preparing the papers now, if you must. She's not safe yet, and I'm not returning her." *Ever.*

"You fucking prick—"

"Spare me the insults, Mason. We've traded them already. I'm sorry things didn't turn out to your liking. Do you love her?"

"Of course." His younger brother bristled.

Duke had known that, but hearing it was still a machete to his heart. "I assume you'd prefer her safe rather than dead."

"Damn you, Simon. None of this makes any sense. What

the devil is going on? I should be with Felicia on my honeymoon, not wondering where the hell she is and if she's going to be all right."

"Keeping her safe is my number one priority, I promise."

"Make certain that's *all* you do with her."

Mason tried to cover his apprehension with demands. Typical Mason. Duke wasn't in the mood.

"Why did you wish to marry her if you knew she didn't love you?"

Duke heard the fury in Mason's hesitation and smiled into the phone. *Score*.

"Don't be ridiculous. Felicia loves me," he blustered. "She has for years."

"Really? She referred to you as her best friend."

"Best friend, yes. Fiancé. Lover." Mason let that last word sink in, and it worked. Possessive heat poured off Duke in waves. He gritted his teeth, fighting the urge to crush his phone in his fist.

"Felicia loves me," Mason assured him. "She'd never have spent so much time with me, trusted me with her house keys or finances, or agreed to marry me if she didn't. She merely has trouble saying the words."

Perhaps, but . . . "You admitted your love prior to your wedding and she balked, which means you hadn't confessed your feelings previously."

"So? I'm hardly a walking greeting card. Why are you digging into our relationship? Hoping to find a way to part us? I know that woman inside out, her likes, her dislikes, her demons. She's *mine*."

Wrong. Duke *knew* she felt something for him that she didn't feel for Mason.

"Why is she afraid of men? Of love?" Whatever spooked Felicia stood between them far more than his brother did.

"Simon . . ." he warned. "There's only one reason you want to know this, and I'll be damned if I'll help you take her from me."

"I have to earn her trust so that she'll let me keep her safe. Every time I try, she grabs me with one hand and pushes me away with the other. Why?"

Mason paused, and Duke's guts seized up. He'd played his hand too heavily, and no doubt his younger brother would tell him to shove off. Damn it, he needed to know what frightened Felicia away from him.

"She didn't tell you?" Mason laughed, low and ugly. "Then she's still mine."

Felicia swiped the last of the tears from her face, furious with herself. Running away and crying were a coward's actions. Everyone around her, Hurstgrove especially, had bent over backward to keep her safe. She needed to stiffen her spine and do her part.

I won't rest until your heart is mine. Those words echoed in her head, striking fear inside her. Yet yearning settled in with it. She could still feel his kiss possessing her mouth until she couldn't think straight. Until he tugged at her heart.

Somehow she must fully bond with him without falling for him. She hadn't the first bloody clue how.

First action, find Sabelle. The other woman would have information she needed to make informed decisions without Bram breathing down her neck. Then she had to act quickly.

Wandering up from the bowels of the caves, she followed dark and twisting passages up several flights of stairs until she heard bustling and female chatter. Breaking into the main seating and adjoining office areas, she found the Doomsday Brethren's mates all staring at the door, as if awaiting her.

"There she is," Sabelle said with a smile.

Kari and Sydney smiled her way, then dove back into what looked like packing the household into boxes.

Felicia frowned. "How did you know I was coming?"

"Everyone's magic stopped working." Olivia winked.

Oh. "I'm preventing you from getting something done. Sorry. I came to ask you if I could help read through some of Merlin's books, but I'll leave you to your work."

Sabelle shrugged. "No worries. Stay. We're nearly finished. If you'd like to lend a hand . . ."

"No problem." Then she frowned. "Are you packing up to leave? If it's because I inhibit your magic—"

"No. It's not your abilities," Sydney promised, tucking a strand of long auburn hair behind one ear and reaching for a big mirror on the wall. "Bram is a cautious git."

"That he is," Sabelle seconded. "Shock warned us that he could only keep Zain and Mathias away for so long. We must be prepared to leave."

The witch turned to help Sydney with a large gilt-edged mirror on the wall.

"Careful," the redhead cautioned. "That's my favorite mirror."

"You have a favorite mirror?" Felicia blurted. Was Caden's mate that vain?

Sydney laughed at her confusion. "Not for grooming. It's the magical equivalent of a television camera for broadcasting the news. I've become magickind's correspondent about the Doomsday Brethren, Mathias, and the war."

"I see," Felicia muttered. "Somewhat."

Kari glanced at her watch. "It's after midnight. We need to finish this up."

"When will you leave?" Felicia didn't know them well, but all these women had welcomed her despite the danger she'd brought. If she let herself, she could become friends with them.

"*We*—meaning you as well—will leave once Bram gives the word. For now, all the warriors except Duke have been out for hours, trying to lure Mathias out of hiding with the Doomsday Diary as bait."

"Morganna le Fay's book?"

"The very one. But a female must transport it. Mathias knows that and isn't taking the bait, it appears. Shock is nowhere to be found, and none of the other avenues my brother has used to reach Mathias appear to be passing the information he planted. In case it smells fishy to him, Bram's asked us to be ready to bolt at a moment's notice."

"With your prized possessions?"

"Yes. Merlin's tomes; Mathias's mistress, Rhea, who is in our dungeon; and the Doomsday Diary."

The dungeon? Then again, if this Rhea was Mathias's mistress, she didn't need to be with her master, wreaking havoc.

Felicia winced. "Will I have any effect on your dungeon? If I undo magic or—"

"No, she's far down, and the cell should hold her without problem."

She sighed with relief, then realized that Sabelle and the rest of these women had their hands full. Her requests would only take the witch from her duty. "I'll leave you to it."

In the background, the other women continued packing books and papers into boxes. Sabelle stepped closer. "Though I can't read your mind, your expression is easy to decipher. Tell me what's troubling you. I'll help however I can."

"I hate to interrupt you . . ." Felicia glanced at all the women working.

"You're not."

She bit her lip. "I'll be brief. Can we talk somewhere quiet?" *Private.*

"Felicia and I will return," Sabelle called to the others. "If you're not certain of something, set it aside."

With nods and murmurs, the other women carried on, and Felicia followed Sabelle to the kitchen. They sat at a big wooden table carved with modern lines and a glossy polish. No way could they pack this. Would they simply leave it behind, along with everything else she'd seen here? Did they live in constant danger, looking over their shoulders?

Sabelle pulled out a chair, and Felicia did the same. "Coffee?"

"No thanks." Felicia clasped her hands. "I know you don't have a lot of time, so I won't waste it. Bram says that Hurstgrove's signature didn't change much after our mating."

The witch shook her head. "Sorry."

"But Shock said it would. He didn't lie . . . unless that's merely the truth as he believed it." Felicia sighed.

"I can't say. I can read Shock's mind only when he allows it. His gift in that area is far greater than any I've encountered."

"I see." But Felicia didn't like it. "Bram suggested that my ancestor changed her imprint on her mate's signature because they were not only mated but . . . um, intimate."

"You and Duke haven't been, and you're asking my opinion?"

Felicia paused. "I know it's mad. I don't know you well, and you'll likely side with your brother."

"Well . . ." Sabelle smiled. "You know I can't lie to you."

Despite the difficult situation, Felicia returned the grin. "No one can."

"Nor can I answer your question. This is uncharted territory, since none of us have met an Untouchable. Recently,

Raiden and Tabitha, his encinta—that's the witch carrying his child—found the Untouchable family tree. The last name on it had been erased. But the date and location fit you. I popped over to Newham General Hospital for a bit. With a little magical persuasion, they confirmed what I suspected. You are of *the* bloodline."

That wasn't good news. Nor was it unexpected.

"Tabitha actually visited you on the night of your birth. I don't know if this helps you, but . . . your parents didn't give you up because they didn't love you. They knew you were destined to be in danger and they wanted to give you a chance at a normal life."

Felicia told herself that didn't matter right now. But hearing that they'd given her up to help her, not abandon her, hit her square in the chest.

"Are they . . . ?"

"Gone. Your mother lived a mere two days after your birth, then died of a fever. After your adoption, your father disappeared. He returned to London less than a month ago and passed away. Perhaps he was looking for you. I don't know."

Now, Felicia never would either. Grief ripped through her. Her father had been alive mere weeks ago. Had someone painted a target on her birth father's back because of her? For his sake, she hoped he'd died in peace.

"Your bloodline is both revered and feared, Felicia. Some of magickind dislike the fact that Untouchables are meant to . . . balance us. They've been hunted for millennia. If you hadn't stumbled onto magickind by meeting Duke, it's likely Mathias could have sought you yet failed to find you for years, perhaps for the rest of your life."

The witch's words sank in, and Felicia realized that she didn't regret her current path entirely. As appealing as peace and security sounded, if she had married Mason and settled into comfortable suburban life, did it follow that she would have been happy? If she hadn't come on this whirlwind journey, she would have never really known Hurstgrove. He might be too frightening to love . . . but he was too fascinating to regret.

"Thank you for that."

Sabelle nodded. "I have more details about them, names, biographical history, locations of graves, if you ever want them."

In Felicia's estimation, the witch was part psychic, part angel. "I will. But right now, we must deal with the immediate issue. Hurstgrove's signature."

"Yes, of course. I can't honestly tell you if sex with Duke will make a difference in that respect. But I think it will in other ways. His ability to protect you increases when he has adequate energy, for instance."

"And he wouldn't go to a . . . surrogate?" The thought of enduring that again agonized her.

"No. A mated wizard never chooses that option unless he must. Not only that, if you and Duke cemented your bond, you would be more prepared to work as a team through the danger. Ice and I had our share of troubles whilst running from Mathias with the diary. But now that we've completely bonded, I swear sometimes I know exactly what he's feeling and thinking, though I can't read him the way I can others."

Felicia believed that. Since exchanging vows with Hurstgrove, she'd felt an invisible thread tugging her insistently in his direction. Even now, she knew he prowled the perimeter of the caves, restless desire filling him. How was such knowledge possible?

"Do mates usually . . . love each other, the words of the bond aside?"

"Deeply. There are exceptions, but it's rare."

Sabelle's answer struck a chord of fear in her chest. Felicia had mated with Hurstgrove for a "rare" reason. Did that mean she might possibly be one of the exceptions to the whole love business? But was she willing to bet her heart on that? "Thank you. I must decide what to do quickly."

"Only you can." Sabelle patted her shoulder. "I know you've only known me a handful of hours, but I'm here if you need to bend my ear some more."

"Thank you for everything." Felicia bit her lip. "But I must ask for one more favor. Merlin's books about Morganna's tomb—"

"I'm ahead of you. Whilst reading for anything about Untouchables, I've been skimming for mentions of the tomb. I've set aside a couple that I believe contain relevant passages. But they require closer scrutiny. He was brilliant but not orderly. I'll continue searching, but if you'd like to start reading—"

"I would. I need to see what I'm up against. Hurstgrove will try to stop me, no doubt, but I'm certain we won't be able to avoid that tomb forever."

Sabelle nodded sagely and rose. "I'll show you where to find them."

As she followed the witch back to the cave being used as an office, Sydney stood in the open door. "Where do you want this for safekeeping? And which of us will take it?"

It was a book with a slightly battered red cover and yellowing pages. An intricate pattern of rubies adorned the cover, raised and dazzling. And worth a serious fortune.

"What is that?" Felicia asked.

"The Doomsday Diary." Sydney held up the book.

"Notice the symbol all decked out in rubies on the front?" Olivia pointed out. "The letter underneath is an M. The piece that locks it is the L. My great-great grandmother believed in bling."

Felicia felt her jaw drop. "Morganna le Fay was—"

"Yep. Don't I have a fun family tree?" Olivia quipped.

Stepping closer to Sydney, Felicia reached for the book. Thinking better of it, she looked back at Olivia and Sabelle. "May I?"

The two women glanced at each other and shrugged. "Have a look."

A sense of electricity overcame her when she grabbed it. Not that she felt magic from the book. But to think she was holding a piece of ancient history that most humans would never know of . . .

"Why have you sacrificed everything to protect this book? Is it worth that much money?"

"It's more critical than mere money," Sabelle said. "It grants wishes."

Felicia stared at her, then the book. "Wishes? Like click your heels together three times and . . . ?"

"Not exactly, but not far off." The gorgeous blonde cocked her head to one side with a considering look. "Open it. I'm curious what you'll see."

Shrugging, Felicia gripped the binding and opened the front cover. Immediately, she saw a very bold script, old, angry. She skimmed the words. "A curse?"

"You can read that?" Olivia's mouth dropped open.

"It's right here." Felicia pointed.

"Not for us," Marrok's mate said. "Magic erases the ink from our view once the wish comes true. That curse was one Morganna put on Marrok a millennium and a half ago. Once it was broken, he could no longer see the words."

Felicia flipped ahead, skimming. "The curse's end is visible on the following page."

"Um . . ." Sydney said. "Maybe you could skip a few pages there that I—"

"Too late." Felicia grinned. "You have quite the imagination."

Sydney flushed pink. "It worked."

"I can see why you caught your man. He must be quite happy."

The redhead laughed. "I like to think so."

Felicia turned another page and read again, before casting a gaze to Sabelle. "It truly must grant wishes. Ice is whole, alive, and with you."

The witch nodded. "I wrote in the diary when Mathias had captured Ice. I didn't know what else to do. The moment Ice reappeared beside me was one of the happiest of my life."

"Why doesn't someone just write in the book to bring Tynan back, if this grants wishes? Or kill Mathias. Clearly, I can't, but . . ."

Sabelle sighed. "It's not that simple. The book has idiosyncrasies. One is that the person writing the wish must be female. It won't respond to a man at all. Their ink simply disappears off the page."

"Believe me," Olivia added. "Marrok tried."

Felicia winced. "I could tell."

Olivia snickered.

"The second catch is that the wish must be the writer's fondest, something she wants with all her heart," Sabelle supplied. "A wish she somewhat hopes will come true won't suffice."

"And saving Tynan is no one's fondest wish?" Felicia grappled with the concept.

"Oh, we very much like him," Sabelle rushed to answer.

"Absolutely," Sydney added. "Tynan is smart and brave."

"Marrok says he's a workhorse," Olivia tossed in. "But

the diary only works when you really, *really* care about the person in your wish."

"I see." The book's methodology dawned on Felicia. She felt sorry for Tynan. "Since the woman who loved him is gone . . ."

"Mathias murdered Auropha," Sabelle said. "The rest of us have spent enough time with the diary to know its limitations."

Kari sniffed. "It makes me so damn sad. Tynan has been a great friend to me. A shoulder to lean on. But as much as I care about him, when I tried to write in the book once for his happiness, my wish was ignored. I don't think this time would be any different."

Amazing. Magic so vast and complex, reaching across the centuries and looking into a woman's heart. Morganna le Fay might have been a total bitch, but she was clearly talented.

"What about killing Mathias?"

"I don't think killing is in any of our hearts," Sabelle said. "No matter how much we'd all like Mathias dead."

Which made complete sense.

Flipping through the book a bit more, Felicia found page after blank yellowing page. Until near the end.

She lifted her head to Sabelle. "Emma . . . isn't she Bram's missing mate?"

Everyone froze. Bram's sister stepped closer.

"She is. Do you see something?"

Felicia nodded and pointed to the page in front of her. "She wished for Bram to be unable to find her."

The women all looked at each other, stunned. Apparently this was news to them, and not of the good sort.

"What exactly does it say?" Sabelle asked with a worried frown.

Looking down at the page, Felicia recited, " 'I've made a

terrible mistake. Bram Rion has captured my heart and will hate me once he learns what I've done. I will miss him always, but I can't stand to see the betrayal in his eyes. Please make it impossible for him to find me, follow me, track me. If he tries to locate me, confuse him. Frustrate him. But don't let him near me. I would rather him believe I left him than to know the truth.' "

"Oh God," Sabelle breathed.

"That was her heart's desire." Sydney shook her head in disbelief. "He'll be crushed."

Though Bram had been a thorn in her side, she felt somewhat sorry for him. "What did she do?"

"Stole the diary from him." Olivia shook her head. "The question is, why?"

"And why did she then give it to my assistant?" Sydney mused aloud.

"All good questions." Kari sighed. "As often as I wanted to rip out Ronan's eyeballs when we first met, the one thing I would never have wanted was to make it impossible for him to find me. He angered me, but I loved him too much to stay away."

Olivia nodded. "I think that's true of all of us with our mates."

"And if you have even a hint of doubt, once those mating words are spoken . . ."

"Like cement," Kari agreed.

Their words staggered Felicia. She, too, had been impacted by the Call and her own Binding. But that was magical, so how could it be possible? Or did the words merely reflect what was in her secret heart of hearts?

"Do we tell Bram?" Sydney grimaced.

Olivia wrung her hands. "I don't know what passed between him and Emma in that one night, but—"

"It was profound," Sabelle finished. "I've never seen my brother like this. He was always snappy, on top of life, and happy for virtually any energy source. Now . . ."

"Won't he want to know that it's her conscience, not her heart, keeping her from him?" Felicia asked.

Sabelle hesitated, then nodded. "Knowing this *will* kill him, but I don't think it would be fair to withhold the information. He should—"

A series of gongs and bells interrupted Sabelle. The witch frowned. In fact, all the women did.

"What is it?" Felicia asked, her senses on alert. "Trouble? Should we flee?"

"No," Sabelle was quick to assure her. "It's Anka."

"Lucan's former mate?" Felicia asked.

"Precisely. She'd never come here unless something was terribly important."

The blond witch darted from the room and headed up the stairs. A few moments later, she appeared with another woman. Gorgeous. Centerfold dimensions. Pouting red mouth. Pale ringlets any red-blooded man would love to sink his hands into. Large breasts, tiny waist, lush hips, flaw-less golden skin. Felicia had always been termed classically pretty. This woman stopped traffic. If Anka hadn't looked so anguished, Felicia would have hated her on sight.

"Hello," she addressed everyone nervously, her gaze skit-tering over the other women. Then Anka looked her way. "Oh. Oh my . . . Are you with Lucan?"

Anka's expression made it clear that even asking the question pained her. Felicia's heart broke for the witch, who clearly had feelings for her former mate. So why was she with Shock?

"No. I'm . . . um, mated with Hurstgrove."

"Who?" Lucan's former mate asked.

"Duke," Sabelle supplied.

"Indeed." The relief on Anka's face was palpable. Felicia wanted to tell the woman that Lucan still loved her. But clearly more stood between them than their feelings.

Anka peered at the space around her. "You have no signature."

"Because I'm an—"

"Is something troubling you, Anka?" Sabelle cut in, then sent Felicia a quick glare.

Right, then. Sabelle wanted to keep the Untouchable thing mum.

"No." Anka shook her head. She appeared teary, disoriented. "Where is Bram?"

Sabelle hesitated. "Out with all the others. Except Duke. He and Felicia mated earlier tonight."

Surprised skittered across Anka's face. "He's let you out of bed already? When Lucan and I mated, I don't think I saw daylight for nearly a week."

Dear God. Surprise coiled through Felicia—along with a jolt of heat. Was that a figure of speech or did being magical give them . . . other abilities? That had never occurred to her. Thinking about it now made her blush twenty shades of red.

"It's been a hectic night," Sabelle segued back to the subject at hand. "You know that Shock took Tynan to Mathias earlier this evening, yes? We're desperately trying to rescue him."

"I didn't know." Anka spoke the truth. "Shock and I don't talk much."

The women exchanged glances. Felicia could feel their surprise. After escaping Mathias, Anka had left Lucan for Shock. Did she now regret it?

"Can I help you?" Sabelle asked.

"Don't shut me out and treat me like the enemy! I'm not.

I know you don't like Shock or trust him. He's . . . not who you think. Living with him, I've come to see a different side. Something in him is broken. I can't stay there anymore."

There was no hiding the surprise on Sabelle's face. Or any of the other women's. "You wish to stay here?"

"Yes. And I want Marrok to train me. I want to fight."

Olivia gaped. "Mathias? You want to be a warrior?"

Anka nodded before the question ended. "I want my revenge, and I won't get it hiding behind Shock's leathers. I need to do this."

Sabelle hesitated. "I'll bring it up to Bram, but . . ."

"Convince him. Please. Shock is on a bender. He's totally drunk. It's not the first time." Fresh tears pooled in Anka's amber eyes and she let out a shaky breath. "Or the tenth. I can't stay there."

Sabelle's eyes nearly popped from her head. *Shock?* Even Felicia was stunned. That didn't fit with the sharp, sarcastic wizard she'd met earlier. But the woman wasn't lying.

"The war is tearing him up. He fights with his brother constantly. It's vicious, and they've threatened to kill each other. He's at Mathias's beck and call. Sometimes, Shock returns looking shaken, and he doesn't want to talk, just drink." She bit her lip, then whispered, "We barely . . ."

Upon closer inspection, Anka looked exhausted, and Felicia understood. Shock wasn't spending much time between the sheets with this witch.

"But that's not my reason for leaving," Anka explained. "I . . . I need to fight."

Dead silence. Felicia certainly didn't know what to say. She tended to keep her feelings to herself, and yet Anka had poured everything out in minutes. The confusion and anguish in her voice . . . Felicia couldn't fail to be moved by it.

Olivia crossed the room and put an arm around Anka. "Why?"

"I shouldn't have hidden away after my rape. I was stunned. At the time, I wanted someone who would shelter me and wouldn't demand much of me. Or so I thought. But I see now that I *need* to stand on my own. I won't feel safe until I can defend myself. And I won't be at peace until Mathias is dead."

Felicia understood and admired Anka for surviving the horror and emerging stronger—but she was worried that the woman pursued a path that would ultimately kill her.

"I don't know if Bram will allow a female warrior," Sabelle admitted. "And Lucan will give him twenty kinds of hell if he lets you anywhere near Mathias."

Anka's eyes slid shut. Regret etched deeply into her face. "Why should he care after what I've done? Hiding behind Shock like a scared girl and sleeping with the enemy . . ."

Olivia drew closer. "Anka, you went through hell. No one blamed you for retreating into your shell. We just all assumed . . . Well, you and Lucan were always so in love that—"

"You assumed I'd come back." She sniffed back new tears. "I . . . can't. I'm not the same woman. He wouldn't want me if he knew the whole truth."

"I don't think he expected you to be exactly the same. Everyone knows such an experience would change you," Sabelle assured.

Anka closed the subject with a tight smile. "Can I wait for Bram here?"

Sabelle and the other women exchanged glances again. Personally, Felicia couldn't imagine throwing this anguished woman out. "If I get a vote, it's yes," she offered. "Mathias is chasing me like mad, and I understand your need to fight."

Anka approached her and smiled. It was sad, wobbly, not perfect. But it was genuine.

"Thank you," the witch whispered. "Duke is a good man. I wish you every happiness."

"It's . . ." *Temporary.* Or was it? After this, could she leave Hurstgrove? Marry Mason?

I won't rest until your heart is mine.

Her heart skipped a beat. If she stayed, how could she possibly insulate her feelings from a man like Hurstgrove? Two kisses and a few words, and she was falling under his spell. What would happen if she allowed him to take her to his bed?

Felicia swallowed. "It's . . . complicated."

Anka laughed. "He's complicated, so that's no surprise."

A sudden crash of the door against the wall, coupled with a feral growl, startled Felicia. Her blood froze and her heart flipped over. Fearing attack, she whirled.

It wasn't Mathias and the Anarki. Instead, she found danger of another kind.

Hurstgrove. His hair was uncharacteristically mussed, as if he'd raked a hand through it over and over. His pupils were dilated. A flush darkened his bronzed face. His wide chest, visible beneath his half unbuttoned shirt, rose and fell with each agitated breath. Need jumped through her belly, then pulsed lower.

"Felicia." His normally cultured voice rattled across the room, echoing off the walls. Stark. Aggressive.

Sexual.

Oh dear God. His intent was unmistakable. He'd come to claim her.

CHAPTER 11

FELICIA BIT HER LIP as her gaze traveled down, over Hurst-grove's hard abdominals and narrow hips to see— Bloody hell. He was aroused. Very.

In response, her body throbbed, the ache deep, strong, demanding. She released a ragged breath, her yearning to touch him so deep, she clenched her fist to contain it.

From the corner of her eye, she saw the other women exchange meaningful glances.

Felicia frowned. "Hurstgrove, I—"

"Damn it! My bloody name is *Simon.*" He charged across the room and clasped her in a feverishly tight grip. "You are my mate. Say my name."

She hesitated. If she did, would the added intimacy give him the green light to ravish her and draw her deeper under his spell? They should seal this union. But as desperately as she wanted him, how could sharing a bed with him not affect her heart?

No doubt he was the sort of lover who made lying back and thinking of England impossible. She shivered. It wasn't merely the sex—at which Felicia had no doubt he'd be quite skilled—but the intimacy. His kisses. His touch. His sensual heat. His whispered words. His possession. All would deepen her feelings, put her heart in peril. The part of her that had never stopped weeping after Deirdre's death was terrified of being that unguarded with anyone again.

Felicia tried to ease away from Hurstgrove. His grip held like iron. Both panic and excitement zipped through her.

He glared at the other women. "Get out. Now."

Jaws dropping, Kari exited quickly, followed by Sydney and Anka. Olivia paused to pat her shoulder on her way out the door.

"Wait!" she called after them.

They went on, falling quickly out of sight. Only Sabelle lingered in the doorway.

Felicia tried to swallow her rising desire and anxiety. "What's happening?"

Hurstgrove's fingers dug deeper into her shoulders. "What should have happened the moment you spoke the Binding. I'm going to kiss you, then sink deep inside of you until you know exactly which brother you belong to."

Felicia sucked in a breath, her insides pulsing at his words.

"It's mating fever," Sabelle murmured. "His instincts . . . He kissed you some days ago, sending his body into awareness. Once he spoke the Call, he became a ticking bomb." Regret spread over her soft features. "Sorry. I should have realized . . ."

That Hurstgrove would become sexually demanding? Felicia looked up into his blunt, dominating stare. He wanted her; he meant to take her.

Ignoring her attraction was her best means of self-preservation. Two days ago, she could have. The past twenty-four hours had peeled back his layers, proving he was brave, committed, smart, self-sacrificing. Nothing like Alexei. After fleeing through the night with Hurstgrove, kissing him, Binding to him, something in her had changed. She'd cleaved to him in some way that had nothing to do with the words they'd exchanged and everything to do with her feelings for him. Knowing he'd visited a surrogate had ripped her open with a hurt she didn't want to experience again. But if she refused him, she would.

Doing without him now would hurt her more.

Felicia rubbed at her forehead in confusion. For the first time, she was tempted to indulge in the heady rush of sensations and emotions coursing through her . . . even at the risk to her heart.

Still, if his fixation with her faded, Hurstgrove could crush her. If? No, *when*. But what would happen if she rejected him now, didn't seal this union? Mathias would find her and kill them both.

"What happens now?" she whispered to the witch.

Hurstgrove leaned closer until Felicia felt the heat of his body pouring off in waves. A drumbeat of desire pounded inside her. "Buckle up, Sunshine. I plan to strip you bare and taste you, before I sink my cock inside you, so deep for so long, you won't remember ever being without me."

Felicia's desire ramped up viciously.

"It's a fever. It will pass," Sabelle assured. "If you don't want this, I'll call my Aunt Millie. She can sedate him. She'll only need to keep him under for a few weeks. A month at most."

A month! Everything inside her rebelled against that. It was too cruel. And too dangerous.

Hurstgrove had risked everything to save her, done his best to respect her boundaries, even allowing himself to sink into this fever, rather than press her. Even now, with every muscle taut and trembling, he restrained himself, awaiting her reply.

"If we don't sedate him?" She heard her own voice shake.

Sabelle hesitated, looking as if she was deciding how to break bad news.

Having no such qualms, Hurstgrove gripped Felicia's chin and forced her to meet his gaze. "There isn't anything or anyone that will stop me from taking you in every way I possibly can, every moment of every day, until you know you're mine."

Sabelle nodded. "That sums it up."

Felicia's belly flipped over. Did the man have any idea that the utter possession in his words were a blowtorch to the ice around her heart?

But, a voice whispered, *how long could that devotion last, especially when magic didn't truly bind them together? When he didn't actually love her for her?*

"Felicia?" Face tense, eyes burning, Hurstgrove demanded an answer.

The way he said her name turned her knees liquid. Then he cradled her head in a desperate grip and leaned closer, hot breath fanning over her lips. His male, musky scent shot a million tingles through her.

She'd never felt as alive as she did right now.

"Should I call for Millie?" Sabelle raised a golden brow.

She had to decide. Here. Now. Say no and protect her heart—or embrace the frightening, burgeoning feelings she had for Hurstgrove, knowing that, once done, he would have more power to hurt her than she'd ever allowed any man?

Felicia licked her lips and stared. Her heart seized, then thumped wildly in her chest. She knew the answer to her question.

"I won't need Millie."

"Good choice." Sabelle smiled, then slipped out.

Before the door closed behind the witch, Hurstgrove gripped Felicia tighter, shaking with restraint. His touch seared her. "Be very sure. The fever is strong. Once I start . . ."

He wouldn't be able to stop.

It was mad, but deep down, that fact thrilled her. It was probably foolish, but she wanted him to want her more than he could bear. She wanted him to ache and need—and take her as though he couldn't get enough. As though everything between them was real and lasting. Because she felt all those things as well.

So dangerous . . .

Felicia met his dark stare. "I'm sure."

She'd been trying to suppress her feelings for Hurstgrove since the moment they met. Hour by hour, he'd crept deeper into her thoughts, burrowing into some corner of her heart. Spending another minute denying the fact that she needed to feel him wasn't possible. This once, she would give herself to him completely.

Without warning, he growled again and lifted her, wrapping her legs around his waist. Felicia had no opportunity to react before he covered her mouth with his. Single-minded and savage, he kissed her, his lips raking over her own, pressing, demanding that she open to him. The second she did, he barged in, sinking deep. His rich taste intoxicated her, flooding her senses, bursting her need wide open.

As desire bombarded her, she curled her fingers through his silky hair, pulling him closer. She met every thrust of his tongue, every silent demand for more, with one of her own.

Gripping her hips, he prodded her against his erection and crossed the room. The friction had her gasping into their endless kiss.

A second later, he backed her against the stone wall, then crushed her breasts against his hard chest. Felicia arched to him. He took all she offered and more, his mouth hungry, decimating hers, before nipping his way across her jaw, down her neck. She gasped under the gentle yet rough scrapes of his teeth and the insistence of his hot and hungry lips. Tingles burst and scattered through her body.

What had ever felt so perfect?

Slowly, Hurstgrove set her on her feet and tore off his shirt. She shivered under his broiling stare. Built lean and muscled, his chest, shoulders, and arms all bulged, hard and so very male. Restlessly, Felicia shifted and pressed her thighs tightly together, but that only deepened her ache. She'd never imagined this kind of desire, like something out of a movie, never believed it could chip away at her resistance, obliterating all but the need to connect completely with him.

Hurstgrove reached for her shirt and unfastened the top button before she could blink. Her heart, already tripping into overdrive, revved up more as he quickly plucked away the rest.

When the last of her buttons came free and he shoved the garment from her shoulders with impatient hands, her need surged.

His stare flared and darkened as he fixated on her white lace bra. He fisted his hands. Hesitated.

A terrible thought occurred to Felicia, and she swallowed down fear. "You . . . don't like—"

God, why humiliate herself by asking if she wasn't as sexy as he'd imagined? He'd had sex with so many women. Actresses, models, beauties both human and magical. How could she compete?

Felicia scrambled for her shirt and covered herself. With a growl, Hurstgrove ripped the garment from her grasp. As her chest rose and fell with sharp, anxious breaths, she felt more exposed than ever.

"Don't like what I see? Is that what you think?" His eyes narrowed, his voice was like a whip.

"I, um . . ." She exhaled, shuddering to momentary silence. "Yes."

"You're mad, Sunshine. I'm trying to figure out how I can sate my immense need for you without utterly terrifying you. You're already apprehensive."

Yes, but not for the reason he imagined. His seduction wasn't too much. Her feelings for him were.

"I've never felt anything like this," she admitted with a trembling voice.

He froze. "Like what?"

"This . . . consuming desire." She bit her lip, struggling with the next words. "I don't know how to fight it."

"I couldn't from the moment I met you."

His words took her breath. Leaning forward, she pressed her mouth to his lightly. Then a bit harder. Hurstgrove braced himself against the wall, knuckles white, shaking with the effort to remain still and allow her to lead at her own pace. His trembling told Felicia that such restraint cost him deeply. Her heart flipped all over again.

With every touch, their connection deepened, their desire grew.

Taking her hair in his fists, he thrust her head back and sank into her mouth, turning the kiss into a ravaging that left her breathless. Felicia shivered as he delved deep, his hands roaming her bare shoulders, her back, before settling on the fastening of her bra. In the next second, it gave way and met her shirt on the floor.

Cold air and his hot stare grazed her nipples. Hurstgrove gazed in wonder, as if he found her the most beautiful woman he'd ever seen. As if he couldn't hold out another second.

"Felicia." He cupped one mound in his hot palm, thumbing the stiff peak, and she gasped at the hot rain of sensation. His touch heated her skin, raising the fever, before his mouth settled over her and he sucked hard.

With a gasp, she arched toward him, clutching his hard, bulging shoulders to keep him near.

Quickly, he shifted to her other breast, captured it between his lips, sucked, nipped. The need expanded, jettisoning her remaining worry and thought.

She moaned. The ache inside pressed down on her, demanding not just sex, but *him*. All of him. A dangerous yearning to share her mind and heart, her fears and tomorrows with him invaded her, frighteningly strong. He was alluring, potent. Forbidden.

Panting with each breath, Felicia eased his zip down, shoving his trousers away with desperate fingers. She wrapped her hand around his erection and stroked down his length, gratified when he groaned long and loud.

Dear God, he was hard. And big. Soon, he'd be inside her, cementing the bond she knew she shouldn't want but could no longer deny.

With a tortured groan, Hurstgrove grabbed her wrists. "I'm trying to go slow, love you the way you deserve. You're killing my good intentions."

She shook her head. "I don't need them. Just you."

Black eyes scanned her, nostrils flaring. With a muffled curse, he lifted her and pushed her to the couch, tossing aside the decorative pillows.

He laid into her jeans, ripping them open with barely concealed violence, dragging them down her hips and to the floor.

Felicia lay completely bare before him, desperate for his touch. Hurstgrove's smoldering stare said he'd never wanted anyone half so much as he wanted her now.

She knew better than to hope that would be true forever.

He covered her body with his. Feverish skin seared her as he kissed his way down her neck and sucked ravenously at her nipples, tightening that invisible vise inside her. She moaned in surrender.

Restlessly, he wended down her body, laying kisses on the underside of her breasts, over her abdomen. Felicia clutched his shoulders, her nails sinking into his skin as he circled her navel with his tongue, awakening nerve endings she hadn't known existed.

"That's it, Sunshine. Dig those pretty little nails into me. Once I'm deep inside you, give me more of that. Promise me."

His words burned her to the core. "Yes."

With a faint smile of triumph, he wriggled his way lower. Felicia parted her thighs for him. Her head spun, dizzy with desire as his breath ruffled her damp curls. His intent became instantly clear.

"Hurstgrove, I've never, um . . ."

He froze and glared up at her. "It's Simon. You're going to say it. Scream it. Over and over as you come until you get it right."

Her belly rolled, dropped, even as her heart soared. She tried to rein it in. No such luck.

"I'm not terribly orgasmic," she admitted softly.

"You are now."

His scorching hands pressed her thighs wider. The muscles stretched for him, a sweet ache. She trembled as he lowered his head, nipping at her thighs, trailing his tongue over her hip, awakening so many nerve endings.

Restlessly, she lifted to him in a silent plea. He gripped her hips in his hands and held her down. "Oh, I'm going to taste you. The scent of your arousal has driven me mad since last night."

He'd *smelled* her? Before she could process that, he trailed his fingers through her slit, groaning when he encountered her slick flesh. She gasped as sensation and ache coiled tight right where he touched.

"So wet," he praised, brushing a finger over her clit.

She gasped, tensed. With a smile, he repeated the movement, pressing harder, circling, lingering. Blood roared in her ears. Then he added his tongue to the mix, laving the little bud, sucking it into his mouth, swirling around until her entire body shook.

Felicia shifted restlessly, mewling, drowning in their connection as it deepened and rushed over each of her senses. With a hungry touch, he caressed her as if he knew precisely what she wanted. She responded with abandon.

The pressure rose. And the pleasure. Dizziness assailed her as he worked his tongue and fingers in an insistent rhythm that had her gasping. Pleasure ran liquid through her veins, tightening until the explosion seemed but a breath away.

He turned ravenous, sucking her clit into his mouth. His fingers scraped a sensitive spot deep inside. Felicia hadn't thought it possible, but pleasure climbed again, teetering dangerously on the edge of something wonderful. She raced for it, straining. So close . . .

Suddenly, Hurstgrove eased back. "When you climax, scream *my* name."

"Others will hear," she protested.

"Then they'll know who you belong to, just as you should. Tonight, tomorrow. Always."

Possession rang in his tone, infusing her with both joy and panic. In his mind, this wasn't a one-time event. He meant to take her body again and again.

And her heart, as well.

Dread and insidious joy infused her at once. "No. This is . . . It's just once."

He speared her with a scorching stare. "Like hell."

Before she could say another word, he slid his tongue over her again, augmenting the sensation with teasing brushes of his fingers. He read her body like a book, knew exactly what she needed and when.

Her head told her that she should be objecting. This hedonistic devouring went beyond mere sex. Exposing her need down to its raw core wasn't necessary. He made her toes curl, her muscles strain. He kept her on the edge, never applying enough friction to send her hurtling into ecstasy. She let out a keening cry.

"Scream for me," he whispered, his fingertips circling her clit. "My name. Not Hurstgrove, not Duke. My first name on your sweet lips."

Felicia grabbed blindly for the couch cushions. Her heart wanted to open to him, shouted at her to comply. But she was so afraid of how easily he could crush her.

"What—*ooohhh*!" She melted at his next touch, then forced herself back on task. "What are you about? Let's—oh dear God!" Felicia struggled against the pleasure. "Get on with it."

Hurstgrove bared his teeth in a snarl. "I am your mate, ready to claim you *in every way*. We'll 'get on with it' when you surrender to me."

Before she could reply, he eased his fingers back inside her, skillfully rousing her even more with a deft thumb.

"Oh!" She tossed her head back, legs splaying wider, as pleasure bathed her.

"That's it. I'll give you everything you need as soon you open your heart. No more hiding. No more artificial barriers. I won't have your guilt or fear between us."

"I *am* afraid." She sobbed out, the razor edge of pleasure and anxiety welling up inside her, forging something so big, she thought her chest might burst.

"Trust me," he panted. "Scream my name. I won't let you down."

God, how badly she wanted to believe that.

As if he considered the matter settled, he lowered his mouth to her again, laving, lingering. Pleasure skyrocketed. Blood rushed, roared, filling her head as her heart pounded, loud and unrelenting. *Thump, thump, thump.*

Felicia's defenses melted beneath his onslaught, and she gripped his shoulders. Against her logic, her heart softened, her soul opened. And her surrender unfurled, leaving her exposed, vulnerable. There wasn't a damn thing she could do to stop him from filling all those empty places inside her as the pleasure crashed over her.

"*Simon!!!*" she screamed long and loud, her nails deep in his shoulders.

Her entire body convulsed as ecstasy rolled through her, raining fire on her, sealing something between them.

Was escaping with her heart unscathed even possible now?

Duke slammed his eyes shut. *Careful,* he reminded himself. He couldn't just slam into her as he so desperately wanted. It wouldn't serve his purpose. He must tie her to him using every weapon he had. Overcome whatever fear she had of him, men, and love. It was time.

It was true that making love to her might change her imprint on his signature and that once she trusted him with her body, protecting her would be easier. But that wasn't why he craved her. No. He needed Felicia because she was *his*, and he'd quickly come to love the shy-but-sassy woman.

In the back of his head, Duke had known that mates usually bonded emotionally, even those who exchanged vows in unusual circumstances. What he hadn't counted on was falling completely in love. He needed to feel her beneath him, his in every way.

Now that he knew she not only responded to his touch, but gloried in it, nothing would keep him from claiming her tonight. And every night for the rest of their lives.

Felicia scrambled back on the couch, her hands covering the soft swell of her breasts.

He was having none of it. "Put your arms over your head and grip the arm of the couch."

She hesitated. "S-Simon . . ."

"It's good to hear my name on your lips." He dusted kisses down her cheeks, nipped her lobe. "Do as I've asked. Trust me."

She hesitated.

"You wanted to get on with it," he pointed out. "Let me."

"You're going to overwhelm me," she accused.

If by "overwhelm," she meant give her another orgasm, then yes. "I'm going to fortify this mating and keep you safe. Arms over your head, gripping the arm of the couch."

Slowly, she lifted them away from those gorgeous breasts with the candy-sweet nipples that drove him mad, and held tight.

"Good girl." He traced a light finger between her breasts, over one nipple. It sprang up, beaded hard, under his touch. He smiled. "You look beautiful."

She breathed harder, watching him with that skittish doe gaze.

His heart clenched as he lowered his body, gritting his teeth at the sublime sensation of his bare skin against hers. Every curve clung to him, as if she was made to fit against him.

Gasping, Felicia looped her arms around his neck. As much as he loved her embrace, Duke grabbed her wrists and repositioned her grip back on the couch. "For my restraint. Please."

With wary blue eyes, she nodded.

Brushing a pale curl from her cheek, he filtered a soft kiss over her plump lips, trying to give her something gentle to savor. The fever was slamming him, hurtling over his self-control, and his urge to thrust home, go deep, and pummel her with every bit of his passion rode him hard.

"Spread your legs for me."

A flush colored her cheeks, and she bit her lip. "I . . . I haven't, um . . . Not in a while."

Duke froze. Hadn't Mason been availing himself of her sweetness at every opportunity? If not, more the fool he. If that was the case, Duke knew he had to dig into his reserves and make this tender enough to be good for her. Somehow.

Sweat broke out across his brow as he propped up on his knees. Under his watchful gaze, she parted her thighs a fraction. That would never do. He needed her to offer everything to him. The fever demanded it. The wizard in him needed to know that his mate was *his*.

He pushed her legs farther apart, revealing damp, pale curls and swollen folds. He licked his lips, desperate for another taste, but he forced the craving aside. Later, when she was sated and docile and wouldn't balk, he'd indulge his desire to spend more time lapping at every delicious inch of her. Now, he needed to be one with her.

Gripping her lean, feminine thighs in his hands, Duke murmured, "Tell me you're ready."

Desire and uncertainty both crossed her face. "I am . . . but this is going to change everything, isn't it?"

Even if he could, Duke refused to lie to her. "Yes. You're mine and you always will be. You'll know that after tonight."

"Not forever. I-I don't want that. You can't possibly either."

Duke stifled his frustration. He could argue with her, but words now meant nothing. She'd have to feel them together, sealing this bond.

Bracing himself, Duke positioned himself at her entrance, fitted the sensitive head of his cock right against her slick welcome. Then he pushed.

And sucked in a stunned breath. "Bloody hell, you're tight."

She shifted beneath him with a whimper.

He let out a shuddering breath. She'd barely taken a quarter of his length. He checked his instinct to ram deep, claim her in one stroke.

Balancing on his knees, he parted her folds with his thumbs and pushed in slowly, watching more of his erection disappear into the hot, silky depths of her body. Beneath him, she thrashed. A pale flush crawled over her cheeks, now spreading to her chest.

"Hurt, Sunshine?"

She thrashed her head from side to side. "Too slow. Deeper."

Joy burst through his heart. Felicia yearned to complete the bond—even if she didn't recognize the emotion. She was everything he wanted, everything he hadn't known he'd been searching for through countless meaningless trysts.

She gripped the couch and raised herself to him. He sank a bit deeper. God, she felt delicious. His thoughts short-circuited, and he could hardly catch his breath. Sweat broke out over his skin.

The little noises Felicia made in the back of her throat

were driving him mad. Moans, whimpers, mewls, pleas. Each told him what she wanted. He'd be damned if he wouldn't give it to her.

Because Mason never would again.

The thought spurred him on as he gripped her hips, gritted this teeth, and pushed in the rest of his length with all his might.

"Simon!" she gasped.

Amazingly, she contracted around him with a scream, her flesh sucking him in deeper, caressing his length until Duke thought he might lose his bloody mind. A second later, he drew back until just his tip remained tucked in her sweet sex, then he grabbed the arm of the couch above her head, and surged into her. Fast. Hard. And she cried out again, now digging her nails into his back.

Thrilled, he set a mad rhythm, blistering, blinding, as he captured her mouth beneath his. *Yes!* He tasted that unique blend of elements, spices, and her own personal something that screamed the fact she was made for him, as he was made for her.

Beneath him, Felicia opened to him in every way, her skin flushing darker with every thrust. Her eyes looked so blue, moist with a plea that had her near tears. Duke read her need as clearly as if she'd spoken because he was inside her in every way, connecting more than their bodies, even more than their hearts. They were one need, one soul. His chest tightened. He couldn't imagine ever wanting anyone else again.

Cupping her face in his hands, he layered his mouth over hers, plundering deep with his kiss as he did with his body. She clutched desperate fingers around his wrists, blue eyes wild and clinging. Her end was near. So was his. He tightened, slowed, hoping to stave off the inevitable. He wasn't willing to give her up. Ever.

Felicia deepened their kiss, raking his shoulders with her nails. He hissed in pleasure. Then, to his shock, she pushed him up to his knees . . . and kept urging him back.

Uncurling his legs, he lay supine on the couch. Felicia climbed over him, determination and craving evident in her concentration and burning eyes. She moved over him, then took his length inside her, deep, deep, deep, setting a pace that made him gasp—and made holding back damn near impossible.

"Felicia, I— Shit. Wait. Bloody hell!"

Frantically, she shook her head, her nails digging into his shoulders and her hips crashing down to him again and again. "No. Please . . ."

When she ground into him, rubbing erotically, peppering kisses up his neck, fire licked across his skin. He wasn't going to last.

Then she whimpered and her sex pulsed hard all around him. *"Simon!"*

Hearing his name on her lips again rocketed him into the most brilliant pleasure ever, stripping away his control.

Ecstasy pummeled him. He exploded, smashing away memories of any other pleasure, of any other woman, leaving only Felicia behind.

Slowly, his breathing returned to normal. His heart stopped revving. The woman in his arms wilted across his chest with a long sigh of satisfaction. Neither moved.

"Sunshine," he murmured in her ear.

"I'm dead," she croaked, her voice ringing with exhaustion.

He smiled. "How ever shall I revive you?"

The thought of taking her in the luxury of a bed with hours at their disposal, feeling her complete willingness and trust, knowing he had her love, made him hard again.

Lifting up, he thrust slow and deep.

Her startled gaze flew to his. "Already? Us mere mortals need a bit of time to recover. You don't?"

"Because we generate energy from sex, wizards are pretty much ready every moment of every day." He surged inside her again.

As he closed in on her mouth to brush a warm kiss on those candy red lips, the phone in his trouser pocket began to vibrate loudly.

"Damn lousy timing . . ." If this was Bram, his problem had better be life or death.

Leaning for his clothes, he groped until he retrieved the mobile. He fumbled it in his grip, and it landed on his chest, display up.

Felicia clapped eyes on it and froze.

Duke snatched it and glared at the lighted display. Mason. *Fuck!*

Bloody impeccable timing. He silenced the little device and tossed it to the floor even as she started pulling away.

"Felicia, don't."

She shoved against his chest, but Duke gripped her hips, holding her in place. Guilt and uncertainty crept across her face. Damn if she wasn't retreating back into her shell.

She shook her head. "This isn't right. It isn't real."

"The hell it isn't," he rasped. "We were as close as two people can be, and not just physically. You can't deny it."

Her face closed up. "Try to understand. You say I'm your magical mate. But I'm still your brother's fiancée, and he's expecting a wife. I don't know where that leaves me."

Duke's mind raced. Females—witches and otherwise—didn't experience a wizard's mating instinct. How could he convince her they were meant to be?

"You planned to marry Mason for children. I'll give them to you. As many as you want."

She shook her head. "I also sought a companion. A friend. But this, you . . . it's more than I can take."

"What does that mean? If you wanted children, you knew you'd have a lover, as well. Did you expect to spend your entire married life feeling nothing beyond friendship?"

She didn't say anything. But her face spoke volumes. Yes, she'd fully intended to marry her friend Mason, procreate, but never expand the boundaries of their relationship.

Duke refused to settle for that.

"This conversation is pointless." She lifted away from him and started fumbling for her clothes.

He let her go—for now. Though he really wanted to make love to her again, talking was more important than sex. If he worked through her issue, her anxiety wouldn't interfere with their lovemaking again.

"How so?" He reached for his jeans and donned them.

"We've consummated the bond. That's all that was required, correct? Hopefully, your signature's changed and we won't have to . . ."

"Have sex again? That's where you're wrong, Sunshine. I promise you, this was the first time of many."

Her fists clenched and her red lips pursed together. "That wasn't what I agreed to. Our mating is temporary, to shield me from Mathias. I've spoken words I don't agree with and now done this." She pointed to the couch, fighting tears. "There shouldn't be more."

She sniffed the sobs back, jaw clenched. Damn, he couldn't bear to see her hurting. Clearly, their lovemaking had gotten to her, scared her. He could remind her that she'd enjoyed it as well, but that was counterproductive. Duke knew he was affecting her emotions. He must tread carefully until he earned her complete trust.

"But there is, even if my signature has changed. Those

words that didn't mean anything to you, meant everything to me. You are the only one for me. I love you."

Felicia gasped. She *knew* he wasn't lying.

Hand to her chest, she backed away with terror all over her face. "How is that possible? You've known me for two days."

"I suspected the first time I saw you from a distance, months ago, that I would fall for you. I knew it for certain when I kissed you. I'm even more sure now."

She backed away another step, turned her back to him, scrambling into the rest of her clothes. "Love is...a fallacy. It's what men like you say to women like us when you want sex. Then you'll claim you fell out of love when you become bored."

Duke found himself wanting to pound someone's face, and he would—just as soon as he figured out which man deserved the honors. "Who the hell broke your heart? I know it wasn't Mason. You chose him because he was safe."

Felicia grabbed her bra and shoes, shot him a glance rife with anguish, then headed for the door. "I'd never let anyone have that chance."

Her answer stunned him to the core. He should back away, think, let her do the same. Already, he'd said too much. But he couldn't simply let her go.

Before she could escape, he grabbed her arm. "I'm not giving up on you, Sunshine."

She jerked from his grasp. "You will. It's human nature."

"Remember, I'm not human."

That reminder exploded across her face—even as an actual explosion rattled the walls and doors around them. The retort died on her tongue. Screaming nearby sent a chill down his spine.

He grabbed Felicia's hand. "Damn it! We're under attack. Come with me."

CHAPTER 12

Felicia gasped. "Mathias is *here?*"

"Likely." Duke pulled her out of the room, into the hall.

"How did he find us?"

That question had already flashed through Duke's mind. None of the answers were good. "Shock must have told him either where to find us or how to follow your imprint on me."

"So . . . you abducting me, us hiding and mating, was all for nothing?"

He curled an arm around her and held tight, needing to feel her close. "No. You're still alive. If I have anything to say about it, you'll stay that way."

As he guided her down the hall, he pulled out his phone and hit the button to dial Bram, who answered on the first ring. "Did you seal the deal with Felicia?"

"Bugger off. We're under attack." Another explosion rocked the hallway around him. The lights flickered ominously. Men shouted above.

"Where are the women?"

"Finding them now."

In the dark, narrow hallway, he ran into Sabelle. "Mathias and the Anarki are here."

"Tell her to abandon!" Bram shouted in his ear.

Duke held the phone far from his ear. "She heard you. We all did."

Bram grumbled, "Get Felicia out fast. Once you do, we'll teleport back and fight."

He hated leaving the rest to fight, but getting Felicia to safety was first priority. "I'll call you once we're safe."

He rang off, then turned to Sabelle. "Escape routes?"

She nodded. "There's a tunnel. Ice's father was paranoid and dug a path from here to the village. In the office, look behind the bookcase on the left. On the shelf, there's a key to one of Bram's cars. It's a late-model Volvo. Gray. Parked in front of the butcher shop. Go."

"You and the others coming with us?"

Another explosion rocked the caves. Loose rock and dust showered them from the ceilings and walls. Duke swore. Felicia grabbed his arm for support. He drew her close, fear edging through him.

Sabelle shook her head. "Once you're gone, we'll teleport to Kari's pub."

He hesitated, hating to leave them, but they'd get to safety faster magically than by car. "Be careful. Um . . . has my signature become more . . . normal?"

She shook her head, expression rife with apology. "No."

Felicia sighed. "I don't understand."

They'd have to figure out why later. Now, Duke grabbed his mate's hand. "Let's go."

Felicia dug in her heels. "What about the diary? We can't leave it."

"I'll take it." Sabelle's face turned grim.

"I can . . . if you'd like." Felicia touched the witch's shoulder. "I'll guard it with my life."

Sabelle gnawed on her lip, hesitating.

Duke's first instinct was to refuse; he and Felicia didn't need extra danger. But now that Mathias had gotten close enough to see Felicia's affect on his signature, a plan to keep her safe dive-bombed his brain, so simple . . . so perfect. It would keep the diary safe as well.

He smiled. "We'll take it. Mathias will expect you to have it, Sabelle. As long as I keep Felicia near the diary, he can't use it. And I think I know how to make certain he doesn't get anywhere near her."

Another explosion crashed around them, this one sounding closer than the last. A door crashed open above. The clomp of heavy footsteps stormed above.

The Anarki were inside.

Sabelle grimaced, facing Felicia. "I left a few books for you in the office. The diary is there as well. Call when you can."

With that, Sabelle spun away. Duke turned to Felicia, but she was already running down the hall—closer to the encroaching footsteps. He charged after her, back into the office they'd just vacated. The couch was rumpled and the air smelled thick with musk and sex. The urge to keep her near, not let her beyond his reach, nearly drove him mad, but he had to check it and focus on the bigger picture.

She darted to the bookcase and shoved the keys Sabelle mentioned into her pocket, then snatched the diary and clutched it to her chest. An instant later, she started scooping up more books.

"All of these?" he demanded. "We can't take this many."

"We must. They're Merlin's."

And Bram would chap his hide, rightfully so, if he didn't protect them.

"I want this information," she explained, snatching up one of the yellowing tomes. "Running from Mathias isn't the answer. We're going to have to face him someday, and I'm going to be ready."

Fear exploded in his chest. He couldn't stand the thought of Felicia anywhere near Mathias. But Bram had dreamed it. Damn, he could only hope there was some way to change the future. Because if Mathias got his hands on her, he would use her . . . and kill her.

And that would destroy Duke.

Felicia shoved the rest of the books into his hands, then pushed her shoulder against the bookcase. Duke dove in to help.

The rapid drumbeat of the Anarki's footsteps drew near. Another explosion rocked above, louder, closer. Bloody hell, Mathias had brought conventional explosives. So they knew Felicia was here . . . just as they'd soon know she was gone— if they got out alive.

Male shouts and mingled voices reached them. The Anarki were just outside the room!

With a mighty shove, Duke opened the portal behind the bookcase. He shoved Felicia into the dark space. "Run! I'm behind you."

Thank God she did as he asked and dashed down the narrow, shadowed tunnel. Duke slammed the door, praying the Anarki hadn't seen them.

The thick walls buffered the sounds of the attack, but he still heard the blasts, the shouting. He felt terrible about leaving the rest of the women to fend for themselves, but Sabelle and Anka were capable witches. Sydney, Kari, and Olivia knew exactly how to assist. They'd practiced for this eventuality. Felicia must be rescued at any cost. For magickind's sake, Mathias could be allowed nowhere near Morganna's tomb.

Books tucked under one arm, Duke darted after his mate, catching up to her in moments. Even in the shadows, her hair flew out behind her like a golden banner.

"All right?" he asked.

She merely nodded, clutching her books, and kept on, the pounding of their footsteps and labored breathing eventually smothering the battle noises as they slipped farther away.

About three kilometers later, they reached the end of the tunnel. Duke fumbled in the dark, then found a knob and opened the door. It squeaked, and he winced. Beyond lay a dark flight of stairs leading up to a cold, starry night.

Together, they plodded up the steep path, only to encounter more stairs. As Felicia mounted them, she panted heavily beside him.

Duke grabbed her elbow to assist. "Can I carry you?"

She shook her head resolutely. "I'm . . . fine."

Stubborn to a fault, too. "You're tiring. I—"

"I can do this! I refuse to be helpless."

Unlike the night he'd abducted her, Felicia now understood the danger and insisted on doing her part. Duke had always respected her, but now his esteem for her climbed another notch.

At the top, he looked about for any stray Anarki loitering in the village. No one appeared in this sleepy little town in the dead of night. He breathed a sigh of relief.

Through the inky night they crept, around a corner, past a streetlamp reminiscent of the village's bygone heyday. In the distance, the ocean rumbled into the bay. Every muscle tense, Duke kept one arm around Felicia and both eyes watchful for unwanted visitors.

A craggy little butcher shop sat off to one side. Its brick walls were surrounded by bare trees, their branches swaying with a stiff January wind. On the side of the building sat a strip of asphalt. And a gray Volvo.

Beside him, Felicia's teeth chattered. Cursing the fact he'd had no opportunity to grab her a coat, Duke pushed her to the car. "Give me the keys."

She set the books on the hood. He noticed then that she still clasped her bra in her fist.

Remembering exactly how he'd disrobed her and what

had followed made Duke ache to sidle closer and slide a hand down her spine, toward her luscious backside. Bloody inconvenient time for the need to reassert itself. But keeping his hands off her was ridiculously difficult.

With a flush staining her cheeks, she shoved the bra in one pocket and retrieved the key from the other, then thrust it in his face. "Here. Where are we going?"

She was all business. Sighing, he pulled away. There'd be time to seduce her later, once they were safe.

He unlocked the car. "Get in and I'll fill you in. I have a plan."

With a sharp nod, she grabbed the books and climbed into the passenger seat. "I assume you're going to drive as ridiculously fast as you did the last time?"

Probably faster. He merely smiled, revved the engine, and sped off.

Mile after mile of Welsh countryside passed in relative blackness while Duke gripped the wheel, downshifted to tackle tricky corners, then floored it on open stretches of road. He had to put miles between Felicia and Mathias to keep her safe.

"So what's the plan?"

Felicia would balk. But in every other way, the plan was brilliant. It would keep her alive, and that was all that mattered.

"We're going to London. Mathias, like every other wizard, knows there are lines he cannot cross without earning the wrath of the Council."

"Council?"

He sighed. Of course she wouldn't understand magical politics. "Magickind's governing board. It's comprised of seven wizards from prominent families."

"Wow. I never imagined . . . but it makes sense that magickind would need a government."

"The positions pass from a wizard to his male heir, much like titles of the peerage. Currently, Bram, Tynan, and Ice all sit on the Council. They vote as a bloc, doing their best to enact policies that will protect magickind and annihilate Mathias. The other four—"

"How could they possibly be against that?" Incredulity widened her eyes.

Duke sent her a cynical smile. "Politics are politics, no matter where you travel. Lucan and Caden's uncle, Sterling, sometimes votes with the Doomsday Brethren. But he has an elder's mentality on some issues. They don't want to act too quickly and risk a misstep. The other three are either corrupt or terrified. They hope that placating Mathias will give him less reason to attack."

Felicia's jaw dropped. "That's absurd. Placating him will make him bolder. History is full of such examples."

"Yes, but Bram, Tynan, and Ice have had difficulty convincing the others. They know little of human history, and care to know even less." Duke sighed. "Recently, the Council gave the Doomsday Brethren license to kill Mathias. That's easier said than done, which is why we've been stuck at this bloody impasse. One thing Mathias could do that would force the Council to throw every resource at him is risk exposure of our kind to humans. Witch hunts—the Inquisition, for example—are too fresh in the memories of many. We'd invite mass murder and extinction."

She sucked in a breath. "That never occurred to me. The Salem witch trials?"

He shook his head, smiling. "Most of magickind remains here in Britain. It's difficult for us to cope without our own kind."

"Right, then." She frowned. "So, the plan is . . . what?"

"Hide in plain sight."

* * *

Felicia peered across the small car's interior at Simon. His profile made her heart stop. Elegant brow, strong nose, chiseled cheeks, full lips, square jaw. The feelings she'd been trying to bury since their interlude on the couch roared back to haunting life. The man moved her on every level. How had he known exactly how to touch her? How had he pleasured her so thoroughly?

Lots and lots of practice.

Shoving aside a sick pang at the thought, she forced herself to focus on the here and now. They were running for their lives. Matters of the heart would have to wait.

"I don't understand," she told him. "Hide among crowds? Blend in to the public?"

"Somewhat." His hand tightened on the wheel. "You recall all the paparazzi hovering about your wedding?" When she nodded, he pressed on. "We're going to use them to our advantage. Our . . . departure together no doubt created a scandal. Paparazzi will be frothing at the mouth to scoop stories on us. We'll keep the tabloids burning, and thus maintain a crowd around us. Since you're Untouchable, Mathias will be forced to scuttle his magic and reach you via human means, which he knows little about. He cannot send more wizards to capture you. They're every bit as clueless about guns and the like as he is."

"What about the explosions at the cave?"

"Formerly human Anarki. Mathias abducts them, magically removes their souls, so he controls them. Without a soul, however, they're dead inside, and the body slowly rots. Walking cadavers are a bit conspicuous among humans, so Mathias cannot employ them in public. Besides, Anarki aren't good at restraining their urge to inflict mortal harm. Mathias needs you alive."

"For now." She clutched her hands in her lap, fear wending through her.

Simon enveloped her hands with one of his own in silent reassurance. "For now."

"In other words, with a crowd about, Mathias will be hard-pressed to find any way to spirit me away to open Morganna's tomb."

"Precisely."

Felicia drank all the information in. The idea had merit. Magickind must be keeping their secret fairly well or it would be all over the news. Of course there had been that one rag . . .

"Wait, didn't *Out of this Realm* run stories about some magical war? Yes!" It was all coming back to her, some paper she'd seen one day on the Tube. "They even named Mathias and the Doomsday Brethren."

"Which is exactly why we sent Caden in to shut Sydney up. She had far too much information. Now she reports for us."

Clever, indeed. "So, we'll milk our scandal, then?"

"And add to it. By the time we appear in London, the fact we're a couple will be old news. I know these vultures. They always want fresh meat. We'll give it to them."

Felicia wasn't sure she liked the sound of that. "Meaning?"

Downshifting, he turned to her with dark eyes full of gravity that made her stomach clench. "We're going to announce our engagement."

"*What?* B-but . . ." Felicia grappled for words.

She was now Duke's magical mate. No denying that. They had consummated their union in brilliant fashion less than an hour ago. But they still had to worry about Mason. Her fiancé. His brother.

"It's perfect tabloid fodder. One of England's most eligible bachelors steals his brother's girl and whisks her away, eventually romancing her to the altar. Naturally, the details of our pending nuptials will be a secret, for which they'll hound us relentlessly."

As much as she hated to admit it, the plan was brilliant. But she saw problems, too. "We must first explain to Mason that we aren't really getting married."

Duke clenched his jaw. "Why be dishonest?"

The truth detonated inside her. Felicia gasped. "Is that your way of asking me to marry you?"

"No." He shifted, and the car lurched forward with a burst of speed. "To me, you already *are* my wife. We've spoken vows. I merely think we should make it official for my family and the human public."

"I've known you for two days! You . . . this—" Felicia nearly choked. "It makes no sense."

"It makes complete sense. I love you. You *know* I'm not lying, Felicia. And I know you feel something for me. Don't deny it."

He could bloody see right through her, and it scared the wits out of her. "Why are you pushing me? Mason would never—"

"Which is why you agreed to marry him, isn't it? He was safe because he placated you, treated you as if you're fragile. You knew he'd let you have your way in the relationship."

Anger welled up, and she opened her mouth to deny every word, but he was right. She had trusted Mason because she'd believed he'd never demand that she let him into her heart. She'd been right up until her wedding day. The ugly truth hurt.

"I won't have it," Simon continued. "Fight with me. Scream at me. Insult me. I'll take it. Or better yet, open up to me and tell me why you're scared. But I'll be damned if I let you hide from me."

Felicia sank back in her seat. Though they traveled farther from danger with every mile, she couldn't remember ever feeling more terrified. "Why me? I'm a nursery school teacher who comes from a family of no import. I have no money."

"I don't give a bloody damn what you do, where you come from, or how much money you make. I want you for *you*. I want the persistent, logical, sharp woman who asked me a million questions the night I took her away. I want the gorgeous one who surrendered herself to me on the couch."

"But you've had . . . dozens? Hundreds?" She flinched. "Thousands of women? I'm not glamorous or sexy or—"

"Not sexy?" he snarled. "Damn it, I have no words for how incredible the sex between us is. I only know that I want more of you and that won't change. Ever."

"You think that now, but what if your feelings don't last?"

He glanced upward, tense, grappling for patience. "If someone didn't break your heart, what the hell happened?"

Felicia drew in a trembling breath. A refusal to answer sat on the tip of her tongue. She didn't share Deirdre's story with just anyone. The pain was too personal, too sharp.

Simon sent a concerned glance at her, and the sincerity on his face made her pause. He had sacrificed so much to save her. He'd risked family dissension, caused a scandal, given up his magical bachelorhood. He'd whisked her from danger twice, and hadn't asked her for half as much, merely for answers. And he was right; she did feel something for him. Those feelings grew by the minute, both warming her and scaring the hell out of her. How could she deny him?

She clasped her hands in her lap and squeezed tightly so he wouldn't see them shaking. "The Saffords adopted me when I was five. My father was a barrister, like Mason. My mother was a self-absorbed socialite who looked forward to club luncheons and galas. I suppose they married because he was wealthy and she was good arm candy. I don't know if his firm frowned on the fact that he had no children or if they thought children would save their marriage. My mother didn't want to ruin her figure with pregnancy. So they visited an orphanage and picked me out, based on a list of desired attributes. Somewhat like shopping for groceries. I was the most beautiful child, my mother said."

"I'm certain you were. But certainly, they came to see how good and intelligent you are."

"She didn't care if I might be sweet, smart, interesting, honest, kind . . . whatever. She mostly concerned herself with whether I looked perfect in Christmas pictures they mailed to their friends and associates." Felicia tried not to sound bitter, but knew she failed. The old hurt never faded.

Simon reached over and squeezed her hand. "I'm sorry, Sunshine."

"At the time they adopted me, they also adopted my older sister, Deirdre. We couldn't be more opposite. She had dark hair like a raven's wing. Glossy, straight. Sleek. When she smiled . . ." Felicia felt her own lips lift as she recalled her sister. "She lit up a room. It's a cliché, I know, but she did. She loved people and life. When she went to uni, she'd come back on weekends and drag me to parties. I was always the wallflower, but by the end of every night, she had men pledging her eternal devotion and women their lifelong friendship. I adored her."

"I can tell." Simon squeezed her hand again. "But why would that make you so violently against love?"

Now the story got difficult. Felicia drew in a steadying breath, praying for strength. "About five years ago, Deirdre met a Russian diplomat's nephew, Alexei. The man had the devil's own good looks. Sophisticated. Beyond charming. Deirdre brought him home for the holidays to introduce him to our parents. He said he loved her." Felicia clenched her teeth, molten fury coursing through her. "I knew he was lying. Deirdre was the only I'd told about my gift, and I begged her to break it off. She insisted they were in *love*," Felicia spat. "She bloody moved to Russia with the bastard.

"About a year later, she called me late one night, sobbing hysterically. Alexei had left her after admitting that he was married. And had a new mistress. Deirdre had merely been a fling. But he'd grown tired of her. God . . ." Felicia clenched her fists. "Her sobs tore at my heart. She begged, told him she loved him. He shrugged and told her to vacate the flat before Christmas."

"Fucking bastard."

"If I knew where to find him, I'd string him up by the balls."

"I don't doubt that," Duke murmured. "I'd help you. What happened next?"

"I wired Deirdre money to return home for the holidays. She came, but Alexei had ripped all the life out of her. She stared at walls with these eerie, vacant eyes. She didn't eat or sleep for days. Just sobbed. I'm certain our parents hoped her heartache would quickly pass. They went skiing for Christmas."

Duke recoiled. "They just . . . left?"

"They were very attentive when it came to appearances, grades. We had all the best money could buy. Emotions? They never knew how to deal with those, so they swept them under the rug." Bitterness slashed a jagged gash in her belly. "I took Deirdre to a counselor, set her up with a support group, rocked her when she screamed. Nothing helped."

Felicia swallowed, unsure she could even say the next words. She struggled against fresh tears. "Deirdre . . . committed suicide a few weeks later."

No avoiding the tears now. They fell in a hard rain as she remembered Deirdre's pale body lying lifeless on the brightly tiled bathroom floor. Felicia slammed her eyes shut and clutched her stomach as the sobs wracked her. "I n-never thought she'd swallow a bottle of sedatives. She was my friend, my sister. All I had."

Simon reached over and wiped away her tears. "I'm so sorry."

"Sh-she said that love was the worst thing that ever happened to her. She wished to God she'd never given her heart."

"And you saw what she went through and vowed you never would?"

"Deirdre shielded me from a lot of my parents' coldness and expectations. She *deserved* happiness, not . . ." Felicia couldn't say another word past her tears.

Simon caressed her back, and she curled her knees up to her chest, almost afraid to believe in his comfort. "I understand how much her death must hurt."

"*Hurt?* It b-broke something in me. I-I miss her s-so damn much."

"I know. But Deirdre wanted you to live. She took you to parties because she wanted you to have fun, meet people. Connect. You're not honoring her wishes."

Felicia clenched her fists, fury pounding in time with the roar of her heart. "You never met my sister. Don't presume to understand what she wanted or thought or believed. She'd want me to be happy above all."

"And are you? Truly? Would you be happy married to a man who couldn't be himself with you, who hid his feelings because he feared losing you too much to pursue the relationship's full potential? And you, refusing to love him but keeping his house and bearing his children—would that *really* be happily ever after? What would Deirdre have said about that?"

That it was pathetic. Cowardly. Felicia shuddered, burying her tearful face in her hands. "Have you ever had your heart ripped out and—"

"No. But neither have you. You've let no man close enough, have you? What about Tristan? Why did that end?"

Wiping away tears, she shook her head. "I don't know. Does it matter? We had little in common. He was a musician, played long hours. I hated the club scene."

"That's scenery. I'm not hearing a *reason*."

At the time, it seemed they simply grew apart. But when had their relationship truly ended? He'd asked her to meet his parents, and she'd been uncomfortable. She'd stopped returning some of his calls, hoping he'd understand that she simply wasn't ready for such a step. It hadn't taken long for him to stop ringing her up at all.

"He wasn't the one," she defended.

"Neither was Mason, but you agreed to marry him because he was willing to take whatever scraps of affection you tossed his way. I'm betting Tristan wouldn't. I bloody won't." He curled a hand around her neck. "Listen, I'm not Alexei. I'd never treat you that way."

Hadn't she just thought a few hours ago that he wasn't at all like her sister's tormenter? Yes. And in her head, she knew that Simon would never abandon her so cruelly. But even if he'd love her madly forever, giving him the power to hurt her terrified Felicia. "What if you grow tired of me someday and want to leave me? If I let myself love you . . ." She shook her head.

It would kill her.

"You're not so weak that you can't survive a broken heart. Even if you gave yourself completely to me and it didn't 'work out,' would you choose Deirdre's option? Really?"

God, he was right. In Deirdre's shoes, she would have never let Alexei defeat her. "No."

"Time would heal you. Completely. Humans fall in love more than once in a lifetime."

"Humans? You say that like magickind is different."

"It is. We are like wolves, in a sense. We mate for life. I knew you were my mate after our first kiss."

"You mean, you knew then that you wanted . . . me?" She almost couldn't wrap her head around the concept. "For life? For hundreds of years?"

He nodded. "I told you, when we mate, we lose all desire for others. We *don't* fall out of love. While I was willing to sever the bond because you wished it, we rarely abandon our mates."

"But Anka—"

"If Mathias hadn't come between them, she would still be with Lucan happily, I have no doubt. Look at Tynan. After losing Auropha, he's had no romantic feelings for another, and he never even formally took her as his mate. Believe me, I am, and always will be, yours."

His declaration ripped the air from her lungs. Felicia closed her eyes. He meant what he said. And she shook. Felicia didn't want to be responsible for anyone else's heart. She was so afraid of her own.

"You can't leave me, ever?"

He frowned. "Technically, I suppose it's possible. As Bram said, mate bonds can be broken. But they rarely are. Me behaving like Alexei should never even enter your mind."

So she had a man who would be faithful and love her for

the rest of his life, guaranteed? Why wasn't she giving in to all the new and warm feelings pouring through her chest? Why wasn't she grabbing on to him and blurting everything in her heart, too? A part of her longed to. If he couldn't hurt her . . . But she still hesitated. Giving in and giving her heart gave him terrifying power over her. She wasn't ready for that.

Felicia squirmed in her seat. "I have to think about this."

He stared out at the road, but she saw disappointment cross his strong features. "It's a big change in a few days. Remember, this isn't a game to me. You're my mate. I want you as my wife."

A million conflicting feelings coursed through her, and she sighed. Marrying Mason now wasn't an option. She couldn't hide behind him any longer. It wasn't fair to him, and she was ashamed that she'd been willing to use him to find a semblance of a happy life, rather than having the courage to actually seek one. But marrying her fiancé's brother? Yes, she was Simon's magical mate, and it was binding in his world. But in hers . . . Could she take him as her husband, knowing he'd do everything possible to work his way completely into her heart?

"I'll play my part for the cameras."

He clenched his jaw, gripping the wheel so tightly his knuckles turned white. "But will you marry me?"

"I'll . . . think about it." Even that terrified her. Simon wouldn't be content with anything less than everything.

"I won't stop trying to convince you."

A sudden smile crept across her mouth. "Why doesn't that surprise me?"

He grinned at her, too. "You're getting to know me."

Neither said anything for a long moment. In the silence, Simon's mobile phone rang. He answered immediately, turning on the speaker.

"Bram, what happened?"

"The women are all fine."

Felicia breathed a sigh of relief. She didn't know the other women well, but the thought of something happening to them, especially at Mathias's hands, horrified her.

"Excellent," Simon said.

"They're at Kari's pub," Bram added. "Caden and Ice are with them. Lucan and Ronan are doing a bit of cleanup at the caves. I've transferred Rhea back to my dungeons so we can guard her there. I think there's enough left to hold her comfortably while we rebuild the house. We'll join up soon to determine our next steps."

"And Tynan?"

Bram sighed. "Still no word."

Simon tightened his hand on the wheel, and Felicia reached out to caress his shoulder. He was worried about his friend.

"Did you find Shock?"

"No. Unreliable bastard," Bram groused.

After what Anka had told her and the other women before the attack, Felicia had to concur.

"What happened with Mathias?" she blurted.

"We found him, but the dodgy son of a bitch got away again. Teleported out when I cornered him. We killed our fair share of Anarki, at least. Lucan zapped Zain with a hell of a spell, but he crawled away like the slime he is. Frustrating night all the way around. I've advised the rest of the Council that Mathias is getting more brazen."

Disappointment slashed through Felicia. The Doomsday Brethren weren't her people, yet she was at the center of their fight. They'd done so much to protect her, make her feel welcome. Yes, she wanted Mathias stopped, not simply for her own sake, but theirs, as well.

"Let me guess. The Council doesn't care," Simon drawled.

"It doesn't affect them and doesn't make them lose face with magickind, so no. It's our problem because we've failed to fulfill our assignment and kill him."

Simon scoffed.

"Where are you taking Felicia?" Bram queried.

"London." A smile played at the corner of his mouth.

"Will we see you?"

"Perhaps. But you'll definitely hear of us. When you reach Kari's pub, have Sydney call me. I need to speak with her former boss. Holly is the perfect person to help me."

"Holly?" Bram choked. "Everything you say will be printed and spread around and—"

"Precisely."

"Have you gone barking mad?"

"No. I'm getting smart about Mathias."

"If you say . . ." Confusion rang in Bram's tones. "When you get settled, we'll set up guard rotation around your location."

Simon shrugged. "It may not be necessary, but it can't hurt."

They ended the call a few minutes later, and Simon and Felicia rode for long minutes in silence. Simon turned up the radio, something soft, romantic. He grabbed her hand.

At some point, she lay her head against his shoulder and drifted off to sleep, lulled by the soft purr of the engine and his nearness. She awoke to a dawning day on London's outskirts, and the sounds of Simon speaking softly into his mobile.

"Thanks, Sydney. I'll call her now."

Then he rang off and dialed again.

Stretching, Felicia listened to Simon's part of the conversation.

"Ms. Rossmont, this is Simon Northam, the Duke of—precisely. Holly, it is, then. I have information that may be of interest to you. I realize that your paper primarily handles paranormal related stories, and I'm sorry I haven't one. But based on our mutual acquaintance with Sydney, I wondered if you'd be willing to handle a story for me?"

A pause later, a woman's voice. Muffled. Felicia couldn't hear the words, just the tone.

"Ah, so the scandal is still alive and brewing." Another pause. "No, I agree. Three days isn't enough time for a story like this to die. I wondered if you'd be willing to help me with something this afternoon. At the Dorchester. Say, four o'clock?"

The woman spoke again, and Felicia's mind raced. Something? The woman worked for a newspaper. Certainly, Simon didn't plan a press conference. Enduring flashing bulbs and barked questions, pretending happiness for the public . . . the thought made her ill.

She grabbed his arm. "Simon, I don't think—"

He held up a hand to stop her protest, and instead spoke into the mobile. "Splendid. I'll make it worth your while."

More silence barely punctuated with a pushy woman's tones.

"An exclusive? Hmm. Under certain conditions."

He listened to her again, a smile slowly creeping across his face. Felicia realized that Simon was playing Holly, getting exactly what he wanted. He knew this game well.

"I'm not certain . . ." he drawled.

The woman on the other end spoke loudly and rapidly. Vociferously. Simon smiled wider.

"Well, if those are your terms, then yes. You can run everything tonight by seven p.m., exclusively, for forty-eight hours. That's my offer."

What was everything?

Silence reigned on the other end for a long moment before she replied. Felicia wished she could hear Holly's words.

"Excellent," Simon finally said. "Glad we could come to an agreement. I'll see you later, then."

With that, he rang off and pocketed his phone, looking very pleased. "We have a lot to do before then."

Such as? "Sleep?"

He laughed. "No, Sunshine. We must get ready to put on a show. This is something I know all about. Trust me."

Felicia drew in a deep breath. Trust him. Did she? To keep her safe, yes. Without reservation. But could she do it enough to let go of her fear and build a life with him?

CHAPTER 13

LESS THAN AN HOUR later, Duke drove into the snarl of London traffic, ready for breakfast, a soft bed, and a passionate interlude with his mate. He would have the first two. The last . . . Duke sighed. He must give Felicia time to acclimate and try to curb the caveman instincts magnified by the fever, but he couldn't let her get too comfortable. He refused to repeat Mason's mistake.

Especially given her story about Deirdre. Clearly, Felicia had loved her sister and Deirdre's death was a wound that hadn't healed. Beneath his mate's cautious shell lay an emotional woman she did her damnedest to repress. He would never win her until he got past her defenses.

When he glanced her way, her face was shuttered again. That she'd closed up so quickly and thoroughly after surrendering so completely in his arms disturbed him.

Bloody hell.

He also had to remember that he'd known her for fewer than three days—not enough time for most humans to fall in love. He sought a passion and commitment she hadn't given to Mason in six years. It sounded fucking hopeless.

But Duke wasn't a quitter.

How could he help her get over the fear of heartbreak she'd developed following Deirdre's suicide? Or was it more? Mason had been in her life before her sister's death, and Felicia hadn't fallen for him then. Nor had she fallen for her previous boyfriend, Tristan. Neither man had been right for her, true, but had something caused Felicia to turn inward even before Deirdre's death? Her parents, most likely. They'd valued her for the wrong reasons and, he'd guess from her tale, emotionally neglected her for most of her life. Now, Felicia did her damnedest to maintain careful emotional distance so she couldn't get hurt. How did he stop that cycle before he became victim number three?

Now wasn't the time to ask her questions. She'd already opened up far more, he sensed, than usual. Though difficult, she'd trusted him enough to talk about Deirdre. It was a good first step. Next, he'd start learning her psyche and seducing her—for good.

As they approached Hyde Park, his mobile rang again. The name on the display surprised him.

"Who is it?" Felicia asked.

"My mother." He grimaced. He hadn't spoken to her since the night he'd carried Felicia away. Duke grimaced, imagining what his mother had to say.

He clicked the button to silence the ringer and let the call slide to voicemail.

Felicia shot him a sharp glance. "You're avoiding her."

"Of course. That's a haranguing in the works."

She laughed at him.

"What is so funny?" he demanded, secretly pleased to see her relaxed enough with him to smile.

"A grown man—a warrior wizard—running from his mother." She giggled again.

"That should tell you just how frightening she can be."

"She was always perfectly lovely to me. We never disagreed about anything whilst planning the wedding."

"Hmm, that's because you kept everything very traditional and acquiesced to her 'suggestion' that you marry at Lowechester Hall. Had you wanted a Goth wedding in an underground club in Soho, I daresay she would have reacted differently."

"Perhaps," she conceded. "But you must face her someday."

"Can I think on that for a bit?" he teased.

She swatted his arm playfully. "Your mother loves you." Then she sobered up. "You can't know how precious that is unless you've never had motherly affection."

As he'd suspected. Had Felicia been protecting her heart since the day her wretched parents had adopted her? What would never being valued or loved for the person she was inside do to a little girl?

If they weren't already dead, Duke would gladly throttle them with his own two hands.

"Does your mum . . . know about you?" Felicia asked.

"That I'm a wizard? No." He sighed, familiar regret sliding through him. "How do I tell her that I'm not quite human?"

"So the magical thing is not hereditary?"

"It is. My ability came from my father's side. He was at the end of his lifespan when he found my mother, so he died shortly after I turned six. The day he died, he said he had much to tell me, but he'd run out of time. I pieced it together eventually," he said, navigating a crowded street and dodging pedestrians. "Mum knows I have some secret. We aren't as close as we once were, and I know my . . . friction with Mason troubles her. But she's still caring and supportive. I do value that."

"So you'll ring her back?"

He smiled tightly. "All right. After we navigate the crowd."

Felicia frowned, peering out the window. "What crowd?"

The sun shone brightly. Pedestrians bundled as they scurried to and fro, their breaths clouding the air, demonstrating how bitterly cold it was.

Finally, Duke turned the last corner and the Dorchester Hotel came into view . . . along with a horde of reporters and paparazzi.

"That crowd."

She gasped, then turned to him in horror. "They're here for us?"

"Indeed." He brought the car to a stop under the low, flat portico in front of the swank hotel, grateful for the auto's tinted windows. He extracted the keys from the ignition, then took her hand in his. Suddenly, a sea of flashing bulbs and shouting people surrounded the car.

"Remember, you must act as if we're in love. Give these people the show they require to provide you a human shield."

Felicia looked shell-shocked but nodded slowly. "Mathias would be an utter fool to reveal his magic to all these people or try some human means to remove them from his path."

"Precisely. Let's go."

He opened the driver's-side door and stood. Immediately, he was swarmed. He shouldered past several reporters with a "No comment," and picked his way to the passenger door.

When he opened it, Felicia shrank back into her seat. "They'll mob us."

"They'll take pictures and shout questions. Ignore them. It will make them work harder." He grinned.

With a sigh, Felicia cautiously gave him her hand. He grabbed it, gratified by the small show of trust.

It didn't take any mustering of effort on his part to drag her against his body and hold her tight, arm curled around her small waist. He let one hand wander low on her hip, just above the curve of her luscious backside. Predictably, flash-bulbs flared all around.

"Are you dating your brother's fiancée?" shouted one reporter.

"Have you been having a sexual relationship behind his back?" another called.

"Did your brother know of your relationship with his fiancée before the wedding?"

"Where have you been since you abducted her?"

Duke put on his coldest face and glared at the group of reporters nearest him. "No comment."

With that, he dragged Felicia toward the Dorchester's door, ignoring their other questions and innuendos.

Inside, the staff greeted them with a smile. "Good morning, Your Grace. Madam. Welcome."

Beside him, she stiffened, and he soothed her with a caress of his fingers at her waist. "I phoned last night. You have a reservation for me, I believe. A suite. With a view." He planted a peck on Felicia's chilled, red cheek—a gesture he knew could be interpreted in more than one way. "And lots of privacy."

"Of course," the desk clerk assured, straightening his proper gray tie. "Luggage?"

"None." Grinning unrepentantly, he knew exactly what the tabloids would make of that.

Within moments, a perky young woman with a modest bun and dark skirt escorted them to the top level of the hotel. Somehow, she managed to keep her gaze averted, but Felicia felt the woman's curiosity. Naturally. The Duke of Hurstgrove was taking a woman to a hotel room, sans luggage, shortly after sunrise. Most people checking into a hotel sans luggage weren't seeking a bed for sleep.

Felicia felt herself flush again, her cheeks even hotter. In the three days she'd known this man, he'd turned her life upside down. Nothing about him was predictable. Or her response to him. Most men were easily brushed aside. If someone got too close, she stopped seeing him. Neat. Simple.

Simon didn't fit that mold. His possessive arm around her waist was a subtle reminder that he intended to keep her close. He monitored everything—her expression, her breathing, her gait—using them to read her, gauge her mood. God knew, Simon could make her body respond to him in any way he'd wished. She feared it was only a matter of time before he made her heart do the same.

Swallowing as the hotel employee opened the door, Felicia peeked inside, her eyes going wide. *Oh. My. God.* It wasn't a hotel room, but a swanky multi-room palace with views that went on forever. It featured exotic hardwood floors, a sitting room with a couch that looked like a chocolate cloud, and beyond that, a massive four-poster canopy bed swathed in the most luxurious silk bedding she'd ever seen.

Simon nudged her into the room, then turned to the other woman. "Thank you . . ." He peered at her nametag. "Ms. Hodge."

"Will there be anything else, Your Grace?"

"Breakfast, please. Twenty minutes, sharp. Eggs, sausage." He turned to her. "You like scones, Sunshine?"

Felicia frowned, grappling to take it all in—the room, his manner, his affection. "I-I don't need anything special. Toast is fine."

"Do you like scones?" he repeated.

"Of course."

With a smile, the turned back to the prim woman. "Scones, tea, and coffee. A newspaper and the manager at my door in an hour."

The woman curtsied. Honest to goodness curtsied. Felicia's jaw dropped.

234   *Shayla Black*

"Right away, Your Grace."

With that, she was gone. And Felicia couldn't hold her astonishment in. "People defer to you like that all the time?"

"Usually." He shrugged matter-of-factly.

"No wonder you're impossible to deal with."

"I get what I want." *And I want you.* His eyes turned dark, silently conveying that fact.

Her belly flipped nervously. "Simon . . ."

He layered a soft kiss over her mouth. "Don't worry, I won't give in to my urge to seduce you . . . yet. First, we have a few items to scratch off our to-do list. Why don't you have a nice, hot shower? After breakfast, you can take a nap."

"You haven't slept all night."

The sexy smile that stole across his mouth made her heart skip a beat. "You gave me enormous energy last night. I feel . . . spectacular. Besides, I'll do nothing more taxing than make a few phone calls, including one to my mother. Go on. I'll wake you when it's time."

"For what? Simon, what is it you've planned? I'm not ready for this public—"

"Shh. You only have to be near me and smile when I ask. I'll take care of everything else. Promise."

Felicia tried not to melt, but it was impossible. Simon frightened her emotionally, but made her feel so safe in every other way. He would handle the press. He would keep Mathias at bay—as he had from the moment he'd spirited her away. Every minute of every day she trusted him a bit more. Somehow, that both comforted and frightened her.

Duke closed the door to the hotel suite after the last of his multitude of guests with a satisfied smile. Finally, everything was arranged. He glanced at his watch. A bit more than an hour to spare.

Perfect.

Duke headed toward the bedroom . . . and a view he couldn't resist. Peeling off the coat of the suit he'd had delivered from his London flat for his meeting with the hotel's manager, he draped the garment over a low-backed, cream silk chair. He slipped off his shoes a few steps later. When he reached the bedroom door, he shrugged out of his pristine white shirt and hung it on the back of the knob.

He looked across the room, pausing to lean on the jamb and study his mate tangled in the sheets. She looked so soft and innocent in sleep. Tousled pale hair flowed across her pillow, her lips slightly parted, hands tucked under her cheek.

Warmth flowed through his chest, an endless pool of contentment and love.

In that moment, he couldn't remember his future ever looking brighter. Yes, Mathias was still plotting nefarious acts. His mother was disappointed in his behavior and had said so in no uncertain terms. Mason was ready to throttle him. Nor had Duke won Felicia's heart yet. But she was *his*. Nothing else mattered. Nothing else ever would.

Shucking off his trousers, he left them near the bedside and slid between the sheets with her. God, she was warm and soft—everything he'd been searching for during a dozen long years of dating tedious models and actresses, pretending happiness.

When he leaned over to kiss her cheek, she stirred. Her lashes fluttered up over sleepy blue eyes. Her gaze was so unguarded, so open, it took his breath away.

"Is it time to get up?"

Duke shook his head. "Soon."

He leaned in and dropped a lingering kiss on her mouth. Once, twice. Then he pressed her to the mattress and half-draped his body over hers, feeling her sweet curves against him.

Felicia tensed.

Undeterred, Duke filtered his hands through her silky curls. "I've missed you."

She hesitated, but he saw her pulse fluttering at the base of her neck. "I've been asleep only a few hours."

"Any time away from you is an eternity."

Felicia nibbled on her bottom lip. "How can you mean that? I-I know you have the magical means of sensing your mate but . . ."

"You don't have that luxury. I'm aware of that." He sighed. "The instinct is magickind's way of ensuring wizards pursue the right female for them. I just wish our women had the same assurance."

"You've sacrificed much to keep me safe. But feelings . . . aren't easy for me."

Impatience chafed Duke, but he curbed it. The mating instinct told him many things about her character that humans spent years learning. The reverse didn't apply, and he had to keep that in mind.

"I know three days seems like a whirlwind romance. What can I tell you about me to help you feel better about us?"

She paused, grappling with her answer. "I don't think it's that simple. I didn't formally meet you until the day before my wedding, and during the months of planning, Mason painted you as the worst cad. Pictures always showed you with new arm candy. None ever lasted longer than a week, and I . . ." She grimaced.

"You wonder if there's any chance at the end of a week, I'll show you the door. You know that's not possible."

"Is it? What if you change your mind? You're only with

me because magic decrees it. Can that last?" She shook her head. "What if your instinct is wrong?"

Duke's heart nearly burst. If she didn't care about him, none of this would worry her.

"My instinct isn't wrong, and I won't change my mind. I wish I had the perfect words to reassure you. All I can say is, you trusted me with your safety. Do the same with your heart. I know you're guarding it and feel scared, but you *are* brave. You took the existence of magickind in stride. You escaped from Mathias, carried the Doomsday Diary with you, though it put you in more danger. Every day you do something new that endears you to me. We'll work this out." He grabbed one of her hands and squeezed.

He kissed her again, more invitation than demand. She stiffened, but he persisted. For a sweet moment, she succumbed, her lips turning soft, clinging. Then she pushed him away again.

"How can you be so sure that what you feel won't pass? Mason told me that you once made love to four women in the same weekend, including his French tutor, and—"

"That was my transition." Damn Mason for passing his bitterness on to Felicia. "When a wizard turns thirty or thereabouts, his magic asserts itself, and he undergoes an intense few days when he becomes more than human. To complete the transition, we require a great deal of energy. Which, as you now know, means sex."

"And that happened in the middle of your birthday party?"

Duke nodded. "I didn't know what was happening. I didn't know what I'd become until my unique magical power emerged. The earth shook—literally—at my command, and I nearly brought down Lowechester Hall's roof."

"You . . . cause earthquakes?" She looked somewhat shaken herself by that fact.

He nodded. "It's not a power I use often. It drains me utterly. And you probably ought to keep that under your hat. Every witch or wizard's unique power is their last line of defense. Somewhat like your built-in lie detector."

"Indeed." She hesitated, staring. "I'm simply . . . What a shock transition must have been for you."

"Utterly. I went through the entire process acting purely on instinct. As regrettable as causing a scene at my party and bedding Mason's crush was, I would have died if I hadn't."

Felicia blinked, her blue eyes incredulous. "So those four women . . . that's not a habit of yours?"

"No." He sent her a wry smile. "I'm hardly a saint, but I prefer one woman at a time. And from now on, I want only shy little blondes with sharp tempers and sweet lips."

Felicia blushed. "You're flattering me."

"One of my favorite things to do."

"Stop."

He smiled. Really truly smiled. "What shall I do instead? I have ideas . . ."

Shifting the lower half of his body closer, he brushed his erection against her thigh. She blinked up at him. "You—you're naked!"

"That's generally how a wizard makes love to his mate. Though I wouldn't object to working around clothing every now and again for something fast and scorching. But having you stretched out bare and warmed by sleep beneath me is a luxury I'll take advantage of every chance I get."

For the first time in his life, Duke wanted to close his eyes and completely give himself to someone, not to rev up his energy, but to exchange love. He ached for Felicia to do the same, but knew he needed to give her some time to open herself to him, be free of her fears and absolved of whatever guilt she felt for betraying Mason. Complete trust in three days was a tall order.

He drew his free hand over her shoulder and down her arm, until he clasped her hand and drew it above her head. Guiding her fingers around the edges of the headboard, he held them there with a gentle, but firm grip. He repeated the process with the other hand. Rearing back, she peered at him with a question.

"Leave your hands here until I tell you otherwise."

"But—"

"No talking. Your only responsibility is to lie back and enjoy the pleasure I give you. Say nothing, think of nothing, only feel."

Duke didn't give Felicia a chance to reply before he wrapped his hand beneath her head and kissed her, urging her lips apart so he could sink into the candy haven of her mouth and stroke deep.

Beneath him, she hesitated, then opened to him. Responded to him. *Perfect*. She was like silken sugar everywhere, sweet, soft, addicting.

With a gasp, she pulled away, wriggled beneath him. "Simon, the danger and Mason—"

"Are not issues at the moment." He pressed her fingers around the headboard again. "Lie still. Let me handle everything. Just feel."

His taking control and removing the appearance of responsibility allowed her to be in the moment. After a long hesitation, she nodded and gripped the headboard. Thrilled, he dove back into the kiss, brushing his mouth over hers, his tongue dancing languidly with hers. Her breath began to stutter. Her body tightened. Her nipples peaked.

Smiling between kisses, he peeled back the sheet to reveal her white bra and knickers.

"But . . ."

He shook his head and tossed the sheet down, to tangle at their feet. "I'm going to make love to you now. And again tonight. Then tomorrow morning, provided I make it through the long night without waking up and needing you."

She sucked in a stunned breath. "Simon, I— That's not a good idea."

"Why? You feel something for me."

"I do, but . . . I'm sorry. You've done so much for me." Regret shone from her blue eyes, even as they became earnest and open. For the first time, Felicia wasn't running from her own emotion. "I need time."

Simon suspected she'd used that line on Mason with great efficiency.

"We have none. The danger is still coming. To fight it, we must stay together. But damn it, I want to be more to you than the means to stay alive."

Her face softened, a mixture of affection and guilt. "You are."

"A friend?"

"Yes."

A safe answer, but an unacceptable one.

"That's not all. We're *mated*. We've bonded. I know most humans don't fall in love in three days. I'll do my best to be patient. Just . . . don't hold yourself back from me."

She shook her head. "I'm not accustomed to this much . . . attention."

"Surely I'm not the only man to want you madly." Felicia looked away, and a suspicion ripped through Duke's head. He froze. "Am I?"

"Well, I . . . Tristan wasn't very sexual. We . . . it was just twice. I never let anyone else touch me after that."

"Except Mason," he pointed out, gritting his teeth.

She squirmed under his hard gaze. "Not even Mason."

Three whispered words, and Duke felt as if someone had punched him in the gut. He gasped, "Mason never took you to bed?"

"No," she whispered.

Triumph jetted through his veins. Felicia was *his*. Tristan? An inconsequential figure from her past. All that mattered was that she had never given Mason the sweet gift of her body. His heart lightened. If Felicia didn't care for or trust him, she would have never allowed him to make love to her, much less reciprocated with such abandon.

Then confusion set in. "But you planned to have children with him."

"Yes, but I told Mason I wanted to wait until we were married. He didn't seem troubled by the request, so I never imagined that he desired me or had feelings beyond friendship until our wedding day."

"Let me be clear: I can't live without you. I don't intend to try. I plan on spending the next thousand years with you. Give me the chance to prove to you that my instinct is right. Lie back, hold on, and feel me."

Bathed in the soft afternoon sunlight, Felicia flushed a pretty pink once more and bit her lip, now swollen from his kisses. Her soft blond curls tumbled around her shoulders, longer strands curling beneath her breasts cupped in peek-a-boo lace. Indecision and yearning spread all over her face.

God, she was beautiful. And—damn it—his. He'd make her see that. He couldn't endure this biting ache for a woman he could see and talk to, but never truly have. He needed her love in return.

He pressed a kiss to her mouth. "Did I tell you that a wizard knows his mate by taste?" At the surprise that crossed her features, he smiled and worked down her body. "So the first time I kissed you, I knew unequivocally that you were mine."

As she gasped, he unclasped her bra and drew it away in a sweep of his hand.

She opened her mouth to protest, but he laid a finger across her lips. "Lie back and feel."

After a long moment, her anxious blue gaze softened. She exhaled in surrender. The sound went straight to his cock.

He laved her nipple with his tongue. She stiffened, trembled. So responsive. Duke smiled secretly against her skin. The sugary-gardenia scent of her lured him. He inhaled deeply, struck again by the rightness of her in his life.

"But what wizards love most is to taste their mate's flavor." He eased a palm down her abdomen, curling his fingers under her knickers and right into her folds. And she was wet. Duke shuddered, nearly coming out of his skin. "Here, where your flavor is pure and most intimate. That, we love."

To prove his point, he whisked her knickers down her thighs and dropped them to the floor. Her damp golden curls beckoned.

"Spread your legs."

Felicia tensed again, but fresh moisture slickened her folds. Damn her fears for making her fight what she wanted. Duke understood, but refused to bend. He must get past this before they could progress.

"That's an order." He sent her a firm stare. "There's nothing for you to think through, only to feel. Let me in, Sunshine."

Biting her lip, her body tense, she did as he asked, oh-so-slowly easing her thighs apart. He could have done it for her but this . . . she opened herself to him like a gift. She trusted him. He was truly grateful.

Easing her folds apart, he breathed in her essence, then

pressed his tongue to her. She gasped, jumped. Duke held her hips down and laved the swollen knot of nerves. Yes, she was aroused. But she wasn't comfortable with it.

He sucked her clit gently, then released it, raking his fingertip over the little ridge. His eyes closed, and she clutched the headboard more tightly, as if restraining her need.

"Why can't you let yourself want me?"

Felicia tried to wriggle away. Duke held her firm, his fingertip working erotic circles over her most sensitive flesh.

"It makes me . . . too vulnerable," she mewled, her body arching.

"You don't want to be close to me."

He kissed her again intimately. Even if her heart was fighting him, her body's defenses were breaking down. With every touch, she slickened, swelled, arched more.

"No." Her high-pitched admission bounced off the wall.

"You think I'll leave you."

"The minute I let myself care . . ." She writhed, fighting the pleasure.

She was dead wrong. His reassurances weren't convincing her. What the hell kept her from tearing down that wall around her heart?

"The minute you let yourself care," he whispered, "I'll be there to fill you up with love for the rest of your life."

Her face told him how much she wanted to believe him, but her head thrashed from side to side in denial.

Duke lowered his head to her slick, tender flesh again and feasted, using slow licks that lasted forever, soft brushes of his fingers. "You're perfect for me," he whispered. "Until you, I never felt as if I belonged anywhere. I never truly connected to anyone. Money and fame insulate. I've often felt alone, even in public or when I had a lover. But you . . ." He lapped at her with a long groan. "With you, I'm at home."

Felicia perspired, her body writhing. She looked at him with fevered blue eyes. "Why?"

"Because you're mine."

"Simon, you—"

"Don't try to say otherwise. Do I make you feel safe?"

"Yes—*oh!*" she cried out as he toyed with her swollen bud again.

"Do I make you feel cared for?"

She paused, then nodded. "You're high-handed."

He smiled. "Part of my charm."

Swiping his thumb across the little bundle, he settled into small circles that had her stiffening her legs and arching her back. "Simon . . ."

"Do I give you pleasure?" He put an exclamation point on the question by drawing her sensitive flesh into his mouth again.

"Oh. Ah . . . I—oh my . . . *Ah!*" Her body shuddered, thrashed as climax racked her.

He stayed with her to the end, easing off as she recovered. "I'll take that as a yes."

"Yes," she admitted weakly.

"I'll do everything in my power to shelter you from pain. I'll never break your heart." Duke gripped her hip with one hand and guided himself to her slick entrance with the other. "Someday, you'll believe me."

He raised himself over her, and eased inside the hot silk of her sheath, gritting his teeth. Felicia's expressive eyes widened, darkened. He drank in her face and sank into her with every inch he had, every bit of love coursing through him to her.

She gasped, a new flush creeping up her cheeks, across her chest. Everywhere he touched her, she scalded him. Sinking in a bit more, he hissed, tensed against the astonishing rise of pleasure. Under him, Felicia moaned, clamping down on his cock. He grabbed her tighter.

Gliding down, down, into her wet perfection, he tunneled deep in a seemingly endless stroke. Finally, he was immersed in her. God, she was incredible. Silken. The most amazing woman he'd ever touched.

"Oh, S-Simon!" Her voice fluttered. "That's—" she gasped, tilting her hips up to him, taking him even deeper. "So good."

Indeed. He'd never felt anything like the electric pleasure racing through his veins.

"Hang on," he warned.

She sent him a shaky nod. And he pulled back, nearly withdrawing, before drowning in her again. Felicia cried out, clinging to him, parting her thighs more and inviting him deeper.

Bloody hell, already she was decimating his restraint. Pleasure shot up his cock, coiling heat low in his belly, curling his toes.

As he invaded her body again, he took her mouth in a desperate kiss. Felicia melted around him, parting her lips, canting her hips up to him, and ripping through his control.

Duke gritted his teeth, growling as he filled her to the hilt again. Felicia's little pants as she tensed drove him mad. He refused to find pleasure without her.

Probing until he found the sweet spot guaranteed to hurtle her into climax, Duke worked it with slow strokes, nonstop friction. Her eyes opened wide as she writhed, trying to catch her breath. A darker flush spread across her gorgeous golden skin.

"Oh! Simon, I need . . ."

"I know," he rasped in her ear. "I'll give it to you."

He did with languorous strokes that sank into forever.

After this, there'd never be a way to untangle himself from her—and that suited him just fine.

"Yes." Her fists gripped the headboard. "Yes!"

With another deep thrust, she came apart, jolting in his arms with a guttural cry.

His self-control followed, and white fire shot down his spine, spreading ecstasy through his body. He needed her so much. Needed to reassure her that his love and desire for her was everlasting. Duke wasn't about to deny that need as he shouted in satisfaction.

Slowly they caught their breath. He kissed her cheeks, the tip of her pert nose, her swollen mouth. He caressed her from hip to waist, then his palm wandered up over her breast, settling around her shoulder. He held her close, their hearts galloping together.

He could stay like this, with her, forever. Being with Felicia was beyond anything he'd ever known. He wanted to tell her that he loved her again, stay in bed all evening, talk her through her fear and clear it away. Then make love to her all night.

A knock on the door reminded him they didn't have that kind of time. He glanced quickly at the bedside clock and cursed. *Right on schedule.*

Felicia went stiff with fear. "Who is it?"

"The people to help us build our scandal," he murmured, then called to the attendant constantly outside their suite, "Ms. Hodge, let them in!"

The door opened with a soft click. Panic raced through Felicia's veins.

"My robe. It's in the bathroom and—"

"You won't need it," he assured softly and pressed his surprisingly hard erection deeper inside her with a groan. "I don't want to leave you, but . . ."

He quietly withdrew. Her body protested. With the friction, nerve endings flared to life, and she gasped. The secretive smile he sent flipped her heart.

Felicia waited for him to get up, find his clothes, and greet his guests. He didn't.

"Your Grace?" called a woman whose voice Felicia had never heard. "Where are you?"

"The bedroom. Follow the stunning city views."

Her jaw dropped and she scrambled to rise. "You can't—"

"Shh." He held her down and eased onto the bed beside her, then drew the sheet firmly over her breasts. He smiled like she was the only woman in the world, and her heart flipped. "You look perfect."

"I need clothes," she whispered furiously. "My hair is mussed and . . . and—"

"Your lips are beautifully swollen, and oops, I left a little love bite on your shoulder." He shrugged with a wicked smile.

The smattering of footsteps drew closer, then rounded the corner. A pixie doll blonde with a Stallone expression stood beside Caden, who had a camera looped around his neck.

Felicia drew the sheet higher and scrambled away from Duke. He brought her closer with an iron grip.

"They've come to take pictures?" she hissed.

"Holly, Sydney's former editor, insisted on the pictures. A forty-eight-hour exclusive in exchange for her help with the press." He turned to the other woman. "You didn't specify what sort, but I assume this will be sufficient to sell newspapers?"

Spoken like a question, but Simon knew the answer. Sex always sold.

Holly smiled widely—a shark with pink lipstick. "Of course."

"They must be released within the hour," he warned.

Holly snorted. "Ten minutes after we're gone, more like. Caden?"

The other wizard stepped forward, camera in hand.

Felicia whirled on Duke, clutching the sheet to her throat. "You're going to let him take pictures of us in dishabille?"

He whispered, "This wasn't my first choice of tactics, but to keep these vultures' attention, we have to stay shocking, at least until we can divert Mathias's attention from you or kill him. Staying in the public eye will keep you safe."

That made sense, but . . . "*Photos?* You gave me no warning. No time to consider. No say in the matter!"

"Ruins the authenticity of the moment." He nipped at her lobe, breathed in her ear.

Despite her better intentions and her anger, she shivered. Her body turned to putty, but she wasn't ready to give up her anger. "Simon . . ."

He frowned. "You're really distressed. Wait a moment, Caden." The other wizard nodded and dragged Holly with him to a corner, then the gorgeous man beside her brushed the hair from her face. "I didn't tell you because I feared the pictures would look staged or posed, and they won't. I not only want everyone to see us together; I want them to *believe* it. Talk about us for days. Weeks. But I never meant to upset or embarrass you. If you're too uncomfortable, I'll call a more traditional press conference. I believe this is more effective, but I'll leave the decision to you."

Felicia bit her lip. Every word Simon spoke was truth. He made sense as well. He not only risked himself to keep her safe and gave up his bachelorhood. He caused scandal again and again, not caring he'd be the target of tabloids, too. Or that he would be further alienating his family. His first thought was her safety.

While she'd been more concerned about Mason and her modesty.

"I'm sorry. You're right. Tell them to proceed."

The smile Simon flashed her radiated pure approval and told Felicia how much he valued her trust. She basked in its glow, warming as if she bathed in golden rays on a summer afternoon. "Excellent. Smile, Sunshine . . ."

CHAPTER 14

AN HOUR LATER, FELICIA's head hadn't stopped spinning. Holly called for extra lighting and a touch of makeup. Caden kept clicking away to "capture the moment," and Felicia blushed.

Between shots, Simon kissed her, long, lingering, deep. Caden snapped those pictures as well, and Simon knew it. After those forever kisses, he'd send her intimate toe-curling smiles, as if they were the only two people in the room. Or on the planet. The world faded away until all she saw was him.

Felicia soaked up her time with Simon, stunned by how much she enjoyed his single-minded attention—and by how much she liked the thought that women everywhere would soon know that Simon had feelings for her. Yes, this was all part of a larger plan to keep her safe, and she normally hated pictures, but he kept her feeling both relaxed and secure.

"Your lips are deliciously swollen again. And there's a bit of whisker burn on your cheeks."

That brought her back to reality. "Very naughty, advertising to everyone that we're . . ."

"An intimate couple, yes. It's shocking, I understand." He nuzzled her neck and whispered, "That reaction, there on your face . . . so perfect and genuine."

As if on cue, the camera clicked several times. Simon added more fuel to the fire by grazing the side of her breast beneath the sheet. No one could see it, but she gasped into his kiss, mesmerized by his touch. A flush crept up her body to her face.

"Ah, you look gorgeous and rosy," he whispered for her alone.

Felicia gulped in a deep breath, trying to keep her wits about her. "Where will these pictures be displayed?"

"*Out of This Realm*'s website for forty-eight hours. They'll create a huge buzz, and everyone will be trying to verify their authenticity. In two days, after we've admitted our relationship, Holly and the paper will make a handsome fortune by selling them to everyone. We'll have another huge crowd around us, and you'll be safe a bit longer."

True, and safety was more important than any embarrassment she might feel or any desire she might have to stake her claim on him. But . . . "Everyone will think I'm your . . . mistress."

Immediately, he shook his head. "Soon, everyone will know differently. I have a plan."

"Announcing our engagement will crush Mason."

Simon's smile fell. "I know. I don't wish to hurt him, but I cannot risk you."

A few minutes later, Holly and the lighting guy left. Caden lingered. "I've spoken to Bram. The Doomsday Brethren will be shadowing you two as closely as we dare while you're in London."

"You have first watch?"

"Ronan and I, yes. As soon as I get these pictures out."

"Any news on Tynan? Have we heard anything from Shock?"

Regret weighed down the other wizard's blue gaze. "Nothing."

Worry slithered through her belly. Tynan had been with Mathias for nearly twenty-four hours. That couldn't be good news.

"Keep me posted," Simon asked. "Make sure these pictures look as if you spied on us without our knowledge and are suitable for most audiences. Evocative, not indecent. Affectionate, not lewd."

The wizards shook hands as Caden left. She was alone with Simon again.

"About the photos . . ." Her voice shook. "I don't want to be a doubting Thomas, and you've done so much—"

"Please, trust me. I know that's hard for you. Others have let you down. Have I?"

What could she say? So far, he'd kept her alive—and surprisingly happier than she'd been in months, years . . . maybe ever. Perhaps she *should* trust him. What were her alternatives?

"No. It's just . . . this isn't easy for me."

His expression softened. "You're accustomed to calling the shots. Mason always let you. Your parents left you to your own devices. Only Deirdre ever dragged you out of your comfort zone. You didn't like it, but I'm betting you realized you needed it. And her."

Surprise washed over Felicia. Simon was right. How had he figured that out so quickly?

She bit her lip to suppress tears. "Stop prying."

He caressed a gentle hand down the fall of her tangled hair. "Sunshine, I'm not trying to pry. I'm trying to help."

Fear followed as she realized that with every moment, he grew closer and closer to finding a permanent place in her heart. "If you want to help, give me time and space."

He shook his head. "Too dangerous. Besides, all you'll do with time and space is refortify your defenses. I'm sure Mason has finally figured that out. What you need is to see us and the love you're hiding from. You need to take a leap of faith and believe."

God, he confronted her over and over. Pushing, shoving, being so damn right. In her head, she knew he would do anything to keep her safe. She knew every word he'd said about mating was true. He couldn't leave her, couldn't make love to anyone else, couldn't fall out of love. She *knew* it. She also suspected she was *this* close to falling in love with him . . . yet didn't know how to make her heart trust.

She whispered, "It sounds too good to be true. I keep waiting for the catch."

"The only catch is that I need your love, too."

Another knock sounded on the door, and he dropped a kiss on her nose. "I also love punctuality, but I should have pushed this appointment later. Coming . . ."

Appointment?

He rose, striding naked across the dusk-shadowed room. She blinked, her gaze glued to his incredible backside. She'd known the man was beyond beautiful, but every sculpted inch of him wowed her. Wide, yet elegant shoulders tapered to a narrow waist and hips. Hard buttocks and thighs, bulging calves . . . *mmm*. She'd never been one to ogle a man, but it was impossible not to stare at Simon.

He disappeared into the bathroom and emerged wearing one of the hotel's thick robes. He tossed the other at her. "You'll want to shower now. When you come out, I'll have a snack waiting. Then there's work to be done."

Before she could ask what, his footsteps across the hardwood floors faded, finally reaching the door. Someone entered; from the sounds, a husky-voiced woman and a man with heavy footsteps. Soon both headed her way.

Felicia tore out of the bed and dove into the bathroom. She shut the door behind her in relief, then turned the faucet. The woman who greeted her in the mirror was a stranger.

Sensual. Tousled hair, swollen mouth. Red cheeks. Utterly sated. The satisfaction on her rosy, relaxed face was unmistakable.

And all of England would see it once those pictures went public.

She closed her eyes, happiness warring with embarrassment. She wanted to stay safe, but feared revealing herself to everyone. Revealing herself to Simon. In a few days, he'd seen through her, all the way to her soul.

That terrified the hell out of her.

Voices on the other side of the door brought her out of her stupor, and she ran for the shower. The hot spray revived her as she tried to put the past few days in perspective. Impossible, really. From Mason's bombshell to Simon's abduction, the revelation of magickind, Mathias's pursuit . . . all of that was staggering, but nothing she couldn't handle. However, her mating to Simon, his possessiveness, his insistence on having her love bowled her over. She hadn't wanted to give her heart to anyone, ever. Slowly but surely, he was prying it from her cold chest and filling the dark space with affection, caring, warmth.

As she rinsed her hair, a pang tore through her belly. How did she trust the idea of him always being in love with her, happily forever? And if she didn't figure out how to stop her feelings for Simon from growing, his abandonment would hurt more than anyone's ever had.

A part of her wanted to trust him, hungered to give him every part of herself the way he seemed to share all of himself with her. But even if she did, would that be enough? Was she too damaged to give him what he needed and deserved? Would he realize that something in her was perpetually broken and elect to break their bond?

Finally clean and having no other means of stalling, Felicia dragged on her robe and cracked the bathroom door. Just outside, a tray with fruits, soup, and a hot sandwich sat on ornate china, along with water and tea in a matching cup and saucer. An older scrap of a woman dressed in head-to-toe black paced in front of the windows, her salt-and-pepper hair perfectly in place. She held a brush in one hand. The other was clenched in a fist.

Biting her lip, Felicia stared at the woman. Who was she? Her presence might have been troublesome, except that nothing sexual existed between her and Simon.

"Thank you for your patience, Amelia," he drawled.

Slowly, Felicia emerged from the bathroom, clasping the lapels of the robe together. Her gaze connected with Simon's. Something wild and intense pinged between them, ricocheting through her body like a bullet, doing maximum damage. He sent her a smile, like a lover who knew her secrets. She flushed and looked away.

"Eat, Sunshine. It'll be a long few hours. After your meal, you can meet Amelia."

Cautiously digging into her food, Felicia watched as Amelia cut a glare at Simon. The older woman sniffed in Felicia's direction. "The pictures of her in the tabloids over the past few days show that she has long hair. That takes time."

So Amelia had come . . . to do her hair?

The woman turned back to Simon. "You're expected elsewhere soon, yes?"

Simon lifted one shoulder. "If we're fashionably late . . ."

Amelia rolled her eyes indulgently. "How like you to assume the world will wait on you."

"I hardly care if they do. But they'll wait for Felicia, I have no doubt."

Amelia wielded an arched brow. "Is that your arrogance talking, or are you finally in love?"

Felicia paused mid-sandwich, but Simon merely smiled. More nervous than hungry, she pushed her meal aside, rose, and faced Amelia. "I'm Felicia Safford."

The older woman's dark gaze scanned her from the top of the towel covering her head to her bare toes, then walked a slow circle around her. After a long, measuring stare, she looked sharply at Simon.

"I'll need three hours and at least one assistant if you want her presentable."

"Indeed?" He looked mildly amused.

Felicia frowned. "Who are you exactly? And what's the matter with me?"

"Amelia Lawine."

She nearly swallowed her tongue. Amelia was the hairdresser and image consultant to the rich and famous. Everyone who was anyone wanted Amelia's advice. But she was always busy and notoriously selective. And she made last-minute house calls for Simon?

"I see you've heard of me." Amelia dragged the towel from Felicia's hair and filtered the wet strands through her fingers. "Not bad. Seems in good shape. The length is a bit long."

"I like it." Simon's voice was suddenly steel.

Amelia shot an arch stare at him, then shrugged. "I'll make it work. Her forehead is a bit oily, her cheeks dry. She needs a thorough shaping of her brows." The little woman picked up one of Felicia's hands, then made a sound of disgust. "Have you been filing your nails with a chainsaw?"

"I had them done three days ago," Felicia protested.

"By an amateur." Amelia let her hand drop and continued her visual path downward. "You need a good moisturizer for your skin all over, and that pedicure predates the Jurassic period."

Simon leveled a reproaching stare at her. "Amelia, nice to know I can always count on you to be polite."

The little woman snorted. "I'm honest. And you could use a haircut yourself."

"I'd never let anyone else touch my hair."

"As well you shouldn't. But you I'll deal with later." She turned snapping dark eyes back on Felicia. "You, come with me. By tonight, I'll make you look like the most stunning creature any man ever beheld."

"I-I really don't—"

"In my opinion"—Simon crossed the room and took her hand in his—"she already is."

Amelia turned a sharp stare his way. "Keep this up, and you're going to force me to gossip shamelessly about you."

He laughed. "As if I could stop you."

The fifty-something woman smiled ruefully and took Felicia by the hand. After dragging her back into the bathroom, Amelia attacked her hair with a comb and scissors. Moments later, another woman crowded in, giving Felicia a pedicure under Amelia's exacting direction. After buffing her heels and nipping her cuticles within an inch of their life, the little bird of a woman at her feet started in on her fingernails. All the while Amelia kept digging items out of her bag of tricks. Goop, then different goop, all applied to her hair, along with lots of tsking and a curse or two.

A long two hours later, Felicia shifted restlessly at the vanity and shouted over the blow-dryer. "Nearly done?"

Amelia snorted. "We haven't even started makeup."

Splendid. What the devil was Simon doing while Amelia and her friend were playing Frankenstein?

She heard people come in and out. A hotel employee cleared away the dishes; Simon's valet appeared with his clothing. Simon and a third man Felicia couldn't identify discussed something in hushed tones. The man stayed nearly an hour. What the devil was that about?

"Your attention is wandering," Amelia chided.

"I'm not accustomed to this much grooming." The woman plucked at her eyebrows, and Felicia flinched. "Ouch!"

"It shows."

What seemed like forever later, Amelia finally brushed a final coat of lipstick across her mouth and stepped back to survey her results. She gave Felicia a pleased smile. "Beautiful. You'll turn every head tonight. I'd say that Hurstgrove will become lovesick, but I daresay he already is. Look."

On wobbly legs, Felicia stood and stared at herself in the mirror, blinking furiously. She almost didn't recognize herself. Her naturally wavy hair had been fluffed into shiny, artful curls that accentuated her natural highlights. Her eyes, rimmed in soft brown, had never looked more blue or exotic, while her cheekbones had definition. The rest of her face glowed. Amelia had painted her lips a vibrant coral, and they looked nothing short of pouty.

"Oh my word . . . wow!"

Amelia began cleaning up the tools of her trade. "My work here is complete. Your dress and everything to be worn beneath are hanging in the closet."

Felicia made her way to the adjacent space and flipped on the light. She gasped at the flow of golden silk cascading from the hanger and falling toward the floor. "It's gorgeous!"

"The color is perfect for you. Shoes are in the corner. Hurstgrove has your jewelry for the evening. Good-bye, dear."

"Good-bye. You're a genius."

"You're welcome."

With that the woman and her assistant left. Felicia stared

at herself in the mirror, and her confidence surged. A woman like her could attract a man like Simon.

Perhaps, but that didn't make her immune to heartbreak.

Her smile faded as she reached for the dress.

Moments and several troubled thoughts later, Felicia tied the sash around her waist. Amazing. Everything fit perfectly. Slightly Grecian with a twist of Katharine Hepburn, the silky dress hugged her breasts and cinched in at the waist, accentuated by the wide strip of silk, then fell like a dream to her feet. She stepped into strappy black shoes that were clearly expensive and felt like a cloud.

A moment later, Simon knocked on the door. "Ready? We're beyond fashionably late."

She opened the door. He cut a handsome figure with a fresh haircut and a form-fitting tuxedo. Debonair and smooth. Lethal to her heart.

When he clapped eyes on her, his jaw dropped. "Stunning." He blew out a harsh breath. "I always knew you were beautiful, but tonight . . . hmm, you're so sexy, Sunshine. I wish we could stay in."

"Great idea!"

He shook his head regretfully. "Nice try. All part of the plan."

Felicia stifled a curse. "Where are we going? And how many people will have seen our pictures by the time we arrive?"

"It's a benefit dinner, and probably everyone. Just smile. I promise I'll take care of the rest." He took her hand in his.

In the bedroom, he handed her a delicate black wool coat. Around her neck, he clapped a gorgeous string of huge lustrous black and golden orbs decorated with diamond rondelles. He attached matching strings to her ears.

"These are gorgeous!" She gasped. "Are they pearls?"

He nodded. "Black and golden Tahitians."

"They're perfect," she breathed, fingering them in the mirror.

"Then they match you."

Such over-the-top flattery, yet when he spoke the words, there was no mistaking his sincerity. Her heart thawed a bit more.

"Aren't these very rare? And very expensive?"

"So I'm told."

A shocking thought hit her. "Tell me you borrowed these."

A ghost of a smile crossed his face. "If you don't like them, they'll go back tomorrow."

Felicia nearly choked. "You *bought* them?"

Simon shrugged, which she took to mean yes.

"I can't take something this extravagant."

"You're not taking; I'm giving them to you. No more arguments. Now . . ." He handed her a heavy, coordinated champagne bag. "The Doomsday Diary is tucked in there. Amelia put your lipstick inside as well, and I'm to tell you on penalty of death that you must retouch."

Despite the nerves fluttering in her belly, Felicia cracked a smile.

"Hmm. I may have to smudge it myself, just to test your dedication to reapplication."

"Simon . . ."

"Ah," he said regretfully. "Another speech where you tell me to keep my distance. Hasn't it occurred to you yet that I'm not listening?"

No, she'd gotten that, loud and clear. "So my wishes don't matter?"

"That's not it." He took her hand, pressing his forehead to hers. "You're hiding, not just from me, but yourself. Once you see what it's like to be truly loved and to love back . . .

well, if you'd like to return to your walled-off existence, I'll do my best to give you what you want. But I don't think you want to spend the rest of your life alone."

Felicia sucked in a breath. He got right to the heart of the matter so quickly. How did he voice her biggest fears and make her see them from a totally different angle? What if he was right?

And then what if something parted them?

"You're thinking too much." He tugged on her hand. "Let's go."

In the chilly evening, the valet brought the car around. The paparazzi hovered, jostling and shouting.

"Pictures of you and your fiancé's brother are circulating the Internet. Are they real?"

"How long have you been lovers?"

"Your Grace, your brother is denying that you have any sexual relationship with Ms. Safford. Given the recent pictures, how can that be true?"

"No comment," Duke said firmly, then hustled her into a sleek silver limousine that stopped inches from them.

Felicia's teeth chattered when she got inside, not just from the cold, but the apprehension. People *had* already seen the pictures. Mason, too? Cold dread slid through her stomach. What must he be thinking?

"May I use your phone?" she said to Simon as he climbed in.

He hesitated, then handed it to her. "Is something wrong?"

"I can't do this to Mason. He stood by me, held my hand, assumed so many of my responsibilities after Deirdre's death. I don't want him to discover . . . us from a bunch of tabloid pictures."

Simon grabbed her wrist. "I inspected them before I allowed Holly to post anything. Caden watched our back. The pictures are sensual but tasteful. They don't look posed at all. Will Mason know from looking at them that we're lovers? Yes. But I made certain they should neither hurt nor embarrass you." He released her slowly. "Call him."

Felicia did. It was a frustrating but guilty relief to get his voicemail. Not knowing what to say in a recording that wouldn't crush him, she simply hung up.

"I admire you for wanting to soften the blow," Simon said softly. "When you do talk to him, he may say that he loves you, but I'll do whatever it takes to fight for you and make you believe in me."

She swallowed her emotions. With every word and deed, Simon demonstrated his devotion. He took care of her in every way. Would a man with no feelings for her trouble himself to do that? No. That trembling part of her again asked how long his love could possibly last. Her head knew forever was the right answer. Her heart balked for every night as a child when she'd cried in her bed, aching with longing for someone to love her.

Only Deirdre had cared about her, and anguish pummeled Felicia when she remembered walking into the bathroom and finding the only person she'd ever let herself really love dead and cold. At Deirdre's funeral, she'd held in the furious tears until everyone had gone. With a stab in her heart, she still recalled wading through grief for the next days and weeks, but no one really reached out to her. Even Mason hadn't insisted she grieve. He'd pushed her to resume a normal life and hadn't tried to make her face the feelings she'd known she couldn't deal with alone.

But Simon . . . if he knew she'd never really let herself cry for Deirdre, he'd be stunned and appalled and insist she do so now.

How could she not love such a man? It was impossible, and her heart knew it.

"I'm trusting you." Her voice shook as she put her hand in his.

He'd likely interpret her words to be about the evening, but it meant so much more. She was too afraid to tell him, but Simon was smart. He would figure out soon that she'd all but fallen for him.

Minutes later, the limousine stopped. Felicia peered out the window. Brown Hotel, another exclusive place for the rich and famous. The driver opened the door, and Simon climbed out. Immediately the press swarmed, shouting lewd questions that rattled her. He ignored them.

Placing her shaking hand in his outstretched one, she clutched her bag with the other and stood on wobbling legs. Flashbulbs went off, one after the other, until the effect was like a strobe light. She clutched his arm.

"Relax," Simon whispered. "They can't do anything to you."

She took a deep breath. He was right. But there was no doubt these vultures had seen the pictures. What were they saying about them? Her?

Felicia turned to him, frowning. "If they can't do anything, why are you so watchful?"

"There may be trouble tonight."

"Mathias?" Horror crept through her voice.

"Perhaps. Just remain cautious and stay close to me."

They pressed slowly through the shouting paparazzi. Cameras and aggressive gossipmongers blocked their way, but thankfully, they were soon at the door, striding through the palatial, expansive lobby, winding their way to an over-the-top ballroom that shouted exclusivity and money.

Everyone around them glittered with diamonds and silks, sparkling teeth and perfection. Felicia stopped in her tracks. She recognized actors, politicians, pop stars—a virtual who's who of British wealth.

This was Simon's world, and he looked very comfortable in it. Even without all the magical and Mathias problems, their relationship would be a challenge. She went to work every morning in something faded and cotton, trainers and ponytails. Simon never wore anything less than perfectly pressed designer couture. She winced.

"I don't belong here."

"Don't be silly," he murmured. "I don't like all this pretentious crap, honestly. But you must look comfortable, or they'll eat you alive." He gestured to the other guests.

A gasp nearby startled Felicia. Within moments, the room began to buzz. Stares swerved their way. Felicia felt their dissecting gazes and shifted restlessly, wishing for a hole to hide in.

Simon wrapped an arm around her and nuzzled her, whispering, "You look gorgeous. Elegant. Their opinions, whatever they are, don't matter. Take a deep breath. We can last a few hours."

Felicia took a deep breath, swallowed. Simon needed her to play her part. If they were going to keep the press buzzing, she had to look happy and in love, not scared to death.

"Sorry." She pasted on a smile and turned to him. "Better?"

"Hmm, not yet, but we'll keep working on it." He snagged a glass of champagne from a passing waiter and thrust it into her hands. "Drink."

She wasn't terribly fond of alcohol, but this was light and sweet and a surprising godsend. "Thank you."

"You're welcome. Let's dance."

"I'm not very good," she admitted.

"Good thing I lead and you follow." He smiled.

The orchestra played an old and romantic standard, *Someone to Watch Over Me*. How apropos. Felicia swayed in Simon's arms. Here, she felt safe, warm, despite paparazzi snapping pictures through the windows and guests staring. For a few perfect minutes, the world shrank to just her and Simon, dancing sublimely close, his heart beating against hers.

With a pass under his arm, Felicia felt light, happy. He was, not surprisingly, very light on his feet. A firm but smooth leader. He dipped her low, and Felicia bent over his arm.

Only to see Mason storming their way. She scrambled upright and turned to face him, butterflies colliding in her stomach and guilt coursing through her veins.

"What the hell is going on between you two?" Mason snarled at his brother, glancing once at her with open anguish.

Something in her chest crumpled. No doubt, she'd hurt Mason, perhaps even broken his heart in the way she most feared having hers broken. She felt two inches tall.

"We're dancing." Simon carefully shifted Felicia behind him. "And unless I'm mistaken, you're not on the guest list."

Fury contorted Mason's face. "You son of a—"

"Mason," she said gently, stepping closer to him. "I tried to call. I want to talk calmly about this."

He turned a furious glare on her. "The fact he carried you off to 'rescue' you, and you what, fell into his arms?"

The room turned deadly silent. Felicia gaped for something to say. "Mason, I *am* in danger and—"

"Really? From whom? Are you going to tell me the waiters are armed?"

She hesitated, wondering how to explain Mathias without

revealing magickind. Mason's face tightened brutally in the silence.

"It's complicated." Simon stood between them protectively.

"The only danger to her is *you*. Look me in the eye and tell me you didn't fuck her."

Felicia recoiled. He spit the words with contempt, his face a snarl. It wasn't concern, but resentment. She hardly knew what to say.

"It's none of your bloody business," Simon insisted. "You don't ever talk about her that way again. She's terrified of her own feelings, and she invested six years in trusting you. After Deirdre's death, sharing any part of herself wasn't easy. I know you know that. If you really care for her, are you going to humiliate her in public now?"

Simon's words melted everything inside her. She clutched his hand tighter.

Betrayal distorted Mason's face, but he shook his head. "No, I'm not going to humiliate Felicia. But I have the ability and authority to make you regret ever crossing me."

Mason turned and motioned to someone at the door. Moments later, two men wearing distinctive tall, dark blue helmets came at them with purposeful strides. Felicia's stomach clenched. The Metropolitan Police.

The one on the left, wearing a commander's badge, stopped in front of Simon. "Simon Northam, Duke of Hurstgrove?"

"Yes." He froze.

The sergeant beside him whipped out a pair of handcuffs and slapped them around one of Simon's wrists. "You're under arrest for Felicia Safford's kidnapping and rape."

CHAPTER 15

FELICIA GASPED AS THE officers whirled Simon around and cuffed his hands behind his back. Around her, the room buzzed as surprise and malicious interest swept through the crowd.

Rape? "You can't do this!" she protested to Mason.

But he could. As the prosecutor and the barrister drafting the charges, he would have latitude the average citizen wouldn't. He could say anything he bloody wanted, at least until someone talked to her and looked at the tabloid pictures. Then, any fool would know the truth. Right?

Or could Mason turn Simon's proceedings topsy-turvy, forcing him to prove his innocence? Apprehension gripped her chest.

"We have a warrant for his arrest," the sergeant pointed out.

"Can we do this elsewhere?" Simon hissed. "This is a benefit dinner. There's no need to keep the cause from making money so that you can make an example of me."

The sergeant speared Simon with a hard stare. "Are you admitting your guilt?"

"I'm refusing to air legal laundry in front of an audience."

"Wait!" she demanded. They had to see this was all wrong. "I'm Felicia Safford."

The commander turned to her. "Are you all right? Do you need medical attention?"

Medical attention? They truly believed she'd been attacked? "No, of course not. I'm fine."

The older man sent her a kindly glance. "Then we'd like you to come with us and tell us what happened. We won't let anyone hurt you anymore." He glowered at Simon. "Let's go."

God, everything was happening so fast. If they took Simon away, her protection would go with him, yes. But she was more concerned about him. She cared for him far too much to let anyone take him from her.

She swallowed, realizing the enormity of her feelings for him. They'd crept up on her and crowded in. He'd barged into her psyche, making himself almost as necessary to her as air.

She loved him. Dear God. How had that happened?

The policemen shoved Simon through the stunned crowd, out the door to the front of the hotel, past the paparazzi. Anxiety, incredulity, and dread rushed through Felicia as she ran after them, through the barrage of questions and flash-bulbs. Mason chased after her, shouting. But she didn't slow. Somehow, she had to get Simon out of this mess.

As the peelers moved to place him in their car and refused her entrance, she grabbed the sergeant's arm. "Stop! You're making a mistake!"

He cast a curious glance between her and Mason, who now panted beside her. "You can tell us your side of the story at the station."

The sergeant pushed Simon in the waiting police car and pivoted away. Felicia darted for the limousine, shaking all over, the press following. Damn, she must keep herself together.

A glowering Mason followed in his sensible sedan.

Nail-biting minutes later, they all arrived at the station. The two officers ushered Felicia into a small interview room, then left. She paced, wondering how long it would be before they allowed her to see Simon.

Mason must have convinced someone to let him in because he barreled into the little room moments later and grabbed her arm. "I filed these charges to help you. Now is your opportunity to tell the truth, Felicia, without Simon to coerce you. You didn't leave our wedding voluntarily with him."

Not for anything would she admit that now.

"You're using your position to prosecute your own brother?" She felt betrayed on Simon's behalf. She understood how Mason could feel as if his brother had wronged him, but how could Mason do *this*?

"No, to *protect* you," Mason insisted. "Make certain he's punished if he forced himself on you."

Simon had gone to another woman and engaged in something less than sex to avoid forcing himself on her, his own mate. "He would never do that."

Mason's face thundered into a frown. "He's seduced you. Did he tell you that he loves you? Don't put anything past him. He'd charm his way into your affections merely to turn you inside out. Felicia, whatever you think you know about him, he'll break your heart and he'll relish it. His 'feelings' for you . . ." He shook his head. "They're all about hurting me."

Two days ago, she would have believed it and run scared. After all, she'd known Mason for six years, and Simon a mere three days. Now, she suspected that if she asked Simon to cut out his own heart and serve it up for her on a platter, he would.

"Aren't *you* trying to hurt him with this stunt?" she demanded.

The door to the interrogation room opened, and the two arresting officers walked in, minus Simon. They frowned at Mason.

She jerked her arm from her former fiancé's grasp. "Where is he?"

"Hurstgrove is in custody," the sergeant growled. "Pending interrogation."

Felicia shook her head. "This is a huge misunderstanding."

"Is it, now?" The commander sent her a searching gaze. "Not according to Mr. Daniels." Then he frowned. "Sir, you shouldn't be talking to the victim until I question her. I'll have to ask you to leave."

Mason raised a brow. "I'm both the prosecutor and her fiancé. She's been hurt, and I've just recovered her. I'm not leaving."

"Simon never hurt me," she insisted.

The commander hesitated, and Mason kept on. "You know me. I would never do anything to jeopardize this investigation."

The older man sighed, clearly not liking it, but he nodded and turned Felicia's way again. "Did the Duke of Hurstgrove carry you away from your wedding against your will?"

"Is that what everyone thought?" She pretended an amused laugh. "Ridiculous."

The older man's bushy gray brows slanted down ominously. "Mr. Daniels claims that, after kidnapping you, His Grace forced you to engage in sexual activity against your will."

Felicia was almost afraid to turn and look at Mason. Now, she had to choose publicly. With one word, she'd likely ruin her relationship with her best friend forever. Inside, she wept, hating that she'd come between brothers. But there was no choice.

"No, he didn't force me to do anything I didn't choose to."

She looked Mason in the eye. His eyes slammed shut, and the pain on his face was a stab to her chest.

"He *carried* you away from our wedding," Mason insisted. "I watched him. So did dozens of others. I've brought their statements."

Felicia forced herself not to flinch. "I went willingly. He only carried me as a romantic gesture and so that my shoes wouldn't be ruined by the snow."

"Your bloody shoes?" Mason railed. "You'd only met Simon the day before. He was a virtual stranger. You were furious with him."

He had her there, and Felicia panicked for a moment. If she didn't think of something plausible to say, he could ramrod these charges through and have Simon prosecuted. He'd proudly made a life of putting violent offenders behind bars.

"He's protecting me. Someone *is* after me." *Please don't let them ask about Mathias.*

"Why not come to us, Miss?" the sergeant barked.

"Simon knew of the threat before I did. I-it all happened so fast, and then we were running for our lives, hiding and unsure whom to trust. But he didn't abduct me."

The policeman cast a glance at Mason. "And the charge of rape? Did Hurstgrove sexually assault you or force you to enter into a sexual relationship?"

"As I said, nothing was against my will."

"Will you sign a sworn statement to that effect?" said the older policeman.

Felicia couldn't look at Mason, knowing he'd stuck his neck out professionally to bring her home safely, and she was rejecting his help. But she nodded.

"You're certain?" the commander asked.

"Yes. I was completely willing," she murmured.

"You *let* him fuck you?" Mason sounded shell-shocked. Betrayed.

Felicia hated that she'd hurt her best friend so deeply. He'd tried so hard to be her everything. She'd do almost anything to take her words back, except hurt Simon. "Mason..."

The commander pulled out a chair. "Sit down so we can get the facts."

A long hour later, the commander put a piece of paper in front of her, typed with her formal statement. "Sign here."

"Felicia," Mason pleaded, looking pasty white. "You can't mean any of this . . ."

"I'm sorry," Felicia whispered, then signed the statement and handed it back to the commander. "Will you bring Simon to me now?"

The younger policeman looked at her as if she was a Stockholm syndrome victim to be pitied. "Are you certain that's what you want? It's not too late."

She didn't care what he thought. She knew the truth. "I'm certain."

The commander made a call to the jail. Moments later, two policemen ushered Simon in and uncuffed him.

"You're free," the older man said, sliding Felicia's statement across the table in front of him. "Miss Safford made a written account of events that exonerates you."

He paused to caress her shoulder in an affectionate gesture of thanks, then plowed toward Mason. "You jealous bastard! How could you do this to Felicia? You know sharing the intimate details of her life is hard. But you forced her into telling all."

Mason raised a dark brow. "She apparently found a way to share everything with you. Her past, her fears, her body. I saw those pictures online. You shared her with the whole fucking world." He turned to her, anguish contorting his face. "Didn't I love you enough? Didn't I give you the space and time you needed? What else could I have done?"

Felicia closed her eyes and clutched her stomach. God, this hurt. She'd always known that being left by someone she loved would cause untold pain, but she'd never imagined that being the one to cut someone's heart out would hurt so deeply as well.

"You did everything," she murmured. "I'm sorry . . ."

"Sorry? With a word, you think my pain just . . . goes away? I wanted to love you for the rest of your life, and I was willing to accept whatever terms you needed."

"It's my fault," she choked as guilt slammed into her. "You were my crutch when I was afraid. After Deirdre died, that was all the time. You never demanded more of me, and I . . . walled myself off. I'm sorry I never let you in. I'm sorry I let you be my strength instead of standing on my own two feet." Hot tears rained down her cheeks. "You've always been a great friend, and I never meant to hurt you. I really am sorry."

"That's enough." Simon pushed between them and glared at Mason. "Don't you dare take your anger out on her. If you'd like to hit me later, I'll stand still and let you. Sue me, hate me, disown me if that will make you feel better."

"Don't worry. I will."

In the wee hours of the night, Duke climbed into the limousine with Felicia at his side, paparazzi still chasing them.

"Don't these vultures ever sleep?" she muttered.

Despite all the tension of the evening, he laughed. "They're robots missing their off buttons."

She shook her head and curled up next to him on the seat, exactly where he wanted her.

"Thank you for everything you did tonight." He hugged

her tightly. Of course he also appreciated the fact she'd come to him wanting affection.

She turned to him with solemn blue eyes. He'd never grow tired of the sight of her. He hoped he saw her every day for the next thousand years.

To his surprise, she planted a soft kiss on his lips. "Are you truly surprised that I defended you?"

"Mason had no basis in fact when he tossed the rape charge out, as I'm sure he was aware. He'd seen the pictures on *Out of This Realm*'s site and become angry." He sighed. "Frankly, I don't blame him. In his place, I'd be an unhappy bastard, too. But I'm surprised you told Commander Bradford that I hadn't abducted you against your will. That wasn't precisely true."

She caressed his face. "From eavesdropping, I knew I was in danger and suspected only you could help me. I balked because it was so sudden." She bit her lip. "And because you scared me."

"I'd never hurt you."

A smile played at her gorgeous mouth. "But you were much too charming and seductive for my peace of mind."

He returned the smile tenfold. "Ah, liked me a bit too much for comfort, did you?"

"Now you're just being cocky."

Duke clamped his hands around her waist and lifted her. She shrieked as he settled her over his lap, thighs straddling his hips. Then he lifted up to her so she could feel his erection. "Not yet, but lose those knickers, and I will be."

"You're incorrigible." She scrambled back to the seat beside him, casting a fretful glance at the driver.

As Duke raised the privacy glass, his heart lurched. "But you do like something about me?"

He almost cringed at the desperate note in his voice. In

the back of his head, a nagging voice wondered if she'd lied to everyone tonight not because she cared for him as a mate, but because she didn't want to lose her magical bodyguard. He didn't want to think that, but as much as Felicia had revealed in the past few days, she was hardly an open book.

She bit her lip. "I like you very much."

Felicia liked him. Duke didn't have the courage to ask her if she loved him, or ever could.

The rest of the ride passed in silence. Because he couldn't stand to be too far from her, Duke held her hand. Though she clasped his in return, he knew tonight had rattled her.

After dodging the paparazzi outside the Dorchester, they dashed through the deserted lobby and into a waiting elevator. The doors slid shut, and he turned to Felicia, caressing his way up her bare arms. "Are you all right?"

She frowned. "I wasn't the one arrested. What about you?"

"Fine."

"How?" She shook her head. "Mason is your brother. This discord between you isn't right. It's my fault."

So that's what troubled Felicia.

A heavy weight settled in Duke's chest. He was aware that he and Mason were quickly approaching a point of no return. Another stunt like this, and Duke would be hard-pressed to forgive his younger brother. On the other hand, if another man had stolen his most precious gift, his very heart, Duke could well understand such hatred.

He'd kill any bastard who took Felicia from him.

"Our problems aren't your doing. They started long ago." He sighed. "Mason has every reason to despise me. He wanted you for himself, and I took you. With your statement, he knows he's lost you. And I'm not letting go, Felicia."

Silently, she looked away, pulled her hand back. A physical withdrawal. Duke cursed under his breath. Did she feel too guilty about hurting Mason? Or, as Duke feared, did she not love him enough to choose him forever?

In their suite, he tore through the dark rooms, frustration edging to the fore. Damn it, with Felicia it was always two steps forward, one step back. He didn't want to lose her, and pushing her now would only induce her to put new walls between them. But would she ever open her heart and give herself completely to him?

"It's wrong. I've come between two brothers and—" She choked. "I feel terrible. Nothing ever came between Deirdre and me, ever. Until Alexei."

And that had ended in the woman's death. Duke's gut twisted.

"Mason is your friend, yes?"

"He was. I don't know if he'd still say the same."

"His anger toward you will abate." Duke couldn't believe he was consoling her, when all he wanted to do was wring Mason's neck. But anything to take that haunted look off her face. "In time, he'll heal. Move on."

"But your relationship with him will never be the same, and I don't know if I can live with that."

"Even if I'm willing to bear it?"

"Simon . . ." Her voice pleaded with him.

Perhaps she meant what she said, but Duke couldn't help but think that she merely used Mason again to keep distance between them.

"What if you find one day that I'm . . . not worth it?"

"That will never happen, but I could assure you until I'm blue in the face, and I'm not certain you would ever believe me. You'll have to realize that for yourself."

Tamping down his agitation, he gritted his teeth and

closeted himself in the bathroom. The warm spray of the shower felt heavenly, and washing the stench and filth of jail off himself soothed him.

Long minutes later, he emerged to see that Felicia had taken off all her makeup and slipped into one of the negligees he'd had delivered to the room. Eggshell silk trimmed in delicate lace. Demure but sexy. She looked stunning. All the relaxation from his shower fled, replaced by a desire that made him edgy and hard. He ached to make love to her. To stake his claim anew.

But she needed time to come to grips with tonight's events. Damn it, somehow he'd have to give it to her. They were making progress, just not as quickly as he liked.

On the bed, she reclined, her knees curled up, a book resting on them.

He frowned. "Is that one of Merlin's books?"

She glanced up, saw the towel wrapped around his middle, and flushed. "Ah . . . yes. It is. I, um . . ." She swallowed, staring at his chest. "I'm trying to find something useful in this book. Tonight proved to me we cannot keep living in this gossipmonger bubble to avoid Mathias. The only way to deal with him is to head off this threat."

"You mean, go to Morganna's tomb?"

"I don't see another choice. We're merely avoiding the inevitable."

He understood her logic . . . but no. "Chasing Mathias is tantamount to a death sentence. I won't let you do anything to endanger yourself."

"*Let me?* I'm a grown woman. An Untouchable. The magic in that tomb can't hurt me."

Duke grabbed her shoulders tightly. "Listen, Sunshine. That's a *theory*. No one knows that for a fact. It's also possible that you could step one foot inside and die instantly."

"Hiding in plain sight won't work forever. You can't keep inventing a new scandal every day."

As much as he wanted to refute her, he feared she was right.

"And how long before Mathias gets desperate? What if he takes a cue from terrorists and starts bombing buildings and killing innocent humans just to reach me?"

Duke wouldn't put anything past Mathias. But how could he simply let Felicia walk into one of the most dangerous places known to magickind?

"Have you found anything useful in that book?"

She shook her head. "Odds and ends, really. The tomb was created for Morganna, and Merlin himself distilled her essence into a bottle to store there."

In other words, she'd learned nothing that would guarantee her safety. Likley because no such guarantee existed.

"What if we led Mathias into the tomb, destroyed Morganna's essence before he could carry out his plan. Perhaps then we could find a way to destroy him?"

The thought horrified him. "Too risky."

"But is it possible?"

Duke said nothing. He didn't know the answer and didn't want to encourage her.

"I think we should talk to Bram," she mused.

"We aren't going to the tomb, period."

"I won't keep running. I'll never have a normal life unless Mathias is no longer a threat."

Bloody hell. That was true. Question was, what did she now see as a normal life? One with him, or merely one in which she wasn't always looking over her shoulder for evil incarnate?

Cursing, Duke rose and found his phone. Bram answered on the first ring.

"Are you out of your bloody mind?" he screeched. "Why not take out an advertisement telling Mathias exactly where to find you and how much you love Felicia?"

Duke gritted his teeth. "Can we save the parenting for later? We have a question about Morganna's tomb. What would happen if we managed to get inside the cave and destroy her essence? Felicia would be basically useless to Mathias, yes?"

"That's possible. Mathias might come after her for mere spite, but he'd have no other reason. If Morganna's essence were destroyed, she'd be well and truly gone forever. Another threat extinguished."

Duke paced to the next room, away from Felicia and the argument he knew she'd put up. "I can't send her in there, Bram. We need to find Mathias and kill the fucking bastard. Now!"

"Haven't we been trying? We can't even find Tynan yet, and the clock is ticking. Maybe it's time to think about letting her try the tomb."

Duke cursed. "Would you send Emma there, not knowing if death awaited her?"

"Because of who she is, Felicia must face either Mathias or that tomb. Duke, you may not be able to spare her both."

"Shut the bloody hell up." He jammed the button, ringing off, breath harsh, heart beating furiously.

Charging back into the bedroom, he found Felicia lying across the bed with Merlin's book again. "You can't protect me from everything. I appreciate your effort but . . . I'm looking for some reference on how to destroy Morganna's essence."

Duke pulled the tome from her grasp and slammed it shut. "You are *not* going in there. My mission is to keep you safe. Bram and the others will have to take care of Mathias."

"They can't enter that tomb without me, and they don't know how to kill him. Be reasonable, Simon. You don't want to see me in danger, and I adore you for it. But you can only protect me from so much."

That fact hurt like hell.

"Bram saw you with Mathias in his dream."

"I remember." She swallowed. "Maybe that's simply destined to become reality."

He hovered over her on the bed, faces inches apart, unable to deal with the thought of her in Mathias's grip, in pain, hurting, dead. Anguish crashed over him. He wanted so badly to grab her, kiss her, make love to her.

She read the intent on his face and looked away. "I'd like to go to sleep now."

Just like that, she shut him out again.

Panic zipped through Duke. He wanted to force her to look at him, force her to admit everything in her heart. But he was too on edge, and pushing her tonight would only be counterproductive.

"You must be tired," she prompted him. "You haven't slept in two days."

He lay down beside her and put his arms around her, relieved when she didn't resist. "Will you let me hold you?"

When she nodded, Duke placed a soft kiss on her lips. "Sleep."

Felicia curled up with her pillow. Moments later, she dropped off. He wrapped his body around hers, quaking inside.

Felicia was brave enough to run into the tomb and face the danger—but so scared to tear down the walls between them. What would it take for her to have the same courage when sharing her emotions? She cared enough to make love with him, enough to issue a statement about her relationship with him in front of Mason. What was it going to take for her to admit that she loved him?

The following morning dawned blustery and gray. Simon herded Felicia out of bed and into a waiting pair of jeans. A big down coat followed, before he urged her to throw on her trainers.

She frowned, barely awake. "It's not even seven o'clock in the morning. Where are we going?"

He thrust a cup of tea in her hands. "Will you trust me and come along?"

He was secretive, a bit edgy. But he'd never hurt her. How could she say no?

"All right. No hints?"

Duke took her hand with a grim expression and led her out of the room.

In front of the hotel, a horde of reporters awaited, loitering near the entrance, springing into action as soon as they appeared.

"Did Hurstgrove rape you?" shouted one.

"Did you lie about the abduction to set him free?"

"Do you have Stockholm syndrome?"

God, she was bloody tired of their questions. "No comment."

She darted away from the scene, Simon holding her hand and running with her. They dashed into the waiting limousine and Felicia waited to hear his instructions to the driver, but he said nothing as the car pulled away.

"What is this about?" she demanded.

He swallowed. "You'll see. Then we'll talk."

Minutes later, they wound down a series of familiar roads. Buildings thinned out. Wrought iron gates appeared, age-worn but strong, with horror she recognized the cemetery where her entire family was buried.

Felicia tensed. "Why are we here?"

"When was the last time you visited your sister?"

The day of her funeral. She'd arranged to have flowers laid at Deirdre's grave regularly, but hadn't found the fortitude to bring them herself.

"What does that have to do with anything? Take me back to the hotel!"

"When?"

"I'm not going out there. Mathias could—"

"Bram and Ice are meeting us for protection. Mathias won't come near you."

"It's cold," she blurted.

"I'll keep you warm. But that isn't your real objection."

"Why are you doing this?" She cried out as he opened the car door and tugged on her hand. "Don't . . . please."

He clenched his jaw. "It goes against everything inside me to force you to do anything, but I want to help you. You need to face your fears. Deirdre died and you let part of yourself die with her. Or did it happen even before that?"

Fear struck down to her very core. Felicia dug in her heels, seeing Bram standing a hundred meters to her left. Ice hovered like a statue an equal distance to her right. Even if she ran, they'd catch her. Or, if he was hovering near, Mathias would.

"Is this your way of making me vulnerable to you, to rip me wide open? I-I won't. God, don't make me."

"Yes, I want you to open up to me, love me. But do you think I'd hurt you voluntarily to get my way?"

No, but saying that was like giving him permission to unravel her past and shove it in her face.

"I'm sorry you think that." He clenched his jaw, eyes looking suspiciously glossy. "I love you, and I wish like hell you could believe me—and yourself—and trust that I'm doing this for you so you can find peace. And eventually feel free enough to love."

She grabbed Simon, her gaze imploring. "Please. If I see her grave now, it will be as if she died all over again. I can't face that."

"Did you ever really accept her death? I'm not certain you moved past anger—at Alexei, at your parents. Were you angry with her as well? I think you were and you used your rage to close yourself off."

Felicia shrank away from him. He'd seen her too clearly and stripped her bare, down to her soul. That fact perversely pleased and terrified her. "Please, don't."

The wind whipped through Simon's hair, and he hesitated. She prayed he would let this go, understand that if she completely accepted Deirdre's death, she'd have to admit that, Simon aside, she truly had no one.

"I'm sorry. But regardless of what happens between us, you need to put her to rest and heal. You'll never be whole until you do."

With that, he picked her up and carried her, crying and fighting, to Deirdre's grave. Felicia buried her face in Simon's neck, squeezed her eyes shut. He pried her away from him and set her down, then spun her around.

"Stop. Face her. You loved her in life. Why have you abandoned her now?"

The sight of her tombstone beside her parents', all decorated with the smatterings of the dried wreaths she'd had laid at Christmas, stared her in the face. Fading red ribbons flapped in the breeze. Leaves blew across the cold earth. The sight was a blow to her stomach, a rending of her heart. Years of fear and loneliness rushed over her, a tidal wave of emotion she couldn't hide from.

"Abandon *her*?" Felicia screamed. "She abandoned *me*. They all did! My birth parents gave me away. My adoptive parents left me to nannies and servants."

"Your birth parents gave you up to save your life. Your adoptive parents were shallow and incapable of love. That's not a reflection of you or your worth. Despite them, you have a huge heart. Let it heal."

She shook her head as tears streamed down her wind-chilled face. "Deirdre was the one person I let myself love. After Alexei crushed her, I would have continued holding her hand, helped her through anything. But she left me alone. Sh-she didn't even say good-bye."

God, Felicia couldn't breathe. The pain was like a tsunami, growing and growing, then pulling her under until she was drowning in misery, loneliness, anguish. Glaring at Deirdre's headstone, she dropped to her knees. "Why the hell did you leave me like that? You never even said good-bye! No note, no . . ."

She dissolved into sobs.

Then Simon's arms came around her, lifting her to her feet. He felt warm. He was a life preserver in a raging sea. "Shh. Deirdre didn't leave *you*; she left the pain. All that you're going through now? She *ran* from it. You're stronger. You *will* overcome it. Once you have, you can accept, open yourself to love. Be happy. You could have been her anchor, but she shut everyone out. Don't make her mistake. I'll help you. Please let me."

He was right. She clutched her middle, not sure if she had the strength to reach out for him.

The realization only made her cry harder.

To take the leap of faith he proposed, she'd have to cross a chasm of black terror. She'd have to invest totally in someone else again. She felt nowhere near ready . . . but Simon had burrowed into her heart. Even with her guard up, she'd come to *need* him. Now, without him, Felicia feared she'd wither, die. What the hell was she going to do?

Back in the limousine, Duke sank into the buttery leather seats beside Felicia. She was quiet, eerily so, her face pale and shell-shocked. Biting back a curse, he wondered if he'd pushed too hard, too fast. But Felicia needed to deal with her demons so she could heal. And yes, some selfish corner of his heart had done it with the hope they could have a future.

Now, it was all in her hands. As much as he wanted to wrap her in his embrace again and keep encouraging her to open up, he couldn't push her more. She'd fought against this moment for years. Grief wasn't like a light switch a person could turn off at will.

He stared at the privacy glass. "I didn't take you there to hurt you."

Slowly, she nodded. "You're right. I couldn't love Mason as more than a friend because of my fear. I've hurt him terribly. I don't know if he'll ever forgive me. I know you think he will, but . . ." She shrugged, then turned glassy blue eyes on him. Tears trembled on her dark lashes. "I don't want to hurt you as I've hurt him. I . . . I can't shut off my feelings for you in the same way. It's frightening."

A fist squeezed Duke's heart. It was the closest thing to an attachment that she'd admitted. "Then don't."

Felicia turned quiet, pensive. "For all we've been through, I've spent a mere four days with you. I-I . . . need your patience."

"Sunshine, I'll give you whatever you need. I want you to be whole and happy, no matter what you do."

The tears shimmering at the edge of her lashes fell. "I've

been such a bother to you. Dragging me from danger, dealing with my woes. I don't deserve you."

He smiled gently and teased, "Well, there's something you can strive for."

She leaned forward slowly, slowly, eyes fluttering closed, lips gently parted. Everything inside him leapt to roaring life. As always, Duke hungered to get her under him, soft and willing. But now he wanted to see the love shining through her eyes and feel the complete acceptance in her body. Soon, he promised himself.

As he laid his mouth over hers, they shared a solemn moment, a breath. His heart filled with love, nearly burst.

Then his phone rang. He yanked it from his pocket and stared at the display. *Bram.*

"What?" Duke barked.

"It's Tynan." Bram's voice sounded strained.

Duke leapt to instant attention, breath held. "Tell me."

"We opened Kari's pub this morning and . . ." Bram paused, sighed. "Fuck. We found his body. Mathias tortured him. I've never seen anything so terrible. He was gutted alive, most of his body burned. He must have suffered . . . unimaginably."

Sick finality slid through Duke. This was their worst fear come true. *Dear God . . .*

Beside him, Felicia gasped. She'd overheard, damn it. Bram was scaring the hell out of her. But maybe knowing the worst of magickind's danger would convince her that she didn't belong anywhere near Morganna's tomb.

He clutched the phone. "Bloody hell, how did we let this happen?"

"We tried to stop Tynan from going to Mathias. The dumb fucking wanker insisted." Bram sighed again, sounding so tired. "Since Shock took him to Mathias and did nothing to prevent Tynan's death, I guess this tells us where his loyalties truly lie."

Duke had suspected the truth for a long time. To be proven right only made him more angry. "I vote we kill the son of a bitch."

"Amen. Tynan's death throws the Council in another bloody mess, too."

Indeed. With Tynan gone, the Doomsday Brethren had lost a great deal of influence on the magical Council. Now instead of needing just one vote—that of Sterling MacTavish, Lucan's and Caden's uncle—to swing the Council their way, they'd need two. Since Tynan had died without heirs, no telling who would replace him or how Mathias-friendly that wizard would be. Damn! The last thing magickind needed now was more turmoil.

"I think you and Felicia should join us, stay somewhere near Kari's pub," Bram said. "My house is nearly rebuilt. I've had people working day and night. We must regroup. Safety in numbers. Felicia can distance herself from the others enough so that she doesn't interfere with our magical security. We'll reinforce her protection with manned watches." He sighed. "This game you're playing with Mathias . . . we're down a warrior, and Mathias is beginning to show us what he's truly capable of. The danger is greater than ever."

Indeed. "We'll be there soon."

"Until then, be careful. I don't have to tell you how bad it would be for us all if Mathias got his hands on Felicia."

The mere suggestion made his heart stop and fear burn through his veins. Bram's dream, the one where Mathias captured her, came back to him in a rush. Duke broke out in a cold sweat.

Moments later, heart and mind heavy, he rang off. He looked over at Felicia and saw her trembling. Her eyes filled with tears. Desperate to comfort her, Duke opened his mouth to assure her that she'd never suffer as Tynan had, then he closed it. That was one promise he couldn't make, no matter how badly he wanted to.

"I'll do everything in my power to keep you safe from Mathias."

"I know."

Silently, Duke wondered if it would be enough. He closed his eyes, certain Felicia wondered it, too.

In the somber silence, his phone rang again. He looked at the display. Mason. Duke hesitated. Now wasn't the time to deal with his brother and the drama of jealousy.

"Let me answer it." She swallowed. "In my heart, he's still my friend. I need to tell him how sorry I am that—"

That what, she wanted to continue to lean on Mason as a crutch? Damn. "Answer it."

Felicia grabbed the phone and pressed the answer button. "Mason, I'm glad you called. I—"

"Not Mason, dear." A deep velvety voice purred in her ear. "Mathias. Mason is with me. You and I haven't met yet, but we will. If you want your fiancé and your lover's brother back alive, you know what I want. Bring the Book of Doomsday and come to the tomb tonight."

CHAPTER 16

CASTING A CONCERNED GLANCE at Felicia, Duke climbed from the car in Glastonbury, near a little pub that cashed in on the town's mythical heritage as the fabled Avalon of Arthurian lore. She'd spoken very little during the entire trip from London, merely buried her head in Merlin's tomes. She was anxious. Bloody hell, so was he. He must keep her safe. And what the devil would he tell his mother if anything happened to his brother? Felicia was already mired in guilt and anger . . . If Mathias killed Mason, what would that do to her? God knew, he'd carry his own cross of guilt for the next thousand years.

"Killing Mason doesn't help Mathias's cause," he tried to reassure her, as much as himself.

While a sadistic bastard, the evil wizard usually had a reason for everything he did. Tynan's murder made sense for Mathias. Eliminating a member of both the Doomsday Brethren and the Council was a big win. Mason was merely leverage . . . at least for now. But if Mathias got what he wanted? Mason would be expendable, and Duke feared his brother would be six feet under.

Felicia stepped from the car, determination stamped across her feminine features. "But he'll do it if we fail to follow his terms. I won't let Mason suffer as Tynan did."

Yes, Simon had seen the horror of it for himself mere hours ago. The gruesome sight had turned his stomach. The brutality of the slaying brought this war to a whole new level, and every one of the Doomsday Brethren knew it. So damn sad that the wizard had dedicated the last months of his life to avenging Auropha's murder . . . only to join her as another casualty.

Whatever enmity Duke and Mason shared, he'd never wanted his brother dragged into this dangerous world. He must save Mason . . . but damn it, not by risking Felicia.

"Which is exactly why you shouldn't be here," he argued. "If Mathias captures you as well . . ."

"He can't use magic against me. I'm reading up for some way to destroy Morganna's essence so that I'm no longer valuable to him. I'm the only one who can help Mason. And after all he's done for me and all I've done *to* him, I must."

Duke knew that protesting was pointless. They'd argued this very point while packing up their hotel room and stopping by Kari's pub. They'd reached an impasse, so she'd enlisted Bram's help the second they walked through the pub's door. While Duke had argued that there must be another way to confront Mathias and rescue Mason, when Bram asked for suggestions, Duke had nothing. There was no other bloody way. They all knew it.

Winter bit through Duke's coat as he slammed the car door with all the frustration seething inside him. Felicia sent him an apologetic glance, but it changed nothing. As worried as he was for Mason and for her, another demon ate at him: Felicia would risk her life for Mason, but with her own mate, she refused to risk her heart. Didn't that tell him in no uncertain terms that she wasn't ready—or willing—to let go of her past and embrace their future? An ice pick to the chest would hurt less.

As they approached the unfamiliar pub, the door opened. Bram, Ice, and Marrok, looking grim, stood inside the empty place, waiting. Ice and Marrok held pints in white-knuckled fists. Bram looked tense and shaky, strung out on fury and adrenaline.

"Glad you made it," Bram said. "The pub owner is a friend of Kari's. He says we can leave your car and any other gear here until we return."

If they returned.

Felicia nodded. "Good. What other arrangements must we make? With Mason captive, we must begin tonight."

For the first time, Bram hesitated. "I can't say exactly what we'll face. Marrok has brought his sword. Duke, Ice, and I will be with you. When Mathias appears, you won't be alone."

"We can't let him hurt Mason," she said with determination.

Bram nodded. "And we can't let him resurrect Morganna. Under any circumstances."

"Let's not dwell on our fears," Ice suggested. "What do we know about the tomb and anything inside it?"

"Precious little," Duke growled.

Felicia paced farther into the little pub. She looked about its dark wood interior and expansive windows, which allowed moonlight to filter in. Stale air, ale, and cigarette stench aside, Felicia looked like she belonged. The pub boasted a celestial ceiling and pictures of the Glastonbury Tor, along with big paintings of King Arthur, and the ethereal witch Morganna. Marrok stared at the last with a grimace as Felicia faced Bram.

"I've been reading in the car. I found a few things. Apparently the tomb has some manner of magical sentry at the door, designed to ward away rather than harm."

"That," Bram jumped in, "I know of. My grandfather was quite fond of using compulsions to keep people out when he wished to hide anything. I'm sure he's used it here. So anyone human or magical who approached the cave entrance would feel inexplicably compelled to turn back."

"Which is why the tomb has never been disturbed," Ice added.

"Exactly."

"If everyone is compelled to leave, how will Mathias get in?"

"He's a snake." Duke raked a hand though his hair. "He'll be devising some means to slither in, no doubt."

"I'm fairly sure Mathias cannot enter before you, Felicia, or he would have already tried," Bram pointed out. "After you've gone in, two of us will linger near the doorway to ensure he cannot enter behind. We'll follow as quickly as we can."

She nodded. "There are four levels inside. Merlin was very coy with his phrasing. One task requires us to be brisk. Another will require us to be brave. The third will force us to 'believe,' whatever he meant by that. The last . . ." She shook her head. "We must have possession of the Doomsday Diary and it's probably deadly. That's all I know."

"You have the diary with you?" Bram asked.

She gestured to the pack on her back. "It's here. Being Untouchable, I can't use it, but . . . how will having it save Mason? We can't simply bypass all the traps and allow Mathias to walk inside. He'll kill Mason as soon as he's gotten what he wants."

And Felicia as well. Duke mulled that likelihood over but didn't know how to stop the danger. How could this end without death?

Duke despised this edgy, impotent feeling. He was a man of action, used to making decisions and carrying them out. No hesitation. No undue deliberation. But the consequences of failure now were gut-wrenching.

Felicia shook her head. "Perhaps there will be a way during one of the levels to . . . I don't know, catch Mathias in one of the traps. Maybe if I can dart ahead enough, the tomb's resident magical safeguards will take over and doom him?"

Perhaps. Perhaps not. Duke hated leaving so much to chance, but what were his other options? Mason must be saved, Mathias no longer answered his brother's phone to negotiate, they knew precious little about what to expect from the tomb, and Felicia refused to stay back.

Bram shrugged. "What, if anything, does the book say about resurrecting Morganna?"

"Almost nothing." She sighed, paced. "What do you know?"

"My grandfather was one cagey bastard. If he wanted to keep something a secret, he had many ways. I'm sure Morganna's tomb was one of those things. Some of this . . . we may have to simply deal with as issues arise."

Not what Duke wanted to hear, but he couldn't fault Felicia or Bram. They'd done their best to find the information. Though it was far more than they had known previously, he was painfully aware that it may not be enough.

"Why is it even possible to resurrect her? Why didn't Merlin simply kill her outright?"

"It's hardly that simple." Bram sighed. "She was a powerful witch who practiced deep into the dark arts. She would have had safeguards against sudden death. Besides, I think Merlin wanted her to suffer. Merely killing her would have been too kind."

And they were all suffering for that now.

"I see. I did find one interesting, unrelated note," Felicia said. "About Untouchables. According to Merlin there were instances where magic could affect them. But I didn't know what he meant. The whole thing was couched in terms of covenants. Does he mean a pact?"

Bram's gaze slid toward Simon. "Or a mate bond."

A puzzled frown drifted across Felicia's face. "Do you think that's what Shock meant when he said that my ancestor, Fayre, was able to hide her imprint on her mate? Her bond to her wizard was somehow different and allowed him to use magic in her presence?"

"Possibly. But we know it's about more than speaking the words because Duke's signature . . . It's perhaps not quite as transparent, but it still shows your imprint. Bloody awkward. I can only guess that Fayre trusted her mate completely and allowed him under her Untouchable barrier. It's perhaps the only way a wizard would have free rein with his ability around someone like you."

In other words, for Duke to use his magic near her, Felicia would have to open her heart to him completely. She must give him her love without reservation or barriers. Given her past and all that had happened to her? Why should he hope that he'd managed to accomplish in four days what Mason hadn't in six years?

He risked a glance at Felicia. Her gaze was downcast, her face pensive. She understood the ramifications of Bram's supposition. And she wasn't reaching out to Duke.

"That could be a bloody fantastic weapon against Mathias," Ice said. "He'd never expect it."

Yes, their veritable ace in the hole, but . . .

"Have you tried using your magic recently?" Bram quirked a brow at Duke. "With Felicia near?"

Not since the night he'd abducted her. "No."

A long moment passed. Duke nearly didn't want to try. He feared failure, the physical symbol of their imperfect mating.

"Go on," Bram urged.

Felicia faced him, and he took her hand. "Will you try?" he asked.

She shrugged, then nodded. "What do I do?"

"Focus on relaxing." He leaned closer and whispered, "Try to open yourself and trust me. Let me inside your walls. Remember that I would never hurt you."

"I know."

Her reply was a mere breath across his cheek, and everything inside him seized. Duke wanted this to work so badly, and not just because it would help the cause.

"Go ahead." She closed her eyes and took a deep breath.

Duke figured he'd best start with something small, and focused on unzipping her rucksack. He closed his eyes, pictured it, tried to muster that indescribable force inside him that provided magic. But like every other occasion around her, the sensation was like screaming down a motorway at breakneck speed, then smashing into a brick wall. His magic fell in shambles around him.

With a curse, he backed away.

Ice scowled at them. "What the fuck is the matter with you two? You're mated but not together? Get your shit together and fix it before someone dies."

Duke turned a glower on Ice. "We're working on it."

God, what more could he say? That Felicia was afraid of her own heart? That after being abandoned so many times in her life she didn't know how to love without fear? The words were too personal. He swallowed them.

"It's too soon," he said instead.

"That's crap. I knew the instant I met Sabelle—"

"But she didn't know the instant she met you," Duke returned. "You earned her trust over time. Allow Felicia the same."

"We don't have that luxury." Bram's glance was full of reproach.

Felicia bit the inside of her cheek. "Unconditional trust isn't something any of you simply gives away. I'm no different."

They all fell silent. Duke took her hand, half for show, the other half just to touch her and tell her that he understood her fear—even if her resistance to their love hurt more than he'd imagined.

"Keep working on it." Bram reached around and picked up a pack, strapping it onto his back. "It's nearly ten o'clock. We should see if we can get in the cave now."

She nodded. "That's what Mathias demanded. He's got Mason, and we can't afford to anger him."

Bram nodded. "We'll see how far we progress tonight. Knowing my grandfather, the tomb will be enormous. And we'll all need rest before we face too many challenges. We can't afford to be sloppy."

As much as it chafed Duke, Bram was right. "Let's go."

The others reached for their packs and slung them on their backs. Duke glanced Bram's way. He looked as thrilled as the guest of honor at a public execution.

"We stay together."

They nodded, and he led everyone to the back of the unfamiliar pub, out a rickety door, and into a dark alley. They made their way through a picket fence that had seen better decades, which led to a wide-open field. A stone path bisected it for long minutes until they reached what appeared to be a cellar door of warped wood built into the side of a hill. But in the upper right corner a small symbol had been branded into the grain: a sword spearing a round table. They were in the right place.

Everything that had happened to him and Felicia had

been because of the contents of this tomb. Duke sensed that whatever transpired in here would determine his fate with her. A million things could go wrong. Mathias could kill Mason—or kill them all. He could resurrect Morganna and wreak havoc. Or they might foil this mad scheme . . . and Felicia could still choose the safety and familiarity of a loveless life over the passion she had found with him. Tonight could well be the beginning of their end.

Bram pulled the heavy wooden door open, and Duke frowned. "How can you be certain the tomb hasn't been disturbed in all these centuries or that Mathias hasn't beaten us inside?"

The other warrior raised a brow. "Ice, Marrok, take Felicia down the path, back to the alley. We'll give our doubting Thomas a dose of my grandfather's magic."

Duke tensed. "I don't want her out of my sight."

"Trust in us," Marrok said. " 'Twould be a bane for us all should Mathias capture her for his own evil purposes."

"Absolutely," Ice added. "We'd be fucked, so it won't happen."

"Three minutes," Bram said. "If you want to know why I'm so confident, give me that."

"I'm fine," she assured Simon softly.

Before Duke could say more, Ice and Marrok escorted her down the long path, out the rickety gate, and down the moonlit lane, watchful and tense. The trio finally disappeared.

Slowly, the atmosphere around the door changed. At first Simon felt a vague discomfort, then a growing agitation. Within a minute, he itched to run, not walk, away from this place. He almost feared it, as if he stood before the gates of hell. Finally, he backed away, physically unable to stand near the door without being ill. Bram was right beside him.

Duke swallowed, clutching his stomach. "Point proved. Dear God . . ."

Never in his forty-three years had he felt anything like that. Not having grown up with magickind, he had never understood why Merlin's name was often whispered with reverence and awe. If this was but one of the wizard's tricks, Duke had a whole new respect for Merlin.

And Merlin's blood flowed through Bram's veins. Perhaps he should ponder a new respect for the Doomsday Brethren's leader as well.

Shuddering, Duke withdrew his wand and pointed it upward. A white arc of light slashed through the night sky toward Felicia and the other men. To the human eye, it might look like a very low shooting star. Ice and Marrok would know exactly what it meant.

Quickly, the illness abated, followed by the fear. Soon, Simon could creep closer and felt no discomfort. Then Felicia came into view, silhouetted by silvery moonlight and flanked by the two warriors.

"Amazing," he admitted to Bram. "And everyone who comes near here . . ."

"Feels compelled to leave to the point of illness? Yes."

"Then Mathias hasn't beaten us in."

"I don't think he would have troubled himself with a human captive if the didn't know for certain that he needed Felicia."

Probably not, Duke conceded.

Once more, Bram pulled on the door. It squeaked open as if protesting, then revealed a dark chasm. No one could see what was inside, especially given the pitch-dark night. Collectively, they peered in, and Duke had a sense of infinity beyond that door, as if one could walk or fall forever and not find the end.

"Keep your eyes open for any hint of Mathias. Torches?" he asked.

Bram and Ice each pulled a flashlight out of their pack. "We all have one. We should rotate using them to save batteries. We've no idea how many hours or days it will take to find our way through the caverns to the tomb."

Good point.

Bram entered first and was immediately swallowed up by the dark. Ice followed.

"Everything all right?" Duke asked. No way was he sending Felicia in next until he knew it was safe.

"Fine," Bram said.

"And bloody dark," Ice groused.

Grabbing Felicia's hand, he looked to her. "Ready?"

She nodded. "We must do this. Having all of you to help makes me feel much safer."

"I don't like this."

Felicia sent him a regretful stare. "We can't leave Mason to Mathias's devices."

Duke closed his eyes. She was right. "Go. I'm right behind you."

With a nod, he urged her forward until the dark enveloped her. If not for her hand tight in his, he would have thought she'd disappeared. He charged after her, relieved when he made it inside, and hooked an arm around her waist. She was safe. In one piece.

God, if he was this nervous now, how would he cope navigating multiple levels and traps to reach the tomb?

Shoving aside the question, Duke looked around. Or tried to. He'd never seen blackness so impenetrable. It was like staring out into nothingness forever. The sensation was unnerving.

There was a shuffling behind him, a dusting of rocks. The

sensation of something brushing just past him, disturbing the air.

"Marrok?"

"Morganna oft made me regret knowing her," he muttered.

Duke turned. The big human warrior hovered near the doorway.

Marrok groused, "The consequences for going to her tomb had best be different than those for going to her bed."

Bram laughed until the big warrior punched him in the arm. As Marrok shut the door behind him, darkness enfolded them. Bram stumbled back with an *oof* if the scrabble of trainers on gravel was any indication.

"Take a joke, mate."

"Piss off," Marrok insisted.

"Are we all inside?" Duke asked.

"I think so."

"Where are the torches?" Felicia asked, clinging close to Duke's side.

Bram flipped his on, and it projected a thin stream of light that the dark swallowed almost instantly. The tiny glow illuminated his hand and wrist, faded into charcoal . . . then nothing. Ice followed suit with the same results.

Bloody hell. How would they ever get ahead?

"Does anyone know what's next?"

"Unfortunately, not a clue." Bram cursed.

Together, they groped for walls to try to feel their way around the opening of the cavern. But it was enormous, and they were soon shouting to be heard. Using their echoes, they found their way back to the opening and shut the worthless torches off. They would have to plunge ahead in the dark and hope that no one fell. Risky . . . but they were running out of options.

"Perhaps we stay here for the night?" Felicia suggested. "It's possible that, if we open the door again, morning may illuminate this space enough to see."

"We can't leave the door open for Mathias. With you here, it's an invitation to enter the tomb and perhaps kill us all."

She sighed. "Brilliant."

Duke wrapped an arm around her. She was afraid, and why not? The cavern leading to the tomb was daunting and creepy. They were dealing with incredibly powerful magic. Duke had become accustomed to its existence over the past thirteen years. Felicia had known of it for less than a week.

"Press ahead?" he asked of Bram.

"I think so. Perhaps this leads to somewhere with more light and we'll rest more safely."

He sincerely hoped so. Felicia trembled beside him, and he hated like hell that being here scared her.

"Are you certain you don't want to turn back?" Duke whispered.

She batted his arm away. "I'm not a coward."

They'd been through so much in the past few days. She'd been a bit frightened but never had he questioned her bravery. She'd always come through. "I didn't mean to imply that."

When he pulled her close again, she relaxed against him.

"Find the person nearest you and grab on to their pack," Bram instructed.

Duke latched on to Felicia's, and he felt someone behind him, likely Marrok. At the head of the group, Bram called, "Going forward. Whatever you do, don't let go."

And they walked. Minutes turned into an hour, then two. The pack dug into his shoulders. Despite the chill, he began to sweat, and he wondered how Felicia was holding up.

"Sunshine, you all right?"

"A little tired. Otherwise good."

He didn't like that note of exhaustion in her voice, but could hardly expect anything else.

"Bram," he called. "Perhaps we should stop soon."

The other man didn't answer, but stopped dead in his tracks. They all halted, crashing into one another. Then they heard it. A deep voice. A growl. A high-pitched scream. They sounded far away, but with the echoes in the endless caverns, who could tell?

"What is that?" Felicia's voice trembled.

"Perhaps more of Merlin's magic meant to discourage anyone who made it this far."

Duke sincerely hoped the other wizard was right.

"Let's investigate," Bram added. "Be certain that we are, in fact, alone. God forbid Mathias slipped in or Morganna found some way back from the dead herself."

Felicia gasped, and Duke winced. Terrible possibilities.

The group trekked forward until suddenly Duke heard a shuffle mere feet away from him. Bram cursed.

"Did anyone hear that?" he asked.

"The scream and whatnot? Bloody hard to miss." Bram sounded annoyed.

"No, that other noise. The shuffling."

"You mean me tripping over my own two feet in this blasted darkness?" Ice growled.

Duke frowned. Maybe that's what the sound had been. He hoped.

Suddenly Felicia lurched forward and began falling. He could barely maintain his grasp on her pack. Then the ground fell out from under him.

"Stairs!" Bram yelled. "Lots of them."

Indeed, they recovered their feet and descended into the earth. Down, down, down, gingerly feeling their way, the twisting path tricky. Duke wondered if these stairs would end abruptly, subjecting them to a freefall that ended in a pit of stakes protruding from the floor or something equally awful.

Instead, they emerged into a chamber. A giant fire illuminated the space, and Duke recognized it as an eternal one. It couldn't feed itself more wood while Felicia was near, but for the past fifteen hundred years, it had been self-fulfilling, thanks to Merlin's magic. *Amazing* . . .

Beyond the fire were hundreds of doors of all shapes, sizes, colors. So many that Duke stared, blinked.

"Now what?"

"This is the task that requires us to be brisk," Felicia warned. "I think that means we must choose quickly."

"How the bloody hell do we do that?" Ice asked. "The right one isn't exactly marked."

Marrok grunted. "And we know not what terrible happenstance will befall us should we choose unwisely."

There was that. Duke was thrilled finally to have some light by which to see, and he noted quickly that Felicia looked none the worse for wear. Then he noticed the fire slowly dissipating.

"The right door won't be a small one," Bram surmised. "Merlin was tall. Hated small openings of any kind."

"Wait!" Felicia called out. "The passage in the book said something about the task being 'natural.' Is there an opening created by the earth, perhaps?"

"Likely, yes. So none of these doors before us. They're all manmade," Bram pointed out. "My grandfather would use something provided by Mother Earth herself whenever possible."

Collectively, they scanned the walls in the slowly dimming light, moving around and in between the seemingly endless row of doors. Duke stuck close to Felicia.

"Here!" she called a moment later.

Duke peered over her shoulder. There was a craggy arch and a huge, age-worn slab of stone covering it. Someone—Merlin?—had leaned the oversized slab up against the arch eons ago. It looked a bit off kilter, and Duke frowned. But he suspected his mate was right.

The others came running. Bram took one look and nodded. "This would be like him . . . though uncharacteristic to have even that small bit of the door uncovered."

"It's possible the earth has shifted a bit in the last fifteen centuries."

"True," Bram conceded. "Marrok, can you move that stone out of the way?"

"Wait!" Ice said. "Do you think we'll be subject to one of Merlin's traps if we do?"

Bram shrugged. "Felicia is with us. She's the best insurance we have."

Reluctantly, Ice nodded.

Without a word, Marrok lifted the heavy stone with Ice's help. Slowly, surely, they pulled it away from the arch.

The fire behind them flickered, sputtered. Darkness crept in.

Bram rushed through the arch, into another pit of black. He reached back for Felicia, who followed, Duke right behind her. He waited for something terrible to happen other than the dwindling fire. But as the blackness grew, the air remained undisturbed.

"Ice," Marrok grunted with the weight of the stone. "Go."

The warrior nodded and charged through unscathed.

"Now Marrok," Bram coached. "Turn and put the arch behind you. Back up until you . . . shit!"

The ground trembled and Duke lost his balance, tumbling

to the rough ground with Felicia in his arms. Suddenly, a barrage of boulders fell from above. Marrok heaved the stone over his head to protect himself, and the rocks pounded onto it in a deafening rain.

"Bram!" Marrok shouted, his voice sounding increasingly distant.

"Bloody hell! Drop it and run through the arch!"

He tried, but the archway quickly began to close over, obstructed by the boulders, taking away the light and the sight of Marrok's face—until both were completely gone.

CHAPTER 17

"MARROK, CAN YOU HEAR me?" Bram shouted, panic in his voice.

"Aye. 'Tis fine I be."

Felicia breathed a sigh of relief. "Thank God."

After losing one of their own today, she knew the Doomsday Brethren would be devastated to lose another warrior.

"How can we get him through with us?" she asked.

The blackness of the underground cavern was so thick, no one could see a thing. Cautiously, Duke felt his way to the pile of rubble, and Felicia sidled toward it, pausing beside him. At the foot of the stones, she bumped shoulders with someone.

"Sorry," Ice muttered.

"Let's pull these stones away," Duke suggested.

Together, the men worked in pairs to heave the boulders elsewhere. Based on the sounds, Marrok did the same at the other end. Cautiously, Felicia scaled the rubble, trying to find any hole at the top through which she might be able to see Marrok. Nothing.

"Bollocks!" Marrok shouted. "Felicia, you've come closer to the doorway?"

At the top of the pile of rocks, she froze. "Yes."

"Back away. Blackness has near swallowed the firelight."

"The eternal fire," Bram explained. "It cannot feed itself as long as you're close."

"Sorry!" she called to Marrok, then scampered down the pile into Duke's waiting arms.

Together they backed away from the others. She felt so safe beside him. There was no denying this cavern was creepy, and she suspected murderous tricks lay at every turn. Felicia had to restrain herself from holding on to him tighter.

After a steady rhythm of grunts and boulder tosses, as the scent of male sweat filled the air, a small shaft of light from the other side beamed into their dark cavern. *Progress!*

Suddenly, another tumble of boulders crashed down between them, smothering the pinprick of light. And, based on the sounds, adding even more stone to the pile than before.

"Bloody hell!" Bram shouted, panting.

Ice seconded that with a nasty curse that made Felicia wince. "Marrok?"

"Aye!"

She could barely hear his voice.

" 'Tis useless. The wall has grown."

"And I wouldn't put it past my grandfather to have built in this human booby trap as an added security measure. Which means the wall will only grow every time we whittle away at it."

"If I back away more and you're able to use your magic?"

Bram scoffed. "What we've encountered is designed to dissuade an overly curious and able human. No doubt good old Merlin built in some even more terrible magical impediment to keep a nefarious witch or wizard out. It would be designed to kill."

"Bloody hell," Simon muttered.

"So you're saying there's nothing we can do? We can't leave him there!" Felicia protested.

"I am a warrior grown. I can find my way out."

Silence. No one wanted to leave Marrok in this cavern of horrors. What if more dark magic awaited any who tried to leave? What if he died?

"Perhaps it's for the best if we stop trying to get Marrok through. Without our mates or surrogates, Ice and I can only expend so much energy and we've still a long way to go to reach the tomb." To Marrok, he shouted, "Return to the pub. Ring the others and tell them we've made it through the first level. Help prepare Tynan for burial."

"Aye. Be careful."

"As I told Sabelle and the others," Bram began, "if we have not returned within a week, assume we are dead. Don't come after us."

Felicia didn't imagine for a moment that Sabelle would do nothing to rescue her mate and brother, but kept the thought to herself.

"Exactly," Ice added. "My mate is to step nowhere near this tomb or she will feel my hand on her backside."

Marrok chuckled. " 'Tis certain I'll be to share that."

After a quick good-bye, the faint sound of Marrok's heavy footsteps retreated on the far side of the wall. Then nothing.

To be minus a member of their party unnerved Felicia. It made the danger feel more real.

"Do we push ahead or stop for the night?" Duke asked, rubbing her hip in a comforting gesture.

His touch felt incredible, and she melted against him, too tired and emotional to waste the energy fighting what she longed for.

"We stop." As always, Bram made the pronouncement like a consummate leader.

"Wonderful. So bloody tired . . ." Ice groused.

She heard multiple zips coming down at once, then the slither of nylon. Everyone was fishing their sleeping bags from their rucksacks. She had best do the same.

Before she could sling the pack off her back, Duke moved in behind her and pulled her sleeping bag out. His grunt and the rasp of synthetic material told her that he did the same with his own. After a curse and more sounds of metallic teeth moving, he took her hand and pulled her into a little alcove around the corner and down to the ground with him. As Felicia felt around, she realized that he'd joined their sleeping bags together to make one pallet for them both.

"Relax," he whispered. "Hungry?"

"Please."

After a fumble or two in the dark, she managed to find his hand and the beef jerky he offered. She grimaced at the first salty bite, but it provided protein and energy.

They ate in silence, and she wished more than anything that she could see Simon's face. Was he looking at her? Was he angry that he'd been unable to perform magic around her when they'd tried earlier? It wasn't that she didn't trust him with her life, but opening herself so totally . . . God, did she even know how? Would he want her forever if he really knew her?

Still, Felicia knew she must continue to try. Having a warrior capable of magic if they were forced to face down either Mathias or Morganna would be critical to winning. And with every step, they marched closer to the tomb. She had days—perhaps only hours—to figure out how to allow Duke's magic to function in her presence.

Moments later, they heard Bram's soft snore on the other side of the wall. Across the cavern, the sounds of Ice settling in reached her ears. Bless them both for giving her and Duke as much privacy as possible.

"Duke?" Ice called.

Beside her, he tensed. "Yes."

"You're the only one here who can recharge your magic. The only one with the possibility of using it when we reach the tomb. Whatever problems you two have, get over them. Fast. I want to see my mate again."

The sounds of Ice burrowing into his bag took over for minutes, then he fell silent.

Mortification and anxiety twisted Felicia's insides. Ice was right. If they failed, it would likely be her fault . . . unless she found some way to scale the huge walls she'd been building around her heart all her life.

"Where do we begin?" Her voice trembled, and she hated that. But she couldn't hide it. Simon was too perceptive not to notice.

"Sunshine . . ." He caressed her hair, no doubt wanting to reassure her.

But it wasn't all right. She knew that. When only their relationship had been at stake, she had the luxury of going slow and taking baby steps. Now, that was gone.

She tensed, thinking about just how emotionally intimate opening herself totally to Simon would be. What if he discovered he really didn't like her after all?

"I know Ice is right," she whispered. "We must solve this. I can't keep standing in your way. I can't be the cause of any warrior's death. Or Mason's."

I need you and I don't know how to tell you.

Simon was silent for long moments. "I don't want to be necessary for the sake of your conscience. I want to be necessary to your heart. But I can't force you. I've done everything I know to help, Felicia. The rest must come from you."

She closed her eyes. He was dead right. Which meant that she was going to have to let him into those uncomfortable parts of her heart and psyche, and trust that all the caring he'd exhibited was real . . . and lasting.

Heaving a long sigh, she rolled into his arms, placing her palm over the strong beat of his heart. "I hardly know where to start."

"At the beginning, with your parents?"

She nodded. *Time to let go.*

"I resented them. That sounds terrible. They adopted me from a gray, unfeeling place. But at least at the orphanage, I expected that. When Deirdre and I were adopted, we had such high hopes. At first, it was all lace and fancy dresses, dolls, trips, and new toys. Then I realized my father was never there, and my mother was too busy with her social climbing to pay us girls much mind. Deirdre took on the motherly role, making sure my homework was done and I was tucked into bed with my prayers. But after a while, I became her mother in a sense. She had suffered abuse as a young child. For years, no amount of affection, attention, reassurance was ever enough. We were each other's rock all through adolescence. I held her hand through a string of failed relationships. But as we grew older, she finally grew more confident, started making better choices. She began to shine."

"Then came Alexei?"

"He stripped her back to that frightened girl. Years and years of progress, of assurance and hugs . . . all gone in months. I tried to rebuild her. Day and night, I stayed with her, talked to her, cried . . ." Felicia felt something inside her give way, and her chest all but caved in. She shook with the first sob. "It wasn't enough."

Simon wrapped a comforting hand around her shoulder. "Maybe Deirdre didn't want to be saved. You invested yourself in her. She was the only person you'd ever totally been yourself with, given everything to. The only person you let yourself truly love."

"Y-yes."

"And she left you."

"I . . . wasn't enough for her. Why would I be for you?" She grabbed his shirt in a fist, a fresh dose of anger pouring through her. "Dragging me to the cemetery was awful and low—"

"And necessary. No matter what happens, if you're ever going to be happy, you must heal. You can't keep blaming yourself, your parents, Alexei, or anyone else for Deirdre's choice. I know you hurt like hell. It wasn't your failure or even her bad relationship that led her to her end. It was *her*. She lacked the will and the strength to heal. I refuse to believe that of you."

Felicia choked back the retort on the tip of her tongue. Oh God, he was right. It wasn't that she feared becoming suicidal. After she hadn't been enough to save Deirdre, she'd feared being crushed again, regressing back to that little wide-eyed girl who'd first climbed into the Saffords' car, feeling so alone, with high hopes and fairy tale dreams, only to be disappointed by reality.

Had she feared never finding happiness so much that she'd never allowed anyone but Deirdre the chance to be close to her? Yes.

A bitter realization.

"You've done so much for me," she whispered to Simon.

"You owe me nothing." His voice turned to steel.

Simon sounded angry, and in his shoes, she supposed she would be as well. To continually reach out to someone only to be rebuffed and have distance shoved between you would be excruciating. He was so strong, she'd never considered that he might have needs or fears that he'd like to unburden on her.

"I owe you an apology. I've asked a great deal of you, put you through a lot. I'm sorry."

He merely grunted, and Felicia wasn't sure what to make of that, so she pressed on.

"What about your childhood? Losing your father must have been difficult?"

"It was. But my mother was all I could have asked for in a parent. My stepfather was kind."

"W-what about you and Mason?"

"We were close until I turned thirty and became a wizard. I had this instant obsession to understand what I was, and spent all my free time learning about magickind. Mason was an impressionable kid, and must have felt like an outsider suddenly. I didn't even stop to think . . ." And Mason had come to resent him.

"I know you never meant to hurt him."

"The only time I knowingly hurt him was when I took you."

Felicia sighed into the silence. She didn't want to be the cause of dissension between brothers, but nor did she want to risk a broken heart. A part of her was still furious that Simon had dragged her to the cemetery to face Deirdre. But she'd needed it, as she'd come to need *him*. If she wasn't able to admit that she loved him, even if allowing him the power to hurt her terrified her, how long would he stay? And why should he?

Damn it, they needed to continue forging their bond, but she didn't know what else to say or do.

Beneath her touch, his heart beat low and strong. The hard flesh and light dusting of hair under her palm made her remember the times he'd locked her in his embrace and claimed her completely. Her lips tingled with the need to feel his kiss, to feel her bare skin pressed to his.

"Simon?" She edged closer, following the delicious scents of midnight and citrus and man until she placed her lips on his stubbled cheek.

He tensed, but Felicia ignored him, chasing the line of his jaw to his delicious cleft chin. Then she crept up to his mouth, laying a seeking kiss directly on his firm lips.

"Felicia." He grabbed her shoulders. "Not because Ice shamed you into it. Please."

"He was right, but that isn't why." She surged free of his hold and covered his mouth with hers.

Felicia understood Simon's reluctance. She'd kept secret the fact he was special and dear to her, that she'd fallen in love. Now, she tried to let go of all her fears and just be with him, shivering when he kissed her back, growing bold as he sank deep into her mouth, his hand clutching her nape.

Then he pulled away. "Don't do this if you don't mean it."

His voice resounded with pain, and she ached as well. "I mean it. Very much. I've . . . missed you. I want to be close to you."

"Why?"

Simon wanted her to give more than her body. He wanted something deeper. But rather than opening her mouth to just spit out the contents of her heart, couldn't she simply show him?

When she moved her mouth to his again, he grabbed her shoulders and held her at bay. "Why?"

"You're . . . important to me," she whispered. "Very much so."

"So is Mason," he growled. "Or we wouldn't be here now."

Yes, but it wasn't the same. He had to understand that. "I've never allowed myself to be this open with Mason. Please . . ."

She caressed his cheek, and he allowed the touch. Still, she sensed his upheaval, and something inside her wept with both frustration and disappointment in herself. She needed to let go and find a way to tell Simon how she felt.

"But you've also risked yourself for him in a way you never have with me." He sighed heavily. "I've pledged to you my heart, my devotion, and my eternity. I've tried to be patient and understanding. I've tried, in my way, to help you heal. But you can't say three words to me. I don't want you to if you don't mean them. Without them, though, I don't know how much more there is to say."

Fear struck her heart, made it shudder and quake. Was he giving up?

"You're leaving me?"

"No. Merely . . . protecting my heart."

He was closing himself off from her. Just as she'd done to him.

And the pain was immense.

"Don't. Please," she gasped. "I—" *Love you.* She swallowed, aching to say it. But fear seized her.

"You . . . ?" Even in the dark she could feel his intent stare.

"I feel more for you than I ever thought I'd let myself feel again. I know I'll never feel this way about anyone else." *Please let that be enough for now.* Love felt too new, towering and raw, to blurt in the dark when she couldn't see his response in his eyes. When she was still trying to put Deirdre to rest.

Simon hesitated for a tense minute. She sensed his mind turning, deciding.

Suddenly, he cut her off with a kiss, his lips a hard demand on hers. Felicia savored his male taste, their connection, with the bittersweet joy churning in her heart. His tongue swept inside her mouth, and she leaned in, fused to him by the pleasure of his kiss and the need building in her heart.

The kiss seared her, making arousal soar in her belly. Until Simon lifted his head, panting.

Waiting for her to make the next move.

Without hesitation, Felicia sat up, peeled away her coat

and shirt, tore off her trainers, shimmied out of her jeans. Beside him, she barely felt the cold cavern air.

Then she reached for his hand—and placed his palm over her bare breast.

"Felicia?" he whispered thickly.

Her heart clamored in her chest, answering with a beat of love. "Thank you for everything. For taking me from my wedding and hiding me from Mathias. For mating with me to keep me safe. For showing me both parts of your life. For doing so much to heal me and make me feel adored." Her heart jumped into her throat, and she choked out, "Don't give up on me."

Before Simon could react, Felicia pressed her bare skin against his sleek, tight-muscled body and covered his mouth with hers. He stiffened. For a terrible moment, Felicia feared he'd reject her, realize she hadn't told him that she loved him and put more distance between them, perhaps permanently.

Instead he groaned, "I can't stay away," and possessed her lips with a single-minded intensity that made her blood sing.

Even more, something in Simon's kiss was different. Desperate. More demanding. He wasn't treating her like a fragile doll, but giving her the full force of a man's desire. She'd felt hints of that before. But now, it overwhelmed her. His touch was like a brand preparing to claim every part of her.

With a shaking hand, he caressed his way down her nape, traced the line of her spine, caressed her hip, gripped her buttocks. She tingled everywhere he touched. She shivered when he urged her to her back and the soft welcome of their blankets.

He spread hungry kisses along her jaw, nipped at her neck. A hazy roar of pleasure charged through her as he moved down her body, his tongue taking unrelenting swipes at her nipples, sucking on her until she gripped his hair and cried out his name.

Nothing in her life had ever felt this right.

Bliss built in her body. She turned achy and wet. As Simon inched up to consume her with another fiery kiss, Felicia lifted her hips to him in frank invitation.

"I want you," she whispered. "Only you."

"You tempt me so damn much . . ." Simon groaned as he unzipped his jeans, shoved them down about his hips, and tunneled inside her.

Felicia welcomed him with a gasp as he filled her, thick, pulsing, so full of need. She could see nothing, but felt every emotion naked between them, stark, pulsing, bright. Hot need coiled deep, rolling like waves on a stormy sea. The urgency in his touch reached deep into her heart.

He withdrew, and Felicia stifled a whimper—until he grasped her wrists and held them above her head, fusing their mouths together as he began to ride her with urgent strokes.

Felicia nearly exploded in a pleasure so sublime, it did more than awaken her body; it dug deep inside her, cementing him in her heart forever. She latched on, feeling the muscles of his powerful shoulders bunch up and roll as he thrust deep. She knew what the faster pace and harsh male groans meant.

"More," she gasped. "I need you. Oh God . . . yes!"

Her chant seemed to unleash something inside him. His fingers tightened on her wrists, matching the urgency of his hard, driving strokes. With every thrust, he possessed her more. The scent of him filled her, mixing with the heady sound of his heavy breaths and moans. Pleasure spiraled out of control. Felicia threw her head back and whimpered his name.

"Simon . . . Simon!"

"Yes. That's *me*, inside you. No one else."

"Never anyone else," she vowed.

The pressure built, and her flesh quivered as she tightened around him. Her breathing escalated, out of control. Her heart revved like never before. More enthralling was the way she *knew* he was focused, as if every sense and pore were attuned to her.

Love swelled in her chest, threatening to choke her. Desperation seized her. If she opened up to him, would he really stay with her, even after the danger had ended, even if his own brother would hate him for it? Would he really still want her?

He kept swearing yes. Felicia clung to Simon, holding tight, wanting so badly to believe.

Her body raced out of control. Arousal flared even hotter now, streaming up her belly, down her legs. Every breath was hard to steal.

"Yes!" she cried into his chest. *Don't ever stop.*

Every muscle in Simon's body tightened, back, biceps, shoulders. God, how she wanted to see his face. Then thoughts fled as her world exploded. She screamed as ecstasy careened inside her, filling her to the brim with love. He followed her over the edge with a harsh cry of satisfaction, then held her close all through the night.

The group woke, but without light of any kind, it was impossible to know if morning had truly come. No one sounded refreshed. After that gritty, moving lovemaking with Felicia, Duke slept hard and woke hopeful. Something had shifted between them last night. He'd *felt* her in a way he never had. Would he be able to get under her barriers and use his magic now? She hadn't told him that she loved him, but damn it, he'd sworn he could feel it in her touch.

Surreptitiously, he tried to use his magic to beam a simple spark of light from his wand. At first, he felt the magic gathering, building, then actually traveling. Another second and he'd succeed . . . but then he slammed into the thick walls of her barricades. She gasped. Duke knew that she must have felt his attempt. His enthusiasm for the day turned to dust.

"Simon—"

"Not now." He was so damn disappointed, he couldn't be responsible for what he'd say.

Was he deluding himself? Would she ever really allow herself to love him?

The others joined them. Together, they walked a few short minutes before they spotted a literal light at the end of the tunnel. It wasn't sunlight or artificial light, but a low fire. The sounds of water and the scent of mold hung heavy in the suddenly humid air. A downpour of rain deluged the cavern ahead, emanating from the grayish stone above and into a swelling river.

"More magic?" Felicia asked.

"Yes. As you approach, the rain should stop, but something about this looks too easy. Be mindful of tricks," Bram advised.

They emerged into the firelight, illuminated by wall torches in each corner of the room. The rain tapered off as she approached.

"This task calls for bravery." She frowned. "To brave a downpour and a river?"

"See the bridge?" Ice pointed. "It exists for a reason."

"Too right." Bram edged closer to the moat. "I have a hunch. Anyone have something plastic they don't need back?"

Felicia paused, then pulled a hair clip from her pocket. Bram took it, then knelt to the water and dipped the tip in.

To Duke's dismay, the entire end of the little hair ornament was suddenly gone, the jagged edges smoking with a burning chemical destruction.

"Acid?"

Bram nodded. "The rain, all the liquid in the river. All deadly."

"What now?" Felicia asked, wide-eyed. "Since I'm here, can we simply walk over the bridge?"

"I suspect it's largely decorative."

"So that's why Merlin said anyone completing this task must be brave."

Bram rolled his eyes. "Probably my grandfather's tongue-in-cheek synonym for 'stupid.' This task will come with a catch. I'll go first. I have a better chance of anticipating Merlin's schemes."

Felicia frowned. "Shouldn't I be near? If I make magic . . . dissipate or whatever, won't I be helpful?"

"You're close enough there."

Bram headed to the bridge. Despite his assurance, Felicia followed, and Duke hovered nearby, determined to do everything in his power to keep her safe.

The bridge shook, rattled, shuddered. Still, Bram placed one foot on the warped wood. It swayed but held. Then he placed the other. It clattered violently for something so fragile looking. Bram raced across and landed with a jump on the other shore.

"Now you," he called to Felicia.

She turned to look at Duke, and he read need in her eyes, the same sort he'd felt in her touch last night. She couldn't say the words to him, but damn if those blue eyes didn't make him feel like the only man in her life. He prayed it wasn't his own wishful heart convincing him that he had a future with this woman.

If they could escape this damn cavern alive.

"Come with me." She held out her hand. "We should conquer this together."

"Be careful," Ice called. "That's a damn rickety bridge."

Yes, but if he was going to go down, he'd rather go with Felicia. With that thought, he put his hand in hers.

She stepped on first. Shockingly, the bridge didn't move an inch. It was literally a placid walk in the park for them, and they stepped across to the other side without incident.

The trio looked back at Ice.

Just then, more of the mysterious moans echoed through the cavern. A female shriek. Then a man's voice, "No. God, man. No!"

Duke froze. He knew that voice.

"Mason!" Felicia gasped and ran away from the bridge, to the other side of the cavern.

Duke charged after her at a dead run. He wished the voice was a trick of the mind, but if so, how had he and Felicia heard it at the same time? Could Mathias have snuck in behind them? Passed them and headed closer to the tomb as they slept? The range at which Felicia suppressed magic was certainly wide enough for any of those possibilities.

Whatever the explanation, he must stop her before she ran into danger. For all he knew, Mathias was using Mason to lure them somewhere to spring a trap.

"Felicia, stop!" He caught up to her, grabbed her arm just before she raced down a flight of steep spiral stairs that led to a hellish black pit of nothing. "Stop."

"I heard Mason."

"I did, too. But we must think smart. Ice, Bram, and I are with you for protection. You can't dart off without us."

"But what if Mathias is hurting Mason, killing him?"

Duke fought to hide his grimace. It was quite possible. "Running into a trap won't save him. Please, stay with us. If he's actually here with Mathias, we'll find him and save him. For now, let's turn back and collect Ice."

She sent him a shaky nod. "Sorry, I wasn't thinking. I heard his voice and I panicked."

In truth, he was panicked as well. For all that he and Mason had fought over the past decade, the thought of his brother dying because Duke had chosen to enlist in this magical war and had never found the courage to tell his family what he was made his stomach nearly upturn.

Together, they walked toward the others.

"Bloody hell!" Ice yelled. "What was that, man?"

Duke and Felicia both broke into a run. The sight that greeted them was the bridge slowly sinking into the pool of acid.

Bram cursed. "The bridge was actually suspended. Once it had been breached, and Felicia walked away, magic cut the ties."

"And the bridge bloody fell," Ice groused.

"So now what?" Duke asked.

"He was your fucking grandfather," Ice said to Bram. "Figure something out."

"Duke, take Felicia to the far end of the cave again. See if the bridge will rise again, by chance, once she's gone. If the acid rain begins again, come back quickly."

Personally, Duke didn't think the odds were good, but . . . he nodded and clasped Felicia's hand in his, jogging again to the threshold of the stairs that led to the next level of this hellish cavern.

He turned back and peered across the empty space. The bridge wasn't visible from this distance, and Ice wasn't budging from his place on the far side of the river.

"Oh my . . . It's my fault Ice can't get across." Regret lined Felicia's face. "I'm sorry."

Minutes later, a slump-shouldered Bram approached. "He'll have to stay back. The bridge isn't coming back up."

"Can he freeze the river? Conjure something to cross it?"

"We tried both. The river only began boiling, then swelled and swallowed up the sheet metal we summoned."

"So there's no way across."

Clearly discouraged, Bram shook his head. "I told him to make his way as close to the entrance as possible. Without fail, at least one of us must reach the tomb, save Mason, defeat Mathias, then rescue Ice and Marrok as they leave."

"We're in this together," Felicia insisted.

Bram looked up at him, and Duke felt the gravity of that worried stare. "The reality is, some of us may not make it out alive."

Felicia excused herself for a moment. She knew she couldn't step too far away from the men. God, for all she knew the whole cavern would crumble and collapse on top of them if they moved too far from the Untouchable.

But she needed a minute to collect her whirling thoughts. Mason might be here, subjected to Mathias's cruelty. Marrok and Ice had now been cut from their party. Bram didn't think they would all leave this hell alive. The reality was beginning to overwhelm her.

A week ago, she'd had nothing more to worry about than making sure the flowers for her wedding were perfect and hoping it didn't rain. She'd never considered herself either brave or adventurous. And these past few days had been fraught with danger—and emotional upheaval. She'd given her body, lost her heart. And as ridiculously frightening as all this was, Felicia felt incredibly alive and grateful to share it with Duke.

"You all right?"

Felicia whirled at Bram's approach. "So much is happening."

He nodded grimly. "Have you and Duke tried using his magic again?"

She couldn't meet his gaze. "He tried this morning."

Bram closed his eyes. "Damn it. I don't presume that I can . . . solve you in one conversation, but you failing to allow him behind your barriers demonstrates your lack of faith in him."

"But . . ." It wasn't about Duke. It was about her. He was perfect, and she had to figure out how to break out of her shell to let him know that.

"Do you know the hell that wizard has resigned himself to enduring for you?" Bram hissed.

She didn't like the sound of that. "What do you mean?"

"When you mated, I told you that you could break the bond. It would be painful, but eventually you wouldn't remember a thing."

"Yes." Felicia had a terrible feeling there was more.

"What I didn't tell you is what would happen to Duke. For a wizard, losing a mate is like losing a part of your soul. You've seen Lucan?"

She cringed. Lucan was a haunted shell of a man. "Isn't that just him missing Anka?"

"In part. But what you see now is a thousand percent improvement. Mere weeks ago, he was chained to a bed like an animal, feral and crazed. None of us knew if he would live. Duke saw that. And he still mated with you, knowing full well you planned to break your mate bond and leave him. And *if* he survived, he would likely be forever alone, since the chances of a second mating are slim. No home, no joy, no children." Bram clenched his jaw. "While you've been worried about Mason and having a 'normal' life and protecting your heart, he sacrificed his entire future so that you could have one. And he never once let on about his pain. Think about that next time he needs to use his magic."

CHAPTER 18

FELICIA FROZE, STUNNED, AS the information sank in deep. All the implications exploded in her head . . . and her heart.

Simon loved her. *Really* loved her. God, to keep her safe, he'd given up more than she'd ever guessed. She was humbled. And shamed. How could she have been so blind not to have seen his true feelings? Because she'd been too selfish to risk her own misery, too terrified to endanger her heart.

No more.

The emotions that Felicia had locked in a cage for so long sprang free. She knew exactly what she had to do. After all he'd done and all they still faced, she couldn't hide from Simon anymore. And she didn't want to.

In the back of her mind, she knew Mason needed them now, but Felicia also knew it could likely help him if she gave in to her urge to race to Simon's side. Joy, nerves, and impatience all pinged inside her as she grabbed his hand and stared until he looked into her eyes. "I know this is a very bad time for me to say it, but I . . . I love you."

She sighed with relief, hope lacing her veins. Telling Simon had, in fact, been cathartic, like a claustrophobic released after spending the day in a small cupboard. Her fear hadn't been totally rational, but now that she'd conquered it, that panic had been worse than the actual act of opening up.

To her shock, Simon turned to glare at Bram. "What did he say to you?"

"Say?" She frowned. "It doesn't matter. Did you hear me?"

"I heard." He looked down, his face set in tense lines. "Felicia, don't tell me what you think I want to hear. I'd rather you say nothing." He shook his head and turned away. "We must worry about Mason now."

Simon didn't believe her. Was she too late?

"Wait!" She grabbed his arm, her heart bloody near breaking. "I'm saying it not because Bram told me to or because I'm placating you. Simon, I'm saying it because it's true. I realized it when we were in London and I was too afraid to tell you. You've given me everything, cared for me, protected me, stood beside me, understood me. Last night when you held me, I hoped you could feel it. But I want to make certain you know. I want you to hear it from my lips."

The yearning on his face nearly killed her, but he still looked skeptical. "My magic didn't work this morning."

"You caught me off guard. Perhaps with some warning, I'd be better prepared to—"

"We're not going to get any warning," he growled, raking a hand through his hair. "We've heard screams and voices in this cave twice now. If you weren't here, I'd think that was Merlin's way of scaring people. But you're Untouchable, so they must be real. You and I both heard Mason, which means Mathias is likely near. I don't know how he got to the tomb before us. Perhaps he's been sneaking around us all this time, using your ability and his wits to get ahead. Which means we will be walking into something lethal. And we'll get no forewarning. He'll appear and we'll have a split second to act."

And if she didn't take the wall around her heart completely down, they'd die.

"I know." Tears filled her eyes, and guilt flooded her. They needed to be running to Mason's rescue. But Felicia feared if they didn't work this out now, there might not be a later for any of them. "I know that I've disappointed you and hurt you. I'm so sorry."

Simon blew out a huge breath. "I love hearing the words, but . . . until you can back up your words by letting me under your guard, we're all in danger. And I'm not certain I can believe you."

"I know you wouldn't have risked your entire future by mating with me if I didn't mean something to you. I wouldn't be risking my heart to tell you that I love you if you didn't mean everything to me."

"So that's what brought this on? Bram told you what would happen to me if you broke our bond?" He cursed. "So I mean 'everything to you' because of what you perceive as my grand romantic gesture?"

She searched his scowling face. "No. Because of *you*. I knew immediately that you weren't the spoiled, arrogant aristocrat Mason painted you to be. You're the most wonderful, selfless person I know. We're going to get out of here alive because you're going to use your magic, then I'm going to spend a lifetime showing you that you made the right choice."

Simon opened his mouth, but it wasn't his voice she heard next.

"Oh God. No! You can't—"

Mason's voice again, resounding from the bottom of the nearby stairs. A chill wound through her. What if Mathias was hurting Mason even now?

Clearly, she and Simon weren't going to resolve their problems before they had to dash to Mason's rescue. Maybe he'd believe her when the moment of truth arrived and she showed him that she meant every word of her devotion.

Felicia took his hand. "We can't wait anymore."

Simon nodded. "Damn it, we've had no time to try my magic."

"I'll make it work. I swear."

He shrugged, as if he knew he could do nothing more. "I hope you can. Let's go."

Felicia watched as he turned to Bram and motioned for the other wizard to follow. Nail-biting frustration ate at her. Mason was in grave danger. And Simon didn't believe in her love. Though why should he? She'd done nothing to prove that she was able to follow through on her promise. Yet. But she would let him completely into her heart and soul without a moment's notice. Failure wasn't an option, both for everyone's safety and for Simon.

Wordlessly, he took her elbow. A zing of rightness flowed through her as he guided her down the steep spiral stairs. Bram followed. Whatever it led to had been swallowed in darkness.

Damn, she hated the dark parts of the cavern. She felt blind, vulnerable. She hadn't wanted to say it, but in the pitch blackness, she was too painfully aware that Mathias could be under their nose, and she'd have no clue. In fact, he likely had been all along.

But now, the terror in Mason's voice rang in her head. They had to get to him. This nightmare must end.

At the bottom of the stairs, the darkness suddenly gave way to a blast of fire. It raged from the far wall several hundred meters away, striking out with hot, frightening flares, almost like a snake's tongue. The wall went on endlessly in both directions. There was no getting around it.

With a gasp at the scorching heat, Felicia pressed her back against Duke's chest, and he braced her with hands on her shoulders.

"C-can your magic bypass that?"

"Perhaps." Simon shrugged. "Normally."

"But nothing about any of Merlin's traps will be normal," Bram chimed in. "What did you say about this task earlier?"

"It requires you to believe."

"In what?" Simon asked with a frown.

"Isn't that the question of the hour?" Bram shook his head. "Bloody brilliant codger. Wish he hadn't been so fond of his own skills."

"Is there any chance that, like the other fires, this one will simply dissipate if I'm around it long enough?"

Bram cocked his head. "Possibly. But I'm going to guess we won't be given that kind of time."

They already didn't have it. Mason was somewhere in this cavern with Mathias, she suspected, and God knew what the terrible wizard had done or would do to him. Apprehension clawed through her. They really couldn't waste time.

As they walked closer to the inferno, the heat was immense, blistering. It daunted her, and she paused more than once.

Simon wrapped his arm around her. "Maybe the task requires us to believe that we will survive?"

That interpretation sounded as likely as any, but when she thought of walking into the blaze that towered over her head, everything inside her balked. How could she believe it was possible to survive that? Not without some serious magic.

She turned to Simon with a searching gaze. He remained focused on the task in front of him, looking tense and grim. Even he had his doubts.

Finally, they got within lashing distance of the blaze. Then the ground began quaking and shuddering. Felicia braced herself against Simon.

"How is this possible if I repel magic?"

"Feel the whole ground shake. The entire mechanism that powers this magic is deep underground," Bram muttered, "far from your influence. Merlin knew of Untouchables. It doesn't surprise me that he would devise magic meant to thwart even your kind. Question is, what the hell do we do?"

As if the question had been heard, the middle of the fire twisted, lurched, then took the shape of a bearded face.

"Merlin?" Simon's shocked stare jumped to Bram.

"Indeed," he muttered. "Show off."

"What you seek lies beyond this wall," a deep voice boomed around them, echoing loudly. "Only those who are pure of heart can enter."

No one said anything for a stunned moment.

Bram sighed. "I'm fucking screwed."

"Why wouldn't you be pure of heart?" Simon peered his way. "Your ambition?"

"I don't seek any personal gain with Morganna's essence, but the black cloud . . ."

Simon grimaced. "Indeed. You're fucking screwed."

Felicia gaped at them. "What black cloud?"

"A few weeks ago, we had Mathias cornered in his lair. He unleashed this spell at Bram. It was a smothering black cloud. He was unconscious for days."

"It bloody near killed me. It latched on to the more . . . ambitious part of my nature and made me a tad irritable."

Simon scoffed. "It made him a bloody pain in the arse we all wanted to kill."

Felicia's thoughts whirled. "How would this elaborate magical trick know whether *my* heart was pure?"

Bram shrugged. "If the magical trigger is far below us, out of your range . . ."

Merlin had been clever, indeed. "So what do we do?"

"I'll try to accompany you," Bram said. "But I'll bet the fire will destroy me if I get too close."

Which would leave her and Simon alone to face Mathias if he was, in fact, already in the tomb. "We can't do this without you."

He grimaced with regret. "You may have to. You have each other. Duke is a damn fine wizard. If you can solve your problems, there's no way Mathias can defeat you."

"Do you believe?" the overhead voice boomed.

Then, with the grinding of gears, the ground broke open, and a path rose slowly from a jagged crack in the earth. The "trick" was mechanical, rather than magical. The fire didn't burn at the front of this path, just below the fire-formed face. All they could see was a door.

"Prove now your pure heart." The voice was so loud it vibrated inside her. "Or perish."

With a nod at Bram, Simon ushered her onto the path, aligned now with the break in the fire. Bram followed.

As they approached, Felicia saw something—no, someone—lying across the path, near the door. She gasped at the pool of blood. "Do you see that? It looks like . . . a body."

Immediately, Simon put her behind him. "A woman's body. She's dead."

Bram edged closer, only to be driven back by a lash of flames that singed his clothing. A warning. "I can't come closer."

The earth rumbled again. The cavern shook.

Simon cursed. "And this path will only last so long. We must go now."

Felicia followed Simon closer to the body, gaping in horror. "How did she get here? How did she die?"

The two men turned to each other, as if deciding whether to impart bad news. She lost her temper.

"Who or whatever is in there, I'm going to face them soon enough. It's Mathias, isn't it? He's beaten us here. He's got Mason."

"She *is* a sharp little tack," Bram quipped.

Simon shepherded her ahead. "Yes. I can only guess how Mathias managed it, slithering around us like the snake he is, no doubt, hiding in your wake. Damn!" He looked at the woman's body. "He's pulled her heart straight from her chest."

Horror rolled across Felicia. Mathias had just reached in and . . . ? She grimaced. What sort of monster were they dealing with?

"Because she was pure of heart," Simon said with a sickened cast to his voice. "He took it."

"And somehow used it to trick this passage into thinking he was the pure one?" Felicia actually felt herself trembling, despite the terrible fire all around.

Simon nodded, guiding her ahead. "And he passed into the tomb."

"Oh my God. If he did this to her, what has he done to Mason?"

Simon clutched her shoulders. "We have to believe in order to succeed. Believe he's alive, that you and I can conquer this trial, that everything will be all right."

"That I'll be open to your magic on the other side, if needed."

He hesitated, then nodded. "That, too."

Simon turned back to Bram. "If we're able, we'll meet you somewhere between here and the entrance in a few hours. If I don't make it out . . ."

Felicia lifted a searching gaze to him. Simon never failed to reassure her. He didn't meet her gaze now.

Horror gripped her. Simon *had* to make it out alive. To do that, she must help him, be completely open to him.

Bram nodded. "I'll take care of her."

Suddenly, the earth rumbled. The path began to narrow. Simon grabbed her hand. "We must go now."

"Be careful," she called with a last look back at Bram.

He replied, but the inferno had come too close, was too loud, and swallowed up the words.

Then they sprinted for the door at the end of the path. Again, a metallic *clank* like giant gears screeched. At the enormous dark door, Simon pressed the latch, and darted through the doorway.

Then he came to a dead stop. Felicia hovered beside him, eyes going wide with shock.

CHAPTER 19

INSIDE THE SMALL TOMB, Mason sat on the floor, leaning against the wall, his hands bound behind his back, a filthy brown rag shoved in his mouth. His dark eyes were wide with terror. Hovering over him was a face Duke knew well: that of an urbane man with flowing tawny hair who oozed charisma. Blood stained the front of his white shirt as the silk clung to the discarded heart in his pocket.

Mathias.

"Welcome." He smirked as he pointed a gun at them.

Duke put Felicia behind him, then said over his shoulder, "Go. This is too dangerous."

"No," she argued. "We came here to save Mason. We stand a better chance together."

Damn stubborn woman!

"How charming." Mathias stepped forward, and the smell of blood reeking from his clothes nearly dropped Duke to his knees. "You're protecting the Untouchable. And you've made her your mate, I see. You've hidden her imprint on you. Clever."

They'd hidden Felicia's imprint on his signature? Duke's mind raced. Did that mean they were well and truly joined by more than words? But Bram hadn't noticed. Because it hadn't happened until Felicia had actually spoken of her love out loud? If so, did that mean she actually loved him as she'd claimed? As he so desperately wanted?

He couldn't ponder that now. Without question, Mathias

would try to kill him. He was nothing more than a potential thorn in the evil wizard's side. Expendable. Duke's most important issue was staying alive long enough for Mason and Felicia to escape.

How? Perhaps he could use the martial arts training he'd received from Marrok to knock the gun from Mathias's grip. Before the other wizard pulled the trigger? Mathias was too far away. He couldn't leave Mason and Felicia unprotected.

There was no other way. He must try to use magic to secure his mate's and his brother's freedom. If Felicia loved him, then she should let him beneath all her barriers. *If.*

Yes, she'd seemed different when she'd told him of her feelings. Her expression had been open, earnest, but her voice unsure. Then she'd hung her head. Mathias had realized that her imprint on him was camouflaged . . . but one glance at Felicia's tense face said this was the last situation in which she'd let her guard down. Duke shook his head at the mixed signals. He had no idea what they added up to, and he had no time to hash it out. He'd simply have to try magic and hope for the best.

Concentrating on the bonds around Mason's feet, Duke turned his attention inward. He gathered energy, rolling it up. It raced through his veins like fire. Just before it burst outward, Mathias cocked the gun.

Duke stopped instantly. He bit back a curse, aching to know if the spell would have worked.

"Are you trying to use magic?" he asked.

He rolled his eyes. "You know that's impossible with Felicia here. Let my brother go. He has nothing to do with this."

"Imagine my surprise to learn that he's merely human. I gathered very quickly that he had no idea what you are. Keeping family secrets, are you?"

"As if you care."

Now what? He needed to distract Mathias and try his magic again. He'd only get one opportunity, as closely as Mathias watched him. Which meant he needed to make it powerful magic. The only magic that was, perhaps, strong enough to thwart a menace like Mathias: Duke's unique magic. The ability had revealed itself during his transition, to be used as a last line of defense. If ever such an occasion existed, it was now.

Duke eyed the thick stone walls, the low-hanging ceiling made up of a network of large slabs of stone and elaborate tiles. Using his magic here would require enormous amounts of energy, more than he'd ever expended in a single spell. Felicia would have to be more than open; she must accept him in every way, in every corner of her being, or they would fail. Bloody hell, he needed time to catch Felicia's attention, forewarn her. If he startled her with an attempt to use his power and she shut him down, they'd all be dead.

He scrubbed a hand across his face, then forced himself to stare down Mathias. "How did you beat us here?"

"Not difficult, really. I had Katherine with me. You saw her outside the door, I presume?"

"The woman whose heart you ripped out?" Felicia panted in horror.

"Indeed. She was pure of heart. And quite accommodating in bed."

"B-before that? In the caverns leading to this tomb?"

"We stayed close to you, Felicia, and your ability often aided us. The darkness all around was handy, and you were all loud enough to mask our sounds—except when I wished you to hear us. Keeping track of you was a simple matter. Though I daresay Mason didn't enjoy the sounds of you fucking his brother."

Mathias laughed, and Duke read the angry truth in Mason's dark eyes. He could almost feel the guilt emanating from Felicia, and he cursed. That was the last emotion she needed to feel if she was going to open up her barriers so they could merge to defeat Mathias.

"Katherine had outlived her usefulness, and Merlin's final test loomed, so . . . I used her one more time. She rather thought I loved her. Pity she was so gullible. It was actually amusing."

"Oh my God." Repugnance rang in Felicia's voice.

Duke hated that she was witnessing this horror firsthand. But he could do nothing more now than try to get her and Mason out of here quickly and alive. He turned to her to get her attention, but Mathias had her full focus.

Duke gripped her arm, and addressed Mathias. "You wanted in the tomb, and here you are. I want my brother back."

Mathias's attention shifted to him. "For a nobleman, you lack social graces. I not only wanted inside the tomb, I want the book. Your mate knows that. I also require her."

Duke paused. So that's why Mathias hadn't killed him on sight. If Duke died, Felicia, as his mate, would be too distraught to perform whatever task he required. The minute she fulfilled his request, however, Mathias would kill them all.

He turned to look at her over his shoulder, hoping she would look his way and read the message in his eyes. They had to use magic and quickly.

She blinked, breathed deep, then her gaze snagged on his. He willed her to understand. After a second's hesitation, she bit her lip, then gave him an imperceptible nod.

"You mate is very pretty. She would make a lovely toy," Mathias mused.

Duke swung his gaze back to the bastard. "You don't touch Felicia!"

"Tsk," Mathias sent him an expression of mock concern. "I don't think you understand who's in control. Let me clarify the situation."

Then he pulled the trigger. Pain exploded through Duke's shoulder, red hot, shocking, and debilitating.

He collapsed to the ground.

The sound of the gunshot was deafening in the small space. Felicia screamed as Simon clutched his shoulder and fell to his knees.

Oh God! At least he wasn't dead. Yet. But could he bleed to death? She knelt to him and ripped at his shirt to assess the damage.

"Stand up," Mathias commanded, then motioned her a few steps away. "Over there."

"But . . ."

The pure evil on his face stopped her from saying another word.

Frantic and terrified for Simon, she tried to recapture his attention. Could he even use his magic now? She had no way of knowing. His eyes were clenched tightly shut as he fought the pain. Blood oozed over his fingertips.

With Mason bound and Simon hurt, no one stood between Felicia and Mathias. It was up to her to save them. And she had no idea how.

"With your Untouchable mate beside you, you have no way to magically heal," Mathias told Simon, sounding altogether too pleased. "In case you're wondering, you can thank Shock for teaching me my way around a weapon. He's quite handy, and I especially owe him for delivering Tynan O'Shea to my door."

Anger ignited in Felicia like a flash fire. The man had taken pleasure in ripping the life from a heartsick warrior.

That smarmy smile told her that he'd enjoy doing the same to Simon. Even the thought of it made her rail with fury.

"You awful bloody bastard!"

Mathias sent her a mock pout. "You don't approve? Tynan's death was some of my best handiwork, if I say so myself. Should you and your mate choose not to cooperate, I'll be forced to perfect those skills on him. Your fiancé can be easily dispatched, and will make for fun sport. Then you and I will be all alone. And I can think of many delicious uses for you."

At Mathias's leer, Felicia resisted the urge to shrink back and tremble. Now wasn't the time to be intimidated. She must stand tall and fight. And use the one bargaining chip in her arsenal: the diary.

"Why do you need both me and the book?" Maybe if she could keep Mathias talking and learn something useful, she could find some way to thwart him.

Carefully, he bent to retrieve a bottle at his feet she hadn't noticed before. Its base was wide, its color such a deep purple it was nearly black. The silver filigree around the glass stopper tinkled gently as he gripped it. "Merlin left this beside the bottle containing Morganna's essence. It's a little scroll with instructions. To resurrect her I must bring her a new heart, the blood of a woman and of someone magical, as well as the Doomsday Diary."

She sucked in a breath. Would he kill her and Simon to complete that spell?

"Now that you're here, I have all the essential ingredients. Only your futile resistance stands in my way." Mathias peered at her as if they were conducting a simple transaction, rather than bargaining over lives. "You did bring the diary, yes?"

Did she admit that she had? Felicia glanced down at Simon, wondering . . . worrying.

"Don't look at him," Mathias barked. "Answer me, pretty. Or do I need to shoot him again to get your attention?"

"No!" *Please don't. Please don't.*

"Again, do you have it with you?"

No matter how much she wanted to, Felicia didn't dare look at Simon. "Yes."

"Splendid. Bring it to me." He held out his hand.

"No." Duke insisted, glaring at Mathias. "She'll exchange it for Mason. As soon as my brother is halfway across the room, Felicia will set the diary on the ground so you can pick it up."

"That won't do! First, this isn't a negotiation. I hold all the cards. And really, how stupid do you think I am? I know from dear Sydney that a female must *hand* the diary to its next owner or it will disappear to its last resting spot. Felicia will tuck it beneath my arm, right beside Morganna." He held up the bottle. "Problem solved."

Simon shook his head. "What's to keep you from killing her for her blood once she hands over the book?"

"Simply because I'm in this tomb doesn't mean I can leave unscathed without her. If I'm unable to resurrect Morganna here, I'll have to carry the witch's essence out. I rather think Merlin would have frowned on that and put extra traps in place. So an Untouchable may be necessary."

Damn it. He was right. None of them knew enough about the tomb and how it worked to be certain, but from everything Bram had said and Felicia had experienced, that conjecture seemed likely. Plus, that plan didn't free either Mason or Simon. And if she went with the terrible wizard, she felt certain that Mathias would shoot her as soon as they exited the cave.

The wizard pinned her with a glare. "Come here. Unstopper this bottle."

Felicia's heart beat wildly. That meant approaching Mathias, getting within grabbing distance. But she had no choice if she wanted to keep everyone alive.

With her heart in her throat, she edged toward Mathias until she stood in front of him. Felicia swallowed. How could a man be so hypnotic, ooze such sexual magnetism, yet be so purely evil? She suppressed a shiver as she lifted the little purple and silver filigreed stopper.

"Good." Mathias turned to Mason. "Stand up."

With wary eyes, he shimmied up the wall. After a glance her way, then at Simon, he looked back at Mathias.

"Come here," the wizard instructed.

Mason complied slowly, but eventually stopped beside her. Felicia took some comfort in his nearness, but was painfully aware of the ticking time, of the amount of blood Simon was losing. What if she managed to save them, but it was too late for him?

Panic threatened to engulf her, and Felicia shoved it back. There was some way out of this mess. She simply had to find it.

Mathias tucked the bottle under his arm, careful that nothing inside trickled out, and pulled out a small object from the front pocket of his jeans.

Triumphantly, he held it up. A pocket knife. It didn't look very menacing, but it was still more weapon that she possessed . . . and it would hurt like hell stabbing deep in her flesh. She gulped.

"Turn around," Mathias barked at Mason.

Oh God, would Mathias literally stab him in the back? Use that terrible little blade to disable Mason and leave her all alone?

She cast a glance at Mason that begged him not to comply. He shook his head. He had little choice, and they both knew it. Mason tried to send her a comforting smile, then stepped between her and the wizard, presenting his back to Mathias.

Felicia winced, bracing for the blow, the scream of pain, the blood. Instead, Mathias grunted, sawed . . . then Mason's arms were free.

"Face me," Mathias demanded, then thrust the bottle at Mason. "Go to your brother and collect some of his blood. A few milliliters will do. Let it ooze from the wound directly into the bottle, then return to me. If you deviate from my instructions, I will shoot your fiancée."

She held her breath. There was no question Mason would comply. He'd always been protective. But what would he do to Simon? The last time the brothers had been face to face, Mason had accused him of kidnapping and rape.

Wordlessly, he approached Simon, who looked pale, his breathing labored. Blood spread all over his dark shirt, and her anxiety ratcheted up again. Surely, there could be no way he'd find the energy to use his magic now.

Mason unbuttoned Simon's shirt, carefully pushed it aside, and tipped the lip of the bottle against his wound. Were the brothers communicating with their faces at all? The back of Mason's dark head blocked everything, and she hoped they were trying to team up and find a way to escape, but given their history, what were the odds?

Seemingly endless minutes later, he stood and returned to Mathias without expression.

"Excellent." Mathias smiled at Mason, then looked her way. "Now, the stopper, my dear."

Felicia trembled, sensing a trap. She was the only female here, and he needed her blood.

As she reached out to place the stopper in the bottle Mason gripped, Mathias struck out like lightning, slicing the knife across the back of her hand. A ribbon of blood appeared immediately, the cut deep.

"Dear God!" Mason cried, then looked at Mathias with murder in his eyes.

"Not a word," he warned. "It would be very bad for her health."

Mason stifled a snarl, but seethed with fury.

Pain was a delayed reaction. By the time her blood began to drip, the tingle at the incision became a deep burn. Felicia hissed.

"All for a good cause," Mathias crooned, then turned to Mason. "Tip the bottle under her hand and collect her blood. Now!"

He complied, looking at her with deep apology in his eyes. And rage. He wanted Mathias to pay.

A few minutes later, Mathias pocketed the knife, then took the bottle from Mason's hand and peered her way again. "Now put the stopper in place."

Felicia couldn't control her trembling hand as she capped the bottle. Mathias now had everything he needed to resurrect Morganna except the book. She knew exactly what he'd say next . . . and she had no way to stop him from killing them all if she complied.

He raised a golden brow to her. "The diary. Give it to me."

She hesitated, her mind racing for *any* solution to this dilemma. But she was utterly blank. *No!* She must forge ahead and hope some opportunity presented itself.

Suddenly, Mathias raised the gun to Simon again, aiming this time for his heart. "Give it to me now or he dies."

Felicia's breath froze in her body. Her heart nearly stopped. Somehow, she had to stall for time, see if she could buy their freedom with her life.

"You'll let Simon and Mason leave alive if I give it to you now?"

"Of course," he drawled. "You'll find I can be very agreeable."

The stench of his lie nearly overpowered her. She staggered back, clutching her stomach. Not only was he never agreeable, he'd kill both men on the spot as soon as he had the book.

Oh God!

There was no help for it. She was going to have to catch Simon's gaze and hope he had the strength to use his magic. Hopefully, she could find some way to give him the strength.

Felicia gave him a shaky nod. "G-good. I'll . . . get you the book, then."

She was a terrible liar, and hoped sincerely that he couldn't see through her or she was doomed.

Shrugging off the heavy rucksack, she dropped it to the ground and turned toward Simon to unzip it.

She risked a clandestine glance at him. He was pleading with his eyes for her not to give Mathias the book.

She did her best to send him a placid smile, then mouthed *I love you.* He froze, then his eyes flooded with love . . . and regret.

They weren't going down like this. Together, they'd fight, damn it.

For a brief second, she placed a hand over her heart. Then she closed her eyes and consciously removed all of her barriers.

A split second later, he gasped, startled. Hope rushed inside her. Could he feel her naked soul completely open to him?

"What the hell are you doing? You're taking too long," Mathias insisted, then pointed the gun at Simon again. "Give me the book now."

With shaking hands, she dug through the pack, looking

for the Doomsday Diary under all her clothes, packaged meals, and toiletries. Buried at the bottom, sandwiched between two of Merlin's other books, she spotted it.

She dragged out the other items unnecessarily, hoping that Simon would try his magic. But she must produce the book now.

That didn't mean she had to hand it over nicely.

With a glance over her shoulder, she saw that Mathias sent Simon a menacing glare. He was looking forward to pulling the trigger.

It was now or never.

Suddenly, she turned and lunged at Mathias, throwing the diary at his hand—the one that held the gun. Mathias cursed his surprise, and when the book struck him, his weapon clattered to the ground.

Felicia felt a presence around her, inside her, something big and protective, hopeful and pure. And love . . . God, so much of it, Felicia was nearly overcome. It brought tears to her eyes.

Simon!

As she lowered her barriers to welcome him, the ground began to shake violently, walls heaving. The ceiling overhead rumbled, and tiles shattered. Rocks fell.

Mathias steadied himself with a hand on the wall, then sent a sharp confused glare to Simon. "Magic? How are you using yours? Impossible. Shock never mentioned this."

Felicia didn't take the time to celebrate. She crept along the wall toward Simon.

"Run!" he shouted at her and Mason. "Get out of here."

And leave him here alone to die? Never.

Mathias growled as he lunged for the gun again while more of the ceiling rained down. He pointed it at Simon, who concentrated too hard on rattling the tomb, trying to bring it down, to notice.

Felicia jumped toward him, but the shaking room sent her off balance.

To her surprise, Mason charged Mathias, kicking him in the gut. The wizard doubled over with a grunt, clutching himself. Then Mason clasped his hands and chopped down on Mathias's back. The wizard dropped the gun once more and staggered to his knees.

More of Simon's energy and spirit filled her, pure white-hot heat . . . and love. The tomb quaked harder, throwing Mathias off balance.

Felicia turned to Simon with a smile. It died when she saw him shudder violently with effort. He looked pale and was panting. Blood and sweat covered him.

Larger chunks of the ceiling fell directly over Mathias's head. One struck Mason's shoulder. With a grimace, he clutched it in agony.

Just as Mathias rose to his knees.

Mason planted a hand in her back and pushed her toward the door. "Simon is right. Go!"

Felicia stumbled, stopping her momentum with her hands on the door. She wasn't leaving until they could escape with her. And if she left now, would Mathias attain his magic again? Too risky.

She glanced down at Simon. He contorted with effort, teeth clenched, exhausted. She had to help him.

The ceiling rattled ominously, but she caught sight of metal barely a meter away. *The gun!*

She lunged for it, grabbed it in her shaking hands, and spun to see Mason kick Mathias square in the chin. The wizard tumbled to the ground.

He rose to his feet again, glowering at Mason with murder in his eyes. Felicia didn't know what he had planned—and didn't want to know.

Gathering her courage, she lifted the gun, aimed—and shot Mathias in the chest, right in the heart. The blast of the bullet knocked him flat on his back, sprawled out in a death pose.

Felicia turned to Simon and skidded to a stop on her knees. Though still using his magic, she sensed it weakening, sensed him waning fast. He looked spent, at death's door.

She cupped his face. "Simon! It's enough. Let's get out."

"You . . . first," he mumbled.

Mason knelt beside her. He covered his head as more of the ceiling fell and shouted, "We've got to run for it."

She wasn't leaving without Simon. "Help me."

Suddenly, the ceiling on the far side of the room caved in completely, tumbling a deluge of heavy stone and broken tile on top of Mathias. He grunted, then fell silent. If the bullet hadn't killed him, she hoped to God something had hit his head hard enough to finish the job. But one glance at Simon told her they couldn't stop to be sure. He needed medical attention now or he would die.

Simon's presence left her suddenly. He fell dead still, looking pale as a specter. Though the rumbling around them stopped, the avalanche of the ceiling continued like a line of dominos, rolling ever closer to them.

Her heart stopped, and she screamed at Mason, "We have to get him out of here!"

Mason didn't hesitate. He lifted Simon and staggered toward the door. Felicia picked up her rucksack, frantically searching about for the Doomsday Diary, but saw no flash of that red cover amongst the rubble.

The roof just to her left caved in. Adding in a terrified scream, she darted for the door, opening it for Mason and Simon. They rushed out, and she followed, slamming it behind her, leaving Mathias behind.

She prayed he died in that tomb, if he wasn't already gone. If not . . . She didn't want to think about that. Hopefully, given the fact Mathias was wounded and had no way out, he would soon die.

And he would remain trapped here forever.

Her biggest concern now was Simon. *Please God, don't let him die trying to save me.*

CHAPTER 20

FELICIA WALKED THROUGH THE blustery Monday afternoon. The wind whipped insistently at her trench coat, the trees around her, the grass beneath her feet. She tried to keep herself focused on the moment . . . but Simon crept into her thoughts. Again.

Mason had carried his brother out of the tomb, which turned out to be significantly easier to leave than enter. After finding Bram and the others at the pub there in Glastonbury, they'd taken one look at Simon's waxy face and asked what had happened. She'd explained in a rush, and they'd hustled her above stairs to a room, shoved her in bed with him, and told her to stay put. A wizard healer had come and gone without much improvement in Simon's health.

He'd nearly died. Bram hadn't spelled that out for her, but she knew. Once Simon had used up all his magic in the tomb, Felicia felt the loss of connection to him—and she'd known he was hanging on by a thread.

For a feverish night, she'd held Simon, kissed him, told him over and over how much she loved him. He'd remained largely unconscious, barely responsive to her affection until deep in the night when he'd rolled over and made love to her wildly, with a passion that stunned her, before sliding back into a deep sleep. In the morning, Bram's Aunt Millie had appeared. Though Simon still slept on, the older woman pronounced him "right as rain."

After breakfast, Ice had appeared to teleport Simon and

Mason back to Kari's pub in London. Bram piled her into the car for the long drive back and drilled her with a million questions about the events in the tomb. His agitation had only increased with every kilometer.

Once she arrived in London, she asked to see Simon repeatedly. Finally, Sabelle had appeared and, looking as if she stifled her pity, had said he'd be detained for a few days.

Felicia could only find one translation for this behavior: her reluctance to admit that she loved him had nearly gotten him and Mason killed. Simon might be mated to her magically, but he didn't want to see her right now, maybe never. He probably despised her. Not that she blamed him.

God, she'd become her own self-fulfilling prophecy. She'd been so terrified that she'd lose her man that she'd driven him off with her behavior.

As Felicia shoved her hands in her coat pockets and walked on the little stone path, regret pounded her. She should have let go of her fear sooner. Right now, she'd give anything to see Simon again with love in his eyes, that amused little smile on his mouth, just before he kissed her.

Would that ever happen again, or would he merely use her to keep his magic charged and eschew anything more emotional? Or would he go back to surrogates and keep her at arm's length. If that happened, she'd do whatever necessary to stay with him, fight to make him see how very much she loved him and no longer wanted to live without him.

But she was painfully aware that she couldn't force him to truly be with her simply because she now wished it. That hadn't worked with her parents or with Deirdre. But this time if she lost, she'd have no one to blame but herself. As she stepped through the slightly soggy grass in jagged little rows, Felicia fought back tears.

After long minutes, she stopped at Deirdre's headstone and knelt to place the yellow daisies she been clutching.

"Hi, D. I brought your favorites, daises. I miss you." She sighed. She did miss her sister—every single day. "I'm sorry I . . . stayed away for so many years. When you left me, I-I didn't know what to do. I wish you'd have let me help you. But I know now that you didn't want to feel the pain anymore." She choked back a nearly overwhelming surge of tears. "I'll be coming to visit more often. Hope that's okay. I love you."

"She had a different path to take," said a familiar voice behind her.

Felicia whirled to Mason. "How did you find me?"

He shrugged. "Bram put a GPS chip in your car, hoping you'd drive it at some point. He's been looking for you for days."

She rolled her eyes. Why didn't that surprise her? Sure, Bram was smart and brave, a born leader. But he could be a manipulative bastard.

"Is Simon all right?"

A sad shadow darkened Mason's eyes before he looked down, nodded. "Fine."

But he didn't want to see her. If he did, he'd be here. And really, she didn't blame him.

Soon, she hoped to talk to him, try to make him see exactly how much she loved him. She refused to give up without a fight, but . . . when she looked over the past few days, she saw so many moments when she'd evaded and hesitated. God, how she regretted them now.

"Where have you been since Friday?" Mason asked.

"My flat." She shrugged. "I figured Simon would call if he healed and he . . ." *Needed me to share his bed.* Would he ever want her for more again? Could she convince him?

He'd loved her once; she knew that. But would he ever trust her to be his mate in every way? The question had haunted her for the last three sleepless nights.

She took Mason's hands in hers. "I couldn't have carried Simon out of the tomb, and he would have died without you. Thank you for saving him. I'm sorry you were dragged into all that."

He gaped at her as if she was mad. "As you were. The two of you saved me. I could never have saved myself from Mathias."

"I'm sorry about . . ." *Betraying you, not loving you, falling for your brother.* "Everything."

He nodded, his conservative dark hair moving with the breeze. "You love Simon?"

"Yes. I won't even ask if you're angry and hurt." She reached into her pocket and withdrew the engagement ring she'd taken off what seemed like a lifetime ago. "You really deserve someone who's marrying you because she's madly in love with you. Not because you make her feel safe."

Mason clasped the ring in his fist. "You're right. I wanted you so much and . . . I behaved badly when I didn't get my way. I hope you can forgive me."

A smile played at her mouth. "Having Simon arrested was low."

He winced. "Not one of my finest moments."

"It's not for me to forgive you. That's between you and Simon."

She hoped someday they would work out their differences, and that she wouldn't be a constant reminder of the reason for their strife.

"Did you two talk?"

"We did." Mason shrugged. "I never knew. A wizard. It boggles the mind, really." He smiled wryly. "No dull family

Shayla Black

tree here. I don't think Mum knows. She always said her first husband was extraordinary, but had a very secretive side. I suppose I now know why."

Indeed. "I don't want to come between you and Simon. I love him, and that will never change. I'm not certain his feelings for me are the same, but that's neither here nor there. You're brothers and—"

"Simon explained that you're his lifelong mate and what that entails. I understand now that he never took you away simply to hurt me. After meeting Mathias, I certainly comprehend the danger he spoke of at our wedding. In fact, I understand everything, perhaps more than I'd like, at least where you're concerned." Mason sighed. "Neither of us would ever hurt you. I'm sorry I let my jealousy get the better of me. As for Simon's feelings, you'll have to discuss those with him."

Yes, and that terrified her. But for him, she would. If he chose not to live with her as his mate and broke her heart, she'd earned it. And she'd live with it. It would hurt like hell for the rest of her years, but she would survive.

Felicia pasted on a smile and nodded. "I will later. At the moment, I'd like to return to work and—"

"Let's talk about our future now."

That voice sent a shiver down her spine.

Simon.

She whirled around to find him standing a few meters away in an impeccable charcoal coat, black trousers, and a black shirt. He looked exhausted . . . but perfect.

Her heart froze, got stuck in her throat.

"You do love him," Mason murmured in her ear.

She turned to Mason with a question in her eyes. What did she say? Do?

He just smiled. "Be happy. I'll be around if he grates on

your nerves, as he sometimes can, or to talk. I'll be your friend. Always."

As he gathered her up for a hug, she embraced him in return, desperately aware of Simon's gaze on her. After a long moment, Mason pulled back, kissed her forehead, and walked away. He paused to clap Simon on the shoulder before exiting the cemetery.

Leaving them alone.

"Are you saying good-bye to Deirdre?" Duke asked Felicia as he approached her in slow, measured steps.

She looked exhausted and as nervous as a cat in a room full of rockers.

"Good-bye . . . hello." Her gaze never left him. "It was time I both accepted her death and voluntarily paid my respects."

"Where have you been?"

"My flat, mostly. I thought it best if I left for a bit, especially since Bram didn't seem pleased with what happened in the tomb."

Duke didn't remember anything after the ceiling began to cave in. According to Bram, he'd been making his way out when Felicia emerged from the tomb into an open cavern they'd never seen. Mason had carried him out, running at a mad pace. Bram joined in and helped. Shortly after they emerged into daylight, the doorway they'd exited from had disappeared.

After escaping to the little nearby pub, the next day was a blur of fever, dark visions . . . and Felicia's sweet touch. Then healing sleep.

He'd awakened to Bram's rantings. A long meeting ensued. Duke had finally found a few moments to see to some unfinished business and grease a few palms. Once he'd returned, Felicia had been gone. He ached to know why.

Softening his expression, he shook his head. "You couldn't have known that Mathias may not die in the tomb and that he's likely working hard to resurrect Morganna as we speak—if he hasn't already done so."

"I pieced that together from Bram's rantings, but I don't understand how it's possible. I know Mathias had the ingredients, but . . ." She looked confused and terrified at once. "I shot him."

"The moment you left, he could magically heal his own wounds."

She hung her head. "I'm sorry. I'd feared that, but I'd hoped he was already dead. The ceiling fell on his head. Between the bullet and the rocks . . ."

"Mathias can heal from most anything a human would consider fatal, with the possible exceptions of pulling out entrails, burning, and beheading. But even that may not be true. He was exiled once, and we thought he died. If so, he came back to life. Who knows what will be necessary to kill him now?"

"Oh. But . . . Mathias said he didn't think he could leave the tomb without an Untouchable. So wouldn't he be trapped forever?"

"Hard to say. If he could revive Morganna, they'd be able to leave quite easily. She was a very powerful witch, and certainly knew many ways to thwart Merlin's magic. If not, we may catch him yet."

She swallowed, looking sick to her stomach. "And you think he's escaped now . . . with her?"

He shot her a grim stare. "Perhaps. Bram wants you and me to travel to the tomb again tomorrow so we'll know for certain what we're dealing with. So forgive him for being less than pleasant. And me for being tied up in discussions . . . and other necessary business."

"I . . . of course." She looked as if she wanted to say more, but didn't. "What is the Doomsday Brethren's next move?"

Duke shrugged. Their options were limited. "We must try something totally different. If Mathias has, in fact, resurrected Morganna . . ."

There would be nothing but hell—and lots of it.

"Y-you're very busy. I understand."

He frowned, his internal alarms sounding. His insides jumped with anxiety. He'd loved Felicia for scarcely a week, and yet it felt like forever since he'd held her. "Why did you leave on Saturday?"

"I figured I'd give you some space to heal and . . ." Her breath caught on a sob, and she turned away.

"And what?" He approached silently and cupped her shoulders.

Felicia loved him, and he knew that. But damn it, would it always be hard for her to admit? He'd pursue her to the ends of the earth if necessary, but just once, he'd like the assurance of knowing that she came to him because she desired his company, trusted his counsel, wanted his nearness.

"I've been terrified that I waited too long to tell you that I love you and now . . ." She sobbed.

It hurt like hell to see her in pain.

Suddenly, Felicia flung herself into his arms. "I know you mated with me because you were compelled and you didn't really know me and . . ." She hugged him tighter. "I love you. Let me prove that."

"And you thought I was angry with you? That I no longer loved you?" He stared down into her miserable blue eyes and felt his heart catch.

"Yes." Her sadness crested, then she shook her head. "You once loved me. I didn't know if you still could. I *felt* it when you used your magic. You've been open almost from the start about your feelings. I didn't know how to be. I . . . don't deserve you."

He guided her away from the cemetery, toward the little park across the street. When they reached a quaint wrought iron bench, he sat Felicia down and glanced at her with reproach. "I hope you really don't think that, or we're doomed to a miserable life together."

"I want to be with you. I'll be here for you always. Give me a chance. Please. I'll endeavor to deserve you."

"You can do that . . ."—he pulled the small object from his suit coat and knelt at her feet—"by marrying me. The human way, in front of friends and family."

Felicia gasped, staring at the ring. He'd purchased it during their stay at the Dorchester, hoping he'd have the opportunity to propose to her after the charity ball. Then she looked at his face, so full of hope and tenderness. The tears started again.

"I've arranged for a small ceremony on the beach in Barbados, if you say yes. But Sunshine, I want you to have the choice this time. Stay with me not because you're compelled by magic or guilt. Stay because you love me."

She blinked, fat tears spiking her dark lashes. Her eyes looked so achingly blue and happy. "Truly?"

"Always."

A smile broke out across her face, with the beauty and promise of a new dawn. "Yes. Yes! A thousand times yes."

He slid the ring on her finger, then lifted her chin until she met his gaze. "Why?"

"Because I love you, more than I ever thought I could ever love anyone, Simon. Forever."

He dropped a perfect, sweet kiss on her lips, ripe with the promise of years of happiness to come. "I'll hold you to that. Because I love you forever, too."

Turn the page
for a special look
at the next exciting Doomsday Brethren novel

EMBRACE ME AT DAWN

by
Shayla Black

Coming soon from Pocket Books

Anka MacTavish held her breath as the most beautiful man she'd ever seen stormed toward her, one heavy footstep after another. Lucan, her mate.

Former mate, she reminded herself. He hated her now, with good reason. She had no one to blame but herself.

His full mouth thinned into a grim line, blue eyes narrowing, as he drew closer. At the sight of his obvious anger, she turned away, toward the surprising warmth of the January sun, praying the golden rays would chase away the perpetual chill that had plagued her these last four months.

It almost worked. Then Lucan seized her arm and spun her around to face him, dragging her close to the familiar heat of his body. Suddenly, she didn't need the sun at all. Their gazes connected, and heat bled through her veins. Her heart lurched in her chest. She felt a jolt of connection all the way down to her soul.

As quickly as he'd grabbed her, Lucan yanked his hand back as if she'd burned him. Sadly, the connection she felt was all one-sided.

"Are you out of your mind?" he growled. "No. The answer is absolutely no."

Anka let her lashes flutter down, breaking the pull of his furious stare, then forcing herself to step away from his beloved warmth. She didn't pretend to misunderstand. "So Bram told you that I want to join the Doomsday Brethren."

Admittedly, asking the leader of the warrior wizards dedicated to ridding magickind of the evil Mathias D'Arc to allow a witch to join their ranks had been a long shot. But damn it, she had a personal stake in this fight. Those who followed Bram into this terrible magical war all sought peace, to make magickind safe again. Admirable. Once upon a time, she'd wanted that, too.

Now, her heart stabbed her chest with every beat, wanting only revenge against the wizard who had destroyed her once-perfect life.

"Yes, he told me." Lucan leaned into her personal space, his glare intimidating, as he no doubt meant it to be. "And it's mad! I won't have it."

That familiar woodsy-musky scent of his hadn't once failed to arouse her in the two hundred years they'd lived and loved together. Nor did it fail today.

Inching back, Anka sent Lucan a sad smile. Not for one second did she imagine that he loved her enough to be concerned for her safety. Four months ago, before her world had shattered around her, absolutely. No mate had been more protective than Lucan. Today? She winced. He rejected her now because he didn't want to have to fight beside her. Bloody hell, he didn't even want to see her. He'd made that painfully clear.

This was the longest they'd spoken in weeks, maybe even since Mathias had abducted her last September, before everything had changed. Before the terrible wizard had forced her to break her mate bond with Lucan and ravaged her until she barely knew her own name.

Even the thought of those harrowing days as the madman's captive made her want to crumble. For a long time, she'd done nothing more than hide, fighting off one nightmare after another, licking her wounds.

No more.

Shoving aside both regret and tears, she tossed her head

back and met Lucan's damning stare. "It's no longer your decision."

Instantly, his jaw clenched, his nostrils flared. Those blue eyes of his could look so tender, but now they glowed with fury and condemnation. "You're right; it's not. And as much as I hate Shock, I know him. There's no fucking way he'll allow you to fight with us."

Shock doesn't care. Anka kept the thought to herself. The last thing she wanted to discuss with her former mate was her current lover, his enemy, Shock Denzell. At least, Shock was her lover when he was sober. Lately, that was never. Which suited Anka. More and more, Shock had been escaping into the bottom of a bottle. Anka hadn't tried to stop him.

Lucan didn't care about her personal drama with Shock. The only thing that mattered to him was that she hadn't returned home after escaping Mathias and his torture. In fact, Lucan probably thought she'd done her utmost to rub salt into his wound by giving herself into Shock's protection. Never mind that breaking the mate bond had obliterated her memories of Lucan for weeks afterward. Never mind that she'd been barely alive and instinctively sought a safe haven, in case Mathias hunted her again. When she'd first reached Shock, she'd been dangerously low on energy. And he'd been more than happy to share hot exchanges of frequent, raw sex to repower her magic and keep her alive— at least at first. Her former mate didn't know or care that Shock almost never touched her now, or that Anka no longer wanted him to.

Lucan only cared that she had betrayed him.

"Shock's opinion on the matter shouldn't concern you. I've offered to lend my wand to a fight that's desperately outnumbered. The decision to accept or not is Bram's. If you're so against me joining, talk to him."

A muscle ticked in his jaw. "The second Sabelle gave me the news, that went on my agenda."

Anka pressed her lips together to hold in a curse. Of course, her old friend and Bram's sister would spill the secret. Sabelle was worried about her and still believed that Lucan cared enough to stop Anka from endangering herself. Sabelle's attempt was sweet in a fashion, if futile.

"Be my guest." Anka gestured across the expanse of Bram's winter-brown lawn, dormant roses swaying with the slight breeze. The Doomsday Brethren's leader's massive new house beckoned, workers in the distance adding finishing touches to the structure built directly over the site of the original estate, which Mathias had destroyed. "But you won't stop me from trying to convince Bram that I can be an asset to your fight."

Lucan scowled at her as if she'd lost her mind. "After what Mathias did to you? Why would you imagine that you'd be doing anything more than putting yourself—and the rest of us trying to save you—in more danger?"

It was a fair question, but she refused to be cowed. "I'm not the same woman I once was."

Lucan clenched massive fists as his side. "I noticed."

He was trying to restrain his temper. Anka had seen this behavior more than once during their mating. She bit her lip to hold in a bittersweet smile. How much she missed his face and every one of those expressions she knew so well. If Bram refused to allow her to join the Doomsday Brethren, would she ever see them again?

Despair bottomed out her stomach into a endless chasm of dread. It was unreasonable to assume that she would forget two centuries of sublime happiness in mere weeks, but even tragedy and rape couldn't obliterate love. Such joy would never be hers again . . . no matter how much she wished it could.

"I have to go." Anka couldn't bear to look at him again and wonder if this would be the last time.

But when she turned toward Bram's home, she saw a familiar narrow-hipped giant sauntering her way. Shock. He wore black leather from top to bottom, like something out of a motorcycle gang—or a fetish club. A goatee framed his full mouth and square chin. Sunglasses covered his inscrutable eyes. She knew without seeing them that he glared at Lucan.

Her former mate shifted his weight to the balls of his feet, clearly itching for a reason to charge Shock. "Why are you here?"

The arch of Shock's black brow popped above his dark-tinted glasses. "I need your permission to be here?"

Lucan hesitated. Anka hadn't thought it possible, but his body grew more taut. "After you dragged Tynan away last week, took him to your boss, then tossed him aside when he was only suitable for a body bag, you have a shitload of audacity to show your face."

"Could you read Tynan's mind?"

No, but Shock could. And everyone knew that since Mathias had murdered the love of Tynan's life, Auropha, upon returning to magickind months ago, the wizard had had a death wish. Shock had done nothing more than grant it.

The night of Tynan's death, Shock had sunk further than ever into a bottle. Given the depth of his black mood, Anka was surprised to see that he'd crawled out.

"You could have saved him," Lucan growled. "And you didn't."

"You think Tynan would have thanked me if I had?"

Shock crossed his arms over his chest and waited for Lucan to concede. That was never going to happen. These two together had always been like oil and water. She'd cared deeply for both of them for centuries. Now, like then, divided loyalties were tearing her up inside.

"I'm leaving." She spun away from the two men.

"Where are you going?" Lucan demanded, grabbing her arm, his hold sizzling though her entire body, settling with a gentle ache right between her legs.

Shock took hold of the other in an equally tight grip. "Where have you been?"

They were both aggressive, demanding. A chill wound through her, killing the spark of arousal. She knew better than to jerk away. Either—or both—would do everything in his power to hold her until they got answers.

"I'm here to talk to Bram. Let go." She glared at them both.

Lucan dropped her arm with a curse. Satisfied, Shock slowly unwound his fingers from her wrist. Anka knew that if she turned her back on them, it wouldn't be long before they began to argue—with their wands and their fists. But neither man was her responsibility any longer. Lucan's magical signature revealed that he was brimming with energy, and Anka wondered who he'd been taking to his bed to generate it. If she stayed to ponder the question longer, she would only cry.

And she'd left Shock a few days ago. This was likely the first time he'd been sober enough to notice her absence. But no matter what he said, she wasn't going back. They were slowly killing each other.

Anka turned toward the house again, this time to see Bram striding toward them, grim purpose filling his sharp blue eyes. In a glance, he took in the scene. His tawny hair moved with the breeze. He was so focused, he didn't notice or care.

"Shock?" the Doomsday Brethren's leader stopped in front of the other wizard, his brow lifted as if to ask *why the hell are you here?*

Clearly, Shock wasn't popular with anyone here. Then again, he never had been. No one trusted him. Anka only did because he'd kept her secret for so long—just as she'd kept his. She'd always known that if one of them went down in flames, they'd be going together.

Smirking at Bram's arrogance, Shock pretended he didn't see the other wizard's impatient expression. "Yes?"

"No bloody stupid games. I hear you've come to see me. Out with it, then. And this had better be about stopping Mathias and Morganna le Fay's antics. They've been so busy of late that everyone in England thinks the sky is going to fucking fall months before the Mayans supposed."

Shock's posture lost some of its starch. "That's exactly why I've come. When Mathias resurrected Morganna in her tomb a few weeks ago, he planned to meld her power to his and—"

"Be magickind's most dastardly supervillain or whatever the hell, I'm sure." Bram raked a hand though his already-mussed hair. "But did he have to take all that energy and direct it against humans? My God, if humankind discovers that we truly exist, the Inquisition will look like a friendly game of croquet."

"Did you want him to direct his power at magickind?" Lucan glowered.

"It's only a matter of time before Mathias comes after us, too," Anka murmured. "We all know that."

She, better than most.

Shock growled, "Fucking listen! Mathias had nothing to do with the decimation of the Tower of London last week or the death of all those tourists. Morganna is beyond control."

"Even Mathias's?" Bram quizzed.

Nodding, his dark waves brushing his shoulders, Shock confirmed what some of the Doomsday Brethren had long suspected: Morganna wouldn't be tamed. "Completely. And she is obsessed."

"With what?" Bram looked skeptical.

A gruff laugh slipped from Shock's throat. "Do I look stupid enough to spend more time with the shrew than I must? No. According to Mathias, she is completely absorbed in looking for something. He has no idea what."

"Or claims not to." Bram put his hands on his hips, skepticism hanging heavily around him. "So you're saying he has no sway over her actions and no idea what she's seeking? Convenient, isn't it?" Bram mused.

Shock rolled his eyes. "Focus, you stubborn wanker. I'm telling you the truth."

"Maybe I should fetch Felicia to see if that's the case?" Bram threatened slyly. "The Untouchable will know if you're lying."

Indeed. Felicia could sniff out any lie, and Anka knew that Bram had come to rely heavily on her skill, made only stronger by her recent mate bond with Duke.

"Feel free. I've nothing to hide."

Bram pulled out his mobile phone and sent a quick text. In less than thirty seconds, Duke and Felicia appeared on the wintery brown lawn, the wizard's arm protectively around his mate's small waist, her long golden hair brushing his shoulder and chest.

"Say it again," Bram insisted.

"Mathias has no control over Morganna and no idea what she's searching for so desperately."

Every eye turned to Felicia, who shrugged. "He's telling the truth. Or at least the truth as he knows it."

So if Mathias had lied to him—or Shock had intentionally allowed Mathias to do so—Felicia had no way of knowing. Bram sighed, and Duke shuffled his mate behind his body, out of Shock's path.

The big, leather-clad wizard shook his head at Bram with a sigh. "I'm telling you the absolute truth. And despite your derision, I'm going to do you a huge fucking favor to tell you that Morganna is determined to kill you and your sister."

Felicia quickly nodded.

Fear gripped Anka's throat. Not so much for Bram, as he was one of magickind's most capable and talented wizards. Her fear was for Sabelle. The young woman was a gifted witch, but in Morganna's league? No. No one was. Bram, along with Sabelle's devoted mate, Ice, would both willingly give their lives to keep her safe. And still it might not be enough. If Mathias couldn't handle Morganna, and Bram or Ice died trying, who would save magickind?

Bram frowned. "Morganna wants us dead because we have Merlin's blood in our veins?"

"Exactly." Shock crossed his arms over his chest. "This is merely a guess, mind you, but I suspect she'd see it as payback for the fact Merlin managed to keep her soul imprisoned for the last fifteen centuries. By the way, she's more than a bit vocal about the fact she could feel pain, thirst, deprivation and agony while trapped in that cave."

Payback, indeed. Anka swallowed. Morganna had never been known for her restraint. Saddled with this sort of fury, what would the witch be capable of? Suddenly, Anka didn't want to know.

"I understand. Warning received. Thank you." Bram sounded almost grateful before he nodded dismissively and turned away.

"Wait! There's more. Mathias knows now that Morganna

must be stopped. And wishes like hell that he'd never resurrected the bitch." Shock drew in a big breath that lifted his massive shoulders. Anka frowned. He was never nervous about anything, but whatever he had to say next unnerved him. "He's tried . . . but he can't put her down alone."

Everyone froze. Felicia didn't refute Shock, and Anka gaped at him. How was it possible that she'd lived with this man, yet knew nothing of this revelation? Then again, he rarely spoke to her anymore.

Their last coupling had been nearly two weeks ago, and even then, he'd barely touched her, as if he found her distasteful. It had taken everything inside her not to push him away, but she'd needed energy as badly as he . . . and the guilt for taking to his bed was already festering in her heart. Sharing Shock's sheets once more shouldn't have mattered. Still, with every moment, she'd thought of Lucan—and barely managed to hold her tears at bay until Shock had groaned out in completion—then immediately zipped up his leathers and abandoned their bed.

Though hidden behind his sunglasses, Shock turned his eyes on her now. Anka felt his gaze sharpen, as if he was dissecting her. She winced and intentionally turned her thoughts to the situation at hand.

Bram narrowed his eyes at Shock. "Are you telling me that Mathias wants *our* help to end Morganna?"

"Either the bitch will go on the sort of rampage that will bring human authorities down around magickind's ears or she'll come after you and your sister with every twisted trick she's got. Deal with those issues or help Mathias kill her first. Your choice."

"No, there's another possibility." Lucan surged at Shock, shoving his face directly into the other wizard's. "You and your boss have cooked up this elaborate scheme to lead us into a trap and straight into our demise. That would leave Mathias and Morganna free to live creepily ever after, with you as their trusted advisor."

Shock stared back at Lucan as if the barb hadn't bothered him a bit, but Anka sensed the fury he barely kept on its leash. A moment later, he reached out to her and wrapped an arm around her waist. Horror spread over her as she realized he was publicly staking his claim to her—right in front of Lucan. "Bitter much?"

The two caustic syllables had barely left Shock's mouth before all hell broke loose.

Printed in the United States
By Bookmasters